Fifty Shades Of Chocolate Presents....

The Blacka The Berry

Anthony D Green

Copyright © 2023 Anthony D Green

ISBN: **978-0-578-27916-9**

DEDICATION

To Kimberly "Strawberri" Taylor
The impact you had on this part of my life is the memory I will take
with me everywhere I go. I thank the man above for the time you
were on this earth and the many lives you touched.

Contents

1 A Knaughty Experience

Alexis struggled and strained to free herself from the bonds that were holding her upright, but despite her many attempts prior to this she was still very unsuccessful. She could feel the black ball gag that was placed in her mouth. There was something about feeling and being helpless that turned her on. She smiles as she thinks about the fact that less than 6 hours prior, she was sitting at home in her bed, scrolling through her emails when a message popped up across her screen.

Are you bored with who you're fucking? Does that toy still leave you unsatisfied?

She was about to close the screen out thinking that it had to be some type of pop up until…

Alexis Cum Join Me

Startled that whoever sent that knew who she was. As she clicked to respond it took her to a blue screen with a hyperlink of five words sitting in the middle that read

Fifty Shades of Dark Chocolate

When she clicked that an address and time flashed at the bottom of her screen. She was very intrigued to find out who the hell would send her a message like that. Everything in her consciousness told her to ignore it, but there was something about those questions that made her get dressed and go to the address to find out what it was all about.

As she arrived at the address, she was surprised to see what looked like a normal chocolate colored two story home. She parked, checked out her makeup in the mirror, got out of the car and proceeded to the door. Her heart was beating hard as hell as the door opened and a woman greeted her.

"Hey Alexis, we've been expecting you" the woman said signaling her to come in.

"I was told to come to this address, and who are we?" Alexis said a little worried.

The woman walked to the desk, grabbed a clipboard and pen, and handed it to Alexis.

"You'll soon find out, but first I need you to fill out this paperwork and bring it to me when you're done." The woman said as she walked back to the desk and sat down.

Alexis skimmed through the packet of paperwork that she was given and was utterly shocked because every page was a nondisclosure agreement, but it had her name and a different gentleman's name on it as well. Her mind was working a thousand miles an hour trying to figure out who and where all this came from, but without much hesitation she signed each one and handed the packet back to the woman at the desk.

The woman glanced over the paperwork, smiled at Alexis and tapped the bell that was sitting on top of her desk.

"Someone will be here in a few to get you." She said with the biggest smile on her face "Enjoy."

Unsure of how to really take that gesture and response. Alexis took a seat closest to the door just in case she needed to make a quick dash for the door. About two minutes later two dark skinned brothers in black suits entered the room.

"Alexis," one said.

"That's me," she said standing up.

"Come with us" he said reaching for her hand.

They walked through a door that was off in the corner and before she could get a good look at where she was one of the guys stood in front of her.

"I'm sorry but we have to blindfold you" one of the guys said pulling the blindfold out of his pocket.

"Blindfold me?" she said nervous about what was going on.

"Did you not read the packet? Are we not following rules already Alexis" he said?

Remembering that she had read that in the packet she signed Alexis nodded her head, telling them that she understands. After she was blindfolded, the gentlemen guided her to a room which sounded to be empty from the echoes of their conversations. They started carefully taking off her clothes until she was standing there completely naked.

"Open your mouth" said one of the gentlemen.

As she opened her mouth the guy put a black ball gag in her mouth. The other one placed these leather and metal shackles on her hands and feet. The ones on her hands were then secured to a chain that was hanging from the ceiling.

What they needed to do was done as they made their way to the exit, closing the door behind them. Alexis couldn't move at all. She was slightly terrified as to what was about to happen to her but part of her was sexually aroused and curious about what she signed up for. All of a sudden she heard a door open and the sound of someone walking towards her. Unable to see who it was she was helpless to whatever they had planned for her. She felt the smooth hands of someone caressing her breast and fondling her pussy lips and the dick of another person on her ass.

"Do you want to cum?" said the person that was standing in front of her.

"Yes" she moaned through the ball gag.

She then felt a hard slap to her ass as the gentleman behind her responded "I want to hear yes sir."

"Oh shit, yes sir" she muffled as she bit down on the ball gag.

The gentleman standing in front of her began fingering her pussy. She moaned as his fingers stroked in and out of her. She grinded against his hand, trying to push his fingers in as deep as she possibly could before she came, but he wouldn't allow her to.

"I didn't tell you that you could cum yet, did I?" he said as he began squeezing her nipple.

"No sir" she moaned "No sir."

He got down on his knees, lifted her legs up on his shoulders, and begin to lick her throbbing pussy. His licks were constant with a light amount of pressure to her clit. She couldn't resist wrapping her legs around his neck.

"You can cum now" said the gentleman standing behind her as he firmly grips her nipples and give them a slight twist.

With one last flick of his tongue, she experienced one of the most amazing orgasms she ever experienced. She couldn't hold herself any longer and collapsed off his shoulders. With one last flick of his tongue, he and the other gentleman turned and exited the room, once again leaving Alexis there tied up.

About two minutes later she once again heard the door open and the sound of what now were three people walking in the room. She was unhooked from the chain that had her upright and carried over to what appeared to be a bed. She then felt someone unstrap her feet from the restraints and before she had a chance to think he grabbed her hips and slammed his hard dick inside her wet pussy.

"Fuck" Alexis screamed as he wrapped his arms around her hips using the floor for extra support to increase the deepness of his thrust, each one causing his balls to slap against her pussy while her breast slapped together.

The only sounds that could be heard in the room was her moaning. She moaned out for him to fuck her rougher, make his thrust deeper. At this point there was no concern of fucking her insides up she just needs all he had to offer. But moans were the only things that could escape her lips because of the ball gag that was put in there during her first session.

The more she screamed into the gag the more he slammed his dick inside her. She couldn't control her orgasm as they tore through her body violently as he was fucking her. His speed increased more and more as his grunts and her moans seemed to echo through the room they were in. All of a sudden, he stopped and his movements became almost motionless. After a few seconds she felt the throbbing sensation from his dick as he came inside her pussy.

As quick as he came he was just as quick to leave, leaving Alexis bound with her legs forced apart. Two men in black suits entered the room to free her of the restraints. She could feel the pain from her last encounter as the cum leaked from her pussy. She was sure it was over as they released her arms from the restraints. But she was sadly mistaken as one of the workers quickly placed her arms and legs in a different type of restraint as he grinned at her with the deepest amount of lust his eyes and smile could give out.

She was carried to another room where there was a mattress in the corner of the room. She smiled because she knew that things were about to get interesting.

"I'm going to feel this shit tomorrow" she thought to herself as she was tossed onto the mattress as the two guy left the room.

She was truly enjoying herself. This was something she had never done but always imagined what it would be like. Her moment to think was quickly interrupted by a hard slap to her ass from her next subduer. She moaned and squirmed as he caressed her body. He was rougher than any of the other men that came before him but she was really enjoying how it felt.

"I need this gag out to hear you tell me how good it feels." he said as he undid the gag she had in her mouth the entire time she's been there.

He turned her over on her back and slid his dick inside her pussy as far as it would go.

"You got anything to say" he said as he slammed his dick in and out of her causing the cum from her last encounter to gush out.

"fuck me" she said with a hint of aggression.

That comment charged him up as he then flipped her back on her stomach to deep stroke her pussy from the back.

"fuck you say to me" he said as he slapped her ass.

"you heard what the fuck I said" she moaned out "stop being gentle with this pussy and fuck me."

His stroke got harder and faster just as she requested. He was gon make sure he did exactly what she asked for. She moaned uncontrollably now that her mouth was free from the gag as his dick sunk deep in her pussy. He controlled her movements for his pleasure as her screams filled the room that was once silent.

"You about to make me…." she said before her words were cut off by his loud

"Fuck" as he buried his dick inside her to cum

She clinched the sheets to embrace it all.

This was definitely an experience she would feel and be thinking about for quite some time.

2. Fever

I thumped on Cyn's entryway pondering what welcome I would be welcomed with this time. She put the V in attractive and I was overly excited to see how she had decorated her 36-29-45 outline tonight. For those of you who think fine ladies just wear a size five I can't help but to disagree. Cyn stood 5'2 with a body the God's had to craft, and as far as looks go, baby wasn't half stepping in that department either. To be honest the very sight of her turned me on.

We've known each other for quite some time, introduced through a mutual friend, we shared a few friendly conversations but that was as far as it went. To be honest she intimidated me a little, so the idea of pushing up on her stayed in the back of my mind but I never actually brought it to the forefront and addressed it. Cyn had what I like to call a flighty personality. She wasn't the stay-at-home type of woman I was accustomed to. That bored her to the core.

She was the type of woman that was more intrigued with adventure. She was eager to always find things that were exciting and new, whether that is random trips with the girl or night out on the town, she was sure to have the time of her life. That's what caught my attention to be honest. My lifestyle needed a bit of excitement. The demand of corporate America kept my life overwhelmed with unnecessary but necessary stress. So every distraction was warranted and Cyn provided just that. I had to have what she had to offer.

Cyn opened her door and the sight of her made me hard as hell as it always did each time I saw her. She wore a satin red dress with a deep v-cut neckline that laced in the back. That shit looked painted on her. "Damn" I whispered as I admired her perfect coke bottle shaped frame as I entered her home and closed the door.

"Hey baby…" she said smiling as she wrapped her arms around my neck to give me a soft light peck. Her lips, to be honest, had me think of several situations where they would be extremely useful.

"Hey" I said as I pulled her back towards me, gripping her ass to pull her close as possible. "You know I need more than a damn peck."

It was something about the way she sucked my bottom lip that caused my dick to throb hard as fuck.
After kissing for a minute she pulled back from me with the biggest grin on her face. "Bae….is all that for me," she said reaching for my fully erect dick. "You can't control that shit can you," she asked outta pure enjoyment for what she was doing to me.

She knew what that did to me. I can't lie I am turned on in every way imaginable when it comes to her. "You already know who it's for" I replied with a hint of cockiness as I pushed her on the couch.

"Bae! What are you doing?" she said as if she wasn't aware of what was about to happen. "We can take care of that when we get ba….."

Before she could even get the words outta her mouth I was already pulling at her dress. "We can take care of this now."

She gave the sexiest giggle I ever heard "Seriously I was already dressed. I just needed to slip my shoes…. Mmmmm bae, damn you know I love that shit" she moaned as I ran my tongue up her inner thigh.

"You're gonna get enough of not wearing panties, that's an open invitation for me" I said in between licks to her pussy.

She moaned as my tongue ran through the lips of her pussy. That was her weakness and my expertise. I knew what would silence her complaints. "I'm just gonna taste it a little bae then we can be out."

Who am I kidding? I had other plans in mind and a quick sample wouldn't do. I have been feenin for her for days and I wasn't going to let an opportunity pass where I didn't overindulge.

"Bae" she said in the faintest whisper "I was gon give it to you when we got baaaaaccc… she moaned as the tip of my tongue brushed across the crack of her ass. There was something about licking her ass that caused her to lose all control. I knew licking there would cause her to give in and fuck me before we left. I went all in, spreading her ass to get deep enough to swirl my tongue inside her.

"Fuck, you ain't right. You know what the fuck you are doing don't you"?

"I'm just gon sample a little then we can be gone bae. Promise" I said knowing I was bullshitting. Who the fuck was I kidding. I wasn't gon be satisfied til I felt her pussy sliding on my dick. "Turn over" I whispered in between licks.

"What you on" Cyn said sly. She already knew what I was on but she played along.

I kept her bent over on the couch for another 45 min alternating between sucking her pussy and fucking her from behind before letting her get up.

"I will finish you off later. Go and take a shower and change" I said slapping her on her ass.

"I wouldn't have had to change had your ass just waited" she said pulling her dress off heading towards the room.

"Put on that black dress I love and a pair of heels."

"I wouldn't have to change shit had you just left well enough alone" she said sarcastically.

She already knew that wasn't ever going to fly with me. Every time I saw her sexy ass I was on it. The scent of her turned me on in every way. So if it was left up to me I was gon fuck her every time I got the chance to.

"Bae…. you so fucking nasty!" Cyn replied walking to the bathroom.

After washing up, fixing her lipstick, and putting on the dress I requested she walked back in the living room with her heels in her hand.

"Is this what you wanted to see me in baby" she said while twirling seductively.

Let me be clear about this dress. It was one of those dresses that looked painted on. It wrapped every curve of her body so ridiculously you would've sworn that whoever made the dress had her in mind when they made it. She approached the couch I was chilling on watching her and sat down next to me…

"Hold up baby, take them panties off and put on these" I said, handing her a pair of red lace vibrating panties.

"What am I supposed to do with this?" she said acting like she was confused as hell.

She knew what it was for. She knew that I loved to keep things exciting and mysterious.

"These panties just look better on you baby. Stand up so I can see how sexy your ass looks in them" I said, pulling her up off the couch to get a better view of that beautiful ass she has.

"Are you fucking with me bae?" she said with this look that said she knew I had other intentions in mind.

"Not yet," I said laughing mischievously.

She laughed as she peeled off her panties to put on the ones I had for her. As she slid the dress down her body I hit the on switch to give her a sample of what she was going to be dealing with all night. The look of her face was priceless.

"Baeeeeeeee" she moaned "why are you playing."

"I just wanted you to feel what I planned for you tonight baby" I said as I stepped to her and gave her the most seductive kiss I had in my arsenal. "Now cum so we can leave."

That didn't take her long. It amazes me how much go she has in her. She is one that can literally go round and won't tap out. That's where we matched perfectly. Our sex was the shit they write in books but can't quite describe fully. It's always a competition between the two of us.

We had dinner reservations at The Signature Room in downtown Chicago. I opened the door so Cyn could walk in and I could watch her hips sway and ass bounce as she made her way to our table. Wanting to add some spice to dinner I quickly reached in my pocket and turned on the remote to the vibrator in her panties. If you could see the way she stumbled, paused, and clinched her legs. That shit had me hard as hell instantly.

She looked back and me and with her eyes told me cut that shit off now. I smirked because deep down I knew she was enjoying every minute of it.

"Baby, this is beautiful," she said, taking in the scenery of the restaurant.

We were on the 95th floor at a table by the window. I chose this table because I wanted her to get a full view of the city. Elevation heightens the orgasm in my opinion and I wanted this experience to be orgasmic.

"I am glad you are enjoying this baby. I wanted this to be very special for you. I couldn't help but stare at her. She had the biggest, beautiful eyes I had ever seen. To be totally honest with you, that was one of the first things that attracted her to me along with some of the other amazing features she had that made her the total package to any man walking this earth.

After waiting about eight minutes or so, our waiter came to the table to take our order. I ordered a bottle of red wine, a medium steak, with veggies and mashed potatoes. As Cyn attempted to place her order, I flipped the switch on again. At that moment the only thing she could do was drop her head, bite that bottom lip I love, and clinch the end of the table. Surprised but silent about the whole ordeal, the waiter waited until she was ready to tell him exactly what she wanted. After a minute she got herself together as much as she could and placed her order.

"I'll have the same thing he's having" she said in between sporadic breaths.

Once he finished writing her order down, he turned his back to head to the kitchen to put the order in. I raised that vibration to the next notch on the remote.

"Fuuuuuuuuuuuck" she whispered in the sexiest moan.

I left it on for a few minutes because I wanted to see the look on her face as she came before dinner. I was guaranteed to win this battle tonight at the rate I was going.

"I'm so addicted to you baby" I said while looking at the sexiest look on her face.

There was no doubt about that. From the first time I saw Cyn I wanted her. She was a perfect ten in every sense of the word. The kind of woman that in my eyes was unattainable but that shit didn't stop me from still shooting my shot. Good thing I did because she surprised me by accepting my offer to take her out. From that moment it was on.

"Bae" she whispered, taking me out of my quick flashback. "If you don't turn this damn thing off I gon take these panties off right here at this table."

Knowing that she wouldn't, I laughed and turned it off. "I'll save the rest for later."

We spent the remainder of our time at the restaurant laughing and talking about the experience. With our schedules we really don't get to do that too often. So this was more than needed at this moment.

"Baby you ready to go" I asked after paying the bill and tipping the waiter.

"Yes bae let's go" she said

Hitting lakeshore drive heading home I decided to spice shit up to a whole nother level.

"Bae where are we going?" Cyn asked.

"Just want to pick up some tools needed for tonight. Sit back and enjoy the ride."

"Tools huh?" she said with a hint of uncertainty in her voice.

We pulled up to a toy store she loved to visit often.

"Where are we going bae?", Cyn asked.

"To get you a couple of toys."

"You so nasty."

"But you want a toy don't you?"

"Yesssss…", Cyn laughed.

"Good. Then let's see what they have. I'll get you one on one condition."

"What's that?"

"Allow me to fuck you with it on the way to your house.", I answered as I turned on her vibrator again.

****

Ding, Ding

"About Time" I said as I impatiently waited on Don to pick me up for our date. "Took you entirely too long to get here.

"Woman hush" he said, "I'm right on time."

Who am I kidding, I can't stay mad at this man. He gets on my last nerve but everything about him gives me what we have both called "Fever". Don stood five eleven with the smoothest chocolate skin known to man. My baby looks like the creator dipped him several times over. He had the sexiest brown eyes that I couldn't help but get lost in often. Medium build, more so on the thicker side because he knows I love my teddy bear men with a little muscle.

Our relationship is not like the ideal relationship. We have been reluctant to give each other titles because of the fear of something going wrong. We both have had our fair share of relationships that ended horribly, and we didn't want ours to be the same. But the reality is that we were together regardless of what we both said. Our chemistry was off the chart and we weren't denying that at all.

Our schedules were always busy as ever so tonight was definitely needed. I can't remember the last time he was able to put his hands on me, in more ways than one. But tonight I only need one touch. The only thing that's been on my mind all day is that dick of his. He definitely wasn't half stepping with that and knew exactly what to do with it.

Our sexual encounters were unlike any others I have had in my lifetime. Don was a dominant male in every sense of the word but what I am speaking on right now is his dominant lifestyle. I'm not sure if people really understand much about it but I know I was one that was unaware of it. I see it depicted in movies and thought it was all pain and punishment, but it actually isn't. It's one of the most pleasurable, rewarding experiences I have ever encountered.

In all of my past relationships I found myself being the dominant one so it was quite a big adjustment when we first discussed his dominance. He wasn't bending despite my several attempts to control the situation. After a while it became easier and I now actually prefer it to be this way. I remember our first sexual encounter with each other. He asked me a question that would set us on this path.

"Baby do you trust me unreservedly" he said as he reached for my panties.

"Don't you think it's a little late for that question" I asked sarcastically.

What kind of question is that I'm thinking to myself? He damn near has me naked already. What else is there to do to tell him I do"?

"Maybe I didn't ask it the right way because you look confused." he said as he pulled my panties off.

"Baby I trust you. Why are you asking me this now?" I said unsure of where he was headed.

"I asked because there's several ways to trust but I want your complete trust. I want you to let go and not have any fear at this moment of what I am about to do to you. Whatever I do I want you to know that I will never hurt you in any way possible. There will be moments that you may not understand but I promise when I'm done you will have all the clarity you need" he said as he began kissing my stomach.

Have I ever really let myself go with any man? I can't say that I have but I have always wanted to. I do feel secure with Don. The way he makes me feel is incredible and I think that I want to let him have all of me……

"Cyn is that a deal" I said.

She nodded her head yes as if she really had a choice in the matter. This is what made our relationship exciting as fuck. She was my willing participant and whatever my desire was she was always down to play along. That was my biggest turn on about her.

"Okay great" I said. "Come on" as I got out of the car to go and open her door so we could get a toy or two.

As we entered the store we immediately went to the toy section.

"Baby pick out what you want" I said pointing to the plethora of toys available.

"I don't know what I want," she said, acting coy.

It drives me crazy when I see a woman that I know has a freaky side but acts shy as shit. If you're nasty, be as nasty as you possibly can be. Since she was taking so long to decide on what she would have me but I grabbed toys off the shelf that I knew would spark an interest in her. If you ever wanted to know anything, always watch a woman's eyes. They are dead giveaways to everything you need to know.

Out of seven toys there was only one that really caught her eye. She lit up like a kid on Christmas when I showed her this red vibrating toy that stimulates every hole she had as well as her g spot. Shit I ain't gon lie that shit had my smiling hard as shit at the thought of what I was going to be able to do to her with it.

"Yep this is the one" I said while amping up the vibration.

She damn near fell over trying to clinch her legs closed. I'm guessing she had a thought of exactly how that shit was about to feel inside her. We headed to the counter to pay and the store was willing to give us a demonstration of what all the toy could do.

"Perfect," I said, "can you put batteries in for me now? "I said handing the cash.er my card to pay for my purchase.

We left the store. hit I-55 and headed back to her house.

"Go ahead and take those panties off now" I ordered.

"Damn can you at least say please" she said.

"You can make this easy or we can pull over and make this hard" I said as I clicked my turn signal to get over to the side of the road. "Now please take them off."

Without another thought she quickly threw her feet on the dash and lifted so she could get the panties off quickly. I couldn't help but watch as she pulled them pass those thick chocolate thighs of hers. With her legs spread apart I could see the wetness coming from her pussy lips. I reached in the bag we just got from the store, pulled out the toy, turned on the vibration, and shoved it inside her wet, inviting pussy.

"Daaaaaaamn…..that feels good…so good bae….", she moaned in her sweet sexy voice. I smiled listening to her moan, while silently laughing at the same time. She gets so hood when she's horny. I found that funny. "Fuuuuuck that shit is everything baby?", I replied, playing with her.

She didn't even catch my sly comment due to the moaning she was doing. I buried the toy as deep as I could in her pussy as I watched it swell around the toy. The look on her face told me the pleasure was far greater than the little pain she was feeling and stopping would not be the best choice at that moment. I can't explain the joy I feel to please her. To know that I am in control of everything is the best way to describe it.

After about ten minutes she pulled my hand back to stop me.

"No bae, I'm not ready to cum yet" she said in her whining voice.

Before I could get a word out my mouth she undid my belt, unzipped my pants, buried her face in my lap, and went to work. She had no thought or worry of the other cars that were passing by and was able to catch a glimpse of her round ass through the window. After about ten minutes of sucking my dick she sat up, kissed my lips, then went back to work on it. Trying to control this car while getting my dick sucked was the hardest thing to do but I managed to get us to her house safely. I threw the car in park and snatched her ass out of the car so fast.

We didn't give a fuck how our clothing was as we exited the vehicle. The only thing our mind was on was picking up where the fuck we left off. Once inside the house I locked the door and let my pants drop to the floor. There wasn't shit else to talk about as Cyn dropped down to her knees and went back at it. Lil baby was going to work on me and at the rate she was going she was going to make a nigga bust hard as fuck.

"Damn bae, slow down" I said, gripping her hair in my hand. "This ain't about me right now. This about you" I said, pulling her up and pushing her over to the black leather couch in the living room. It's like she knew what I wanted as she arched her ass up in the air for me. Without another notion I buried my face in. She moaned loud as ever as I circled the tip of her asshole.

"Damn bae, what are you on?" she said while biting on her bottom lip.

I paid it no mind as I continued to lick, suck, and tongue her ass. After about 30 minutes of licking, I flipped her over and began sucking her swollen pussy, trying to take in all the juices she had.

"Ummmmm….". Cyn moaned as she had an orgasm from my tongue penetration.

I allowed her body a second to shake from the orgasm before going back to licking and sucking her clit. I have to say I always heard the rumor about women having sweet pussy and never really believed it but this one time I was proven wrong. Cyn had some of the sweetest pussy I ever had. I sucked, slurped, and stroked my tongue in and out of her pussy.

"Damn I love the way your pussy tastes" I said knowing how much that gets her off.

She wrapped her legs around my head and tried to suffocate my ass. Her thighs were thick and strong as fuck but I didn't let that shit stop me. I'd pass out before I stopped.

"Ohhhhhhhh baaaaaaby…. It's so good. It's so damn good. I'm gonna cum… I can't hold it. I'm gonna cum." she moaned as she tried to contain her orgasm.

"No baby. Don't cum yet" I said while holding her clit on my tongue.
Who the fuck was I kidding. I damn near get off letting her cum in my mouth. That shit is such a turn on for me.

"Okay get on your knees and let me see what damage this toy can do" I said, reaching in the bag we got from the toy store and pulling out the toy.

Eyes widened as far as they could open "okay bae" Cyn said as she climbed on all fours on the couch.

I had been wanting to fuck her doggy style all night so I figured why not use every possible scenario before I gave her some dick.

"You like that baby?" I asked as I stroked her with it.

"Ohhhhhh Yeaaaaaa baeeeeeeee....", she replied.

"You want me to make it rotate while I fuck you bae?"

"Yeaaaaaaaaaa...."

I turned on the rotation control for the vibrator and had it rotated in full circles.

"That feel good so fucking good baby.", she said "Push that shit in deeper bae.", she moaned.

I was more than happy to oblige as I pushed in deep and turned up the vibration.

"Ohhhhh yeaaaaaaaa.....", she moaned as the toy pleased her pussy the way she desired to be fucked. I continued to stroke her with a toy until I felt a gush of wetness running down my arm.

"Damn bae did you just cum?" Already knowing that she did but wanting to see the expression on her face. My baby couldn't answer, she just buried her face in the pillow and moaned into it. "Arch your back more" I said, pushing at her lower back.

At that moment I positioned the toy so it rested on her clit and with my other hand gripped my dick and slid it in her wet pussy. I slowly pushed in deeper and began to stroke faster when I felt her pussy explode all over my dick.

"Fuuucccckkkkkk" she screamed at the top of her lungs.

Despite cumming several times I think this was the orgasm she had been waiting on for a while. I was damn sure that everyone passing by the house outside could hear her at that moment. She didn't hold anything back.

"You got another one in you" I said as I stroked harder.

"Come on bae" she moaned "Why are you doing me like this."

She already knew why. There really wasn't a need for me to answer. It's my job and my pleasure to make her cum as many times as possible. I loved the control she allowed me to have with her body so I had to make sure I was her greatest lover in every aspect of her life.

"Shiiiiiiittttt, I'm about to cum again" she moaned. "You about to make me CCCUUUUMMMMMMM."

There's something so sexy about fucking a woman from the back and having her look at you while cumming. That shit is priceless. Her eyes spoke volumes to what she felt. She was conquered and she loved it. But her look wasn't enough for me. I needed to hear her say it.

"Is it mine" I said while slapping her ass and shoving my dick deeper in her.

"Fuck yeah it is" she screamed.

"Tell me this pussy is mine" I said while slapping her ass harder.

The force behind my slap caused her body to damn near go into convulsions.

"Baby this pussy is all yours, I promise" she moaned.

I started stroking her faster. There was no second guessing what was happening at that moment. It was my turn to let go.

"Tell me where you want it," I said, gripping her waist to get a better grip.

"Wherever you want to put it baby, wherever you want. Just cum for me please. Fuck…... Fuck….. Fuck…..…." she screamed as she came again.

I couldn't hold back anymore. I was ready to cum and I couldn't think of a more perfect place….. inside of her.

3. Confessions Of A Sex Slave

Exposing who I am and what I do has always been a challenge for me. Especially when I am afraid of the judgment that I will receive from what I am about to expose. I have been carrying this secret for the past year of my life. Hello, my name is Devon, I am 34 years old, and I am a sex slave. Now to most this will seem far-fetched because of my lifestyle.

Prior to this year I was a single, established, dark skinned, handsome brother that could have any woman he wanted to have. To be totally honest I was on the brink of something great and had the world at my feet. That was until I met her. Usually in most stories there's always that contributing factor as to why people change but in order to understand me, you have to understand her. Leah or as she likes to be called "Master" was a feisty woman that stood about 5'8, caramel complected, and in my eyes a piece of art crafted like no other. Maybe that's why it was so easy for her to take control of me.

Master told me that I should write about the relationship we shared from the beginning to where we are now. She said she wanted to know what I thought of her, and it would please her to know my thoughts. The other task that I had to complete was sharing it with you, but like any task that she has ever given me to do, there are always rules, and she expects these rules to be followed completely.

Rule 1 – I must be completely naked when writing this. For me this isn't anything unusual because she requires me to have nothing on when I'm in her presence. I will tell you more about this as the story goes on.

Rule 2 – I cannot stop my writing at any point to touch myself. I can't orgasm at all either. This again isn't unusual because I have to get her permission to do either one of these things. My master knows that I have the hardest time not doing one of these things often especially when we're talking or reminiscing about the past, so she has demanded that a video camera be on me at all times.

Rule 3 – In this story I have to be completely honest, not holding anything back for concern of what the punishment may or may not be. She will judge it once I'm done and then she will decide just how severe my punishment will be.

You are more than welcome to comment, share, or send messages to Master or myself. If you do decide to write to us, please understand that I am not the most professional writer. I am only giving you my story, from my point of view. What you will be reading is completely honest. My hope is that once this complete you will have a clear understanding of who I am and what I do. Here goes nothing....

I was 20 when I became curious of the world of bondage and elevating my sexual pallet to another level. To be honest most of the partners that I had had were amateurs. Sex with them was gratifying but it wasn't always fulfilling. In my opinion there was always something missing or lacking from each one. Have you ever had that feeling after you had sex with a person that you just weren't satisfied? Well for me that was often, so my hunger for more intensified. So, to be totally honest the thought of just having fulfilling sex is what brought me to search for this.

I learned quickly that I always had a very submissive personality when it came to the bedroom. It seemed like the right fit for me mainly because of who was in the bed with me. Most wouldn't understand the desire I had to try other things. I felt that most would be alarmed by what I wanted to do to them and with them. So, I wasn't forced into this lifestyle, I chose it willingly, or maybe, just maybe it chose me and I accepted willingly.

How does one take on the role of Master you ask? Well first let's define what the word master really means. Master is defined as one having control, an owner especially of a slave or animal, or the employer especially of a servant. To be totally honest with you either one of these definitions would fit my situation. I bet you are probably wondering how a person acquires a master.

To be totally honest with you it's not as hard as it seems. Most people are born with the desire to serve someone or please them in some way. It's a natural instinct to want to make a person happy but for me it went further than that. Not only did I want to please her, but I also wanted to give myself completely to her, mind, body, and spirit. I wanted her to have total control over me. I got off on that shit and to be honest I wouldn't have it any other way.

Before her I had my fair share of relationships, some boring, some offering a brief moment of excitement before reverting back to what I was accustomed to. To be totally honest I was at the point of saying "fuck it" I was ready to throw the towel in until our unexpected encounter came about. She became the person I would vow to learn and trust enough to give all of me to. The way we met was at a party that a friend of mine was throwing. I was heavily intoxicated as most of the people at the party was. The music was playing and all I wanted to do was hit the floor and try to sweat some of the liquor I consumed out.

You know the story line to most romantic movies where you look across the room and you and that person locks eyes. Well, this shit wasn't anything like that. We met at a party I was hosting with a group of friends. Everyone was drinking and having a good time at the bar when she walked up to the bar.

"Excuse me bartender" she said waving trying to get the bartender's attention.

This spot we were out is always jumping and very busy so there was no way she was going to get the bartender's attention at the rate she was going. Not to mention if you weren't a regular the bartender would get to you whenever they had a free moment.

"Bartender…. Damn what I got to do to get a drink" she said with frustration in her voice.

"Is there something I can help you with" I said diverting her attention to me.

Startled that someone was paying her attention she responded with a remark that would start our back-and-forth game "Baby you too young to help me with anything" she said sarcastically.

Now to most this would be a diss but not to me. I saw it as a challenge and to be honest I just wanted to help the lady get a drink because she was getting angry about not getting served.

"Is that so?" I said stepping closer to her at the bar. "I beg to differ. There's a lot I can help you with" I said surprising myself.

The funny thing about liquor is that it gives you supernatural powers or so we'd like to think. My power that night was courage. Normally I'm not the aggressor at all. I am very shy, and to myself but not tonight. Not with her. Everything about her made me want to push the aggression button harder.

"MMMM is that so" she said intrigued at my confidence.

"That's right" I said while biting my bottom lip "Alyssa can you get the lady whatever she wants on me."

"What if I want you" she said, "Can that be arranged."

"Most definitely" I said, "Without a second thought."

To be honest this shit is freaking me out. I have no idea where all these words are coming from. I did not expect her to entertain me. But there was no turning back now. I got to keep this up because she will definitely sense and deviation for my current position.

"Leah" she said extending her hand for me to shake.

"Devon" I said grabbing her hand and caressing it in mine.

Leah was a bombshell in every sense of the word. She stood 5'8', caramel complected, with the biggest sexiest eyes I had ever seen. I never really had a thing for women that were close to my height, but she definitely set off all radars inside me. Her body was amazing. She had some of the most succulent breast I ever laid eyes on. Either her bra was everything or they were just perky as fuck. She was hippy with a nice little ass that accompanied her hips.

"Are you okay" she said bringing me out of my trance.

"Yeah, I'm sorry, just admiring how sexy you" look I said.

"That was obvious you just look me up and down like I was your next meal" she said laughing to break the tension.

"I can only wish" I said with a hint of hesitation.

Shit who am I kidding she could be my next few meals for the next few years. My mouth salivated over her. Haven't felt that shit ever but I definitely enjoyed the feeling.

"Baby how old are you?" she said laughing "You trying to make me catch a case."

"You won't catch one with me at all, but I'm old enough."

That's the typical line most dudes use when it comes to trying to approach an older woman.

"What's old enough, I'm 42 and I know you ain't that old."

That caught me off guard because I would have never guessed that. She definitely didn't look a day over 30. Whatever she had been doing to take care of herself was definitely working.

"So what were you saying about being old enough "she said taking me out of my thoughts.

"I wasn't about to say anything, but you look amazing. I'm 32 years old. But like I said before I'm old enough "

"We'll see" she said winking at me as if her wink was the seal of approval.

The rest of our evening was spent on conversation, occasional flirtatious comments, touché, and seeing that to be totally honest, could've lasted the entire night. Everything in my body wanted to tear every article of clothing she had off but tonight I was going to be a perfect gentleman. Besides, it looks like she would fuck the shit outta me and leave me with my thumb in my mouth. I made up in my mind I would treat her like a lion to a gazelle and stalk my prey, and when it's time to attack I will do just that.... Attack.

"Well, it's getting late. Are you walking me to my car, or are you going home with me?" Leah said grabbing my hand and heading to the exit.

"Now what kind of man would I be if I went home with you" I said pulling her close to me. "Tonight, just you time and attention were enough for me."

I think I surprised the both of us, but you know the funny thing about being a gentleman is that sometimes it pays off.

"Totally wasn't what I expected but definitely respected" Leah said with a look of admiration.

The rest of our week was spent in social media conversations and hours on the phone.

"Okay baby, although I have enjoyed our conversations and loved our hours of phone sex, I think it's time for the real thing. Playing with my pussy is only getting me so far" Leah said in a sweet moan on the phone as she was playing with herself.

"Are you playing with yourself now. I said, wondering why the fuck she was moaning but already knowing why.

"YES" she said "Can I come play with yo....

Before she could even finish her sentence, I responded with a "Fuck Yeah."

"Okay I'm on my way. Drop your pin" she said as she got off the phone.

I ain't gon lie, right now I'm nervous as fuck. This ain't no amateur I'm fucking with, in all classifications this is what us young folk call a "Vet". For those of you who don't know what a vet is let me break it down in the plainest term possible. Leah knew what the fuck she was doing. She had a few years of practice and I'm sure she knew her way around a dick.

"*Ding.... Ding*" as the doorbell rang sending my thoughts in hyperdrive. I don't know if it was because of the disbelief that she was actually at my door or the sexual tension that has been pent up in my body all week. As I looked at my security display to see her standing in anticipation of me answering my body instantly went the thought of what it felt like having her body near mine. Our only encounter was dancing but I knew tonight there was going to be a different type of dancing. Tonight, there wasn't going to be much talking at all.

"What took you so long? "Leah said as if I kept her waiting too long.

"I'm sorry, I was busy watching you in the monitor" I said point to the security system monitor on the wall by the couch.

I can't begin to describe the beauty that stood before me. She had that 2am look, hair wrapped in a head wrap, a tight pair of grey joggers and a thin ripped white shirt that covered a pair of nipples that were doing everything to poke through the cuts of her ripped shirt. I could tell she had jumped out of bed and rushed over to see me. But I think that's what made her sexier. She didn't need all the glitz and glamour to get me at that moment.

"If you take a picture, I swear it would last much longer" she said giggling at how long it took me to say anything. I must admit I was starstruck.

I guess a response from me took entirely too long for her because her next motion was throwing herself in my arms, pressing her lips against mine, releasing all the sexual frustration she had been reserving for me the whole week. It felt like every part of my body was exploding as I felt her tongue dart in and out of my mouth. We couldn't keep our hands off each other as we passionately explored each other through our clothing.

"This has to be a dream" she moaned in the lightest moan her body could release.

It's shit like that comment heard at the right moment will send a man into an uproar. Leah had me right where she wanted me. I was lost in the sauce with no thought of every coming up. Feeling her body pressed against mine wasn't nothing new but it definitely felt different than the last time. This time there wasn't any restraint, no hands-on hips, I was very familiar with these curves, and I was going to take my time exploring each one of them fully.

With one hand reaching her, gripping her ass firmly, holding it tight in my hand wishing I could snatch these jogging pants off with one pull. I had to pull her into me and grind her against my pulsating dick that lay in wait inside my pants while the other hand made its way to her round soft breast.

"This Damn Bra!!!" I said gripping at the Vicky secret bra that stood between me and the flesh I was ready to sink my teeth into.

"MMMMmmm" she moaned again "you playing."

Crazy thing about sex with someone new is it gives you a newfound courage you never had before. This wasn't me at all, Leah gave me courage. She made me feel things I didn't with those before her. I wanted her to have all my aggression. Each touch to her body seemed to send surges of passion through it. I was hoping that she wouldn't want to have a second thought about it, as I was ready to tear her up right here in the living room.

Breathing deeply, she was able to break away from me, taking a step back to try and gather herself. Before she could completely get it together, I was right back on her, one hand gripping the back of her head to pull her in for a kiss, the other hand wasting no time at all making my way down to her slightly gapped legs. I could feel the wetness of her pussy mixed in with the jogging pants as I rubbed it. She did everything she could to try and prevent the moan that was escaping her lips. I kissed her deeper than before and she willingly accepted, pushing her tongue as deep as it was allowed to reach in my mouth.

The wetness from between her legs was inconceivable, I was almost sure that she came once already. But I wanted to be sure as my fingers found the edge of her jogging pants. I slid inside, slowing inching them down as I move lower, brushing across her soft brown skin, until I finally reached her waiting pussy. Her breathing became sporadic and heavy as she knew what lay in wait for her. There was nothing obstructing my mission, no panties, nothing to get in my way as my finger found her swollen pussy lips.

The heat coming from them was indescribable as I slid lower to find her clit. Her pussy was dripping wet. It felt so good rubbing her hard clit, feeling her pussy opening as if I was inviting me to slip inside for a visit.

"Baby…" Leah moaned as she began shaking uncontrollably.

Her eyes were closed tightly as she slipped her hand in her pants to grip my arm tight as I played with her clit. Moving my thumb to her clit I slip my finger inside her waiting pussy and began to rub and stroke simultaneously.

"Please don't stop" she begged me.

I had no intention on stopping anyway but I enjoyed hearing her say that. Sliding in as deep as I could I continued my rhythmic motion inside her. I could feel her pussy dripping inside my hand as she pressed her pelvis against it for me to go even deeper. As loud and extremely deep moans began escaping her lips, she lost it.

"Don't stop baby, please don't stop, you're about to make me cummmmmmmm" she said as her body tensed up.

I wasted no time removing my hand from her pussy and sucking the juices off my fingers.

"Take your pants off" I said as I got down on my knees.

She didn't oblige as she slipped her completely soaked jogging pants down and off one leg at a time. As she took her right leg out, I motioned her to place it on my shoulder as I buried my face in her pussy. I began to lick and lightly suck her clit with every intention to cause her to bust one more time.

"What you doing to me" she moaned.

As I began flicking my tongue across her clit as I gripped her ass, pulling her closer to allow her to grind against my face. The sensation sent her damn near into convulsions as her body began shaking once again. It didn't take her long to cum this time, but it was deeper and harder than before. Exhausted from the two orgasms she already experienced she stared into my eyes as if to tell me bring whatever I had. She was ready for it.

I wasted no time in seeing just how ready her body was for my dick. I was hard as hell and wanted nothing more than to slip my dick out of my pants and bury it deep in her throbbing pussy. The only thing on my mind at this moment was dominating her and making sure she remembered me the next morning. I twisted her body around quickly and pressed it against the wall as she spread her legs apart and stuck her ass out from me to get a full view of those juicy, dripping pussy lips. I wasted no time snatching my hard dick out my pants ready to slide it in.

Her pussy hole wasn't hard to find at all as I slid my dick in. I didn't want her to completely give her all my dick so I only pushed in a small amount so she could fill the size and pressure that comes along with it. The way her pussy wrapped around my dick would drive any man crazy, but I had to stay the course. Leah's pussy was so wet you'd swear she has a facet buried in there.

"Damn" I whispered, taking it all in.

With one long deep thrust I was buried in her pussy. The way it wrapped around my dick damn near made me bust. I teased her with my dick, only giving her inch by inch as I stroked her pussy. But she had other thoughts in mind as she pressed against the way and took all my dick inside of her. She moaned and tried to catch her breath.

Fuck you are going to make me cum all over your dick…. Fuck" she said as she pushed deep and harder in her stride.

I wrapped my hands around her hips and started to stroke her harder and faster. At this point I couldn't help but watch as my dick disappear inside her, every inch, going deeper and deeper. Her moaning and screaming as she told me how much she was ready to cum drove me crazy. It is such an indescribable feeling at this moment.

I grab on to her hips and started to thrust my dick into her, faster and faster, harder and harder, fucking her like she was continuously begging me to do. She was taking me in whole, every inch, deep, moaning and screaming how much she wanted to explode. I fucked her hard, so fucking hard, not caring and wildly pumping and thrusting my dick into her wet pussy. I felt it drip out, was dripping down my dick and for sure it was dripping down her legs.

She reached back at some point and grabbed on to both of her ass cheeks, spreading them to the side, making me go even deeper inside of her. Clearly liking it because she moaned louder and louder. I could not resist and wetting my fingertips I placed them on her asshole just gently teasing it. That must have hit a nerve because the next thing I knew, after a few more hard thrusts from my dick in her, she started to shake, to moan and scream.

"Oh god yes... fuck I'm going to cummmm... Ahhhh!

Her pussy gripped my dick hard as hell while her hands were grabbing at me, her ass cheeks clenched tight as she lost control again. I wrapped my arms around her, pulling her close to where her back faced my chest, causing he dick to move in an upward direction inside her pussy. That extended her orgasm.

"Fuck nigga......, I can feel that shit in my stomach."

I guess she could feel my dick swelling as I was about to bust myself because her thrust to throw it back intensified. I didn't have much fight in my anyway, I was a few strokes away from bussing hard and shooting what like was going to be a heavy load inside her pussy.

"Shit baby" moaned deep and hard. "You about to make me ccccuuuuummmm."

I don't know if it was her pussy juices or my nut but I felt it dripping down my dick to my balls.

"Baby you made a mess" she said as she reached back and pulled my dripping dick out her pussy.

A mess was an understatement as I watched nut run down her leg.

"Me... no baby that was all you" I said laughing at the comment.

The rest of our night was spent fucking in every room we possibly could.

4 TEMPTING TEMPTATION

I pushed open the door to the auditorium and stepped into the class. She was sitting in the front row, again. At this point, it had to be deliberate, no other way to put it. I looked away and pretended to myself I hadn't noticed a thing. I needed my mind in the right place for my classes, and I had a really busy day today.

"Good morning, Ladies and Gentlemen ," I greeted the class.

"Good morning, Dr. Mike," they chorused back, their voices echoing through the large auditorium.

I smiled at them before taking a moment to run my eyes through my notes while I waited for them to settle down.

"I notice a larger crowd than usual. Did I schedule a test for today?" I asked them.

"No," they screamed, the look of creeping worry on their faces just perfect. It really was a larger crowd than I'd come to expect. It was just a few weeks from the beginning of the semester, and students rarely made it out of their apartments this early in the morning.

"Perfect! Since we have such large numbers today, we'll take our first test today."

They all gave a loud groan.

A hand went up into the air. It was Blake, and he argued all the time.

"I would argue, sir, that we were not pre-informed about this test and are therefore within our rights to refuse participation in such a travesty."

Oh, the boy is good, I thought, laughing, but he didn't have to be. I wasn't giving them a test, and they should've known it.

"Fine, I'll give you a few minutes to prepare," I said, and without waiting for an answer, I stepped off the podium and walked to the back of the class to settle down.

They groaned again and started flipping through their notes, trying to get as much information into their brains as they could. It wasn't possible, but they should've known that by now. These were final-year students of psychology. It should've been immediately apparent what was going on.

I'd noticed Memi hadn't picked up her notes. Her eyes had been fixed on me the whole time, I couldn't guess what her game was, but something was definitely up. At this point, I didn't even believe I wanted to know.

When my timer gave a beep at five minutes, I stood up and walked back to the podium.

"Alright, guys, put the books away. We're starting," I said.

I waited while they put their books away and calmed down.

"Alright, question one, explain the reasoning behind the psychoanalysis theory being divided into three distinct levels. Question two, question one was way too simple, and you're all invited to my house for my birthday celebration," I told them.

I watched their stunned faces for a moment while they analyzed the questions and then watched as their faces broke out in smiles, and whoops filled the room as they screamed their "happy birthday Dr. Mike."

I saw Memi shift forward on her desk, her eyes wide. I almost regretted my decision then. I and my wife Mya had decided to invite the faculty and students to join us at home for a celebration of my birthday. It was going to be a big affair, my first birthday party in a while. I was almost excited myself.

"We'll write the test next class, do make sure to prepare before class," I told them before stepping out of the room and making my way to my office.

I needed to get away from her innocent eyes, her dark brown skin like melted chocolate, and her cat-eyed glasses. I couldn't pretend I hadn't noticed she'd shown an interest in me suddenly, showing up in classes early, coming to my office on flimsy excuses, or even passing her hands over me at the slightest provocation. Like the other day when she had handed me the pen off the table. It really hadn't been necessary, not the eye contact nor the lingering touch.

Or maybe it was just my lust-addled brain confusing me. Mya and I had been discussing introducing a new dynamic into our sex life—either a new female or a new male. The last time had been a man, so this time, we wanted a female. Maybe I was considering Memi. But she was my student, and it would be stupid whether she wanted to or not.

***

Mya's POV

I paced back and forth in front of the window while I waited for my husband to get home from work. I'd been home for about an hour now, and he should've been too, but he wasn't. The man was never early for anything. He would be late for his own birthday party at this rate. Or at least the party before the main party started in two hours. It was an early birthday gift.

I made my way over to the kitchen to check on the food. The caterers had done a good job with it, everything was prepared and well stored. We certainly paid them enough for the quality they gave, but I was grateful anyways.

I wanted everything to be perfect. Mike would be turning 35 today—the big-big 35. And I wanted it to be a party to remember. I'd convinced him to invite some people over. It would be fun.

All that was left was the man himself and the guests. Hopefully, the guest didn't arrive before him.

I made my way out of the kitchen and to the bathroom. I was a little bit nervous about Mike's reaction to my new hair. I'd had it dyed an auburn color at the hair salon. I'd also had the curls teased. They framed my light brown skin and made my brown eyes pop. It had been Millie's idea, all I had to do was go along with it. I couldn't deny that I loved the result. I only hoped Mike loved it half as much.

I stared at myself in the mirror for a moment. I was 32 years to Mike's 35. I didn't look too bad, either. My skin glowed softly in the light of the bulbs, my lips full and pouty. I'd made sure to dress to show off my ass in a flimsy little outfit that was made to be taken off. Mike said that was his favorite part of my body, next to my pretty little feet.

I heard the sound of his car outside and ran my hand through my hair once to create a sexy little bed head. Blowing a kiss at myself in the mirror, I stepped out of the bathroom and made my way to the living room.

I bent over by the couch and waited for him to open the door. I wanted to be the first thing he saw when he stepped into the room, directly in his line of sight. The door opened, and I heard an immediate rush of air leaving his body.

"Well, what do we have here?" He asked. His bag hit the floor, and he made his way over to me in swift strides.

I turned towards him and saw his eyes widen at my scanty little outfit. It had literal stripes across my dark nipples and nothing else. I'd known he would love it.

"An early birthday present," I told him. I led him over to the chair I had set up by the fireplace and pushed him into it.

"Happy birthday, my love. I'm yours to do with as you wish, but first!" I said, leaning in to give him a soft kiss on the lips. He grabbed unto my waist and pulled me closer. He was going too fast, too, too soon. I pulled away and moved from the chair.

"I've got a little something for you," I told him before turning around and making my way out of the room.

I had gotten us a little vacation to the Maldives. Mike had always wanted to visit, but we had never had the money, and now we did have the money, but we never had the time. But I wanted to surprise him with a trip during his mid-year break.

I made my way back to the living room and gave a little laugh when I saw him. His tie was shot, as well as his socks and shoes. He had unbuttoned his shirt and taken it off to reveal a broad chest matted with black hair. His brown arms were crossed over his stomach in a macho pose. He gave me a smile.

"Well, I didn't want to waste a minute," he said when he saw my raised brows. I ran my eyes slowly over him, pursing at his trousers which already had a prominent bulge in front.

"Someone's excited," I said, laughing when he shrugged.

"No arguments."

I walked over to the chair and handed him the brochure. I wanted us to pick out either a guest house or an inn together. But not right now, apparently. I watched his eyes stray to my boobs before he reluctantly accepted it.

"You're deliberately teasing, aren't you?" He asked me.

"Well, what's the rush?" I asked him, settling into his lap, my ass against his expanding dick.

He replaced his eyes with his hands on my body, but I swatted them away and nodded at the brochure.

"Take a look."

"Fine."
He opened it up and then immediately gave a whistle.

"This what I think it is?" He asked, running his eyes over the page.

"I knew you'd love it," I said, laughing.

"Oh honey, you didn't have to," he said, giving me a little kiss behind my ears. I pressed into him.

"I was hoping we could pick out a place together, but we can always get to that later," I said, my voice breathy from his hands on my body. He had trailed it to my nipples, his fingers twirling the nub until they stiffened in his hands. I moaned and rested my head against his neck.

"We should probably move to the bed," he said.

"I like it here," I told him, getting off him and settling on the rug in front of the fireplace. We had about two hours before the party, and I wanted to take advantage of every minute.

Mike made to get off the chair, but I waved him back into it, getting off myself and knelling in front of him. Why not suck him off first. It was his birthday, after all.

I stepped up to him, and I undid his belt as fast as I could, my hands reaching into his shorts to rub at his dick before pulling them down together with his pants. I'd need to pack up fast, but it would be worth it.

"I think I've found someone for us," Mike said when his thick ebony meat popped out.

"Oh," I said, my body quickening. Mike and I had decided to introduce certain dynamics into our marriage. It allowed us to keep our marriage sexy and spicy, allowing ourselves a break from each other and enjoying other people while at it. The sex felt so much better when we got back together, and it was just the two of us.

But no cheating, we had to agree, and we had to be together

while we had sex.

"Who's she?"

"Memi, one of my final year students, she must want me too, and she might be at the party later tonight," he told me with a groan when I put my mouth on him, giving a tiny suck almost immediately. I released him and gave him a couple of teasing licks, my hands fondling his balls as I licked his tip slowly.

"You sure about that? She's your student, after all," I asked him, even as his hands tangled in my hair and my lips tightened around him. I stroked back and forth with my lips, doing my best to keep my lips around his thick girth.

He flinched and hissed in between his teeth. "It'll be consensual. I believe she'll want it as much as we do," he said.

I kept my attention on his dick, my tongue on the tip, egging the pressure I was applying to his body. He gave a loud groan and pulled my head over his dick. I wanted him inside me before he came, and from the way his legs had widened and were moving, he would be on edge soon. I moved my lips down his dick as slowly as possible, taking him in as far as I could, and then gave him a long kick before releasing him.

Mike moaned slightly and opened his eyes. Without waiting a moment to let him get a word in, I sat on his lap and let his dick slip into me.

"Damn," Mike said, releasing a shuddering breath as my own "fuck" filled the room. The rigid head of his dick slid past my folds and into me, the sensation unexplainably good. I raised my hip and brought it back down, Mike raising his hips to meet me halfway. We continued in this way, my cries of pleasure filling the room.

Mike was good, encouraged by the large size of his dick, which was, at that moment, filling me up in ways I couldn't believe. No one had ever been this good. I couldn't believe anyone else would be—not this good.

I felt his hands creep down to my stomach and down to my pussy. His hands rubbed against my clit, fast, then slow, then fast, then slow. It was erotic, and my body felt like it had a will of its own. With each thrust inside me, I lifted and tilted my pussy to meet his perfectly, affording him deeper thrusts and me more pleasure.

I gave a loud moan and felt his hands move to my breasts again. This time, to gently pinch the nipple, the pinch helping me along to my orgasm. I could feel it spreading through me. The heat was all I could think of. I was moist and ready, and very soon, I would be exploding all over him.

"I'll be coming soon, can't take it no more," I told Mike between moans, who somehow managed to increase his pace even more. He was fully in control now, my body too far gone to think of anything else.

"Don't worry," he said, his voice urgent, the movement of his body matching his tone of voice. I threw my hands behind me and wrapped them around the post of the wooden chair he was sitting on, offering him more access to my body.

"Oh Mike, that's good," I cried out in a throaty moan, my head tilted back, my body stiffening in the throes of my orgasm. He pumped harder, his body driving into me spectacularly. He felt him shout my name and then the warmth as he blew his load inside me. He kept thrusting as my body milked his seed from him.

I gave a shuddering breath and relaxed against him. He was breathing heavily, my own breath leaving my body in gasps as the twinges of our orgasms faded away.

"We do get carried away sometimes," Mike said after a moment. His voice was a throaty growl against my ears.

"It's your birthday. That's a great time to get away," I told him, his dick half-hard and buried inside me as he ran his hands through my hair.

"I kept wondering what looked different this whole time," he said, fingering my large curls.

"You like it?" I asked.

"It's a bold color, but you're a bold woman, my Mya. Thank you for making the effort, for being my woman, and for that mind-blowing coitus," he said.

"Only you would say coitus with a straight face, and that's exactly why I love you," I said, getting off his lap and bending over to kiss him softly.

He opened his lips and accepted my kiss, his tongue dueling with mine. If we kept this up, there was no way we'd be ready before the guests arrived.

"We should stop. Our guest will be arriving soon," I told him softly, my lips pressed against his.

"Well, I'm certain they're quite a few of them with voyeur fantasies. It could be our gifts to them," he said with a naughty laugh.

I placed a perfectly round O on his lips and leaned away. I

needed to get a few more things ready before the party, and he could be convincing if he wanted to. I turned away from him.

"I love you, but I'll never be able to live that one down," I told him. I walked away, jiggling my ass at him.

"Well, that's a very provocative way to say no," he said, "and that outfit? How are you still in it?"

"I was wondering the same thing, guess you were too busy devouring me to notice," I said with a wink over my shoulders.

"Nope, I did notice, but it's such a little piece of floss. There's really no need for it anyways," he said, getting off the chair and picking up his tie and shoes.

I bent over slowly in front of him, the skirt riding up and over my ass, my recently mauled pussy, glistening and wet from his cum.

"What do you think now?" I asked.

"We should definitely get you out of it," he said, his eyes bugging. He swept his eyes over me again and took a step forward.

"Nope, maybe later. You missed your chance," I told him, giggling at his disappointed puppy face.

"You're a wicked-wicked tease Mya," he said before giving me a little spank.

I picked up his suitcase and shirt from the rug, and we made our way to the room together. It was time to get ready for the party.

***

Mike's POV

When the sun began to set, I made my way down the stairs to my backyard, feeling excited and a little nervous. I knew that Mya had planned something special for my birthday, and I couldn't wait to see what it was.

As I stepped into the backyard, I was taken aback by the stunning setting that Mya had created. The trees were lit up with warm golden lights, and fairy lights and lanterns had been strung up, casting a warm and inviting glow over the entire space. Mya had outdone herself again.

Soft music played in the background, adding to the relaxed yet elegant ambiance. The dining area had been set up with a beautiful tablecloth and chic tableware, with gorgeous flower arrangements placed strategically throughout. I could hear the chatter of my students and colleagues and the sounds of laughter and music. It was clear that they were all having a great time.

The scent of delicious soul food grilled on the barbecue filled the air, making my mouth water in anticipation. The bar was stocked with a wide variety of top-shelf liquor and fine wines, and bartenders were on hand to mix up any drink the guests desired. Small, intimate seating areas were arranged throughout the yard, with comfortable chairs and sofas that provided the perfect setting for conversation and laughter.

Mya came up to me, giving me a warm hug and a kiss. She led me towards the refreshment table, where she'd laid out a spread of delicious food and drinks. The scent of freshly baked cupcakes filled the air, and I knew that she'd been working hard to make sure that everything was perfect.

"Do you love it?"

"About half as much as I love you," I said before giving her a little kiss and wrapping my hands around her waist. She looked radiant, her auburn hair up in a beautiful bun with a few ringlets framing her face. Her long fuchsia dress had a slit down the side for easy movement while it hugged her curves in all the right places.

Without warning, the birthday song rang out, the sound riotous from the start. The older faculty members sang completely out of tune while the students made more effort to keep their songs in line. They all seemed to be enjoying themselves, though.

"Happy Birthday, Dr. Mike!" one of my faculty members exclaimed as he approached me with a smile. "I hope this year brings you all the joy and happiness you deserve."

"Thank you, I appreciate it," I replied, feeling grateful for the warm wishes.

Another faculty member approached me with a glass of wine in her hand. "Cheers to another year of growth and success," she said, clinking her glass against mine.

I smiled and took a sip of the wine. "Thank you, I couldn't have done it without all of your support and dedication."

Another colleague chimed in, "Speaking of inspiration, have you read that new book on leadership that's been making the rounds lately?"

I shook my head "No, I haven't had a chance to read it yet. Have you?"

"Yes, and it's been a game-changer for me," she replied. "I think you'd really enjoy it, so I got you a copy," she said, handing me a wrapped gift. I gave her a hug and a thank you before moving on to talk to the rest of my guests.

I had noticed Memi alone at the bar, her eyes trailing my every move. She was alone, her glasses perched on her nose as usual. I looked around for Mya and made my way over when I saw her over at the small stage that she'd set up in one corner of the yard. I walked up to her, stopping along to way to speak to a few members of faculty.

"She's over by the bar," I whispered to Mya when I got to her. "In the midi gown."

"Well, she certainly dressed to impress," Mya whispered back, her eyes discreetly scanning the attire, "and she's beautiful. Look at those doe eyes," she added.

"I know, so I talk to her?"

"No, let me handle that. How about we keep her for the night? It'll be a fitting close for such a perfect day," Mya said, looking at me with a smirk.

"She might be a tough nut. Besides, I don't know if she'd be interested," I told her.

"She's been staring at you the whole time. She's definitely interested."

Later in the evening, I found myself in a deep conversation with one of my students about her career aspirations. She shared her dreams of pursuing a career in research but expressed concern about the challenges she might face as a woman in a male-dominated field.

I listened intently and offered some advice based on my own experiences. "It's true that there are still some barriers that need to be overcome, but don't let that stop you from pursuing your dreams," I said. "You have the talent, the drive, and the intelligence to make a difference in the world. And we're all here to support you every step of the way."

As the night wore on, we continued to enjoy the festivities, sharing stories and laughter. Mya brought out the cake, and I cut into it with a round of loud applause from the guests present. It was a wonderful moment, and I felt truly grateful for the amazing people in my life.

I kept my eyes on Memi the whole time, watching as she guzzled down drink after drink, she and Mya had been talking, and she seemed to have loosened up a bit more. She laughed at a joke Mya made, her hands trailing slowly off her arm when she put it there.

So, she's definitely interested then, I thought.

The party wound down with most of the guests saying their goodbyes and leaving their gifts in the house, where a gift hamper had been placed. Mya blew kisses and gave hugs to the faculty members and shared a laugh with the students. They all seemed to like her. But then, everyone seemed to like Mya.
I moved down the lawn and walked over to her.

"Where's Memi?"

"She offered to help with some of the dishes. Isn't that sweet?" She said, looking up at me.

"She's spending the night?" I asked.

"She's the type who's willing to try anything, so maybe yes, but she's not certain. She did say she's in a relationship," Mya said.

"That's a party pooper," I said, my face clouding over with disappointment.

"Oh, don't worry about it. Maybe he'll be interested in joining. We've never had two at once," Mya said with a giggle. Then I realized she was slightly tipsy, probably from guzzling all those drinks with Memi.

We waited while the rest of the guests left, and then I took her hand, and we walked inside together. The backyard would need a ton of cleaning, but Mya had paid a clean-up crew, so that would be easy enough to deal with.

Memi was stacking some plates into the dishwasher when we stepped inside. She turned towards us, startled by our sudden appearance.

"I didn't know it was you, Dr. Mike," she said, cleaning her hands on a dish towel when she was done.

"Call me Mike," I said to her. "And thanks for dealing with that," I added, nodding toward the dishwasher.

Mya held her hands out.

"Come," she said, leading her out of the kitchen when Memi took her hands.

5 The Encounter

I followed Mya from the kitchen and down to the lounge. Their home was beautiful, and it seemed to fit their personality. Or at least my idea of what their personality was.

Except maybe not, Mya had hinted that she and Mike were wondering if I would be interested in joining them in bed tonight. I just hadn't been able to believe that. I never would've guessed they'd do that. They looked too perfect together to need anyone or anything else.

Dr. Mike was my lecturer, and he'd probably noticed me making moon eyes at him by now—probably why they had picked me out of all the other girls. So maybe my efforts hadn't been a complete waste.

I was delirious, the one hitch being the fact that Tye was probably waiting at home for me. He wouldn't be too happy if I didn't make it back home tonight—birthday party or not.

I settled on the couch with Mya and watched as she pulled off her heels, the straps leaving indents on her glistening dark skin.

"The things we do for beauty," I said to her when she leaned over to massage her feet. Mike watched us, his eyes following her movements greedily. Mya suddenly shifted closer and put her hands on my thighs.

"Did you think about it?" She asked, her voice low.

"I did, and I don't believe cheating on Tye would be the best choice right now," I told her, shaking my head.

"Then maybe he would be interested in joining us, our last was a male, but we wouldn't mind having two at once now. Who knows, he might enjoy it," Mike said.

And knowing Tye, he probably would too. Or maybe that was the lust speaking. I turned towards Dr. Mike and stared at him for a moment. I wanted him. And if this was the only way I could have him, then I wasn't giving it up.

I nodded my head slowly and watched as they gave a collective sigh of relief. They really cared about my reply then.

"We should move to our room," Mike said before getting off the couch and extending his hands to the both of us. Mya took my hands and made her way over to him. We went up the stairs together, down the hallway, and into the last room on the right.

"Wow, this is really pretty," I said. The room was done up in warm tones, the walls a pastel color. It was very minimalistic.

"Thank you, we love it," Mya said. She turned to me and asked me to help unzip her dress. My hands shook slightly as I slowly pulled the zip down, exposing the smooth length of her back in small increments. I leaned in and kissed her, her skin pebbling when she felt my lips on her.

"Oh," she breathed.

Mike settled on the sofa opposite the bed to watch. He gave me a wink before working on the buttons of his shirt, his eyes feasting greedily on us.

I pulled the zip down completely, my eyes on Mike. I wanted him as much as I wanted to feel Mya under me. This was the most adventurous I had ever been, and they were apparently about to let me take the lead.

I kissed her shoulders, all the way down to where the zip ended, and then kissed my way back up to her shoulders before pushing the dress off to expose her lace lingerie. I turned her to face me, her body following my lead. I pushed the bra straps off her shoulders, kissing my way down her chest and stomach. I sneaked my hands behind her and pulled the hooks free, releasing her breast into the air.

Her breasts were perfect, the two round globes perky, with her dusky nipples out in the air. I threw the bra to the floor and bent closer, my lips on her collarbone. I resumed kissing, my tongue swiping out occasionally as I trailed my way down her body. I wanted to feast on her.

Moving down to her stomach, I pushed the dress off her waist, and then the lingerie bottoms followed the same way. She was naked now, her body as beautiful as any I had ever seen. Her dark skin glistened in the semi-dark room, her skin taut and smooth. Her brown legs were long, her stomach still flat, probably from a lot of exercises, she seemed like the type. She looked toned; her skin well taken care of.

"You're beautiful," I told her.

"So are you," she replied before stepping out of her panties and kicking them away. She got on the bed and spread her legs out, probably inviting me to eat her out. I'd only ever done this once, but you never really forget. It was like riding a bike, after all.

I got on the bed beside her and placed my lips over hers to kiss her. The kiss started slowly, her lips like melting butter against mine, soft and tentative like she was trying not to overshadow me. I pressed mine forcefully against hers and felt her respond. I pushed my tongue against her lips, licking at hers when she opened her mouth and let me in. We continued kissing for a while, my tongue tangling with hers occasionally.

Eventually, I pulled away and made my way down her body to her wet pussy, bent over to be as near to her as possible. Her pussy had been shaved clean; the lips already swollen slightly. I knelt on the bed, my ass in the air and my legs spread before pushing her legs apart and sliding my hands to her pussy lips.

"Come on, Memi, gimme some more," she moaned softly as my hands made it up her legs. My heart was racing; before me was the most beautiful sight. She was almost hairless, and that was arousing enough on its own. Parting her puffy lips apart with my thumbs, her inner lips were glistening with her juices.

I slid my thumbs into her folds, stretching the skin open and pushing her pussy lips apart to reveal her swollen clit. Her juices were already secreting, the creamy wet juice dripping as I stroked her. She leaned back on her hands, her body flushed and her chest rising and falling with her quickened breathing. I looked up at her.

"Is this want you want, Baby?" I asked.

I leaned in and licked her pussy, my tongue sweeping out to catch her juices as they came spilling out of her. She tasted divine, and my tongue went in once more, digging for more. She moaned and gasped,

"Yes...Oh yes," I repeated the process, and she pressed into my lips, her back arching off the bed. I took my lips off, and she groaned in disappointment. I looked behind me and noticed Mike had lost his pants, and his hands were on his dick, slowly stroking it as he watched us.

I closed my mouth over her budding clit again, this time drawing the sensitive flesh into my mouth, sucking and flicking my tongue over it.

She was gasping now, tilting her hips toward my mouth,

"More Memi, don't stop, please."

If only she knew just how uninterested I was in stopping. As I continued sucking on her, I slid one of my fingers over her entrance to coat it in her juices and then pushed it into her. My hands slid in slowly, first with one finger and then the next.

Her pussy clenched against my fingers. I turned them over, bending and curling my fingers inside her to stroke her pussy walls. Her hips pushed further against my mouth as she panted and gasped.

"Fuck, that feels so good" she moaned loudly.

Well, look who has a dirty tongue. I could feel her muscles tense as she crept to her climax. I continued to suck on her clit and finger-fuck her, my eyes on her face as her body got more wound up, sweat breaking out on her skin. Her legs started to shake, and a moment later, her pussy walls milked my fingers as she climaxed, and I pressed my fingers deeper, letting her ride the wave of her orgasm. I kept at it till she gently calmed after the orgasm. Her chest rose and fell quickly.

"Damn, you're good," she said, smiling when she regained control over her body.

That was exactly what I had hoped to hear. I lay on the bed beside her, my eyes roving over to Mike, who got off the chair and made it over to us.

"Your turn now," he said.

"I'm looking forward to it, but how about you fuck me already? I'm teased enough. I want you inside me," I told him boldly.

I did want him badly, and after eating Mya out, I just couldn't *not* have him. I couldn't take it anymore. I ran my hands down to my body and stroked myself softly, all the while keeping my eye on his. He turned to Mya, and at her nod, he pulled me to the edge of the bed and slipped into me.

I moaned immediately; my starving pussy filled completely by his thick girth. I raked my hands up his back, my body responding immediately as he thrust into me quickly.

"Faster, Dr. Mike, faster," I moaned into his ears. Mya got off the bed and walked over. She put her hands over my pussy and started strumming the clit quickly. It would be over too fast at this rate, and I wanted to enjoy this.

"Get on me," I told her, indicating that she lay on my body with her legs spread out beside me. She complied, getting into the bed and throwing her legs over me before she shimmied down my body, her pussy over mine.

"Get into her," I told Mike. He pulled out immediately and pushed into her with a groan. I watched his face greedily, his pleasure as arousing as his dick in my body.

"Mmmm," Mya breathed on top of me. The friction as her body shook on top of mine was delicious. I worked my hands between us to fondle Mike's balls. He closed his eyes tightly and banged into her, over and over again, until she came on top of me, moaning her orgasm out loud, her body shaking slightly. Then she went limp like a rag doll on top of me.

Mike immediately pulled out of her and slid his length into me, his pace even faster than before. His legs were shaking as he kept up his strokes. He was obviously close to his orgasm. Mya must've noticed the same thing because she got off me and into the 6-9 position, her pussy right over my face while her face went over mine.

She flicked her tongue out and gave me an experimental lick. I moaned loudly and asked for more.

"Gimme more," I moaned again.

"I'm close," Mike panted, his voice a sexy little growl.

"Give me some time. I'll get her off real soon," Mya said, increasing the pace of her sucks and her licks. She placed her hands over my clit and rubbed it fast, her other finger running over my folds in fast strokes.

"Fuck, that feels good, faster, Mya," I moaned. It really did feel good, the stroke of her soft skin against mine pushing me toward my climax. I felt my body getting closer to the edge.

"Can I cum inside you?" Mike asked, his eyes wide as he slammed into me again and again.

"Yeah, do it," I answered.

He pushed deeper, tilting my hips up slightly to afford him deeper penetration. His style was screwed, his body just pushing into mine, chasing my pleasure as well as his. I felt my body quickening and then stiffening.

"I'm...cummming," I screamed, my body lifting off the bed as my orgasm came upon me. Mike came a moment later, his hot cum splashing against my walls as he came.

He must've been holding on by a thread, waiting for me to cum so he could, too, I thought absently.

Mya got off me and dropped like a log beside me on the bed.

"For a first timer, that was pretty hot," she said. "I assume, of course, that you're a first timer," she added, giving me a soft kiss before pulling away and falling on the bed again.

Mike gave a final groan and fell beside us, with me in the middle. I felt cocooned between them, my body sandwiched by their bodies. I loved it.

"Thank you for doing this with us, Memi," Mike said, leaning over me, his head on his hands.

"It's fine. I loved it too," I told him. His dark skin looked epic, completely unblemished by age or injury. I ran my hand over it just because I wanted to know what it felt it. No way my skin felt this good. It was almost velvety to the touch, like a baby's skin or a rich dowager back from the spa.

That must be Mya's doing, I thought with a little giggle to myself.

I stretched out on the bed and closed my eyes, it was late, and my body felt limp from my orgasm. No way I'd be leaving this place on my own legs tonight. Mya shifted closer, and I pushed down to cuddle up against her soft boobs, my head right over her chest.

She placed her legs across mine and closed her eyes. I felt more relaxed as Mike spread his arms over the both of us. Then our breathing slowly evened out as we dropped off to sleep together.

Tye's POV

As I walked into the spacious gym, the aroma of sweat and metal filled my nostrils. I could feel the energy in the air, with the sound of weights clanking and upbeat music blasting through the speakers. The walls were lined with mirrors, giving a clear view of the equipment and the people using them.

The gym was well-lit, with fluorescent lights illuminating every corner of the room. The floor was lined with rubber mats designed to absorb the impact of heavy weights being dropped. A variety of equipment was scattered around the room, including benches, racks, and machines, each designed to target specific muscle groups.

In the center of the gym was a large, open space, perfect for high-intensity workouts or group classes. The walls were adorned with motivational posters and fitness slogans, inspiring anyone who trained there to push themselves harder.

"Alright, everyone, let's get started," I called out to my students, who were scattered around the gym, warming up. "Today, we're going to focus on upper body strength. We'll start with some bench presses and move onto some pull-ups and dips."

I could see the excitement on their faces as they made their way over to the bench press station. "Remember to keep your back straight, and your feet planted firmly on the ground," I instructed. "Don't forget to breathe out as you lift the barbell."

As they lifted the barbells, I walked around the gym, offering tips and advice to anyone who needed it. I could see the determination in their eyes, and it made me proud. They were all pushing themselves to be their best, and that's all I could ask for.

"Good job, everyone," I said as they finished their sets. "Now, let's move onto some pull-ups." I demonstrated the proper form and encouraged them to do their best.

"Great job today, guys," I said as we all gathered around. "Keep up the hard work, and I'll see you all next week."

As I was packing up my equipment, my girlfriend Memi walked into the gym. She looked a little disheveled, as if she had just woken up.

"Hey, babe," I said, greeting her with a kiss on the cheek. "Are you okay? I was worried about you last night."

"I'm fine," she replied with a slight smile. "I just stayed at a party a little longer than I intended to."

"What? You spent the night at their place?" I asked, my brows arched in question.

"The time kind of got away from me, love," she said, looking away from me at the rest of my students who had dispersed to their various mats.

"He's a nice guy letting you sleep over without notice," I said, shaking my head.

"His wife's the hot one. They've invited us over for dinner. What do you think?" She asked, staring up at me, her eyes pleading. Memi obviously wanted me to go with her, and why not? It could be fun. Memi was always talking about her hot male lecturer, and now I get to meet his hot wife.

"We'll talk about it later in my office," I told her with a wink.

I couldn't help feeling relieved that she was safe. I didn't like the idea of her being out late without me.

"Did you come to work out with us?" I asked playfully, gesturing towards the group of students who were still finishing up their workout.

Memi nodded. "Yeah, I need to burn off all 'those calories from last night," she sidled closer and added softly, just for my ears, "there's also the fact that I missed you."

"You can prove that to me later," I told her just as softly before chuckling. "Alright, let's get you set up."

I quickly grabbed a pair of dumbbells and led Memi over to a corner of the gym where we could work out together.

"Okay, we'll start with some bicep curls," I instructed, handing her a set of weights. "Remember to keep your elbows close to your body and exhale as you lift the weights."

Memi followed my instructions, and I watched as her biceps flexed with each repetition. She was a natural athlete, and I loved watching her push herself to be better. Also, she looked damned sexy, and her butt pushed out as she bent over to lift the weights, her glasses replaced with contacts so she could move her body without worrying about them falling off.

As we moved onto other exercises, I could see the other students watching us, impressed by Memi's strength and form. I couldn't help but feel a sense of pride, knowing that she was mine. I could be possessive, but only because Memi loved it as much as I did.

As the workout ended, I could see that Memi was exhausted but satisfied with her effort. I knew she would be sore tomorrow, but I also knew that she would be proud of herself for pushing through.

"Great job, everyone," I said, clapping my hands. "Y'all killed it today. Now, don't forget to stretch and hydrate."

As the students began to disperse, Memi and I made our way over to the water fountain. She took a long drink, and I could see the sweat pouring down her face.

"Are you okay?" I asked, concerned.

"Yeah, I'm just tired," she replied, wiping her forehead with the back of her hand. "That was a tough workout."

I smiled, proud of her effort. "You did great, babe. I'm proud of you."

She grinned, looking a little more energetic now. "Thanks, Tye. I must admit, I feel pretty badass right now."

I laughed. "You are pretty badass, if I do say so myself."

We made our way over to a bench to stretch, and I helped her with some stretches to loosen up her muscles.

"Ow," she groaned as I helped her stretch her hamstrings.

"That means it's working," I replied, grinning.

As we finished up our stretching, Memi turned to me. "Tye, can we talk for a minute?"

I nodded, curious as to what she wanted to talk about. "Sure, what's up?"

"I just wanted to say that I'm sorry for worrying you last night," she said, looking a little sheepish. "I didn't mean to stay out so late, but I got caught up in the party."

I took her hand, looking into her eyes. "It's okay, babe. I'm just glad you're safe. But maybe next time, you could let me know where you are?"

She nodded, looking a little guilty. "I will. I promise."

I could see the sincerity in her eyes, and I knew that she meant it. "Okay, then. It's all good. Now, how about we grab some food and head back to my place?"

Memi smiled, looking relieved. "That sounds great."

As we made our way out of the gym, she linked her hands through mine and talked non-stop about the party. Strange that she seemed more energetic this morning than usual.

"Tye, you need to meet Mya. She's hot; I'm certain you'll love her," she said, sounding enthused.

"Okay? I love her already, Memi, but can we not talk about how hot she is? We're going to the lady's house for dinner," I reminded her.

"I really don't think she minds," she said, turning towards me.

"Now, how would you know?" I asked her.

"They're really laid back, and they swing both ways, if you know what I mean," she said, wiggling her eyebrows suggestively.

That wasn't my Memi. She never would've said that with a straight face, not her.

"That sounds interesting. Would that be why they're inviting us over for dinner?" I asked her suspiciously.

"No need to sound so suspicious, Tye," she said, laughing out loud.

"Well, count me in," I said. If she was as hot as Memi made her sound, then I would not be averse to having a share of the pie. Besides, if it was Memi's idea, then it technically wasn't cheating.

"We'll go see them tomorrow then," Memi said.

We walked the rest of the way home, the pack of takeout swinging in my hands. Memi was silent now, her forehead creased whenever she looked up at me. I pushed open the door and walked in.

"Are you sure you're okay?" I asked her when I had set the satchel on the kitchen counter. She'd settled on the counter beside me, watching as I laid out the meal.

"I'm perfectly fine. I've just missed you an awful lot," she said as she got off the counter.

"Best time to prove it," I told her, my arms open as I waited for her to step into it. She gave me an almost shy hug before placing her lips on mine and giving me a kiss, which was the opposite of her shy demeanor a minute before.

"I want you to fuck me already, Tye," she said, pulling away and getting her sportswear off. Thinking of that, she must've been home before coming over to the gym. She certainly hadn't left the house in that last night. I got rid of my own clothes just as fast and watched as she walked over to the counter and leaned against it, showing off her ass.

I walked over, my hands stroking my dick to get it hard. I slid my fingers into her slowly, testing to see how wet she was. My fingers slid in, her pussy already wet. I removed my hand and replaced it with my dick. Memi was shaking in anticipation.

"Fuck it." She growled as she slid back on me. Hard.

I arched my back in pleasure, a moan escaping me. I grabbed her hips and smashed myself into her, my hips smacking against hers. Her nails reached behind her and scratched across my chest. Sweet pain exploded across my brain. This was one of the very reasons I loved her, her ability to mix pain with pleasure, the pain as exhilarating as the pleasure.

I pressed her into the counter, pulling her hands behind her and locking them with one of mine, my hips jammed in and out, her wet cavern receiving me. I was being rough, and I didn't care. I only cared about the heat of her, like a glove wrapped around me. My hands found her hips, and I ground her deeper and deeper into me as she rocked back and forth.

"Fucking damn!" I called out as she ground against me, repeatedly.

She leaned back against me, and I wrapped my arms around her, enclosing then around her breast. I pinched her nipples hard; her moans and cries filled the room as she threw her head back in pleasure. I kept up my thrusts, my dick surging in and out of her.

Suddenly she leaned into me, her thrusting increased in speed, and her hands splayed out on the counter. Her thighs tightened across my legs, and I knew she was about to cum. She was squirming, her body shaking as she got closer. The thought of her orgasm against me almost made me cum then.

"Fuck!" She shouted out at the top of her voice. Her pussy tightened around me. My hands found her hips, and I ground her hips against mine. Her moans filled the room. I was barely holding on by a thread. All I could think about at that moment was the blinding orgasm surging through my body.

Wave after wave of cum shot out of my dick, straight into her. I roared out my pleasure, the sound loud in the kitchen. My body quivered in pleasure, my arms tightening around her.

I flipped her around, and sinking my hands into her hair, I pulled her into me and kissed her roughly.

She broke away and looked up at me. "We're visiting them tomorrow, right? And we're spending the night."

"Fine, whatever you want," I agreed.

6. "The Meet and Greet"

As Memi and I approached the house, I felt a mixture of nerves and excitement. I wanted to make a good first impression. I'd even worked on my hair somewhat after I got home from the gym. I was looking forward to meeting Mya in person, and I knew Memi was excited to see Mike outside of a professional setting.

As we walked up the drive, I couldn't help taking in the surroundings. Mike and Mya's house was beautiful, with a well-maintained garden and a neatly trimmed lawn. We knocked on the door, and Mya greeted us with a warm smile.

"Hey, you made it!" she exclaimed, giving us each a hug. "Mikes in the kitchen. He's just finishing up with dinner. Come on in," Mya said, gesturing to the living room.

She was a statuesque woman with smooth brown skin, curly auburn hair, and an infectious laugh. She wore a simple yet stylish outfit consisting of black jeans, a white blouse, and a colorful scarf wrapped around her neck. And yes, she was hot. I found my eyes straying to her ass when she turned around to lead us into the house.

We followed her into the house, and I took in the décor. The walls were adorned with artwork and photographs, and there were plenty of books on the shelves. As we made our way to the kitchen, I noticed that the furniture was a mix of modern and vintage pieces, giving the room a unique and eclectic feel.

We walked into the kitchen, and I couldn't help but admire how organized and clutter-free it looked. The countertops were clean,

Mike was at the stove, stirring a pot of fragrant curry. The smell wafting from the stove was delicious.

He turned around as we entered and greeted us with a friendly smile.

"Hey, Tye, Memi," he said, wiping his hands on a dish towel. "Glad you guys could make it."

He was a tall man with short curly hair that framed his face perfectly. He had warm brown eyes, a broad smile, and a confident yet approachable presence. He was dressed in a simple t-shirt and jeans, with a colorful apron tied around his waist as he finished cooking. He greeted us warmly, with a twinkle in his eye that suggested he had a joke or two up his sleeve.

We chatted with Mike as he put the finishing touches to the meal, and I couldn't help but admire his culinary skills. The curry smelled amazing, and I knew it was going to be a delicious meal.

When the meal was finished, we moved together to the table. Mya brought the food out with Memi helping her with some of the platters, and she had offered to lend a helping hand.

I watched them together, noticing the easy familiarity between them. Maybe Mike wasn't aware, but those two must've had sex together. It was obvious, from the way Memi looked up at Mya with a secret smile on her face to how Mya responded to that smile. It was a look of intimacy and one I had only ever seen her wear around me.

"How do you love your classes?" Mike asked Memi when she and Mya had settled down. The food was getting passed around the table.

"Very much, I have a little difficulty with some of the themes, but

I'm certain I'll get them with a little work," she said, smiling at him.

"And Tye, Memi told us you're a fitness instructor. Do you love that?" he asked me.

"Very much so, or I wouldn't be doing it," I answered with a giggle, my mouth munching on the crispy side of prawns they had cooked up.

"You could hook me up with an instructor?" Mya asked suggestively.

"I could be your instructor," I answered just as suggestively—no need for the cat-and-mouse game. I was interested, and I wanted to make it known.

Memi smiled at me before looking away and attacking her meal.

"I'm guessing Memi told you about our...?" Mike said.

"She did hint at something, not sure what," I broke in when he couldn't seem to find the word.

"Well, we're looking forward to experiencing sex with another couple, and we're having you, and Memi would agree to join us," he said, his face kind of blank like he wasn't certain we would agree, and he didn't want to appear too eager.

"We could be, but you and Memi have a professional relationship. Are you certain about this?" I asked, my eyes on him, trying to get every show of emotion. "This could come back to bite her in the butt."

"This is going to be between the four of us. We can always break it off if anything goes haywire," Mike said, looking at Memi and then at me.

I turned to Memi and waited for her nod of approval before I nodded at Mike and Mya to indicate our agreement. Her face broke out in a smile.

Mya led the way out of the room and down the hallway to an open room. We all settled on the bed.

She grabbed my hand and looked at Mike with an impish smile. "Mike, be a good host and take care of Memi," she said and winked.

Mike held out his hands to Memi, and she crawled into them. I watched as she slowly pulled his clothes off him, her lips meshed with his in a kiss. I watched them for a moment as she and Mike eagerly explored each other's bodies.

Then I turned to Mya. She had already slipped out of her clothes. I stifled a groan of disappointment; I would have enjoyed taking her out of them.

"Would you like to watch, have your own fun, or both?" I asked her.

She giggled softly. "We have enough time for all that. Let's get you out of these duds," she said, already unbuttoning my shirt and pulling it off my shoulders. Then she threw it behind her and grabbed my hard-on through my pants. She gave me a few tentative strokes and then rolled over on her back.

"Come on, show me what you got," she said as she waved invitingly to me.

I lay down on the bed, as close to her as I could get, and slowly kissed her neck, my hands caressing down her thighs. She closed her eyes and took deep breaths. I kissed my way to her body and licked at her tits as my hands rubbed gently at her clit.

I wasn't certain what gave her pleasure, unlike with Memi, where I was certain how to strum her body to orgasm. It would be an experience finding out what pleased her and what didn't.

But from the way her back arched off the bed, I knew she loved me kneading her clit, so I increased my pace, sliding my finger across her pussy lips occasionally. After I found the right move, it only took me a few minutes to bring her to a climax.

It hit her in waves, and she moaned softly while her body shook slightly, then she arched her back and moaned loudly. I tried to prolong her orgasm by sliding my fingers into her and massaging her clit until they became too sensitive, and she started bucking against my fingers, pulling away as much as pushing against me.

"That was fast. You've got magic fingers," she said, grinning from her perch on the bed when she had calmed down.

"Anytime, Mya," I said, and I leaned in to kiss her when we suddenly became aware of Memi's loud cries coming from beside us.

We silently turned to them to watch what was going on. Memi had grabbed on to the bedpost and was holding on for dear life, her head thrown back, and eyes shut right as Mike pumped into her from behind with powerful thrusts which pushed her body forward with each thrust in.

Memi cried a loud "Yeah" every time Mike pushed his dick fully into her pussy. Her body looked hot and bent over like that to receive his thrusts. She pushed against him; her slender body spread out for his invasion.

Mike's body was dotted with sweat, his forehead tight as he kept upright behind Memi. He ran his hands over her back and down to her pussy lips, his fingers slipping back and forth over them as he fucked her hard.

Keeping my eyes on the two of them, I stepped behind Mya and slipped my finger into her to check how wet she still was or wasn't. When her juices coated my finger, I guided my dick into her pussy. She spread her legs apart when she felt the tip of my dick nudging against her entrance.

I slipped effortlessly into her pussy and started sliding in and out slowly at first, pushing my dick in to the hilt and then pulling out just as slowly till it was just the tip left in her. I hissed out through my teeth, Mya's moan coming a moment later when I pushed back into her.

I kept it up, but then my thrusts escalated to match Mike's thrust into Memi. I grabbed her tits from behind, and she pressed her head into the bed for support.
We were both panting loudly, Memi and Mike's moans just as loud beside us. They seemed lost together in a sea of pleasure like nothing could reach them on their island of lust.

I increased the pace of my thrusts as I watched Memi shaking, her hands slipping off the bed posts as her orgasm hit hard. She started shaking as Mike pulled out of her and let his seed cover her ass. He used his dick to spread it all over before massaging it into her with his hands.

I focused on Mya then, closing my eyes as her walls tightened around me in a vice-like grip. The sound of her moans increased like a crescendo. She pushed over the edge into the abyss of her orgasm, and I pushed into her finally before I came myself in her pussy, giving her one last deep hard thrust.

We both fought for breath to control the strength of our gasps as I slowly pulled my dick out of her and opened my eyes. It was only then that I noticed that Memi and Mike were watching us.

"I must say you two were really hot," Memi said.

"Well, you and my husband were on fire. No better way to put it," Mya answered.

Then she got off the bed and moved over to Mike. She gave him a quick kiss before whispering in his ears. She waited for his nod before she lowered herself to her knees and took his semi-hard dick into her mouth. Mike closed his eyes and then shook his head.

"Damn, I don't think that's a good idea. You'll have to keep at it for a while," he said, looking down at her on her knees.

"How about I give you some time to recuperate while I clean off your dick?" She said, giggling at his dismayed expression. Not waiting for an answer, she licked his shaft from all angles, cleaning it up nicely. Then she got off the floor and went to the bed to do the same to me.

Memi watched her silently, a speculative look on her face. She turned to Mya.

"Would it be fine if they both fucked me at the same time?" She asked, her eyes on Mya, who was still cleaning me up.

"You mean together?" Mya asked, her eyes widening slightly as she looked at the meat between our legs. "I wouldn't advise that," she said with a dirty little laugh.

"You're right. I've never done that before, I just thought it might be fun," Memi said. I'd never known she might enjoy that. But like Mya said, we were both pretty well hung. It might be too much for a first timer. I'd never even fucked her in the ass before.

"You could fuck them together, though, one in and out and then the next, just not at the same time. What do you think?" Mya asked. She had finished with me and spread out on the bed like a cat about to take a nap. Her breast rose and fell with the movement of her breath in and out. It was mesmerizing to watch.

Even better was the fact that Memi was giving serious consideration to her suggestion. Her brows creased as she thought about it.

"I'd love Tye to go first if that's fine with the both of you," she said finally.

I felt a slight jolt of pleasure that she preferred to have me first before she had Mike. I watched her softly before beckoning her over. She slid into the bed and crawled to me. Mike gave her a light smack when she passed beside him with her ass in the air.

"I love you," I whispered to her. "And you don't have to do it," I added.

"I want to try, but I'd love to rest a moment; the night's still young," she said softly to me.

Then she got off the bed and stretching her hands out to Mya, they moved into the bathroom together. A moment later, the shower turned on, and the sound of their giggles reached our ears.

"Would you like a snack? I feel famished after these things," Mike asked me.

"I could use a drink," I answered him. I picked my clothes off the floor and slipped into my pants. No need to walk around their home with my dick swinging. Not that I thought they'd mind. It was more for my comfort than theirs.

We were still in the kitchen when Mya and Memi reappeared. They were both naked and didn't seem to care. A look at them, and my deflated dick gave a twinge and decided to give its life a second chance.

As though pre-planned, they both bent over in front of us, supposedly rummaging in the cabinets below. Neither of them came up with anything, though, their hands empty when they turned back to us. I watched them greedily as they bounced around the kitchen together.

This torture was deliberate, and I was certain of it now.

***

Memi's POV

I watched with a smile on my lips as their eyes tracked us around the kitchen. This was all fun and games, but I couldn't wait to get back to the room. This was the most adventurous I had ever been sexually, and I really didn't want the night to end. The cherry on the cream being the fact that Tye seemed to be enjoying himself as much as I was.

I wanted to take him and Mike at once, but like Mya had said, it might be a bit much for me. Wishing I'd let Mike fuck me in the ass sometime before now, I watched as his eyes followed Mya around.

Mya had one of the best bodies I had even seen on a woman, not that I'd had the chance to see a lot of naked female bodies. Her hips were slender, and her complexion was rich. She smiled with her whole face except when she was in the bedroom. There, she groaned and twisted and shivered, her loud screams filling the room.

I wanted a chance to eat her up, to have a go at her waxed pussy. I was certain it would taste perfect. I let my eyes stray to the poles which were slowly but surely tenting in front of Tye and Mike. And they weren't making any effort to hide it either.

We stayed in the kitchen for some time, eating small bites and some snacks, and I also opened a bottle of red wine when Mike gave me directions to where they stored them. Mike, Mya, and Tye talked about their jobs and colleagues while I spoke about the daily struggle of being a student in America.

At about twelve o'clock, we went into the living room. Mike and Mya settled in front of the fireplace, with Mya placing her head in his lap. He ran his hand softly through her auburn hair, his face tender.

I settled into Tye's lap on the sofa he had chosen. I kissed him, my eyes open. Tye never kissed with his eyes open, so I almost always kept mine open to watch him while we kissed. I pressed my lips tightly against his, his lips opening when he felt my tongue probe at them.

I ran my hands over his abs, a testament to his job at the gym as an instructor and the many hours he slept there working on himself.

"You are one hot-hot man, Tye Smith," I said to him.

"So are you my love, and to think you're mine," he said to me, nipping at my lips with an exaggerated growl.

I gave him an impish smile before sidling off his body. He

watched me as I captured his dick in my hands and locked my lips around the throbbing length. I kept my eyes locked on his while my hands gave him stroke after stroke. I hadn't had the chance to pleasure him all night, and I wanted to make this count.

Besides, he would probably last a whole lot more now he had already blown his load with Mya.

"Who's your little Dick sucker?" I asked him, taking my lips off to swipe at him with my tongue.

"You, you're also my sexy little kitten," he answered me. He was looking down at me with wide eyes, and I absolutely loved it. He knew he was in for something good.

He sat up on the sofa and spread his legs to allow me more access to his thickening meat. Mya and Mike were still kissing on the rug in front of the fireplace, their kiss more tender than lusty.

"Why don't you lie back and let me take over?" Tye asked suddenly, his brow arched in question.

"Are you certain?" I asked. The only thing better than giving pleasure was receiving it, so when he nodded, I got on the sofa and watched him spread my legs wide and settle in front of me.

"The game is on," he said to me, a wild smile on his face. He started on my belly, spending a few minutes laving at my inner navel before moving up my body to my erect nipples. He stroked me with his tongue, his lips suckling at the extended flesh like a baby. I put my hand behind his head and pressed him closer.

When he took his head off to kiss down my body again, I gave a weak moan of protest, which quickly became one of pleasure when his mouth closed around my pussy. Then he moved away from my pussy, kissing down my thighs and around my lips without touching it.

He continued kissing around my pussy, and my head was thrashing on the bed by now, craving his hot lips, or at this point, even his tongue would've done. Just as suddenly as his mouth had left, I felt his finger penetrate my walls roughly. I was caught off guard, and I released a loud moan before I could stifle it. Not that I wanted to stifle it, of course.

He sniffed at my pussy for a moment and soon was kissing me there. He massaged my clit with his thumb, slowly but surely driving me to yet another orgasm. I'd lost count of how many I had had just this night alone. No way around it, I would be terribly sore come morning, but I wouldn't give this up to save myself the trouble—no way in hell.

Tye began pushing his tongue into my slit, his rhythm matching that of his thumb against my clit. I moaned as I let the pleasure control my body, it's movements and response. I felt my orgasm brewing again.

"I'm gonna cum soon," I moaned aloud to warn him. He kept kissing and licking and tongue fucking me, the combination of all three pushing me to the edge and then over it into a body-shatteringly good orgasm.

"I'm cummminggg," I screamed into the room, my body rising off the couch as the force of it hit me. I wrapped my legs around his head, forcing him to keep at it even while I panted and moaned and groaned my orgasm. I felt my juices spilling out of me and the lapping motion as he kissed it all up.

He kept massaging my clit until I finally released his head as the force of my orgasm receded. When I had somewhat calmed down, he laughed aloud.

"You could've sure as hell strangled me to death, Kitten," he said, slapping softly at my wet pussy. It made a smacking sound.

"I'm sorry," I said to him with an embarrassed little smile. I hadn't meant to press my legs so tightly against his. He got off the floor and, taking my hands, led me over to Mike and Memi.

I lay back down and spread my legs again, and I watched as Mike got off the rug and put his hands to his hard wood, stroking it as he watched me open my legs. Tye slipped into me first, not taking care at all with his thrust.

Memi got off the floor and sat on my face, offering herself to me. I attached my lips to her pussy eagerly, my tongue going to her clit immediately, her moan of pleasure my reward.

"Come on, faster," I panted at Tye behind me. He must've been watching Mya's heaving breast because his pace had slipped. He picked up his pace, pushing into me with one move and fucking with steady, long strokes of his body into mine.

I noticed that Mya's legs were moving randomly as her pleasure built up. Certainly, she would cum all over my face soon.

"Come over, Mike," she said with a voice full of passion. Mike walked over, and she stroked him, our moans filling the room as we pleasured each other. Tye kept pushing his dick deep into my pussy, a grain leaving his body with every push in.

Then without warning, he thrust into me once more and went stiff behind me, his body quaking as his orgasm took over. He pulled out and came all over my ass, thoughtful even as his pleasure clouded his mind.

Mike immediately pulled out of Mya's grasp and replaced him behind me, his strokes softer as compared to Tye's deep strokes from a moment ago. Then he slowly picked up the same rhythm.

He fucked me fast and slow, alternating between the two rhythms. It was all I could do to keep my focus on Mya. He pulled his dick out slowly, and when he was only halfway out, he'd push it back in fast and hard.

Finally, he decided to use his thumb to massage my clit as his thrusts became quicker. In the meantime, Mya had gotten off my face, and Tye was using three fingers to slowly fuck her while he sucked her clit with his mouth.

I knew she wouldn't be able to stand his head game for long, and from the look of excitement on her face, she would be cumming soon. I wasn't surprised when she suddenly dropped her head back, closed her eyes, and just moaned aloud.

"That's it, Tye," she said between moans, her body completely seized by pleasure as Tye continued to roughly finger-fuck her. He only stopped fingering her when her body stopped shaking. Then he leaned forward and kissed her.

I moaned as Mike shoved his dick into me, his grunts resounding. We were not even trying to hold back ourselves. He pushed his dick in deep, and I felt my walls tighten around him as my body exploded into an amazing orgasm. I came first, my shout filling the room, and then immediately after, Mike came with a loud grunt, shooting his load inside me.

Then we just collapsed on the floor together, breathing in tandem. Tye and Mya were snuggled together, their bodies relaxed and at rest. Mike and I tried as best as possible to control our deep breaths.

Fuck, that was great, I thought before I closed my eyes and fell asleep.

7. Avi's POV

I woke up to hands trailing over my skin, tracing intangible words on my body, causing shivers to run down my spine. I involuntarily let out a moan from the sensation and groggily opened my eyes to see a smirk etched on my husband's beautiful face.

"Sorry, did I wake you?"

Sure, he did!

The smirk on his face was still there, so it was obvious that he had done it on purpose.

"Yes, babe, what is so important that you had to use several methods to wake me up?" I didn't make a move to get out of bed or hide my naked body from his gaze. Tariq and I had been married for about three years without children, and we voluntarily decided that. We wanted to explore a little bit before we got saddled up with the responsibilities of children.

"I'm so hard up for you," he grunted, reaching for the button on his trousers before pulling it off and tossing it aside. He slid his hand over his thick bulge. He moved his body between my legs, spreading them wide as his mouth caressed mine. A soft gasp escaped my lips only to be taken in by his. He rocked the tip of his ebony dick that was sticking out from his underpants against the entrance of my pussy, and the throbbing ache grew when he rubbed my clit, making me drip.

He swallowed hard, his eyes searing through me. Slowly he stroked my folds before pushing a finger inside.

"I want to come all over this sweet little pussy and mark it as mine, but first, I'm going to make you come on my tongue." He dropped to his knees and smiled, breathing my pussy in like he had to savor that moment. He gently kissed down my pussy before sliding his tongue across my reddened slit.

I moaned, leaning on my hands as I watched his mouth cover my pussy, and then he licked his way up and down, dipping inside until he reached my little nub. It ached so much that as soon as he sucked it between his lips, I cried out, holding a fistful of bedsheets in my hands, thrusting my hips forward and my head back. I could not stop the orgasm about to invade me, not even if I wanted to.

Tariq growled, sending a vibration over my already throbbing pussy. He kissed my inner thighs and worked his way up.

"Girl, your pussy so sweet you got me addicted." I heard him say. He kissed me hard, thrusting his tongue in my mouth, letting me taste my juice from his mouth. I moaned and sucked on his tongue a little harder, imagining it was his dick.

"Fuck, I want to feel your lips wrapped around my dick like that."

I reached out and grabbed his dick, swiping the bead of cum off the tip and bringing it to my lip, licking it like it was the sweetest thing. He kissed me and thrust his hand into my hair. His tongue wrapped around mine, and I gasped as he pushed his dick in just a little.

"I want you to cum all over my face. Can you do that for me?"

"I don't know," I whimpered, clenching around his dick. I leaned back and stared between them, where his huge black dick practically split my tiny ebony pussy in half.

"Look what you did, baby. I'm tearing your innocent little pussy apart. Watch how you take me in so perfectly… swallowing up my dick," Tariq said, cupping my chin as he lifted my head to look at him.

"You're mine—you and that tight pussy belong to me. Do you want to cum again? Because I do. I want your pussy to suck up all my cum as you scream my name."

His words turned me on more, my body tensed up, and my head fell back. "I'm cumming," I cried out, my vice grip around his dick squeezing his cum out in quick jets. Tariq leaned down, pinning me to the surface.

"Get on your hands and knees. I want to watch my dick fuck your pretty slit from behind."

I did as he said, in the middle of the bed on all fours. A tingle traveled up my spine as I felt the bed shift with his weight. His hands were the first thing to touch me, grasping my hips. He moved over to my ass and gave it a little spank before moving lower and grazing my pussy. A finger pushed in, making me feel so full. How he had always gotten his giant black dick in me was a mystery, but it was pure heaven.

"Fuck me again, Tariq."

He swatted my ass, and I wiggled it a little. "I think you need to learn that I'm in charge."

The tip of his dick brushed past my ass, moving slowly down to my center.

He thrust in, claiming me from behind. Tariq leaned over with his chest pressed against my back, sending him deeper inside my pussy. He gripped my chin harshly. "You're so fucking sexy. I love the way your body fits mine. Kiss me, and I'll make you come."

I tilted my head a little more and kissed him. He pulled back with his hands skimming over my breasts, down my sides to my hips. One hand slipped under and pressed against my clit. I moaned and pushed backward, sending him fully inside me. There was a mix of pleasure and pain which I enjoyed, so I did it again.

After we were done, we lay on the bed, covered in each other's cum and sweat; Tariq hugged me from behind.

"Happy anniversary, babe," he whispered into my ear before nibbling on the tip.

Time passed by quickly. It seemed like yesterday when I just met Tariq. I had followed my best friend to the gym and met him. It was lust at first sight with his brown skin that made me want to trace my tongue over him. He was a fitness trainer with a great body and a six-foot two height that seemed to attract me since I was just a five foot one. I also happened to love his short black hair. He had a tendency to run his fingers through it, giving himself a ruffled appearance but sexy with it. There was so much I was attracted to. His laugh, it was deep, throaty, and like he couldn't quite help himself, I loved the sound and wanted to hear him laughing all the time. He had a soothing voice whenever he spoke, and he also had a great personality that livened the mood of everyone around him.

"Happy anniversary, babe," I giggled as a thought flashed in my mind. "Babe, what do you have planned for this anniversary?"

"It's a surprise, but first, we need to get a shower and get some

food in you. Then maybe I'll be convinced enough to tell you."
He smirked at me.

Every anniversary, Tariq always ensured that he fulfilled one of
my sexual fantasies, and I was so sure that this year wouldn't be
any different.

I closed my eyes as the spray hit my face. It felt so warm and
relaxing. Even better was the feel of Tariq's hands sliding around
my waist. I sighed and leaned back on his chest. "This is so nice."

"Yes, it is," He whispered, kissing my neck from behind. "Let me
help you."
He poured some shower gel into his hands and lathered them up
before rubbing them over my body. This was so perfect and
addicting. Every inch of my body was caressed, worshipped.
After some time, we rinsed off, and he stepped out to grab the
towels, helping me dry up. A moan involuntarily escaped my lips
when his hand came between my thighs, drying my pussy and
wetting it all at once. He took my hand and led me into the bed
once again.

Tariq's hands firmly gripped my hips and pulled me against his
arousal while his mouth invaded mine. I was so desperate to be
touched by him, my body burned for him, and only his touch
could soothe the desire quickly building up in my core. He had
that effect on me, and he knew it. He enjoyed using it to his
advantage. I let my hand explore the muscular ridge of his back as
his mouth left mine. He trailed hot wet kisses over my jaw and
down my neck. His touch was electrical, like a spell that I was
unable to break away from.

I felt wanton under his gaze as his eyes hungrily devoured the
sight of my body, his hands sneaked lower, and instinctively I
parted my legs for him. Tariq ran a thick finger through my folds,
my breath hitched, and I gasped at how amazing it felt. I was so

fucking turned on that I almost unraveled under his touch. His fingers trailed a little higher and made a few lazy circles over my clit with just the right pressure. My body tightened and begged for more.

My breath was released in short pants, and my knees were weak. I clung to his shoulder, hung onto him for dear life as he continued his delicious assault.

"You like that, baby?" His deep voice echoed, demanding and low. It sent shivers through my spine.

"Yes, daddy," I whispered with a gasp. My eyes fluttered shut. I was enjoying his touch, but I wanted more. He trailed his hand south and slid through my folds. The wetness of my arousal coated him, and he smacked my inner thighs playfully. Tariq's long finger pushed inside me, deep and controlled. I widened my legs to give him all the control to do as he pleased. I wanted him, and I wanted it all.

"Fuck, how come you are still so fucking tight?" he hissed and licked his lips, eager to taste me.

I blushed; it was all the explanation I could give. Despite having had sex a lot of times, he still commented about how tight I was. My breathing increased, and that encouraged him to slide another finger and speed up the pace. His black dick was rock hard again, and every dirty thought of him inside me surfaced.
Damn!

I wanted him to fuck my black pussy with that big-ass black dick.

My head fell back as my hip jerked up to meet his thrusts. I was now muttering incoherent words. I felt my nipples harden, aching for attention. As if he had read my mind, Tariq lowered his head and tugged one of my nipples into his mouth. He closed his lips over one of my nipples, sucking and nipping it lightly before moving to the second nipple. They were so hard and sensitive, pushing on pain and pleasure, and his actions caused desire to flood through me.

"Yes," I moaned. My pussy wall clenched around him, and I exploded, legs shaking and heart pounding. He thrust up, driving his dick deep until he came. Both of us rest there completely out of breath.

"Damn, it's gon' be a wild one today."

He slid out almost all the way, leaving just an inch inside, then pumped forward. I cried out, but this time it was a soft moan for more. His mouth took mine roughly as his dick pulsed. He was so close he latched onto one of my nipples, sucking it between his teeth. I moaned, arching and rolling my body until he thrust harder in and out of my pussy. Then, he attacked my neck, kissing, nibbling, and sucking on my beating pulse. My hands run up his sides and over his shoulders, spurring him on to go faster. Slipping his hand under the back of my knee, Tariq tugged it around his waist, driving himself deeper into my womb.

"Avi bear, your pussy is so tight, it's like you never want to let me go."

"I don't. I'm so full. Tariq, uh…you feel so good."

"Avi, are you sure you can't cum once more? I want to feel your pussy squeeze every drop of cum out of me like it's demanding my seed. Do you want my cum?"

"Yes. Give me your cum, please. It's all mine." I whimpered.

He slammed into me over and over with his balls slapping my ass. The sound of our sweaty flesh meeting only made him wilder.

"Sugar, it's all for you. Now come all over my huge dick," He demanded, hanging on by a thread. I tightened up, my nails dug into his skin, and my pussy choked his dick in a vice-like grip. My walls pulsed as he flooded my womb with jets of cum. "That's it, babe. Your pussy is pulling every drop out. Take it all."

I tossed my head back, panting as I rode out my orgasm on his dick. He slipped his hands under my body and rolled with me on top of him.

"Wow," He could take me all over again. His dick, although not completely hard, was still hard enough to fuck my brains out. If I kept rolling my hips on him, it wouldn't be long before he filled my pussy up again. I nestled my head against Tariq's chest, and I felt complete. I felt at peace with his arms wrapped around me.

***

Tariq's POV

I wrapped my hands around Avi. She was the best thing that ever happened to me. When I first laid eyes on her, I was completely entranced by her beauty. She was a black beauty that caused heads to turn wherever she went to. She's also very smart— beauty and brains mixed, and her glasses made her stand out. To the public eye, she was an intelligent and decent woman, but I knew that the latter was far from the truth. She was a completely different person when it came to our bedroom activities. She loved trying out new kinks, and I was very happy to indulge her as long as I was involved. She was my addiction, and I was addicted to her smile and every inch of her body.

"Babe?" She called out to me, but I closed my eyes and pretended to be asleep.

But she was not having any of that. She gently bit some spot on my chest, but I kept up the pretense.

"Babe, are you really asleep?" She got out of my arms. I thought she had given up, but I had no idea she was far from done. "Babe?" I felt warm hands on my dick, and it hardened immediately as her soft hand caressed it.

'Minx,' I swore in my head. She always knew how to get what she wanted and would even go to extreme lengths. I knew what she wanted, but I wasn't ready to let her in on the surprise for our anniversary.

She ran her hand through the full hardened length and the tip. I cussed in my mind, I knew that Avi was deliberately teasing me, but I tried to control myself from acting out.
"Babe, I'm hungry. You've had me nonstop all morning. I want my treat."

I didn't respond, but I carefully cracked an eyelid open to watch her. She leaned closer and took the length into her warm mouth, and I bit my tongue to prevent the groan of pleasure that was about to slip from my mouth. Her tongue dipped out and took a swipe at the bead of cum on the tip, licking it off with a small moan. When her lips wrapped around my dick and sucking me in, I almost lost all control. She pulled my dick from her mouth and ran the tip of her tongue from tip to the base, nice and slow. She slid her tongue over the tip and wrapped her fingers around it.

I was reveling in the moment, but all of a sudden, it stopped, and my eyes snapped open. "Why did you stop?" My voice was filled with desire.

"My job here is done." She gave me a mischievous smile before letting go of my dick. She crossed over my body and strolled towards the en-suite bathroom, sashaying her hips as she went. I was stunned, speechless by the seducer I got in the form of a wife. I only broke from the trance when she had fully shut the door behind her. I looked at my erect dick pitifully and shook my head, knowing that Avi wasn't going to do anything about it.

When Avi returned from the bathroom, she got dressed in a tee shirt and shorts and didn't as much throw a glance in my direction. She immediately left for the kitchen, so all I could do was take a shower, a very cold shower. I changed the sheets that had been soiled in our sweat and cum once again and rearranged the room, putting everything in place before I went after Avi.

"Hey babe, lunch is ready." She smiled at me. I was taken aback. I thought she was going to give me the cold treatment.

We took seats beside each other at the dining table, and Avi immediately started explaining an editing job she was working on. When we were done eating, she cleared the dishes and resumed asking the question that had been long bothering her.

"Babe, what's the surprise? I really want to know." She batted her eyelashes at me.

"You should be patient. Patience is a virtue, my love." I grinned. I enjoyed seeing how impatient she was.

"And procrastination is a bitch. So why don't you tell me now? I promise to act surprised when the surprise happens."

"It's still a no from me," I shook my head. "Be patient, darling. The surprise would be worth the wait. I promise."

"Are we having company?" She stared into my eyes.

I couldn't avoid her gaze. I nodded, "Yes."

"Really?" She grinned. "I should probably go get ready. Looking my best is most important," she rushed off without giving me a chance to speak.

Having a smart wife could be a headache sometimes. Even though she might not be entirely correct, she was able to guess a bit about what I had planned for her. Half an hour later, Avi wasn't out yet. I was about to go after her when the doorbell rang.

It was almost time.

I opened the door and ushered my best friends in. "Hey Brian, Luke. Come in."

"Dude, what's up?"

"I'm good. Everything's great. Where are the girls? I thought they were going to show up."

"Nora is at her parents," Brian replied.

"While Charlotte is at work, she wished you a happy anniversary and told us to make sure that Avi is well taken care of," Luke grinned at the end of his statement. We all knew what it implied because it had happened in the past, twice.

"Babe!" I called out in a loud tone. I heard a door slam shut, and she showed up, wearing a white bathrobe. "Babe, remember my best friends Brian and Luke?"

"Yes. Hello." She came to my side.

"Hello, sister-in-law, happy anniversary," Brian and Luke greeted her simultaneously.

"Thank you," I slowly led her to the guestroom while talking to her. "Nora and Charlotte couldn't make it, but they sent their best wishes."

"And they asked us to make sure that you are well taken care of," Luke added. He and Brian followed at their own pace. "Remember when you said you craved to be stuffed with dicks? It's about to come through," I whispered into her ears.

***

Avi's POV

I wasn't sure what Tariq was planning, but since we were going to have company, I had to look my best. I rushed back to the bedroom and took a long shower. I had shaved my body to make sure it was smooth. Then I got dressed in a two-piece lingerie that Tariq had gifted me on my birthday before I covered it with a bathrobe.

When his friends showed up, I instantly knew why they were there because Tariq had hinted to me about a few things they had done in the past. I was so nervous as he led me to a guestroom. Our bedroom was off limits to outsiders, something Tariq had said about not defiling our sacred space. I didn't know what to expect, so I kept my cool.

As we all entered the room, Tariq started kissing me in front of Brian and Luke. I felt nervous and should have struggled, but I didn't, especially with the way his lips invaded mine, his hands iron grips on my arm and neck, his tongue demanding that I open up to him. As I surrendered to him, his hands relaxed, slipping around my body and stroking my back as I draped my arms around his neck, kissing him back as deeply as he was kissing me. Damn, Tariq was a great kisser, and most time, I had to try and keep up with him. His tongue knew exactly what to do, entwining and rolling with mine as he bent down, lifted me in his powerful arms, and carried me to the bed.

"Damn. Look at Riq. What are you doing there, buddy?" Luke asked as he let out cat whistles.

Tariq dropped me on the bed, "Giving my baby girl the treatment she deserves," he said, helping himself to a seat on the bed before he helped me take off the robe, ripped off my lingerie, and tossed it aside. There were more whistles and comments about how sexy I was. Tariq laid down and hugged me so my back and ass were facing his friends. I blushed and buried my face into his neck, and he whispered to me how beautiful I was.

One of the guys behind me—I'm not sure if it was Brian or Luke, placed his hands on my shoulders and slowly pushed my head down until my ass was in the air. Tariq sat back with my breasts in his face, carrying on with his skillful touches, sucking and nibbling on my nipples, no doubt contributing to the growing throb that was making itself known between my legs. Now that I was bent forward, someone's hands were smoothing over my ass, alternately taking fistfuls of my flesh, parting my ass cheeks, and giving me light, playful smacks. Below me, Tariq opened his pants, exposing his erection. I made to reach for it, his beautiful, hard dick with a glistening drop forming on the tip, but he slapped my hand away.

"No. Not your hand. Lower your pussy on me," he quietly demanded.

I crawled up with one leg on either side of him and balanced over his dick. His thumb flew to my clit, and I suddenly must have him inside me, no matter how ill-prepared I might be to handle him. So I parted my lips with my free hand and slowly allowed his tip inside, then I hovered while my pussy adjusted.

"You good, babe?" he whispered into my ears. It was nice to see that he was still worried about me. But before I could say anything, Brian answered, "Art, I got her nice and juicy for you, buddy."

He was right. I lowered myself, so full of Tariq's dick I almost couldn't breathe. It was like the damn thing had impaled me all the way to my throat. I held myself there for a moment as someone's hands returned to my ass, and when a tongue touched my puckered hole, I started riding on Tariq's dick. That was how good both things felt at once.

While I slid on his dick, I simultaneously pushed my behind into the face of whoever was licking me.

Incredible.

"God, baby, your pussy's always tight," Tariq groaned.

Then, with a sudden movement, he lifted me clear off his dick.

"What... what the...?" I started to ask, but he shifted me until I felt a dick pressing into my pussy from behind. A second later, I was being fucked by someone different.

8. Sex Games

Holy shit.

I realized it was Brian because I spotted Luke out of the corner of my eye. He had pulled his own dick out of his pants and was slowly running his hand up and down the shaft.

Brian drove into me and pulled back out, over and over, so hard that Tariq, who I was still kneeling over, had to hold me in place. I moaned out as pleasure overwhelmed me. Only a minute more, and I'd cum so hard, but Tariq grabbed me and pulled me back down over his dick.

Weirdest fucking game I'd ever played, but I didn't care. I was enjoying the attention. I ground on Tariq's dick, trying to get the release I desperately needed. The surface of my skin buzzed in anticipation, and just as waves of pleasure started to wash over me...

Tariq pulled me off his dick. Again.

"What? What are you all doing to me?" I cried out. Luke moved toward me until his dick was pressed against my lips.

"There you go, baby. With my dick in your mouth, you can't complain." He pushed inside me, nearly to the back of my throat.

I groaned and tried to twist my head, but I was held in place. Brian leaned over my back and put his hands on my breasts. "Don't worry, darlin', we'll let you come eventually."

Fuckers

I was wild with need, and when Brian finally drove his dick back inside me, I clenched with all my might, bouncing back on him as hard as I could.

I have to cum, I thought.

I had to cum. And as I started to buck and moan, even with my mouth full of Luke's dick, Brian continued to pump, giving me what I needed. At last. As I started to cum and my head drooped, he pulled out again and turned me over to Tariq. He filled my pussy in one stroke, and my orgasm continued as if it were never interrupted. With hands, lips, and, well, all three men invading my body, I was coming over and over. And just when I couldn't see straight anymore, there was pressure on my asshole and a burning sensation, and something pushed inside while Tariq was still in my pussy.

I was so not expecting that.

I spit Luke's dick out of my mouth. "Hey, I don't know about this-" I started to say, but Brian just held himself there while Tariq reached down to rub my clit. "Relax, baby," He whispered in my ear. "You can do it."

I cannot do it, I thought.

Brian pushed so gently into my ass without going any deeper, that it actually started to feel good, albeit painful. Like unbelievable. Like nothing I've ever felt before.

"You'd like to be our fuck toy, baby?" Brian asked before pushing deeper into my ass. Well, his dirty talk was the last thing I needed. I exploded into an orgasm that probably scared them all, as well as the people in the next valley over.

I couldn't see, hear, or really even think. Only felt, which was fine. That was what I wanted, needed, and craved. It was like a cleansing or some kind of purification. I started to scoot off the bed with one arm. Tariq caught me and pulled me to his lap, flipped me over his knees, and pushed my head down until my ass was in the air.

What. The. Fuck.

"This isn't over, babe."

Fine. I could kind of understand, but he was so going to pay for this. But strangely, I'd stopped squirming, stopped trying to get out from under his grip. I liked what was happening, even though I knew my face was beet red. After all, his hand on my ass was not going unnoticed. It felt nice. Really nice. And the warmth, the nice gooey feeling, was spreading from my core to the rest of my body.

"What?" I snapped, the warmth in my core turning into something wet between my legs.

But before I could start my tirade, a hand smacked my ass, the sting jolting me and causing a new gush of wetness between my legs. After, Luke didn't lift his hand but instead kneaded my ass, rubbing and massaging the flesh until the sting somewhat faded into the background. And in spite of myself, I moaned, pushing into his touch.

His fingers danced over my ass cheeks like feathers, teasing my heated skin. But he didn't stop there. I shivered when his fingertips moved from my sore ass to my crack. He gently, ever so lightly, brushed them between my cheeks, starting at my lower back and not stopping until he reached my pussy. His touch tickled my pussy lips, now fat and puffy with desire. A drop of my excitement trickled out, and I could feel it dribble through my lips and to my clit.

God-fucking-dammit. I had no control. I felt tired. I had been going at it all morning.

"Please, Luke," I whispered, about to beg him to let me up. But I didn't. "Do it again, please," I murmured, my cheeks reddened in embarrassment.

Tariq's dick surged under my belly as he smoothed his hand over my ass, and I braced myself for another smack. But this time, he stopped cold. "Hey, Brian," he said across the room, "you want to have a hand at teaching this lovely lady a lesson in some manners? She has to understand that we are in charge here."

Brian cleared his throat from somewhere in the room where I couldn't see him. In fact, pretty much all I could see were Tariq's lovely feet as well as the dust bunnies under my bed. That's how far down he had my head.

"Yeah, man. I think she needs it from all of us for it to really sink in. You know, for her to really learn her lesson."

His footsteps got closer on the bedroom carpet, and he positioned himself behind me, I guessed, for maximum leverage.

Whack!

I screamed. That one was hard. I mean, fucking painful.

"Okay, guys, that one was not fun. I get what we're doing here, but if you could go a little easier—"

Whack!

I screamed again.

But Brian, like Luke had done before, massaged my stinging flesh, the pain of his spanking transforming into a deeper, sexier heat. I was gasping, eager for more, when I let out a moan. Tariq's hands magically lifted from my back, and he pulled me to my feet. There I stood, perspiration running down my temples, hair sticking to my face, wetness dripping down my thighs, and I chewed on my button lips.

Brian and Luke stepped right before me, their erect dicks before me. It was then I realized that I was the only one that had an orgasm.

"I'm sorry, guys." I whimpered, biting my lip. "Please let me make it up to you."

"Hell, I never say no to a pretty lady," Luke said, removing his shirt until he was completely nude. They were almost complete opposites, but both seriously hot as fuck. Brian was chiseled with sleeve tattoos that had been covered by his shirts, and Luke was all tense, taut, ready-to-explode muscle, but they couldn't be compared to my Tariq. He was the most impressive one of them all. Luke and Brian were both beyond impressive in the dick category, each of their erections hanging heavy between their legs, ready for...

Me? Again?

As I stood there, I noticed Tariq watching me with amusement in his eyes. "Babe, you'll be fine. Just breathe," I was staring at the two huge, hard black dicks in front of me.

"Don't worry about that, sweetie," Luke said, smoothing his hand over my ass and dipping a finger between my legs. "You just focus on your... lesson. Damn, this woman is soaking wet," he added.

"You are in good hands," Brian added and slipped a finger into my pussy, and I gasped, but he pulled it right out. "You want some more?" he asked, his voice deep and scratchy.

Holy fuck.

"I want…" I forced myself to say, "I want… fuck, I want to feel good!"

"Of course you do, honey," he said, his voice pouring over me like melted chocolate.

"And we're here to help you with that. Just bend over the bed a little so we can see your pretty puckered asshole and juicy pussy, all right?"

Luke stepped forward and, turning me toward the bed, eased my shoulders down until I extended my hands into it for balance, leaving me bent at a ninety-degree angle.

"You got three big guys here to make you feel good, Avi. And we're going to give you something you'll never forget," Luke crooned.
Fear trickled up my spine at the tone of his voice, but I told myself to relax. I trusted my husband. He knew what he was doing. I stared at the fluffy down comforter beneath me and waited. When I turned my head around in curiosity, the three men grinned at me, each stroking their massively erect dicks.

"I'll tell you what I'm gonna do, baby," Luke said, edging up behind me, his dick bouncing against my ass crack, his hands encircling my waist. He reached under my body and began to play with my tits. Then, he jumped onto the bed next to me and propped himself up on one elbow to meet my gaze.

I was getting nervous once again.

There I was, locked in a bedroom with three naked and very buff men. I put a frightened expression on my face and played along.

"If… if you guys let me up, I promise I'll be a good girl," I said.

But Luke just dropped onto his back on the bed and laughed. "Kinda late for that now, isn't it, Avi?" He twirled a strand of hair hanging over my forehead.

"Ok. Good. Now, Brian, can you spread her a little? So, we guys can decide what we want to do?" he asked.

Oh my God.

As aggressive as his words were, which had my heart thumping against my chest, they also left my pussy throbbing in a clash of emotions.

"What are you guys doing?" I mumbled.

"Wait, wait, wait," Luke said, jumping off the bed from next to me. "Let me test her for myself."

He parted my pussy lips with one hand and slipped a finger inside me with another.

"Well. I can tell you all she's no fucking virgin. Tariq, how do you keep her so fucking tight."

Oh my god. Just no. I started to stand up, even though Luke's finger was still inside me. But someone, either Brian or Tariq, pushed me right back down.

"We're not done here, relax babe," Tariq whispered in my ear.

Anyway, back to my experiment," Luke said, slowly pumping me with his finger. "Brian, come here. You put a finger inside her too. That way, we can see how tight she really is."

"Or isn't," Brian laughed.

"Hey, can you guys stop messing around, or you guys can just fuck right off—" I screamed in sexual frustration.

But Tariq bent right next to me, so close I could smell his shampoo. "Honey. If you don't shut up, we'll shut you up."

"What the fuck does that mean?" I screeched in his face and pouted.

Tariq sighed, "Well, I warned you" he picked up one of the guys' neckties off the floor.
"Hope this wasn't an expensive one," he said, looping it around my head to fit in my mouth and tying it over my hair.

Really? He had to gag me. I mean, my hands were free. I could take the goddamn thing off any time I wanted to, but Brian's and Luke's fingers felt so good inside me I decided to play along. In fact, I pretty much already was playing along.

"Cripes, look how wet she is" Brian's finger slipped out of me, and he reached around my head and poked it in my mouth, pushing the necktie gag aside.

"Suck it. Taste your pussy, baby. You got to know your own flavor."

I closed my lips as best I could around the necktie to suck Brian's finger while someone behind me slipped in another and then a third finger. I groaned from the fullness and pushed back as if I could take more.

Could I?

"I'll get the lube," Tariq said and left the room, but he soon returned with a bottle of lube. When I looked back between my legs, I saw that Tariq was using the lube on himself.

"Babe, have you had your ass eaten before?" he asked.

Was he fucking kidding?

He had never tried it.

"Obviously, no!" I snapped, trying to pull my legs back together.

"Get to work, Brian," he said with a laugh.

Brian positioned himself behind me, everyone having taken their invading fingers out of my pussy. He placed his hands on my cheeks, lifting and opening them wide to the point of near discomfort, and then his tongue was back there, flicking against my most private part. It felt good. So fucking good. In fact, it was so good my knees almost buckled. But I was holding myself up on the bed with my arms and wasn't about to collapse yet.

"Oh, that looks good, Brian. Move aside. I want some," Luke growled.

Brian stopped licking my ass for a moment. "Fuck off, dude. You can have it when I'm done."

Were they really fighting over my asshole?

I'd seen a few things but never anything like this.

"Fuck, dude. Be sure to leave some for me," Luke laughed, and I looked back to see him stroking his dick just like Tariq was.

"Come up here, Luke. Let me help you out with that dick," I said and grinned at Tariq. He smiled back at me. He seemed pretty impressed that I was taking everything happening so well.

"Oh hell yeah," he whooped and jumped onto my bed, positioning himself in front of me and lying back with his head propped up on a pillow to watch.

Brian's mouth on my ass was like a switch being thrown, and I wrapped my own lips around Luke. We were a trio, Brian's tongue violating me as I sucked Luke deeper, his hands in my hair controlling the depth of both my mouth on him… and Brian's tongue on my asshole.

"Use some lube. Work a finger in, man," Luke advised Brian. "She's such a petite little thing. She's gonna need lots of TLC."

A moment later, cold lube trickled down the crack of my ass, causing me to jump. Tariq laughed. "Sorry, darling. I should have warmed that up first."
And then strong hands pressed against my asshole until the tip of a finger popped inside me.

It was glorious. I'd always been a girl who wanted to have her ass played with, and Brian knew how to open me up, working one finger inside while Tariq reached under me to play with my clit.

"Oh, baby, suck me like that," Luke moaned as I tightened my lips around his dick head, the same way my asshole tightened around Brian's finger.

Goddamn, it was hotter than hell. Holy shit, If I'd known when

I'd gotten up in the morning that my day would end like this, my head would have exploded. I was caught, half wanting to give Luke the best blowjob of his life, while the rest of me was distracted by the pleasure of Brian and Tariq slipping a third finger into my pussy and ass.

My body flooded with electric pleasure, and even before Brian had pushed his fingers more deeply into my ass, I was already coming, whimpering and shaking while moaning against Luke's dick.

"Think she's ready once again," Brian said to no one in particular.

"Be my guest, brother," Tariq said.

I heard a couple more pumps of the lube, and then Brian's huge dick head rested against my ass.

Luke was getting ready to explode in my mouth, Tariq was playing with my breasts, my clit, and my hair, and Brian was about to give me something I'd never really tried.

He pressed harder, and the stretch burned, almost to the point of my asking him to stop. But Tariq leaned down next to my ear. "You can do it, babe. Push against Brian's dick. It will help you open up."

I was doubtful and ready to call the whole thing off when I tried Tariq's suggestion, and Brian was able to push inside me deeper.

It felt fucking awesome.

It felt so awesome that I pushed back on Brian's dick because I wanted more of him in my ass. I moaned, triggering a flood of precum from Luke in my mouth as he tried to hold back while Brian penetrated me.

"Goodness gracious, you're one of a kind," Tariq whispered, lovingly stroking my back. "Amazing, babe."

His compliment had me smiling inwardly, and when I felt Brian bottom out behind me, I sped up my work on Luke.

"Haven't you always dreamt of coming in my wife's pretty mouth?" Tariq teased.

With that, Luke's entire body stiffened, and he let out a groan that almost scared me as he started to spurt down my throat.

"C'mon, baby," he hollered, pounding the mattress beneath us. "Take it all."

When he was done, I motioned to Tariq to take his place, which he did with lightning speed.

"Oh, I'm going to have my turn now. You made your husband wait so long," he chuckled.

Brian pulled back, and I felt myself driven and split by the two men. It was heady, and within seconds, I was drifting, overwhelmed by the power of the dick in my mouth and the one in my ass. Brian's hands dug into my hips as he sped up, fucking me for all he could.

"Fuck, so tight, so tight… fuck, Avi, I'm not going to last long," he grunted, but I didn't care. I loved every stroke, every renewed fullness, every slap of his balls on my pussy lips as he pumped faster and faster. Tariq was there too, swelling in my mouth as his hips bucked up to meet me. He held my head still, and I was at the complete sexual mercy of two powerful men as they used me, their grunts and gasps telling me even before they tensed when they were going to cum.

Brian was first, his groan followed by the warm feeling of his cum filling my ass. It made me come myself, and my orgasm was only enhanced when Tariq cried out, his lips forming my name as he came down my throat. The three of us froze, and when time started again, I felt Brian pull out, falling to the top of the bed as his legs gave out.

"Holy fuck… you were my first anal, Avi," he panted.

"You were my first, too."

"Two virgins. How lovely," Tariq said. "Did you like that, little minx?"

I nodded.

"Then mind your manners and say thank you."

My mouth dropped open, but I closed it before something rude and smartass flew out of it. "Thank you. Thank you, both of you."

He stroked my face. "And it's not over yet, baby."

I looked at Luke, his dick already hard again. "Are you up for it, darling?" he asked.

"Oh yeah," I assured him, pushing myself up on the bed and laying my sweaty, damp head on someone's thigh as Luke got into position.

It was… erotically beautiful. We all watched Luke's dick disappear between my pussy lips. He sank into me slowly, his powerful body keeping himself from going too fast or hard.

"You good, little girl?" he asked.

I took deep breaths before nodding. "Yes. I am. But that's one huge dick you have, Luke."

He chuckled. "If you can take Tariq's black monster, then you can take me, baby. We'll just go slow."

It took time for him to enter me fully, and when his hips were settled against me, and he leaned down, I was trembling on the edge of cumming for a third time. But as he pulled back, two more sets of hands stroked my body, turning all their attention to my overwhelming pleasure. Luke thrust one more time, and I was cumming again.

I was in heaven.

I lost track of my orgasms, one tripping on top of the next as he drove into me, those thick, glorious muscles drilling every inch into my willing, eager body.

"Avi," he grunted, sending me on a final release that left me shaking and my mind blank.
But I wasn't worried.

How long was I out?

I didn't know, but when I came to, the room smelled of sex and sweat, and of experiences I would never forget. I was alone, and the door was open, a slight draft breezing in. Blinking, I got up and found my bathrobe, pulling it on as I walked out to my living room.

"Babe? How do you feel?" Tariq was the only one in the living room, and I realized that his friends must have left while I was still passed out.

I made my way to where he was sitting and entered his warm embrace, his arms around me made me feel safe and complete. "I'm just a little sore, but it'll pass. How long was I out."

"About a few hours, I assumed that you needed a lot of rest, so I didn't bother to move you."

I could get cranky if I get woken up from the sleep I needed so much. "Oh. Our anniversary is over," I glanced at the clock. It was five in the morning.

"Yes, babe, there is always next year, and I'll make it the most memorable, I promise."

I believed him. He always fulfilled his promises.

"Also, Nora and Charlotte called. They specifically said that you must share the juicy details. No part should be left out."

I nodded and hummed in agreement. As Brian and Luke were Tariq's best friends, Nora and Charlotte became my best friends after I got married to Tariq, and we instantly clicked. At first, I felt a little jealous that they might have had a chance to fuck my husband, but it wasn't a big deal anymore since I had done the same with theirs.

***

Tariq's POV

One year later.

Avi was taking a lot of time to get to the car. I had been waiting for over thirty minutes and was just about to go in search of her when she suddenly rushed out the front door with her purse.

"I'm sorry I took so long. I had to kiss the twins goodbye again. I feel a little bit awkward without them." She kissed my cheeks as she entered the car.

"They will be fine, my love. The babysitter will be here for a week. She'd definitely take good care of them while we're gone," I reassured her. "We have to get going, or we might be late."

It was Brian and Nora's anniversary, and they had invited us over for something they planned in a private resort. Avi and I were looking forward to spending time with them, even though she was reluctant to part with our kids for a week. Tianna and Tommy were almost two years old, but they were the most beautiful thing that ever happened to me, including my wife. When I first laid eyes on them, I knew my life was complete. Most of the time, they took Avi's attention which caused me to gain less, but I was glad I'd have her all to myself in the next few days.

9. **Paige's POV**

Ever since David and I opened our own art gallery, we've been passionate about finding and nurturing new talent. So when we stumbled upon Malik's paintings at a local exhibition, we knew we had found someone special.

We just didn't expect it to go the way it did. Or even to end the way it ended.

David and I had been working with Malik for a few months, helping him market his work and introducing him to influential clients. He was a regular presence in our lives, and we enjoyed his company. But there was something about him that I couldn't quite put my finger on.

One night, after a long day at the gallery, David and I were sitting in the living room with Malik, sipping wine and talking about art. I couldn't help but notice the way Malik's eyes lingered on me when I spoke. And when he brushed his hand against mine as he reached for his glass, a jolt of electricity shot through me.

That was my first indication that trouble could potentially be looming, but who was I kidding? My first thought was *pleasure*— pleasure could be looming.

I tried to ignore the feeling, chalking it up to my overactive imagination. But over the next few weeks, I started to notice other subtle flirtations and touches between us. And I couldn't deny the fact that I was feeling something for Malik that went beyond just friendship.

It was a confusing and scary realization. David and I had been married for years, and I loved him deeply. But there was something about Malik's energy, his creativity, that made me feel alive in ways that David had only ever been able to invoke in me. And I couldn't help but wonder if maybe, just maybe, there was room in our relationship for one more.

David and I had been together since college. Being both African Americans, we had weathered our fair share of challenges as a couple. But despite the occasional stares and whispers, we had always felt like we could conquer anything together. Malik was also black, and it felt good to have another person of color in our lives who shared our passion for the arts.

He was younger than us, but he had a quiet confidence that I found intriguing. And there was something about the way he talked about his work that made me feel like he understood art in a way that no one else could. It was triggering.

One evening, David and I were lying in bed, our bodies pressed close together. I hesitated before breaking the silence.

"David, can I ask you something?" I said, my voice shaking slightly.

"Of course," he replied, propping himself up on his elbow to look at me.

"Do you ever feel like there's something more between us and Malik?"

David's eyebrows shot up in surprise. "What do you mean?"

"I mean...I can't shake this feeling that he's interested in us. And... I think I might be interested in him too."

David's expression softened, and he took my hand. "Paige, I love you. And I know we've been through a lot together. But if you're feeling like you want to explore something with Malik, then we can talk about it."

I felt a weight lift off my chest at his words. It was scary to admit my feelings, but David's support made it feel a little less daunting. "I don't know if I'm ready for anything yet. But I just wanted to be honest with you."

David squeezed my hand. "I appreciate that, Paige. And whatever you decide, I'll be here for you."

"Thanks, Dave. I love you."

I moved closer to him, my body pushing against his firm frame. I pressed my lips to his softly, waiting as his lips slowly opened to accept my probing tongue. The thought of Malik kept snapping through my brain. He would be just the ticket right now.

Suddenly, David flipped me under him and growled at my ears.

"Don't think for a moment that I don't realize you're thinking of him right now," he said.

"Do you mind?" I asked. I really didn't wish for any of this to create conflict between us.

"Sort of, but he's a hot, virile young man. If I wasn't so jealous, I'd be thinking of him too," he said, giving me a nip in my ears. "Not that I don't anyways," he added.

I take his dick in my hand, caressing his hard length with my palm, our eyes finding one another while I stroked them rapidly, my eyes widening, and a little gasp emitting from my lips as he pushed his fingers into me to return the favor.

And we were hungry too, our tongues tangling, my hands on his chest, above his beating heart, fingers running through the hair there, while his finger traced over my thigh to the nub between my legs, little droplets of moisture already gathering.

His finger touched my opening, and I shifted closer, our lips pulling apart, both of us breathing a little harder, and when he found my clit, I gave a little gasp. I leaned into him; my legs wrapped tight around him. I could feel my firm breast against him, the nipple poking into him, and the sound of my sighs as his hand rubbed against my clit.

"Come on, David, I need you now," I whimpered into his ears.

"I love you," He whispered, rolling into me.

I rolled with him onto my back, breathing the words, "I love you too."

He slipped between my legs, his hard black dick pointing at me, his dick slowly spreading the moisture he found there, and my hands found his bum cheeks, pulling him onto me, into me, his hard length sliding into me slowly.

I gasped; my breasts squished against his chest generating even more heat between us. I joined our lips, and he increased his pace, the pleasure increasing with our quickening rhythm.

I thrust my groin against his, trying to take as much of his dick as I could, my nails digging into his shoulders, my warm breath grazing his ears as I gasped and panted.

"Oh, David," I gasped again, "Please."

My pleasure was rising with his, every thrust taking me closer to a crazy orgasm. I was panting now, and I knew I was close, and then I screamed, my body twisting uncontrollably. He became rigid against me while the orgasm spread across his lower half, his belly, legs, and groin, releasing into me, pulsating thick shots of cum while I trembled around him, quivers and quakes of love and pleasure.

"I love you," I whispered, "I really do."

"I love you, too, my love."

We held one another for a while longer, several minutes or more, before turning to our sides and cuddling together. We fell asleep in each other's arms, our breathing gentling slowly.

Over the next few days, we talked more about what this new dynamic could mean for us. It was a strange mix of excitement and fear, not knowing where this road would take us. But we both agreed that we wanted to approach things carefully and make sure that everyone involved was comfortable—everyone being Malik.

As the weeks went by, David and I started to talk about Malik more and more. We would speculate about whether he was really flirting with us or if we just imagined things. We even started to fantasize about what it might be like to be with him together. It was arousing. Our sex together went up a few degrees hotter just from the thought.

But we both knew that this was uncharted territory. We had never been in an open relationship before, and we weren't sure if we were ready to go down that road. And we still had no idea if Malik was even interested in us in that way.

So we continued to dance around each other, our feelings simmering just beneath the surface. And I couldn't help but wonder if, in the end, we would be brave enough to explore what we were feeling.

The tension between us only grew more palpable as time went on. Every time Malik came over, my heart would race as I wondered if he was going to make a move. And every time he left; I would feel a pang of disappointment that he hadn't.

David seemed to be feeling the same way. We would exchange meaningful looks when Malik wasn't looking, trying to communicate with each other without words. It was as if we were both trying to gauge each other's level of interest in Malik without wanting to say anything outright.

Things were escalating quite fast, and they almost tipped over. Malik was spending as much time at our place as we did. It seemed we were delighting in torturing ourselves.

We had all gone out to a fancy restaurant to celebrate one of Malik's recent successes. We were all dressed up and feeling good, the wine flowing freely.
As the night wore on, I found myself sitting closer and closer to Malik. I could feel the heat radiating off his body, and the scent of his cologne was intoxicating.

And then, out of nowhere, he leaned in and whispered in my ear, "You're so beautiful."

I felt a shiver run down my spine. It was like a switch had been flipped inside me, and suddenly I couldn't think about anything else except being with him.

David must have sensed the change in the air because he started to touch me more intimately as well. His hand brushed against my thigh under the table, and I felt a thrill of excitement.

It was like we were all dancing around each other, testing the boundaries of what was possible. But we didn't break those boundaries that day. No, we kept up the torture—our bodies delighting in the chase.

And then the night when everything changed…

***

David's POV

I washed my hands off at the sink and moved to the dinner table. We were all about to enjoy a meal that Paige had cooked from scratch. The scent of roast chicken and rosemary filled the air, and I could hear the crackle of the fire in the background.

The dinner table was set with our best dishes, and the aroma of roasted chicken filled the air. Malik had brought a bottle of red wine to share, and we were all feeling relaxed and happy.

As we ate, we talked about our day and the latest developments in the art world. Malik was animated, gesturing with his hands as he described his latest series of paintings.

Paige and I listened intently, fascinated by his creative process. But I couldn't help feeling a pang of jealousy as Malik laughed at something Paige said. I wondered if I was being ridiculous if her feelings for Malik were getting in the way of our marriage. I couldn't deny that I wanted him too, but I felt pressured to act on it.

But then Malik turned to me, his eyes sparkling. "David, I have to say, your input has been invaluable to me. I don't think I would have made it this far without you and Paige."

I felt a warm flush spread through my body. "Oh, it's nothing," I said, trying to brush off the compliment.

"No, seriously," Malik said, leaning forward. "I feel like you really understand what I'm trying to do with my art. And I'm so grateful for that."

Paige smiled at us both. "Well, I have to agree with him. You have a real talent for marketing and promotion, David."

I smiled back at her, feeling a sense of pride. Paige had always been my biggest supporter, and I loved her for that.

As the night wore on, I signaled to Paige and nodded toward the kitchen.

"I can't stop thinking about it," I said softly as we stood together by the oven.

"I know," she replied, reaching out to take my hand. "I can't either."

There was a long moment of silence as we both processed our feelings. Finally, Paige spoke up again.

"Do you think we should talk to him about it? See how he feels?"

I hesitated for a moment, unsure of what to say. But deep down, I knew that I wanted to explore this further.

"I think that might be a good idea," I said slowly. "But we need to be careful. We don't know how he'll react. He might think it's a trap."

"You want to do the honors?" She asked me.

"Are you suddenly shy?" I asked her quietly.

"No, but he'll be more relaxed if he knows you agree," she said.

"Fine, let's do it," I said, taking her hands and leading her out of the kitchen.

Malik was still at the table, he looked up at our entrance, and something must've been different because he arched his brows and shook his head.

"Y'all don't have to," he said, a small smile on his lips.

"Don't have to what?" I asked, my eyes lingering on his.

"Fuck me," he said bluntly. "It very well might ruin our working relationship," he added.

"We realize that, but we also want you, and we're willing to work around it," Paige said, walking over to him.

"Besides, I know you want us too," I added.

Probably Paige more than me, I thought, my insecurities rearing their ugly head.

Malik leaned back in his chair and ran a hand through his hair. "Look, I ain't trying to deny that the thought has crossed my mind. But I don't want things to get awkward between us if it doesn't work out."

"We understand that" I said, stepping forward. "But we also think that the three of us could have something really special if we give it a chance."

Malik sighed and looked down at the table. "I don't know, guys.

This is a big decision. Can we take some time to think about it?"

"Of course," Paige said. "Take all the time you need. We just wanted to bring it up and see how you felt about it."

"Thanks for being honest with me," Malik said, a small smile on his lips. "I appreciate that."

As we walked back to the kitchen, Paige took my hand and gave it a squeeze. "I'm proud of you for speaking up," she said.

I smiled back at her. "I couldn't have done it without you, chocolate."

I led Paige over to the bed, where we explored each other's bodies, taking our time to discover every inch of skin.

As the night wore on, we found ourselves lost in a sea of pleasure and desire. It was unlike anything any of us had experienced together before, and we knew that we had stumbled upon something truly special. It would be so much better if Malik were in bed with us, and I hoped he agreed.

After a few days of thinking, Malik invited us over to his place. We sat together on his couch as he poured us each a glass of wine. Paige had her hands wrapped around mine, her eyes on Malik as he moved around the room. Her hands were shaking slightly, the suspense getting to her.

"I've thought about it," he said, looking at us both when he had settled down across from us. "And I think I'm willing to give it a shot."

Paige and I exchanged a glance, feeling a rush of excitement and nervousness all at once.

"Are you sure?" I asked him, wanting to make sure he was fully on board.

Malik nodded. "I'm sure. I trust you guys, and I think we could have something really amazing together."

We all took a sip of wine, the tension in the room dissipating slightly.

"So, what now?" Paige asked, her eyes flickering between Malik and me.

"I think we should start it slow," Malik said. "See how things feel between us and make sure we're all comfortable with what's happening."

"Agreed," I said, feeling a sense of relief wash over me. "Let's just see where this takes us."

"However," Malik continued, "I'd like to offer my house to explore this further. I know how important your home is to you both, and I don't want to risk anything that might harm the purity of that space, you know *what* I'm saying?"

Paige and I looked at each other, feeling a sense of gratitude and respect for Malik's thoughtfulness.

"Thank you," Paige said, smiling at Malik. "That's really thoughtful of you."

Malik nodded. "Of course. I want this to be a positive experience for all of us, and I think having a neutral location might help with that."

We all took another sip of wine, feeling a renewed sense of excitement and anticipation for what was to come.

After finishing our wine, Malik led us to a room he had set up for us. It was dimly lit, with candles flickering softly in the corners of the room.

"I thought we could start with a massage," Malik said, gesturing to the massage table in the center of the room.

"You should get out of that," he said, nodding at our clothes. He started getting out of his too.

Paige and I nodded. We undressed and lay face-down on the table, waiting for Malik to begin.

Malik alternated between the two of us, dribbling hot oil on our skins before kneading our tight necks and shoulders. I gave a little gasp when I felt his hands on my ass. I hadn't been expecting that. I could feel my dick hardening from the ministrations too.

"You are way too tense, David," he admonished softly as he started manipulating my ass. "You need to relax."

I bit my lip against a groan as his fingers pressed into them skillfully. The teasing was a bit much. So I got off the massage table and, taking their hands, led them over to the bed. Paige gave a small laugh.

She pushed away from us, shaking out her dark hair and indicating we should sit together on the edge of the bed. She settled in front of us, her hands eagerly wrapping around our dicks as she bent her head and nuzzled into my lap.

She looked up at once and went right down to business, her lips wrapping slowly around Malik's dark dick. She began caressing my dick in her hands. She kissed Malik's tip, then licked it, her tongue swirling around before she took it into her mouth again.

Slowly, she took more of it in, and she cupped her hands around my balls, squeezing lightly as she moved them around slowly.

Malik put his hand behind her head, encouraging her to take him deeper. She pressed her hands against him, taking him deeper until she gagged and backed off a little. Malik groaned appreciatively while I watched them hungrily.

Her hands on my dick were still working them, but just watching her pleasure Malik was arousing me beyond belief. She looked up at me, gave a wink, and, maintaining eye contact, gave Malik a long lick. He inhaled sharply and fisted his hands in her hair. She gave me a dirty little smile and moved to my dick then.

She closed her lips around me, moving slowly at first, then quickening her pace when I moaned. I held off thrusting like my hips wanted to, not wanting her to gag again, and soon I felt my balls tighten.

I pulled her head away, I got fully on the bed, and Paige joined me, Malik coming up behind her. Paige rolled onto her stomach and pushed herself up onto her hands and knees.

I moved around in front of her to see her already sweating face, framed by her hair, her lips parted as she breathed in. I leaned in and gave her a kiss, her tongue seeking me out, and our lips meshed hungrily against each other.

As I lay back on the bed, Malik moved behind her, poised at her entrance, ready to push into her.

"Look at me," I told Paige. Her lips were parted, her breath leaving her body in pants. Her eyes locked on mine, and then she gave a loud moan as Malik slid forward, burying his hard length in my wife. Her back arched, and her eyes slowly pulled closed. She looked ecstatic.

I watched as Malik's muscular chest heaved, his hands wrapping around her hips, as he pushed in and out, his head thrown back. Her body was rocking from the movement of his hard length inside her.

"I want you," Paige said. Her hands found my still rock-hard dick and pulled me up into the pillows so she could engulf my dick with her mouth. I shuddered, a wave of goosebumps breathing across my skin.

Paige bobbed her head up and down on me, her movements somehow matching the rhythm of Malik's thrust into her, his dick pounding into her while she moved back and forth, sucking on my dick.

Faster and faster, Malik slammed into her, like a man on the edge, his face twisted, his muscles strained, a line of sweat appearing on his brows, his panting turned to groans, and he breathed in harshly with each thrust into her.

He slammed into her once more, and his teeth clenched. Paige pushed against him, her voice breaking into a scream which she muffled by putting her lips over me. The reverberations of her screams almost pushed me over the edge then.

Malik pulled out of her and fell to the bed, his breath still coming in harsh gasps. Paige was shaking as her body released itself. When she'd settled down a bit more, she looked down at her hands still wrapped around me.

"You're still hard," she said, her brows raised. She stroked her hands down my length slowly, her eyes on mine. Malik was watching us from his place on the bed. His eyes fastened greedily on Paige's breasts, which were heaving slightly.

He leaned forward and quietly suggested, "Maybe you should fuck your husband now?"

"Only if you're up to it. We do have all night," I said to her with a lewd smile.

Paige guided her hips towards me. I attached my lips to hers and kissed her softly. Malik's hands wrapped around my dick, stroking it as he _ed it to Paige's gaping pussy.

"Damn," I swore aloud. The sensation of his hands wrapped around me was good. Fucking hot. I slid up into her, my hips raised off the bed as my dick slipped completely inside her body.

"Fuckkk..." I groaned aloud at the pleasure. I was so close to the edge from watching them earlier that I had to consciously prevent myself from cumming then. Paige closed her big brown eyes and panted along with me, her warmth tightening sporadically around me.

I pulled out and slammed into her again, my muscles shaking as I tried holding off. A few more thrusts, and I would definitely blow my load. Malik shifted closer and put his hands on her nipple, his other hands swishing between us to rub at her pussy.

Her orgasm tracked across her body, pushing me over the edge. I felt my muscles spasming as my body trembled from the force of my orgasm. The three of us collapsed in a heap on the bed, completely spent.

Paige wiggled between us, her body sweaty. She gave Malik a soft kiss before turning to me and mashing her lips to mine.

"Thank you for this," she said. Like I hadn't just had one of the most shattering orgasms of my life, like this wasn't due to her. I gave her a kiss back, spreading my hands on her body.

"Save the thanks until we're done. The night has just barely begun," I told her. She gave a giggle and fell back on the bed. Malik spread his legs over hers and closed his eyes with a long sigh. The cruise had only just started, and this was only the first port of call.

10. Double The Pleasure

The next morning, after we'd gotten home and fallen asleep, when I woke up, I could feel a twinge of guilt nagging at the back of my mind. I looked over at David, who was still sleeping peacefully, and wondered if he felt the same way.

"David?" I whispered, nudging him gently. He stirred and opened his eyes, giving me a sleepy smile. "Good morning, beautiful. How'd you sleep?"

I hesitated for a moment before blurting out, "Did we make a mistake last night?"

David's smile faded, and he sat up in bed, looking at me intently. "What do you mean?"

"I mean...I don't know. I just feel like things might get complicated between us and Malik, and I don't want to hurt you or our relationship."

David reached out and took my hand, giving it a reassuring squeeze. "We don't have to do anything we're not comfortable with, Paige. We can take things slow and figure out what we both want."

I nodded, feeling grateful for his understanding. "I just don't want things to get messy."

"We won't let them," he said firmly.

I leaned over and gave him a kiss, feeling a surge of love and gratitude for this man who had been by my side for so many years. But even as I kissed him, I couldn't help but wonder what the future held for Malik and us.

A few days later, we invited Malik to the house. We all sat down at the table, and David served us plates of steaming hot stir-fried pasta, some salad, and grilled chicken. The fragrant aroma of the food filled the air, making my stomach grumble in anticipation.

We dug into the meal, savoring the flavors and chatting about our day. Malik told us about a new gallery he had visited, and David and I talked about a potential new client we were trying to woo. As we ate, I couldn't help but steal glances at him, admiring the way his sharp jawline and full lips looked even more enticing with a smear of red tomato sauce.

This was just like any normal evening. After our night at his place, we'd been together a few more times but never at ours. This was just a reprieve to keep our friendship flowing outside the bedroom.

The night ended beautifully, with Malik spending the night in the guest room and still refusing to have anything sexual going on in our house, which at this point, was really pointless. The sexual tension between us was always sizzling hot whenever we were together, irrespective of where.

I spent the next morning cleaning the house out, and Malik was still somewhere around here. I wasn't certain where, though. I couldn't seem to find David either, which meant they were most probably off somewhere together.

I set up breakfast and then rummaged through the house, looking for them Malik's clothes and shoes were missing from the guest room, so I headed over to the one place they were most likely to be found.

I walked into the studio, David and Jackson standing side by side, looking at a piece of art. It was an intriguing contrast: David, with his tall, muscular frame and shaved head, and Malik, with his lean, athletic build and thick, coiled hair.

David's skin was the color of dark chocolate, and he had a strong, square jaw that gave him an air of authority. His eyes were a deep brown, and they seemed to see straight through me whenever he looked at me. He had a warm smile that could light up a room, and I loved the way his deep, rumbling voice made me feel.

Malik, on the other hand, was lighter-skinned, with a caramel complexion that looked almost golden in the sunlight. His eyes were a bright hazel, and they sparkled with intelligence and humor. His hair was a wild, untamed mass of coils that seemed to have a life of its own, and I found myself wanting to reach out and touch it.

David was dressed in his usual morning uniform of a black polo and jogger, while Malik was wearing his bright yellow button-down shirt and slim-fitting black pants from last night. David's style was usually more straightforward and practical, while Malik's was more daring and flamboyant.

As they turned to greet me, I felt a jolt of electricity shoot through me. I wanted both of these men so much, and I couldn't believe that I had the privilege of being with them both. I wanted them right then and there in the studio.

"Get that look off your face, Paige," Malik pleaded desperately immediately he turned to me and saw the look on my face.

"What look?" I asked, strolling casually towards them.

"You look like a bitch in heat, Paige," David said with a little laugh. "Stop scaring him."

"Not you calling me a bitch, David," I said with a pout on my lips.

"I apologize, my love, but you know what I mean," he said apologetically.

I moved forward, keeping eye contact with Malik as I walked toward them. Then I completely ignored him and went to work on my husband.

I knelt before him, my hands pulling down his joggers, and his thick black dick sprang free. I gently stroked his dick, my hands running up and down its length with a soft smile on my face. I moved my hands in circles, my fingertips tracing up and down its length. David gave a faint moan of pleasure.

Malik gave a groan beside me and shifted closer, his eyes fastening on us.

"You should leave," I told him, my eyes on his as I leaned forward and slowly slid David's dick into my mouth.

"That feels really good," David said. I purred and grabbed his dick tightly, making him moan louder.

Running my hands along the length of his shaft, I took a few moments to enjoy the feel of him in my hands. Heat radiated from him; the warmth sweet against my hands. I gave him a wink and slipped him into my wet mouth again. This time my moan joined his.

"Yeeaahh," he loudly moaned as I started moving my head up and down the length of his erect shaft, my tongue swirling around his dickhead.

"You enjoying this?" I suddenly asked, my eyes on Malik. He looked ready to join the fun. I didn't know why I was teasing him this way, but I couldn't seem to help myself.

"Yeah, just don't stop," David replied quickly.

His hands slipped behind my head, his fingers entwining into my hair to hold me steady.

His hands moved down from my hair, sliding down my body to my breasts and fondling them through my tank top. I lifted my hands and waited as he pulled the top over my head and then threw them behind him.

Malik shifted closer; his pants tented.

"You're really going to make me do this," he said.

"You really want to do this." I said to him.

He stretched his hands towards me and then pulled back and walked out of the studio.

"Well, you've gone and done it now," David said, looking down at me.

"Good thing you get to enjoy all the attention."

Well, I had to admit to a fair portion of disappointment, but I put my head down and continued with my task.

David moved his hands to my left breast and flicked his thumb over the distended nipple. I took most of his length into my mouth, my tongue wrapping around his tip. He shivered against me from pleasure and pushed my head further onto his dick.

"Fuck, Paige, your throat's so tight," he mumbled.

I bobbed my head faster, trying to take him all in at once, then I bobbed it even faster and sucked harder, repeating the process as needed.

"Shit," David moaned, his head thrown back as I kept up the assault. "I'm about to cum soon."

His body was trembling and shaking from pleasure, his hands on my nipple, twisting and turning. David thrust himself down my throat faster. I relaxed it and let him enjoy himself. I put my hands on his moving hips and stayed still while his hips pushed in and out of my mouth.

The door was pushed open then, and Malik walked back in. He had discarded his pants and was instead dressed in his shorts. I gave him a lustful stare and watched as he pulled the shorts off roughly and stepped towards me, a tube of something in his hands.

David gave a final thrust into my mouth and came, rope after rope of his salty cum filling my mouth. I sucked harder for a moment and then relaxed. David groaned for a long moment and then pulled out, his legs weak. He kept his eyes on Malik while he settled on the floor beside me.

He gave me a soft kiss and whispered a *thank you* into my ears. Malik placed the tube on the table beside me. It was a tube of lube. He'd probably picked it up from our bathroom.

"What's that for?" I asked, watching him warily.

"For you, if you're interested, of course," he said, leaning towards me and giving me a little smacking kiss. The reluctant Malik from a few minutes ago was completely gone.
"What's it for?" I repeated, still searching his face.

"I was thinking maybe David and I could have you at once," he said slowly, his eyes also searching my face.

I felt my pussy tighten at the thought, and then a second later, I shook my head.

"I've never done that before," I said.

"Always a first time for everything," he said, picking the bottle up and shaking it in my face.

David gave a shrug when I turned to him.

"It's your choice, babes," he said.

I made my choice, getting off the floor and moving out of the studio to the pool area where we had set up a gazebo. It had more space, and a section had been set up with a bed for nights we wanted to spend outside. Besides, it still wasn't inside the house, so Malik should have no objections.

I stepped into it and watched as they walked over to me. Malik stepped into the gazebo and pulled off his shorts, David watching him. He pulled off his top and settled on the bed.

In a second, I reached up and grabbed hold of Malik's dick, slowly stroking it in my hand and marveling at how beautiful it was. My other hand reached out and massaged his smooth, big balls. I heard him let out a little moan, and I looked up to smile at him.

Then I slid my mouth over him and moved my plump lips up and down his shaft, massaging the head with my tongue. Sticking out my tongue, I ran it all the way from the base to the top and gave the head a little kiss.

"Oh god, that's so good." He moaned as I licked and sucked on his balls.

I could feel him squirming around me, and I loved that he was enjoying it. Bringing my head up, I played with his balls some more, my fingers squeezing and releasing the heavy sack.

When he couldn't take it anymore, he pulled it out of my mouth, picked up the tube, and squirted a little into his hands.

"You ready?" He asked me. I nodded softly, uncertain yet willing to try. I lay back on the bed, spreading my legs while I waited for him.

He rubbed his hands together and then slowly pushed one hand into my asshole. I pulled my eyes tightly shut, my back pressing into bed as I tried to stifle my groan of pain. It hurt, no denying that, but I felt the fullest I'd ever been in my life. He pulled his finger out and pushed it in just as slowly again.

"Fuck!" I panted into his chest when a second finger went inside of me. I felt myself pushing away from him slightly, my ass pushing into the air as I tried to pull away.

Malik pulled out completely and gave me a moment before pushing back in. My asshole received him much easier now, pleasure accompanying the pain this time. Then I felt his fingers pull out and go back into my ass.

"Fuck!" I moaned out again as he quickly started finger fucking me.

He grabbed onto my ass cheeks and pulled them apart, exposing my hole to his hungry finger. My eyes watered slightly, and I felt my ass clench around the fingers inside of me.

I looked up to see David staring at us, a hungry concerned look on his face. He raised his brows at me in question, and I shook my head—no. This had the potential to get really fun.

Soon enough, the speed of the fingering increased as my ass loosened up, my moans getting louder and louder. Malik slipped another finger into me without warning, and I clenched my eyes, my body vibrating.

David moved towards us, his hands grabbing my tits and twisting the nipples. I moaned out from the pure pleasure I was receiving at this point.

Malik made me turn onto my stomach, then he held onto his dick and aimed it up at my wet, throbbing pussy. When I felt the headfirst push inside of me, I let out a long, heavy gasp.

With his dick completely covered in my juice, he pulled out and slowly stroked his dick into my asshole. It was intense, and I felt completely filled ready to burst my eyes widening.

He pushed in a moment at a time, waiting for me to adjust before he pushed another half an inch. This continued until he was completely inside me. He gave a ragged groan and held himself inside me stiffly.

"Ooooohh!" I moaned aloud, and my body stretched beyond imagination. I'd never seen this in my future, but it felt good, the pain entwined with pleasure. After a moment, he pulled out completely and pumped his dick into me again. This time his stroke moving with a lot more freedom into my asshole.

He picked up my legs and held them on his shoulders, forcing his dick deeper and deeper inside me. When I'd gotten used to his dick, I croaked my hand at David and invited him to join the fun. Malik dropped my legs and slipped under my body and then into my asshole while David aimed his dick at my pussy and pushed in.

My body twitched and spasmed as he pulled out and pushed in again.

"Fuuuckk, you're going to rip me in two!" I moaned out as both their dicks started moving inside me. My body felt unnaturally full, and when I felt David's dick rub up against Malik's through the thin membrane of skin separating the two, I realized my pussy and asshole were well and truly filled for the first time ever.

"Mmmm" I screamed out as my body started shaking, my orgasm induced just by the feel of the two of them inside me at once. The feeling was like nothing I had ever felt before, I thought I might black out. It was that intense.

I was screaming so loud that David pressed his hands over my lips, stifling my loud screams while his grunt filled the air as he thrust his hard member into me. Malik was doing the same in my ass.

Then, another feeling I had never before experienced hit me, and I screamed at the top of my lungs.

"Fuck fuck fuck fuck" burst out of my mouth as I screamed and started to squirt all over David.

The feeling was great, my body releasing copious amounts of fluid as I went light-headed, the squirt seemingly endless. I couldn't stop moaning if I wanted to. I was in cum-heaven just then.

Even as I came, I felt Malik push deeper into my tight ass, and so did David. They eased deeper into me, then backed out together. Their dicks had to be rubbing together inside me. It was unavoidable.

"Damn, this feels good, and I'm about to cum any moment now," Malik grunted behind me, his rhythm erratic as he built towards his own orgasm. David put his hands on my waist and pushed into me roughly, chasing his pleasure as much as mine.

Then they both exploded inside me, their combined cum sprouting inside my body, spraying my insides with their seeds. They grunted loudly together, and then David pulled out, his cum leaking out of my gaping pussy. He put his dick on my stomach and concentrated on breathing, his shoulder shaking as he inhaled and exhaled harshly, his face dotted with sweat.

Even Malik had stopped thrusting inside me, his body spasming as he pulled in breath after breath under me. I got off him and spread out on the bed, my eyes facing the roof as I thought about what had just happened.

It had been pleasurable beyond measure, the pain quickly replaced with pleasure, and now I had gotten the first time out of the way, I definitely wouldn't mind a repeat. So long as David had no qualms.

I noticed he had stretched out beside me, and I gave him a little kiss on his sweaty forehead before turning over and doing the same to Malik. Exhausted, I fell between my two handsome men and closed my eyes.

***

Paige's POV

Three months later.

I looked up from the stick, the two stripes giving me news I had never in any reality expected, especially not now. I was pregnant!

David and Malik gasped behind me, I couldn't see them, but from their voices, they had to be as surprised as I was. This wasn't possible. I took my pills with almost religious regularity, especially after Malik had joined us in our bed, or after we had joined him in his, to be very specific.

I had been feeling sickly lately, having to keep to my office while at the gallery because I was prone to throw up at any moment, and at home, the smell of eggs suddenly seemed to disgust me enough that I had thrown up just from watching David eat the stuff.

My dark nipples had grown darker and sensitive. After two months of such incidences, it finally dawned on me that I was experiencing symptoms of a certain condition. Hence the pregnancy test and its result.

"That's not possible," I said, my voice almost a sob.

David moved forward and placed his hands on my shoulders, his thumb stroking slowly at the tense muscle under it.

I bent over suddenly and rummaged through the cabinets below, searching for my pills. And no wonder, too, there were three pills instead of the two I should've found.

"Fuck" I swore. "I must've missed a month."

"It's not the end of the world," David said.

I blindly backed out of the bathroom and into the living room. He didn't realize it yet, but he would very soon.

There, Malik claimed the baby was his.

"That's crazy," I said, turning to him. I had, in fact, been expecting the moment I saw those thin lines. Malik was a possessive man; he would never have let it go. "David's my husband"

"Except in the last few months, you've fucked me about as many times as you've fucked him, probably more," he said, pacing across the room.

"We'll get a DNA test when it's born, but for now, it's David's baby," I told him.

"And what if it's my baby?" He asked, staring at me, then at David who was on the couch, his eyes staring in shock.

"We'll cross that bridge when we get to it," I told him, getting off the chair and walking over to David. He looked at me, a soft expression on his face.

"I didn't mean for any of this to happen," he said quietly.

"It was as much my idea as anyone's," I told him. Always the protector, he was already searching out ways to protect me. He got off the couch and spoke to Malik.

"I guess this is the end for us then?" He asked Malik, who was still pacing around the room, his hands in his pocket.

"If you're trying to keep me away from her, then yes. But mind you, I'll fight it the whole way," he said calmly.

"Malik, I and Paige are a family. Surely you don't believe we'll let you take our baby. That's crazy," David said.

I watched the two of them, my eyes flicking to whoever seemed more likely on the verge of an explosion. Malik was being difficult pursuing this.

"I love Paige, and this baby could very possibly be our baby," he said, pointing his fingers between me and him.

"You love me? You can't love me. I'm married, Malik," I said to him. This was getting more ridiculous—all shades of ridiculous.

"You're a young man Malik, you'll find someone for you, but it's not me, I'm married, and I love my husband," I added.

"So what? You were both using me for your own pleasure? With no thought to my feelings?" He said harshly.

"Get off your high horse Malik. You enjoyed it as much as we did," David broke in, stepping beside me and putting his hands on my shoulders.

Malik watched him, his eyes narrowing on my shoulders where David had placed his hands.

"This isn't over, I'll leave, but I'll be back in nine months, and we'll have to have that test," he said before moving out of the room and banging the door on his way out of the house.

"He never gave any indication he could be that way," David said immediately, shaking his head. He bent down in front of me, taking my hands and wrapping his fingers over them.

"Are you okay?" He asked, concerned.

"He's really going to try taking our baby," I said, my voice shaking slightly at the thought. "And if it's really his, what do we do?"

"Stop, Paige. Like you said, we'll cross that bridge when we get there," he said reassuringly.

I leaned my head into his shoulder and relaxed against him. No need to worry about it now. We still had a few months before the baby came. Besides, Malik might have changed his mind about keeping the baby before then.

I couldn't pretend that I hadn't noticed the fact that Malik's feelings toward me had changed. He had suddenly been possessive with me, even extending it towards David, caressing my thumb at dinner, and making suggestive remarks. But I had brushed it off, thinking it was just a phase.

But now, with the news of the baby, it seemed like Malik's possessiveness had turned into something dangerous. David and I had to be vigilant to protect ourselves and our child.

We spent the next few days talking about our options, researching legal avenues, and consulting with our friends and family. It was exhausting, but we were determined to do whatever it took to keep our family safe.
One day, David surprised me by showing up with a bouquet of flowers and a huge smile on his face. "I have some news," he said, "I talked to a lawyer, and we have a case. We can fight Malik for custody of our baby."
I couldn't believe it. Relief flooded through me, and I felt a weight lift off my shoulders. We still had a long road ahead of us, but I knew that David and I could face it together.
As we hugged each other, I knew that no matter what happened, we had each other's backs. We were going to be okay!

11. Passion

I stirred slightly as the light reached my face, my eyes slowly fluttering open to take in the new day. For a moment, I lay there, just basking in the warmth of the sun and the peace of the morning. Then, with a soft sigh, I stretched my arms above my head, reveling in the feeling of my muscles awakening after a night of rest.

I sat up, my long legs stretching out before me as I yawned and rubbed the sleep from my eyes. As I ran a hand through my hair, I took a deep breath and savored the fresh scent of the morning air.

The early morning sun filtered through the window, casting a warm golden glow across the room. As the light crept across the floor, it gently illuminated my husband who lay sleeping in the bed.

His skin was the color of rich, dark chocolate, and his hair was a tangle of wild curls. He was perfect. If only everything else was half as perfect as he was.

With a smile on my face, I leaned over and gave him a gentle kiss. He stirred but didn't open his eyes. He had gotten in very late last night. It was one of the consequences of being an up-and-coming architect.

I rose from the bed and made my way to the window. I gazed out at the cityscape below, watching as the sun continued to rise and paint the world in vibrant colors.

As I stood there, taking in the beauty of the morning, I couldn't help feeling sad. It was a new day, and the possibilities were endless, but for me, I had only one dream now, to cuddle my baby.

Farrell and I had been trying for a baby for months now, and every month brought on a new anxiety. It was straining our relationship, mostly my fault, I had to admit.

I left the window and strolled back to the bed. I slipped in beside Farrell and wrapped my hands around his limp form. He was usually so strong and active, but in sleep, he was as relaxed as a baby. It was one of the reasons I had been first attracted to him. His ability to let go and relax. I didn't have it. Which was the reason I was about to wake him now. Slowly, pleasurably.

I ran my hands over his hairy abdomen while I leaned over to give him a soft nip in the ears. Farrell gave a light stretch and smiled in his sleep. He turned over on his stomach and gave me access to the rest of him. No way this man wasn't awake.

I kissed a trail of kisses down his body, moving painfully slow. It was as much for me as it was for him. I ran my hands over his stomach, over his navel, and wrapped my hands around him. Farrell gave a soft groan and stretched out even more.

"Do we have the time?" He asked softly.

We had a doctor's appointment this morning, and he didn't like being late for anything, especially not for our baby, and this was our first doctor's appointment.

"We can make the time, besides, you want it," I purred at him.

"That I do," he laughed and then surged up quickly to roll me under him.

He leaned in and fastened his lips to mine. I pushed against him, twisting out from under him. I pushed him against the bed and rose over him.

"Lemme do this, enjoy," I said, giving a sexy little giggle.

He fell back on the bed and folded his hands behind his head like a spoiled god. I loved it. Looking at him intently, I pulled his shorts down his leg and off. I threw it out behind me and knelt over him again. Farrell spread his legs and gave me a wink, and I kissed my way up his body and to his lips.

I kissed him roughly, pushing my tongue into his mouth. He latched onto my tongue and sucked on my lips. I felt his dick rising against my stomach.

There we go, I thought.

I gave him a small bite and leaned away from him, kissing my way back down his body to his dick. It was already hard and straining against my hands. I gave it a soft stroke, brushing my fingers over the tip. He inhaled sharply and pulled his hands over mine.

"Keep doing that," he said.

He loved being teased, so I tickled my hands through his short pubic hair, scratching at him softly. I gave him a small smile and stroked my hands up and down his hard dick. He breathed in sharply and exhaled, relaxing into the bed.

I felt his dick twitch against my hands, his face a mask of hot lust. Much as he loved being teased, he would be begging for me soon. I felt my pussy tighten pleasurably; this would be very good.

Taking him into my mouth, I ran my tongue twice over his dick, bobbing my head up and down over him. I sucked hard, my lips a round tight sheath around his throbbing dick, the veins sticking out prominently. Farrell gave a low growl and fisted his hands in my hair. I gave a gag, and he quickly let go.

I sucked his dick deeper and hummed low in my throat, the sound vibrated up and down his dick, and he swore and tightened his hands in my hair. He was already dripping pre cum, and I flicked my tongue out over it. I gave a slight suck and took him in completely, it wasn't easy, but Farrell loved it, and I did what Farrell loved.

I stopped, my head tilted back, and clasped my hands around him more securely. I took him into my mouth again and sucked quicker. He would cum soon, I was sure. I quickened my pace, my tongue flicking out to caress his tip whenever I pulled my head up.

Farrell gave a loud gasp and pulled my head even more forcefully against his body, his balls tightened, and I dropped my hand there, giving him a slow tickle and a squeeze immediately after. It was all the provocation he needed to blow his nut in my mouth. I lifted my head and stuck my tongue out. His cum sprouted all over my face, his groan of pleasure echoing through the room.

I kept at it while he came, my hands stroking him fast. He shuddered and relaxed on the bed, his breath coming in quick rasps. I started kissing up his body to his mouth and gave him a light kiss.

"You like that?" I asked him softly.

"I loved it," he replied, a slight slur in his words.

I got off the bed and moved to the bathroom to wash out my mouth. I'd give him some time to recuperate before I got him up again.

"Where you off to, lady?" Farrell asked from the bed.

"Missing me already?" I asked with a look over my shoulder at my husband. He looked yummy spread out on the bed like that. His legs crossed one over the other.

I slipped into the bathroom and rinsed out my mouth. It had been good to pleasure my husband, but now I was back to worrying about the doctor's appointment. We were thinking of other ways to get a baby since I couldn't get pregnant. It was a difficult reality to live with, but we would be running tests today at the hospital to ascertain that for sure.

The doctor had said he couldn't confirm anything over the phone until he had run the tests. I loved Farrell, and I wanted to give him our child, but if I couldn't do that, then we needed to consider other options. Farrell wasn't too happy about any of this. He wanted our family to be our family, and he was willing to forgo kids if it meant I was happy. But I wanted him to be happy as much as he wanted me to be happy, and I always got my way.

I washed my face with warm water and toweled it dry before moving out of the bathroom and into the bedroom to Farrell. The room was empty. I turned around and snuck out of the room, tiptoeing down the stairs and to the landing. I was certain he had moved to the kitchen to start breakfast.

Farrell was at the counter, mixing eggs with a whisk. He had laid out some things for a pancake. It was his go-to breakfast meal and the only meal he could prepare without burning some part of it. I moved quietly into the room and wrapped my hand around his waist, screaming "boo" directly into his ears.

He gave a jump and dropped the bowl on the counter. He turned to me and picked me up, and he wasn't smiling. He walked down to the living room and dropped me quite suddenly on the sofa. He started laughing then. He knew I hated that about as much as he hated being surprised. I burst out laughing even louder. I hadn't been expecting that.

"I'm a happy man this morning Layla," he said, turning away and walking back to the kitchen.

"And I gave you that," I said to him as I got off the sofa and followed him back to the kitchen.

I had thrown a little slip over my body before leaving the room, and it barely covered anything. Farrell gave me a long look and shook his head, deliberately stepping away from me. But that wouldn't work for long. He just wouldn't be able to resist. I knew that because I knew my man. He was a horny black stallion, especially when I was naked and ready. And I would be very soon.

I followed him back to the kitchen and took out a large mixing bowl from the cupboard while Farrell grabbed the bowl he had dropped earlier and some measuring cups.

"Let's make some blueberry and chocolate chip pancakes," I suggested.

Farrell nodded in agreement, "Great idea. I'll get the blueberries from the fridge and the chocolate chips from the pantry."

I started by measuring out the flour, baking powder, and sugar into the mixing bowl. I mixed it together with a wooden spoon, creating a well in the center for the wet ingredients. Meanwhile, Farrell whisked together the eggs and milk in a separate bowl.

As Farrell poured the wet mixture into the well in the dry ingredients, I continued to mix with the spoon, making sure to scrape the sides of the bowl. Once the batter was smooth, Farrell gently folded in the blueberries and chocolate chips.

"I'll heat up the griddle," Farrell said as he poured the batter onto the hot surface in small circles. The pancakes sizzled as they cooked, and I grabbed a spatula to flip them over once they were golden brown.

As the pancakes cooked, we talked about the appointment.

"Are we leaving immediately after breakfast?" I asked, flipping a pancake over with ease.

Farrell nodded. "It's by ten. We should get out early."

It was eight o'clock now, more than enough time to get ready and out of the house. Neither of us spent much time in the bathroom, and the hospital was only a short drive away. We had made sure of that.

After a few more flips of the pancake, we transferred them onto plates and sat down to enjoy our breakfast. The pancakes were fluffy and delicious, the blueberries and chocolate chips adding a burst of flavor.

I made sure I finished my breakfast first, and then I leaned against my chair and pulled down the strap of my slip, slowly looking at Farrell with a mischievous smile on my face.

"Oh, we're doing that now?" He asked eagerly.

"No," I said, "it's just really warm in here."

"No, it's not, you naughty woman," Farrell replied.

I slowly pushed down the strap, exposing part of my boobs. They were round globes of honey-colored flesh, the nipple a lighter shade. I knew Farrell loved sucking on them as much as I loved teasing him with them.

"No way it's that hot," Farrell groaned aloud, his brown eyes latched greedily on them.

I ignored him while I got off the chair. I walked down to the counter and hopped on to it, giving my breast a little jiggle. It was cool against my thigh, and his only served to heighten my arousal.

"Is it hot in here or what?" I panted as I pulled the slip completely off my shoulders and let it pool around my waist. I was naked from the waist up, and it was all the space I needed right then. I brushed my hands up my stomach and to my nipples. I pinched them hard, all the while keeping my eyes on Farrell's. They looked ready to pop.

"We have a doctor's appointment, Layla," he said, almost begging. "We're going to be late."

"No, we're not," I said, spreading my legs a little wider. His eyes trailed down my body to my legs and then ran over my body, leaving a blaze of heat on my ebony skin. He would be off that chair and to the counter in less than a minute. He just needed a little more push.

I pulled one leg over the other softly, the sound a soft swish in the quiet room, the silence only broken by the chirp of birds outside the window. Taking my hands from my body, I pulled the straps of the slip down my legs and, lifting myself a bit off the counter, pushed it completely off. I was naked now.

Farrell gave a sharp groan and got off the chair with a burst of energy, the chair falling over in his haste to get to me. Like I'd said, he couldn't resist naked, willing me, and that's exactly how I was at that moment.

"You vixen," he whispered against my ear as he bent over me to nip at them.

"You love it," I said with a soft purr. I leaned away from him and looked up at his warm eyes. I loved him, a lot, and I wanted to spend every day, every minute, every second proving that to him.

I gave him a slight kiss, and wrapping my legs around his, I pulled him closer.

"You're way overdressed."

"I'm catching the heat. Get me out of it," he replied, turning away and hopping on the counter himself. I got off and, running my hands to his waist, pulled the shorts off as slowly as possible. His dick was straining against the material, a prominent bulge I just couldn't ignore. I stopped pulling at the shorts and rubbed my thumb over the nub. Farrell closed his eyes and fisted his hands on the counter.

I moved my hands away and continued pulling at the shorts. When they were completely off, Farrell got off the counter, picked me up, and dumped me on top of it.
"You let me do my job now," he said, giving me a little spank on the ass. I had known it was coming, and now it was here. I closed my eyes in anticipation and shivered. His head game was strong, really terrific, and he always gave as good as he got—always.

***

Farrell's POV

"Spread them legs," I said, even as I placed myself between her legs and pushed them apart myself. She helped me, parting her legs as wide as they would go. I picked one up and placed it on the counter. It couldn't possibly get any wider, I thought, until I picked up the other and put it up on the counter too.

Layla was usually loud during sex, but today after the amazing orgasm she had woken me up with, I wanted to make her a screamer. It would just need a little more work than usual. And that I could do. We just didn't have as much time as I wished we did.

"You're gonna eat me out, aren't you?" She asked, a naughty little smile on her round face. She knew how to give what she wanted, and she knew what turned me on. And she was hitting all the right buttons then. I kissed a trail of kisses down her stomach, the taut flesh a subtle reminder of why we needed the doctor's appointment in the first place.

I didn't care about it, but Layla did, and that meant I didn't have a choice in the matter. Whatever made her happy made me happy. I rained kisses on her navel, giving it a lick and a deep bite.

Her navel was an erogenous zone, and she loved me to play with it. I licked at it twice more before moving on down her lush body. I wrapped my hands around her small beaded waist and pulled her to the edge of the counter.

With her so easily accessible, I spread her legs again and attacked her pussy. She gave a loud moan and blindly yanked me closer, her face a mask of pleasure. My tongue flicked out, and I rubbed the rough side against her opening.

Using her hands to hold her legs still and away, I pushed a finger into her painfully slow. I waited for her mewl of pleasure, but she didn't oblige. I looked up and noticed the challenging look on her face.

"Oh, it's going to be that way today?" I asked.

"You think you're up to it?" She asked with a little laugh.

"I'm up to anything with you," I told her, looking away and getting to work again. Sometimes Layla switched things up by forcing me to be innovative, and today I wasn't letting her win. It would be fast, but I would be deadly.

Pushing two fingers into her, I licked up and down her pussy, the moist opening accepting my fingers as easily as it had when it was just one. She inhaled sharply and closed her eyes to focus on the sensation. I repeated the action twice more and then added another finger. Layla gave a breathy little moan and lay back completely against the counter.

I gave her clit a bite and then a full suckle, my mouth sucking at the tiny little bud. Layla gave a hum low in her throat, the sound reverberating through her body. I continued sucking at her, my finger going in and out at a quick pace, in opposition to how slowly I was sucking against her. The two different paces created a clash of sensations, one immediately after the other.

"Come on, get it over with," she breathed out, her voice a testimony to how far gone she was, her body suffused by a light dusting of early morning sweat. She was breathing fast, her chest rising and falling quickly. I added my other hand to the fray, rubbing at her nipples even as my finger went in and out of her, my tongue teasing her to distraction.

"Did I win yet?" I challenged, keeping up the torture.

Getting off the floor, I put my hands around my dick and rubbed the pre cum which had been steadily dripping out over it. Layla was watching me silently, her face a mixture of excitement and lust. Much as I wanted to tease, I was teasing myself as much as I was teasing her.

I stood up, leaning slightly against the counter, then very suddenly, without warning, I slammed my dick into her.

"Fuck!" Layla screamed, bucking against me.

The single slam had induced an orgasm. Layla's legs were shaking, making it difficult for me to control my thrusts. Her enjoyment fueled my excitement. It was all the provocation I needed to keep slamming into her. Over and over and over again.

I stopped and pulled out slowly, this would be done too soon, and I didn't want it to be. I spread her shaking legs and rubbed the nub of my duck against her pussy, penetrating gently with the tip at intervals but never going in too far. Layla pushed against me, trying to drive me into her.

"You want to relax and enjoy this," I said softly.
"Could I die of pleasure? She asked, whimpering. Her mewls of pleasure filled the room, my groan a constant accompaniment. We were headed towards an orgasm together, and I couldn't wait. Pulling out completely, I thrust into her again, this time pushing myself to the hilt. The pleasure exploded in my head, so good it was almost painful.

It would be difficult to hold it in much more, but I didn't want to cum without Layla.

"How close are you again?" I panted against her.

"Close enough, you can go," she moaned.

I quickened my pace, my hips in control of my body. I was burying my dick in her rapidly now, the sound of my body hitting her's a loud smack in the otherwise quiet room. I pulled Layla closer and bent over to suck her tits right as I put my hands on her clit to run frantically at the little nub.

I needed her close. I was really close myself. The pleasure was clouding my brain, it was a lustful fog I couldn't get enough of, and it was only about to get better. I felt Layla tighten around me as another orgasm rushed over her. She was panting now, her hands in her hair as she tried to keep from shouting.

My balls tightened painfully in reaction to her, and I could feel my body preparing to explode.

"I'm really close, Layla," I warned her, panting loudly.

"You can let go, so am I," she said, leaning forward and giving me a sharp bite on my ears. She knew just how to get me over the edge. I felt heat low in my belly, and in the next second, the sprout of my seed into Layla. It was exquisite. I bent over and lay my head on her stomach. The pleasure was so great my legs shook as I groaned out my orgasm.

Layla gave a loud moan and stiffened against me. Her boobs were pressed against my chest, their movement an erotic twist as she shouted her pleasure. I pulled up and kissed her thoroughly, sticking my tongue in her mouth as she came down from her high.

"You like it?" I asked her.

"I loved it. You keep doing that all the time, there won't be no need for a challenge," she said laughing.

"We're late now." I said, getting off her and holding my hands out so she could hop off the counter.

"My legs don't work anymore. Gimme a piggyback," she pouted.

"You'll pay for that later," I said, bending forward so she could get on my back. We would be very late for our appointment at this rate, but it was only nine when I got to the room. We had about an hour to shower and get to the hospital in time for our check. Hopefully, there would be no hang-ups or traffic.

Layla was naked, and she gave me a slow slide down my body as she dropped off my back.

"You keep doing that, and we won't make it to the doctor's office at all," I promised her. I might've meant it too if she didn't sashay off to the washroom, her hands on her waist. She threw a dirty smile over her shoulders.

"I'd invite you into the shower, but you're a scaredy cat," I didn't like the sensation of water beating down on my face. That's why I'd had the tub installed, first thing. Layla loved her showers, so we always took our baths together, just sort of in separate places.

I found a robe and slipped it around my waist while I waited for Layla to leave the bathroom. I didn't want to be in there with her. I might devour her again, this time against the bathroom wall. And we just didn't have the time anymore. We had to leave, and very soon too. Our baby was important, way more important than my undisciplined balls.

12. Foreplay

As we entered the women's health clinic, the sound of beeping machines and the smell of antiseptics filled the air. The clinic was a large, brightly lit space with a reception desk and several waiting areas. The walls were painted in soothing pastel colors, and the floors were shiny, polished tiles. I noticed several people waiting in the reception area, some reading magazines while others were on their phones.

After checking in, Farrell and I were called into the doctor's office, where a friendly nurse took my vitals and provided me with a hospital gown to change into.

As we waited for the doctor, I nervously fidgeted with my fingers while Farrell tried to keep me calm, reassuring me that everything would be fine. When the doctor finally arrived, he introduced himself as Doctor Thomas and asked me a few questions about my medical history and the symptoms I had been experiencing.

"So, Layla, you mentioned that you've been trying to get pregnant for about a year now. Is that correct?" the doctor asked.

I nodded, feeling a bit embarrassed to talk about such a personal issue with a stranger.

The doctor smiled warmly at me, sensing my unease. "It's okay, Layla. Many women experience difficulty getting pregnant, and there are many treatments available to help. We're here to help you."

Dr. Thomas then asked me about any medical conditions I had, my menstrual cycle, and any medications I was currently taking. Farrell chimed in with additional information when necessary, providing support and reassurance to me.

After running some tests, the doctor returned with the results and explained that I was experiencing some issues that could make it difficult for me to get pregnant naturally.

"However," he added, "there are many treatments available to help you conceive, such as fertility medication or assisted reproductive technology."

I nodded, taking in the doctor's words. "What kind of assisted reproductive technology?" I asked.

"Well, depending on your specific situation, options like in vitro fertilization, intrauterine insemination, or surrogacy may be recommended," the doctor explained.

Farrell put his arm around me, offering me comfort and support. We both listened carefully to the doctor's recommendations, taking notes and asking questions to make sure we fully understood our options.

When the doctor was done with us, he directed us to a nurse at reception who would provide us with pamphlets and books on the available fertilization options he had recommended. I felt unusually nervous this morning. Maybe the excitement was finally catching up to me.

"You want to go get coffee?" Farrell asked me gently when we stepped out of the door into the sunlight. Our appointment had taken about two hours. The sun hit the roofs in splashes of gold light, a crisp breeze blowing into my curly hair.

"No, I want to get home," I replied, linking my arms through his as we made our way over to the car. I wanted us to consider our options and come to a decision fast. I needed Farrell to agree now.

"Alright, do we pick something up to eat later?" He asked as he opened my door and waited for me to slip inside the car. He was a macho man who opened doors. What wasn't to love?

"No, I'll cook something later," I replied when he had settled into the car himself. We moved out of the parking lot and into traffic on our way home.

***

Farrell's POV

She looked so beautiful, no scratch that, she was stunning, a creature of sunlight, air, and love. Layla lay snuggled into the sheets, her rowdy curls framing her round face while she snored softly.

I should make a video of this, I thought, even as I moved into the bed with her. She'd never believe she snored without evidence. I know; I've been trying to tell her for a while now. I snuggled against her, my arms around her body. I could feel my hips gravitate towards her round ass, my dick rubbing against her.

"Someone's awake," she mumbled sleepily.

"And someone isn't," I mumbled back. I pressed a kiss to her cheeks, and then just cause I knew she couldn't resist it, I pressed one behind her ears, right on the lobe. She stretched out, turning towards me to give me even more access.

"That's not fair. You know me too well," she said, a pout on her full lips. I loved the lips, the full brown upper lip in contrast to the pink lower lip, both mine to devour. I pulled her closer to me, my hands already seeking out the buttons on her sleepwear. They gave easily, and I pushed the silky piece of nothing off her shoulders, not completely off but just enough.

I started kissing my way across her collarbone, my mouth leaving a trail of heat, my fingers over her nipples, already caressing the distended buds. I got to her lips and gave her a soft kiss, my lips probing at hers, my tongue begging for access. She opened her mouth slowly, and I dived in, kissing her with reckless abandon.

She returned the fervor, her tongue seeking and then wrapping around mine. My fingers kept up the pressure on her nipples, twisting them gently to match the sensuality of our kiss. I broke the kiss and leaned away, looking at her swollen lips. They looked sultry in the morning light, their bright pink color a reminder of our passion.

I continued on my way, trailing kisses from her lips down her chest to her breast. The buds were already ready for me, and they looked like tiny little raspberries, their color bright against the hot brown of her skin. I pressed a kiss unto her breast, making sure to avoid her nipples. I wanted her mewling for my lips on her in no time. The suspense could be just as good as the action, after all.

Circling my tongue on her tits, I pressed a kiss against her skin, the soft flesh almost delicious on my lips. I kissed circles around her boobs, using my hands on the other, which wasn't getting as much attention. Finally, I latched onto her nipple and gave it a soft bite. Her back went off the bed, pressing her body into me. She moaned loudly and snuck her hands into my hair to hold my suckling lips to her nipple.

"You like that?" I asked, leaning away to lavish the same attention on the other nipple. The suckling sound filled the room, and I felt filled with red heat. It was relaxing in a way that lets you know you belonged right where you were, sucking on your wife's nipples.

Releasing her nipple, I kissed my way to her pussy. It was wet and glistening already. I placed a very wet kiss there first before sticking my index finger in to test the waters. Layla gave a loud moan and pressed her legs closed. I laughed aloud; Layla did that sometimes when the pleasure was really good.

"You want me to stop?" I asked her, caressing, teasing, her cries of pleasure, all the reward I needed.

"You better not," she gasped.

I increased the tempo of my thrust into her, my fingers like a piston. The squelching was quite loud now; she was ready for me. I gave myself a caress and then went ramming into her. Her eyes had been closed, but they popped open now, her face tight and sweaty.

I held still to give her a moment, and it took all my might to resist the urge to keep going. When she had marginally calmed, I started moving my hips again, this time slowly, like I had all the time in the world, like we weren't meeting our surrogate today, as though Layla hadn't come up with the craziest idea I had ever heard, as though I wasn't mad at her.

Clasping her hips to mine, I went ahead to slam myself into her, the lengths of my thrust shortening as we raced together towards orgasm. I was angry, and I wanted her to know it. She had me wrapped around her little fingers, and she was about to take advantage of it.

I kept my speed up until I heard her keening as her orgasm washed over her. She pulled me to her and dug her teeth into my shoulder, jerking as she came off her high. I came then, my body tightening as I released. I stiffened and roared out in pleasure. Panting, I fell back on the bed and pulled her to me. Her eyes were tightly closed, and she was breathing in faint gasps.

"You didn't tell me you were that angry," she said when her breath had steadied.

"I didn't know I was that angry," I said. After months of deliberation and recommendations, we had settled on a surrogate. It was the best option for the two of us, and we could have a healthy baby that could still be created with our seeds. Until Layla decided she wanted to be part of the process, right there in the room.

She wanted me to impregnate another woman, like fuck her, with her in the room, a willing participant. I didn't know she had such inclinations, but I didn't. I wanted to be faithful to my wife. It was a promise I had made and one I wished to keep.

"We need to talk," I said, getting off the bed and pulling my robe off the bedpost to slip my hands into them.

"I know, but everything's already settled. She's agreed, honey," she said, a pleading expression on her face.

"Well, I haven't agreed, and you need my dick, just in case you forgot," I said, frowning at her. I didn't know how she'd convinced Lena to agree to her crazy scheme, but I didn't want a part in it.

"It'll only be once," she said, swinging her legs off the bed.

"And if she doesn't get pregnant?" I asked, my brows raised. I didn't want to think of having to do it more than once.

"She will. She's really fertile according to the tests," Layla said.

"Layla, I love you, but we don't need to do this. We can always adopt our baby as long as we love it, nothing else matters," I said.

"We've already gone too far to back down now. This will only take a night, just one night, besides you'll enjoy it," she said with a slight smile.

Lena's flight had been booked, we'd spoken to her on the phone and FaceTime, but we'd be meeting her physically in about five hours, according to the clock. We'd be picking her up at the airport together later.

Lena was beautiful, and she looked like a younger replica of my wife, with the same round face and largely untamable curls. They were also the same complexion. We had been careful to choose someone who looked as close to Layla as we could. I'd gotten my way in that, at least, because the way this conversation was going, I didn't think I'd get my way in this one.

I walked down to the bed and settled beside Layla, picking up her hands and clasping them in mine.

"Are you certain about this?" I asked softly, "I'd hate for you to regret this."

"I'm sure, babes, I need it this way; I want to be physically with her as we make our baby, the three of us, together," she answered just as softly.

I gave her a kiss on the forehead and then turned her hands over to kiss her on the wrist, and then inside her palm. She shivered and smiled.

"Fine then, let's do this," I stated.

"Thank you, love," she squealed happily, jumping off the bed and onto me to wrap her legs around my waist.

"I'm not happy about it, but let's get it over with."

***

Layla's POV

She's beautiful, that was my first thought, followed immediately by, *our baby will be beautiful.*

She was seated in a corner booth, her eyes fastened on her phone, her hands scrolling fast. She had decided she wanted to meet at the coffee shop first to get comfortable with us and to see if we would be a good fit, physically or otherwise, before following us home.

I tapped at Farrell and pointed to where she was seated. His eyes had been roving the shop looking for her.

"My goodness, she looks exactly like you," he said with a stunned shake of his head. No way I looked half as beautiful as that. No way at all.

"No, she doesn't," I said. Lena had beauty, youth, and smarts on her side. "She's so young."

"You're only 27," Farrell said, laughing aloud. "She can't be any younger than 22, don't make us sound like the ancestors."

As we walked up to her, I felt a mix of excitement and nervousness. First impressions mattered. I liked her already. Hopefully, she liked us too. We had seen pictures of her online and had spoken to her on the phone, but this would be the first time we would meet in person. I really wanted her to. She'd be perfect.

As we approached her, she looked up from her phone, and a warm smile spread across her face.

"Layla and Farrell?" she asked, standing up to greet us. "I'm Lena. It's so great to finally meet you both!"

She was a striking woman in her early twenties, with dark hair and brown skin, and from the wide smile on her face, a warm, outgoing personality that immediately put us at ease. We sat down at the table, ordered some coffee, and began to chat.

Lena would be moving in with us, and if she agreed, she'd be staying with us in our guest room for the next two days while we tried making our baby. She'd be flying back home after that. It left us with limited time, but we had to work around her calendar.

Over the next hour, we talked about everything from Lena's background and family to her thoughts on being a surrogate. She was open and honest about the challenges and risks involved but also about the rewards and the sense of fulfillment she felt from helping others start a family.

As we spoke, I couldn't help but feel a connection with Lena. I was struck by how kind and compassionate she was and how much she genuinely seemed to care about our well-being. Her eyes sparkled when she laughed, and I noticed her eyes kept straying to Farrell. *Good, it would make the whole process easier.*

Farrell, too, was clearly impressed with her, by her wit as well as her unwavering commitment to the whole process.

"Why are you doing this?" He asked her suddenly, maybe not so impressed then. I linked my hands with his under the table and gave a warning squeeze. I didn't want him to scare her away. But she didn't need my help apparently because she leaned forward eagerly and said.

"For people like you, who have got nowhere else to go, the money is good, but the joy is even better, when you're holding your baby, and you can't help your tears. That's what I want for everyone. My parents couldn't have babies either, they had to have a surrogate, and now she's my godmother."

"Wow," I said. I didn't know if I'd make her my baby's godmother, but she was good. I felt Farrell relax against me and give me a squeeze back. It was our *agreed* signal. A squeeze from him meant he agreed; we could move forward.

"My wife had a crazy scheme in her head. She says you're consensual, but I'd like to hear it from you."

Well, that was direct, I'd hoped to more gently introduce the topic to her just before we left to avoid any awkwardness that might arise, but here we go.

"Yes, I am. I want to make this as comfortable and as good for you as it can be. You don't have to worry about that," she said with a wink at Farrell.

As we finished our coffee and said our goodbyes, I hugged Lena tightly and thanked her for everything. She'd join us later. She'd said she needed a moment to herself to prep her mind. I could feel the tears welling up in my eyes, and I knew that this was the beginning of a long and emotional journey.

We made it out of the door and to the car, I needed to convince Farrell, and I needed to do it fast. Lena would be perfect for our needs, but I could see that he was still hesitant, especially after meeting her.

"Did you like her?" I asked as he put on the car and drove out of the parking lot. It was three o'clock now, and we were heading over to the beach to enjoy a day out. Farrell had taken a few days off work to be with me while we finalized things with Lena, and we wanted to spend as much time together as we could.

The beach was private property, and it belonged to our friends, the Davis'. They were out of town together with their kids and it fell to us to keep an eye on the property as we lived close by. I wound the windows down and let the air sift through my hair. I was almost deliriously happy. I couldn't help it. I just wished Farrell was as happy too.

"She's not bad," he replied noncommittally. That meant he liked her, but he wasn't sure.

"You said it's fine if she agrees. I want this baby, please" I linked my hands through his free one and gave him a little kiss on his palm.

"We shouldn't, Layla, I feel we're using her. Did you tell the doctor about this? We could get sued," he said, his eyes on the road.

"This is consensual, honey, the hospital won't care, I promise, Lena and I spoke about it," I said.

"You really thought this through," he grumbled loudly.

"Of course," I replied with a laugh.

If I couldn't convince him when he was rational, then I'd just have to find another way to convince him, a much more pleasurable way. I thought of waiting till we got to the beach property, then discarded the idea.

Why not feed him the first course in the car? The second course he might get later on the beach if he agreed. No one had ever said I was ungrateful.

I dropped my hand to his legs and ran them closer to his dick. He quickly brought his hands down, placing them over my hands.

"What are you doing? I'm driving," he said, a note of desperation in his voice.

"Just playing around, love, nothing to freak out about. Besides, there's almost no one on the road," I said.

"Doesn't mean there couldn't be. You stop it," he said, giving me a stern look.

"Yes sir," I replied, giving a snappy salute. I leaned back against the headrest and acted like the good girl I was, for the moment.

When we had gone about half the distance, I once again placed my hands on his legs and then twirled my fingers to his dick. I didn't wait for his protest this time. Rather I started rubbing at him through his jeans. He inhaled and then stiffened in his seat.

"If I crash the car, it'll be your fault," he said.

"But we both know you won't crash the car, right?" I said as I unbuckled my seat belt to give myself more room to work with. He would be fucking me very soon, he just didn't know it yet.

I twisted towards him and, using both hands, unzipped his jeans. He was already hard against the front of his shorts. I pulled that down a little and attacked his dick. I stroked him twice and watched as he became even bigger.

His eyes were bugging out of his head; that alone was arousing enough that I could do that to my normally straight-laced husband. The power was heady. I kept stroking him slowly, and my little baby was growing. Very soon, it would be big enough to play with.

Farrell breathed out shakily and then wrapped his hands around mine, stroking with me.

"You can't blame me if you crash the car now," I teased, laughing when he gave me a thunderous expression. His expression quickly turned to pleasure when I ran my nails softly against his tip, the pink nub throbbing slightly in my hands.

I got up from the seat and knelt on it, unbuttoning my shirt to provide Farrell access to my breast. He didn't need to be invited twice. My hands tightened around him, stroking from the base to the tip. I leaned forward across his lap and put my mouth around him, spitting on him softly before I suckled him.

Farrell swerved the car to the side of the road and suddenly got out. I looked out the window, but it didn't look any different. He opened the back door and stormed in.

"Get back here," he growled at me, his voice a throaty piece of lust.

"Oh," I'd finally managed to drive him to distraction. I opened the door and got out of the car, quickly walked to the back door and got into the car. Immediately I was settled, Farrell whispered in my ears.

"Bend over."

I listened, getting on my knees on the seat and turning away from him to offer my trimmed snatch. He gave another groan, and then without warning, he slid his dick into me. I gave a loud moan and then checked myself. This wasn't home, and it would be difficult controlling my moan. I was a screamer after all.

I felt Farrell's hand cover my mouth, his "scream as loud as you want," following the action a total turn-on. He slid out and slid back in, the action sending hot waves of pleasure through my body. I pushed against him as he pushed into me, the pleasure explosive.

We ran together towards completion, my moans becoming louder as we got closer. Without warning, he lay back against the seat and let me ride. I raised my hips and came down forcefully on him, the sound of our snacks filling the car with the delicious sound of sex.

Farrell gave a long, drawn-out groan and tightened his hands around me. He was close, very close. He would shoot off soon. I increased my tempo, letting my hands drop to my body. I started rubbing at my clit, the sensation aiding me to my orgasm. I moaned louder and felt my orgasm come upon me.

I felt Farrell explode inside me, my insides coated with his seed. I came immediately after, my back arching as I orgasmed. I fell on him heavily, and our breath came in very short gasps. Farrell folded his hands around me and ran his hands through my hair, then down to my back and onto my butt.

It was after-sex foreplay. We never forgot it. It helped to ground us in the intimacy of the moment, the love we had for each other. I sat up slowly, my legs weak from my orgasm.

"We need to move," I whispered to Farrell. His eyes were closed as he tried to get a handle on his breathing.

"Give me a moment," he said, his eyes slowly blinking open. I gave him a little kiss on the tip of his nose before arranging my dress as best as I could and stepping out of the car. I'd give him a moment. I opened the driver's side door and got in.

"You're going to drive?" Farrell asked, a bewildered look on his face.

"Yes, it'll be fine," I assured him, pulling out of where he had packed on the shoulder of the road.

"You really do love me," he said with a laugh. I hate driving. I never drive if we're together. Never. Yet here I was doing just that, for love, I thought fondly. I joined him, my laughter wry rather than amusing. I increased my speed slightly, ignoring Farrell's words of protest. We'd just wasted about an hour on the road. We needed to get to the beach house and back home before Lena arrived.

13. Laila's POV

Farrell and I had decided earlier on to set up in Lena's room. Our room was our sanctuary, and according to him, he didn't want it "despoiled," whatever that meant. I'd had a shower and dressed in my robe while I waited for him to step out of the bathroom. He was taking really long in there, I was certain he had changed his mind when the door clicked open, and he stepped out naked.

I breathed in sharply and looked him up and down, feasting my eyes on his magnificence; he was a specimen, that's for sure.

"You'd like another pose?" He asked, placing one hand on his waist and blowing me a kiss with the other.

"I'll let Lena deal with that one," I said naughtily.

He walked over to the vanity and used a dab of perfume, the musky scent filling the room. I breathed in deeply, enjoying the fragrance.

"You ready?" I asked. We would be heading over to Lena's room soon, I wasn't certain how any of this would go, but I was certainly looking forward to it. Our sex life was great, but I wasn't such a saint that I didn't think it could get better. And Lena might be just the ticket. If only he would let himself relax.

"Let's go," I said, turning to head out of the room. It was getting dark outside, the lights of the town visible through the glass of the windows as I stepped out of the room. I waited outside for Farrell while he found a robe for himself too.

I knocked softly on Lena's door and pulled it open, then stood stock still at the door, shocked. Lena was spread out on the bed in all her glorious, half-naked, black beauty, a mischievous smile on her face. She seemed to love our surprised expression because she gave a small smile before swinging her legs off the bed and sauntering sexily toward us.

The room had been set up too. Candles flickered on surfaces, somehow giving the room the ambiance of a bodega. Petals had been strewn on the floor; the effect was confusing, like the innocence of a prom night beside the obvious sexiness of a brothel. The Lena of this afternoon was gone; this Lena was all woman.

She was dressed in a lingerie set, the red lace setting off her bright brown eyes, she looked to be glowing in the light, no way that was natural, but I liked it anyway.

She pulled at a knot in front of the lingerie and then left it trailing off on its own. Her eyes were fixed on me while she walked up to us. Farrell was still frozen beside me, he certainly wasn't expecting this either. I gave a smirk, he sure as hell was loving this as well.

The knot seemed to be the only thing holding the lingerie together because it started slipping off Lena's body as she walked toward us. She didn't care, continuing her bold stride to us. The lingerie came off completely, exposing her pert breast to my gaze. She saw me sweep my eyes over her body and smiled again.

She swung her eyes to Farrell, who also had his eyes feasting on her lithe body. She seemed to love the attention. Reaching us, she yanked us into the room and to the bed. Obviously, we were to follow her lead.

This was going better than I had ever envisioned. Lena pushed Farrell gently onto the bed and knelt before him. She pulled on his robe ties, and it gave way slowly, baring his body to our feasting eyes.

"You're hot," she whimpered softly, her hands tracing his muscles and then his distinct abs. Farrell worked out regularly to keep a body I loved. Mostly.

"Well, thank you, Layla loves it," he answered, looking up at me. His eyes seemed to ask if I was okay with all this. I nodded and watched him relax.

"I love it too," she said. She stretched her hands behind her and beckoned me to come forward. I walked down to the bed to settle in beside Farrell, but she shook her head.

"Come here, beside me," she said, pointing at where she wanted me. I walked down there and settled beside her on my knees.

Lena bent her head and took Farrell's hard length into her mouth. She lowered her head slowly, his black dick disappearing into her mouth as she took him deeper.

"Wrap your hands around it," she instructed. I shifted closer and wrapped my hands around him, my hands stroking down his length when Lena's mouth came down and stroking down when she pulled up to swipe at his tip with her tongue. Farrell fisted both hands in our hair and closed his eyes. He was certainly loving it.

Lena quickened her pace as she continued sucking, her lips making slurping sounds as she sucked faster. I increased the pace of my strokes to match hers, one of my hands moving to squeeze Farrell's balls. He gave a groan and opened his eyes to look from me to Lena.

She gave a sly wink and continued enjoying the moment. I couldn't take it anymore. I got off the floor, loosened the ties on my robe, and moved to the bed. I pushed Farrell back so he was lying on the bed and then settled myself on his face. His tongue stabbed out almost immediately, right into my pussy. I gave a shaky moan and forced my legs to stop moving.

He attacked me with his hands and then slipped two fingers into me. I was dripping already. His thumb rubbed against my clit quickly. I threw my head back and moaned. Lena must've done something crazy to him because his back thrust off the bed, his tongue going deeper into my body as his body rode off the bed.

I looked back at Lena, who was displaying a mischievous smile. I'd ask her to show me whatever she'd done later. I motioned her to the bed and replaced her on the floor. She climbed on his face, Farrell hesitated a moment, and I gave him a little tap on his dick.

He stuck out his tongue to taste her before devouring her. Just then, I started sucking at him, my hands squeezing at his balls, he would blow his nut soon at this rate, and we needed that inside Lena. We didn't have time to waste.

I climbed onto the bed and slipped him inside me, starting to ride him even as he sucked at Lena's pussy. She was squealing quite loudly. She was a screamer like me then, one more thing we had in common.

I went up and down on him faster, my tempo increasing as my pleasure increased, then I got off. I heard him give a groan of disappointment, the sound reverberating through his body, and I tapped on Lena.

"Replace me, he'll cum soon," I informed her.

She scrambled down his body and pushed herself down his length fast, her body landing with a loud slap on his body. She was good, really good. Farrell gave a loud shout while Lena shuddered on top of him, her brown shoulders shaking.

I crawled up to Farrell.

"Are you enjoying this?" I whispered to him.

"You can ask me that in the morning. I'll be more objective," he answered before groaning aloud. I leaned over him to suck at his nipples, biting first one bud and then the other. I lapped at them, running the rough side of my tongue over them every time. Lena was going faster now, and Farrell was even closer.

"I can't cum without you, come over here," he said, beckoning me to his face again. I didn't hesitate, swinging my legs over his body and settling on his face. His hands came over to my nipple while his tongue slid into me slowly. I moaned aloud, my attention zooming to the feel of his tongue on me.

I would be over the edge soon, I thought. The feel of Farrell's fingers pushing into me, the friction resisting as my body stretched to accommodate the intrusion, Lena's loud moans echoing behind me, Farrell groaning as he pushed closer to orgasm. It was all I could do to stop myself from going over the edge. I pulled my eyes tightly closed, my body responding madly to his touch.

"Fuck, I'm cummminggg," Lena screamed. I blinked my eyes open to see her body going limp on top of Farrell, her arms stiff as her body went through orgasm. We did differ there then, I thought. I was more prone to violent shakes during orgasms.

"How close are you, love? I'm very close," Farrell asked, his eyes fixed on my face. My body was suffused with need, and I couldn't control the movement of my hips on his hands. I was close, very close. I closed my eyes again and felt my body give in.

I started quaking, my legs moving with no control. Waves after waves of pleasure hit me, my body responding to the feel of Farrell cumming inside me. He pushed into me once more and fell back on the bed, his face dotted with sweat.

"Damn," Farrell swore as Lena ground her body on top of his, his spent body still reacting to her. I fell over him, spent like a rag doll. My body thrummed after my orgasm. That was good, very good. Even Farrell couldn't possibly deny it.

I closed my eyes and tried to steady my breath. Lena got off Farrell and spread out beside him, her long legs flung out everywhere. I got off him, too, and lay on his other side, my chest rising and falling as my breathing slowed.

Farrell wrapped his arms around us and pulled us closer, giving me a kiss on my forehead before leaning over and doing the same to Lena.

"Are you okay?" I asked him.

"Never been better," he replied, a lewd look on his face.

I laughed, watching as animation returned to Lena's limbs. She got off the bed, her hips swinging as she made her way to the bathroom. She pulled the door open, threw us a look over her shoulders, and pulled the door closed. She really was a siren.

"She looked so innocent and young," he said, shaking his head.

"Not you gossiping, Farrell," I laughed.

"No, really, she's a vixen in bed, but she looks like an angel out of it. What happened?"

"You don't like it?" I asked, slightly worrying now.

"Are you kidding? I loved it," he said, smoothing my hair from my face. "Was it good for you?" He asked, giving me a little kiss.

"It was perfect. Let's hope she's pregnant," I said, my heart beating fast as I realized that our baby could very possibly be growing inside her right now—a little baby boy or girl that could be ours.

"We should give her room back," Farrell said, making to get off the bed. My gentleman already thinking of her privacy. I picked my robe up and started dressing. He did the same while we waited for her to leave the bathroom.

"Where do y'all think you're going?" Lena asked as she stepped out of the bathroom. She turned to me.

"You're not taking your hunk away already, are you?

"We thought you'd love your privacy," I said.

"Oh no, I'd love for you two to spend the night here. That's not too much to ask, is it? She said, a suggestive look on her face.

"Oh," I said, lost for words. I turned to Farrell, who was looking at her, a confused look on his face.

"You sure you're the person we met at the coffee shop earlier?"

Lena laughed, stepping closer and rubbing her hands over his body,

"I'm not many things, but that was certainly me," she said against his ears. He gave an involuntary shudder, and I laughed. Lena pushed him onto the bed, scrambling up the bed and giving him a kiss. She looked back at me sultrily.

"You're not joining us?"

And there I was, thinking the night was over. I untied my robe and went to join them on the bed. Nights weren't meant for sleeping alone.

***

I blinked my eyes open and sat up. I couldn't recognize the surrounding for a moment until my brain unfroze long enough for me to remember that we'd fallen asleep in Lena's room last night. I scrambled up, trying to get off the bed before she woke up. Except she was already awake and staring at me.

"You're beautiful, and Farrell says I look just like you. Isn't that nice of him?" She said quietly.

"He did tell me that, too," I told her. "Where's he?" I asked, looking around me. Farrell was gone. He'd probably woken up earlier and sneaked out of the house. I wonder why he hadn't woken me before leaving.

"He had to get to work. He left you that," she said, pointing at a note beside me, "and that," this time pointing towards a breakfast tray that had been placed on the table along with fresh flowers.

"Oh, how long has he been gone?" I asked as I looked around me, the sheets had been thrown off the bed, and Lena was barely dressed, her breast peeking out from her lingerie from last night.

I looked away, not wanting to violate her privacy. Plus, they looked good, I could feel myself responding, and that wasn't normal.

"You're not gonna be shy now, are you?" She said, smiling at me..

"No, it's just you look even better in the daylight, and no, you don't look like me at all. You're way prettier," I told her.

She stretched before spreading herself out on the bed beside me.

"Come on, join me," she said, pulling on my hands.

That's not right. I should let her sleep, I thought, even as I spread myself out beside her. She looked at me a moment before pulling me closer and kissing me softly.

Damn, her lips are soft.

I couldn't *not* respond to them. I kissed her back just as softly, the imprint of her lips like a hot brand on mine. She opened her mouth and left it that way. I took the initiative, plunging my tongue into her mouth greedily. I'd never kissed a woman, and this felt different, like kissing a soft teddy.

Her lips fell beneath mine, her tongue sneaking out to meet mine in an erotic game of cat and mouse. I searched her mouth, my tongue sweeping the interior, she tasted sweet, and I realized she must've been awake for a while now.

She pulled at me as she sat up, taking my robe off as she motioned her hands down my body to my pussy. She pushed them in without hesitation. It felt good, like Farrell when he wanted to tease. I focused on the feeling of her finger pushing and retreating, pushing and retreating inside me. I spread my legs and gave her more space to work with.

I'd probably feel more about this later, but for now, the feel of her hands inside me was driving me crazy. She crawled down my body, stopping along the way to stick her tongue in my navel before moving on down to my pussy.

Her hands squeezed my breasts as she sucked on my pussy. My body shuddered in excitement, my legs clamping around her head. I was primed and on edge, my body receiving pleasure. *I'd be over the edge soon at this rate,* I thought absently.

She increased the movement of her hands inside me, plunging in and out fast, my body enjoying the ride as she sucked and fingered me. I moved my hands down and ran them over her breast, my nails scraping roughly over her nipples before pinching roughly, she gave a loud moan, and her tongue went straight into my pussy in retaliation. I moaned just as loudly, as I clutched the bed.

Lena's tongue swirled before she snuck it into me, thrusting it into me quickly, mimicking a dick. She took it out suddenly and replaced it with two fingers. My body was hot and sweaty, and I felt my body start its way to an orgasm. Lena must have felt it too, because she increased her pace, pushing both fingers into me roughly.

I screamed out loud and started shaking on the bed, my body quaking in orgasm. She kept up the assault, pumping her fingers in and out until I relaxed on the bed. Then she trailed my body softly and crawled up the bed to kiss me. Her lips tasted salty, the juices from me still staining her lips.

"You ever done that before?" She asked after a moment had passed.

I shook my head no and got off the bed on shaky legs. My

stomach felt empty, the effect of all those orgasms from last night and this morning. I had to tell Farrell about this morning after Lena had left town, and it was just as well she'd be going cause I wouldn't mind a repeat of that. Not at all.

"You want a bite?" I asked her, pointing to the tray laden with bread and eggs, some bacon, and a closed mug of coffee.

"No, I've had breakfast. I get extremely hungry after a full night of sex," she said.

"Can you stay another night?" I asked and almost immediately regretted it. I didn't want to seem too eager, plus I didn't know if Farrell would want her to.

"We'd planned on two nights, I know, but no, I don't think I'll be able to," she said, disappointment stamped on her face.

"Why? You don't like us?" I asked her.

"That's not it, I'd hoped to be here a day early so I could spend the weekend, but I've got a few things to clear up at school on Monday. I need to get home and prepare for that," Lena was in her final year of college. She'd be done in a month, way before the baby.

"Alright, I'll miss you," I told her. And that was true too. I picked up the mug of coffee and took a long sip from it.

"I'll miss you too," she said, sitting up on the bed to watch me eat.

"You said your parents had to get a surrogate. Why exactly?" I asked her.

"Mom had cancer a little young. She had to give up her womb," she told me, looking away from me out of the window.

"Oh, that must've hurt," I said, getting off my chair and walking over to her. I reached my hands out and waited until she took it before settling beside her.

"It wasn't my pain. Mom says she only ever regretted it when it looked like they'd never find a surrogate," she told me, her eyes filling with tears. She swiped them away quickly. "It's why I'm doing this, to give another hopeless couple some hope," she added.

"And we're very grateful for that," I told her, leaning over to give her a kiss on the forehead.

"I know," she replied, smiling.

"You need some help packing up?" I asked, looking at her stuff which had been hung up in the closet and arranged around the room.

"No way all this stuff came in that pack," I said, looking at her with my eyebrows raised.

"It most certainly did," she said, getting off the bed and walking over to the pack.

I watched her as she picked it back down and walked back to the bed to drop it beside me. She moved around the room, down to the closet to unhang her dresses, and then into the bathroom to pack up her toiletries and makeup.

Then she proceeded to pack them up into the bag, creating space in crevices to put in her stuff. I looked at her, my lips slowly widening into a wide smile as she packed up everything.

When she was done, she bent over in a deep bow and swept her hands out beside her like a magician. I got off the bed and gave a resounding applause like an audience of one. I gave her a kiss and watched as she worked her hands over her hair self-consciously.

"You're good," I told her. I could be a rowdy packer, so I was slightly impressed with her skill. The bag wasn't even full!

"Thank you, thank you," she said.

"You're not leaving this morning, are you? We should spend the morning together," I said, looking at her with entreaty on my face.

"I'll have to go soon, but we can get a cup of coffee together," she answered, walking over to the bed and snuggling into the sheets. She patted the space beside me, and I walked over to the bed and got into it.

***

Lena's POV

Several months later.

I stood at the airport, anxiously waiting for my luggage to arrive. I had just flown in from New York, where I had been staying for the past few months. My mind was racing with excitement and anticipation as I thought of the resin for my trip.

Gwen was one year old, and I was on my way to Layla and Farrell's home to celebrate her birthday party. I had been Gwen's surrogate mother, and her parents and I had become friends.

As I waited for my bags, I checked my phone to see if Layla had sent any updates on the party preparations. I saw a message from Layla saying that they were running a bit late.

Finally, my bags arrived, and I quickly made my way out of the airport and into a waiting taxi. The drive to Layla and Farrell's home was filled with excitement and nerves as I thought about how much Gwen had grown since I had last seen her.

When I arrived, I was greeted warmly by Layla and Farrell. They were still a beautiful couple, Farrell looking dapper in a shirt and pants and Layla in a beautiful two-piece.

The room was loud and filled with the sound of laughing children. I looked around the room and saw Gwen playing with a few other children, her bright smile lighting up the room. My heart swelled with love and pride as I watched the little girl that I had brought into this world.

Layla and Farrell took me to the kitchen, where they had set up a small table with snacks and drinks. I grabbed a glass of water and took a deep breath, trying to calm my nerves.

"I can't believe Gwen is already one year old," I say, feeling emotional. "It feels like just yesterday I was carrying her in my belly."

Layla and Farrell smiled warmly at me, grateful for my role in their daughter's life.

"We can't thank you enough for what you've done for us," Farrell said, his voice filled with gratitude.

"It's my pleasure," I replied, feeling emotional. "I love Gwen like she's my own."

"We know that, which is why we're making you her godmother," Layla said, a smile on her face.

"You did say you didn't think it was necessary," I said, laughing out loud. It was unbelievable. I loved it.

"We changed our mind. Gwen agrees too," she said, laughing.

"That's so sweet. Thank you, Layla," I said, leaning over to give her a tight hug and then doing the same to Farrell. I could admit to a lingering attraction to them. After our last time together, we had kept up our tryst whenever I came into town, but with Gwen in the house now, it would be sort of difficult.

I hoped they would have another baby soon. It would be the perfect way to get them together with me again.

14. Sibling Encounters

Mouths and breaths, hands and bodies twisting over each other. We surged ahead into a wordless space, one where I knew I was about to be inside her. I needed the warmth of her body on mine. I needed to sheath my body in her flesh.

She submitted, no, she directed me to join her. I tore the pants off her ample hips, pausing only to inhale the honeyed fragrance of her before I aligned my body with hers. I couldn't bear to be more than a few inches away from her. That searing heat, that beautiful secret between her thighs. That was all I needed.

She was wet and welcoming, guiding my dick toward her pussy lips with a gentle touch, moving my body into position with hers. She wrapped her calf behind my hip, drawing me to her, making it impossible to resist.

"Yes, Tony baby, I want you inside me," she whispered before I kissed the words away from her.

Shifting slightly, I held her underneath me as I stroked her gently with the head of my dick. With a groan, she wrapped her legs behind my hips and guided me deeper. The first inch was tight, a tense band of flesh that soon yielded, just slightly, to allow me to pass. I tried to be gentle, but I needed more. Every inch of conquest only made me think about how I needed more. I needed her to envelop me completely. I needed to be buried inside her.

We moved together urgently, magically, my body threatening to explode before I could bring her to climax. But she swirled her hips underneath me, taking what she needed from me to my utter amazement. She knew just how to use my dick to bring herself to climax. Her pussy sucked me in further, swirling around my shaft over and over again.

My fingers dug into the mattress to keep from coming until I was sure. Her eyes rolled up and closed as she moaned, shuddering, grasping at my dick with her beautiful pussy walls. Only then did I allow myself to climax inside her, plunging so deep she gasped again, allowing me to release my cum deep inside her, every last bit of it.

With that, I leaned down and pressed a kiss to her lips. It started out slow and sweet, but after a moment, Heather pulled me closer, deepening the intensity as she moaned into my touch. Seizing the opportunity, I swiped my tongue inside her mouth and caused her to let out a loud gasp.

"Was that good for you?" I growled as I broke the kiss.

She wrapped her arms around my neck and dug her fingers into the back of my head while nodding.

"Yes," She whispered hotly.

We quickly got cleaned up and turned to be in each other's arms, where we found solace the most. I kissed her forehead. Heather and I had been married for two years. She had ebony skin, long dark hair which reached her back, but she enjoyed mixing dye to it for her amusement, round brown eyes that sucked me deep whenever we locked eyes, her button nose, and heart-shaped lips.

She was quite petite at five foot one and had an hourglass-shaped figure which seemed more evident under tight-fitting clothes. She could be a maniac in bed, just the way I love her.

"More, Tony. Make love to me." She blinked her eyes, which had become watery for no reason.

"Don't you need a break? There is something we have to discuss..."

"Just one more time, then I'll listen to whatever you have to say. There's also something you should know." She said, cutting me off. Her eyes twinkled in excitement, and instantly I knew it was something good since it only happened whenever she had something really exciting to say.

Her lips hovered just millimeters away from mine, open to allow her sweet, gentle breath to float over my mouth. She tasted good, and we paused for a few tortured seconds, just barely apart. She arched her back to kiss me, moaning gently as our lips began quickly to explore each other with mounting intensity.

I was hungry for her, so hungry I could practically want to drain her of this delicious taste. I wanted her tongue, her lips, and her body wrapped around me. I wanted her arms clutching my shoulders. Her thighs clenched over my hips. I found myself in an immediate, primal frenzy, touching every part of her. Her breasts contract under my palms, nipples turning hard.

***

Heather's POV

My gorgeous husband turned things up a notch. He ran his hands down my sides and over my belly to my hips before pulling me as close as possible.

"I love you so much," he rasped while looking down at my breasts between us. "Fuck, you're so wet."

The next thing I knew, he was running his tongue through my pussy, lapping at the wet folds.

"Ohhhhh!" I cried out, my hands gripping the sheets. "Fuck!" My hips jerked forward, and I pushed my head back into the stack of pillows, moaning.

"You're so wet for me," he rasped hoarsely. "It's sexy as hell, and I need more."

I lifted my head just in time to feel his tongue licking up my folds again before swirling around my clit. Stars sparkled before my eyes, and my hips jerked, but he held me in place and devoured my sweetness. He alternately licked and sucked my clit until my whole body was trembling, and a hot sweat covered my skin.

"Oh!" I cry out. "Tony, I can't … I'm going to…!"

He lifted his head and looked at me, his eyes gleaming. "That's it, baby. You want to cum? I want to hear you scream."

He dropped his head back down and pressed his tongue to my clit as he pushed two fingers inside my pussy, pumping them vigorously. Ecstasy surged through my form, and I screamed, my back arching as my pussy spasmed with pure pleasure.

"Tony!" I screamed. "Uhhh."

Tony continued drinking from my slit, swallowing again and

again as hot gushes of my female nectar streamed down his throat.

Excitement brightened his eyes as he pulled away, and he notched the tip of his dick in my hole before leaning forwards. The pressure was heavenly as my lashes fluttered shut as a long, guttural moan escaped my throat.
"Mm, that feels so good," I gasped. "You're so hard."

"Yes, but you can take it," he groaned throatily. "You're fully relaxed, baby. Just spread your legs and take it all."

Then in a fluid movement, he pressed inside, filling me completely. A strangled gasp escaped my throat at the sudden penetration, and I was full to the point of bursting. But Tony gazed down at me with appreciation in that azure gaze.

"Baby, you feel amazing, and you're taking it so well. I'm never going to get enough of this." His fingers burned into my skin as he pressed my thighs apart, rolling his hips and pumping into me. He went slow at first, but then he picked up speed. His eyes never left mine.

"Your pussy looks so good getting fucked over and over again," he moaned.

I couldn't answer, but a high keening sound started in my throat, and he nodded in understanding. Keeping one hand on my thigh, he ran his other up over my belly and caressed my breasts. I was teetering on the edge of the cliff as he pinched the nipple before flicking at the hard nub.

"Tony, oh!" I screamed. "Shit!"

My back arched, and Tony dug his fingers into my thighs, pumping into me once, twice, and then it happened.

"FUCK!" he roared. "Oh shit!" His enormous black dick jerked inside me, and his body went rigid as he groaned, spurting hot reams of cum into my sweetest spot. My pussy spasmed again, the milking action bringing his fluid deeper into my body.

"Oh!" I cried out, losing myself. "Shit!"

He groaned again, spurting wildly before collapsing on my body.

I couldn't say a word because I was still in the throes of ecstasy. I cried out again, my pussy snapping as my breasts shook. My vision went dim, and I lost all sense of space and time as the world closed around me.

***

Tony's POV

I smiled when I saw Heather, passed out on the bed. I went to the bathroom and returned with a washcloth to clean her up. I lovingly parted her folds and wiped away every trace of our fluids to leave her feeling fresh and relaxed whenever she woke up.

There was something else she needed to know, something I had planned, but I wondered if she was going to approve of it. I didn't have to wait to long to find out because warm hands caressed my back. I turned to see her, she looked a little spent, but her eyes were still twinkling.

"Is there something on your mind?" She raised herself to a sitting position.

I nodded and smiled to reassure her. "My brother invited us to this private island."

"I thought you didn't have a sibling?" She looked confused for a moment.

I chuckled. "It's Nate, silly, my half-brother." She always seemed to forget that Nate was family because he had been away for too long, and there had been no news, calls, or texts from him. When I saw the message requesting our presence, I knew I had to visit to see how much he had changed.

Her face morphed through a series of expressions. "Since we were invited, you don't want to go?"

"I was thinking you might not want to."

"If it's fine with you, then we should go. It's not every day that we get invited to a private island." She tucked her hair behind her ears and grinned. "Let's just call this one a vacation."

And so we did.

The island was ten and a half miles in circumference. There was the marina, the docks, the low, interlocking structures, the nine-hole golf course, swimming pools, and the fortress-like resort. Heather and I were stunned as we were led through all this by a male escort that he had assigned to show us around before we met him. I was dumbfounded since my brother had never given me the details of what the island entailed. I didn't expect it to be so huge.

The bedroom we were ushered into was huge and done up in shades of gray. There were silvery drapes framing enormous windows and also a cream-colored carpet, but it was the bed that had Heather entranced. It was a gigantic king-size with a plethora of silver pillows done up in shiny damask, and she gasped at the luxury. We were on our way to finally meet my dearest, long-lost brother when Heather tugged at my hand to stop us both.

Her eyes were wide and expectant. We surrendered to a few moments of pleasure, kissing each other like no one was watching. Even with a few people around, we made out with passion and lustful desire. Happily, we made our way to the resort, where my brother was waiting for us.

"Hey, brother." He had his back facing us, and he abruptly turned around to take a look at us. When we were just a few steps away, he smiled.

What I felt then, I never felt before. Not until now. A feeling that something was just inexplicably correct. A rightness. And I felt... Happy.

We hugged each other before I began my questioning. "Where have you been? You went on hiatus." I playfully glared at him.

"I was creating this." He glanced around to indicate the island. "Now, before you continue, won't you introduce me to the pretty lady next to you."

"Heather, meet Nate-"

"Your long-lost brother, I get it." She smiled and stretched out her hand. "Nice to meet you."

He took her hand in his and kissed it. "The pleasure is all mine." Then he let go and gave me a knowing look which I easily understood, so I grinned at him. "Come on, brother, let the pretty lady get some rest at the beach. The guides will look out for her. You and I have a lot to catch up on."

I turned to look at Heather, and she nodded at me, so I kissed her forehead before leaving with Nate. We found ourselves in the kitchen since we cooked together in the past. Nate stirred a pot of pasta, humming as the food cooked. We were preparing a special spaghetti and meatballs recipe that we had created. It was a treat because each meatball was humongous and seasoned with a special spice mix, in addition to being made of the finest steak meat. My mouth watered as the aroma hit my nostrils, and I could tell Nate was getting hungry too. He was putting the finishing touches on our garlic bread, and the gooey butter mix looked revolting and yet also delicious.

"You're curious about her, aren't you?" I asked, and Nate nodded, his attention not leaving what he was doing. "She's amazing, one of the best things in my life before you."

He rolled his eyes.

"You're attracted to her," I said. He suddenly stopped and looked at me, then he shrugged.

"Just a little. It's really nothing."

"It is not the first time, you know, this happened in the past." I laughed. I was expecting his response. "What do you say, brother, just this one time?"

He looked surprised. "You don't mind that I'm a little attracted to her?"

"You are attracted to her, and it's just lust. I have strong feelings for her, and I love her; she's mine, but I can still let you have a taste of the heaven she is."

"She won't mind?" There was glee in his eyes. I knew he fancied

Heather, every man does fancy a beautiful woman, but he clearly knew that he couldn't have her since I had already claimed her.

"I've always wanted to try a threesome with her. This could be our only chance. She's a wild one herself. I'm quite certain she wouldn't mind." And then I left the kitchen in search of Heather. The sun was high in the sky, and I quickly realized that today was going to be quite hot.

When I reached a pass, I cut across a path, taking me back toward the beach. To my surprise, I found Heather on the beach, not swimming or tanning but holding her hair back with her hands, staring down the long strand of white sand. When she turned toward me, she raised a quick hand in greeting, squinting and smiling against the sun.

"I expected you to be having fun," I remarked when I neared her. It was hard not to smile at her too broadly. She was smiling at me too. She looked me over with unabashed interest.

"How long can you stay underwater?"
"I can hold my breath for three minutes," I replied.

She raised an eyebrow at me.

"Would you like to see?" I asked playfully.

Grinning, she followed me back to an outcropping of rock, "I don't think I can swim today. I'm not wearing…"

"You won't be swimming," I reassured her with a smile. "Trust me?"

She shrugged. "I do," she confirmed.

"Take off your shoes." I smiled. "Actually, let me." I led her to a smooth, white rock, and she sat obediently as I knelt before her, gently removing her footwear. I set them aside and then pushed her simple, teal-green skirt over her knees. The sunlight caught the hairs on her upper thighs as I exposed them, inch by inch. She shuddered with delight and looked around to make sure we were all alone. After confirming that no one was watching, I pushed her knees apart, and she allowed me to spread her legs, revealing the white lace panties.

I opened her legs further, taking time to memorize the closed bud of her pussy. Her pubic hair was trimmed but not shaven. It barely covered a plump, healthy pussy, one so sweet that it always made my mouth water.

I had to get her into the water. My dick was so hard already I was afraid I was going to come on her feet. Abruptly I stood, pushed her skirt down to her ankles, and slid the sleeveless top over her head. She gasped and bit her lips together, holding back a whimper of surprise.

"It's warm, I promise," I reassured her as I drew her to the water. We waded through knee-high, warm water with barely any ripples and circled a column of stone when the floor suddenly gave way. It was only about four feet deep now, a turquoise-green pool completely enclosed by stone columns. The water was bath-warm and still, with a natural seat on one side. I entered first, pulling her behind me. When she stepped into the pool, I found her hips under the water and maneuvered her floating form to the stone seat.

"Babe, hurry up."

I smiled, eager to feel her yet again. As soon as she was settled, I began. I took several deep breaths in a row, finally holding one, and then submerged myself beneath the surface of the warm water. Notching my knees under the ledge of the rock, I opened my eyes to see the wondrous, brown-skinned spectacle of her open thighs in front of me. Holding my breath, I took a moment to imprint this vision on my memory because I never wanted to forget. The ligaments of her upper thigh were connected to her pelvis, the gradual opening of her pussy lip, and barely visible ruffle.

Pulling her closer, I covered her clit with my mouth. My tongue parted her lips with one smooth movement. She released a sweet pulse of juices into my mouth that I swallowed just a bit of, not wanting to drink too much salt water, but she was too sweet to pass up. Her fingers soon tangled in my hair as I tongued her lips, letting the water flow over each.

I could feel her hips tremble, and her thighs flex as I delved deeper, tonguing her pussy entrance with my tongue as I nosed the delicate pearl of her clit. My lungs began to burn, but I couldn't surrender; my task was just too important.

With two fingers, I reached inside her to find the ridges of her G-spot and stroked them gently as my lips sucked at her clit. She pulled me closer, and her hips slid into the deeper water, but I couldn't let her go. I didn't want to stop until she came in my mouth. Sucking just a bit harder, I pulsed her G-spot insistently. She began to come, her juices charging the water all around us.

Her thighs clamped over my ears, and she twisted a handful of my hair. I sucked her clit until she released me, then I took one last look at her pussy before emerging from the water. Now she was open, blooming like a flower, her petals all flamboyantly displayed. When I took my first breath in the sunlight, for a moment, I was afraid I would pass out as the air sparkled with reflections.

Heaving myself up, I took a moment to sit next to her in the warm, soothing pool until oxygen returned to my blood.

"I think that was more than three minutes," she panted, smiling sleepily.

"Really?" I asked. "Then I broke my record."

"You could have hurt yourself," she scolded me playfully. "You could have died! What would I do without you!"

"It was totally worth it," I smiled, squinting against the light. With water on my eyelashes and the midday sun overhead, it was almost impossible to see. Turquoise spots swam in front of my eyes, obscuring everything but this beautiful vision.

***

Heather's POV
"Just think about it," Tony urged me but I just looked at him without saying a word. "You're attracted to him, right?"

I shrugged.

"My brother may seem like a puzzle, but he is simple to understand. Let's just try it once."

It was late in the evening. Tony and I were in our bedroom, and while I was riding his dick, he was discussing having a threesome with his brother. I didn't see anything wrong with someone joining in on our bedroom fantasies, but I wanted him to plead earnestly. I had a chance to meet with Nate for lunch, and he was a very likable person.

My mouth went dry as Tony penetrated me again, and my head fell back in ecstasy. He was supposed to fuck me hard, but because I was being unresponsive to his suggestion, even though he knew what my answer would be, he wouldn't let me orgasm.

"I agree! Just let me cum!" I screamed in frustration, he had let me reach my peak and stopped when I was on the brink of my orgasm, and it had been going on for too long.

"No, he just came in," Tony groaned softly in my ear. "He wants you, baby, and watching us like this will turn him on."

Holy shit.

I've never considered myself an exhibitionist because although Tony and I fucked a lot more than the average couple, we always did it in the privacy of our bedroom or anywhere else private. I knew that Nate was watching us, but I was enjoying it. I liked seeing how his eyes were glued to my body. I liked how he moved his hand up and down his shaft in time to me bouncing up and down Tony's dick.

But right when I thought that he was going to do nothing but watch, he stepped forward from the shadows, and I gasped. God, this man was gorgeous, his shoulders were broad in the darkness, but I could still make out the heavy, hard muscles of his chest and the tight, toned six-pack of his abs. Now, his dick was fully visible too, and I gasped when I saw that he was dripping from the tip, so much that there was a long gooey string trailing to the floor.

Nate grinned and straightened so that he was positioned behind my ass. Then he notched his tip at my back door and began to press forward.

"What?" I managed to squeal again.

"Push out," Nate commanded in a low voice, his hands steady on my hips. "Like you're going to the bathroom, honey. It'll go in easier that way."

With an audible pop, my sphincter gave it up, and that huge dick slid deep into my ass hole. I squealed again, shocked at the double penetration of two men, one in my pussy and one in my ass. *This only happens in porn, right?*

My ass hurt since he penetrated me without prepping, but the pleasure of two huge black males inside me, their dicks dueling for room as one moved in while the other moved out overwhelmed me. Tony and Nate had a syncopated rhythm going so that I always got a dick in me at all times, and I began to shiver and tremble, my breasts swaying as pleasure crashed over me in waves.

"That's it," Tony murmured while staring up at me with adoration on his face. "Let go, sweetheart. Let yourself enjoy the feeling."

"Fuck, you feel good, Heather," Nate groaned behind me. "Better than I had imagined."

With that, my vision blacked out as ecstasy seized my frame. A loud wail escaped my throat as my body clamped and shuddered, spamming violently on the dual rods buried deep in my sensitive spots. My two holes squeezed violently, and shudders of pure pleasure ripped all the way to my fingers and toes.

15. Heather's POV

I smiled as I came down from the bed, my legs were shaking, but I managed to steady myself. Immediately, Tony and Nate got on their feet, waiting. Their dicks were still hard. Gently, I took them each in one hand, gripping lightly at the base, then stroking them both at the same time. I let my palms slip across the velvety shafts of their dicks. Tony moaned immediately, curling his toes against the carpet. Nate took a sharp breath and glanced at his brother before allowing the sensation to overtake him.

"You feel so good," I whispered to both of them. "This feels amazing."

Slowly I began to stroke them, rolling my wrists as I maneuvered my hands from the bases to the tips. In moments, they were stiff and veiny, their hips bucking against the piston action of my hands.

"Heather," Nate sighed breathlessly as he began to really give in.

He dug his fingers through the back of my hair, pulling my mouth toward his. I could taste the lust on his tongue, the surge of pheromones as he neared release.

Tony drew closer to me, too, his fingers trailing over my belly. He angled his dick against me as I jerked him off and slid his hand down until it reached the top of my pussy. I was swollen, pulsing with desire, and when his fingers slid against my lips, I couldn't help but moan into Nate's open mouth.

More hands cupped my breasts as Nate kissed me senselessly. My body shuddered with the strain of keeping sane while every cell began its relentless climb toward release. I wanted nothing more than to come with them, for us all to come together, unified by our shameless, urgent needs.

I could feel their dicks changing in my hands, and they became harder, thicker.

They switched places, Tony, before me and Nate behind me. Hands gripped my hips so hard that I was sure I'd have marks later as Nate pushed himself almost violently into my behind.

"Fuck!" he shouted as hot male cream jetted into my asshole. "Oh shit!"

Meanwhile, Tony was no better. My husband's expression was intense as his hips pounded up and down into my pussy.

"Fuck," he raged. "FUCK!" virile lashes of semen sprayed all over my fertile fields, and the three of us screamed in unadulterated pleasure as the sensation shocked us to the core. I almost wept with heady delight as the men finished inside me, hot seed dripping down my thighs from both holes.

Finally, we collapsed in a heaving mess, and our skin sheened in sweat as we panted from exertion.

"Oh, you're heavy," I giggled breathlessly.

"Oh, sorry," Nate groaned before pulling out. A huge mess of cum rushed out of my ass when he exited. If anything, Nate leaned forward and tongued my asshole a bit, enjoying the taste.

"Tangy," he remarked. "But really delicious."

Then, Tony pulled out as well, his eyes alight. "Really?" he asked. "Shit, I need a taste too."

The men pushed me back on the bed before spreading my legs and going to town, helping themselves to the sloppy cream pies. Meanwhile, I leaned my head back as my eyes fluttered shut, my nipples going hard again as I laid back, overworked. After all, this was the filthiest fantasy that I've ever had, but now it's not a fantasy anymore. It was a reality. I had two males feasting on my body, and I was going to enjoy every second for as long as it lasted.

When I finally came to my senses again, I realized that I was holding someone's hand. Someone had my hand wrapped in his bigger, stronger hand. Legs were thrown over my hips, and feet covered my feet. We lie in a pile in the middle of the bed, satisfied and drowsy.

The next morning, I woke up with a jolt. I was disoriented and, at first, didn't even know where I was. But then I realized I was in the bedroom I shared with my husband. Was last night a dream? Did I just imagine everything?

The sore feeling in my ass and pussy was real, and when I looked down, there was a huge amount of dry cum caking the insides of my thighs. That was no dream. I was with Tony and Nate.

I stretched my arms over my head, knotting my fingers together as I purred audaciously. There was a soft knock at the door. Grabbing a robe off the hook in the small closet, I wrapped the white, fluffy cloth around me and opened the door just a crack.

Tony smiled from behind a rolling cart with silver service on top of it. "Room service, ma'am?"

My eyes went wide.

"What? Is this… Oh my God, is that coffee?"

"You're going to have to let me in and find out," he smirked.

"Pease, come in! Come in!" I was vividly aware that I was completely naked beneath this robe. Tony seemed to be aware of it too. I could see the hungry look in his eye as he rolled the cart past me toward the small table by the window. My bare feet made no sound on the carpet as I walked across the room, excited to see what he had brought. He poured out a dark, fragrant stream of coffee into a porcelain mug and dropped two sugar cubes into it, plus a healthy dollop of cream.

I tucked myself into the chair on the side of the table, then I held the warm cup between my palms and blew across the top of the liquid as he stood to the side and, with a flourish, removed the silver lid from a small dish. Gleaming pastries sat in a pile, with chocolate chips and raisins poking out at different angles. My mouth instantly began to water. He picked up a pair of silver tongs and clapped them together three times.

"Okay, let me guess," I said, and he smirked. "I am going to say... Yes. Chocolate croissant."

"Wow!" He nodded avidly. "Exactly!"

He winked at me as he plucked it from the pile with the tongs and put it on a small dish.

***

Tony's POV

"Turn over." The look of surprise on her face triggered my animal instincts, and she frowned because she had to leave the food. I loved to listen to her gasp, love the startled, primal look on her face that turned quickly from alarm to desire. She did as I asked, lay on the carpet, slowly shifting her weight so that she rolled onto her belly. I took off the bathrobe and pushed her panties over her chocolate thighs, exposing the curves of her ass. Nate stepped forward and joined me in pulling her panties down, then carrying her to the bed—the food forgotten.

"You're going to love this," I assured her as I generously moistened my fingers in my mouth.

Kneeling in front of her, I took one thick thigh in each hand and pulled her to the end of the bed. Her gasp aroused me further as I gently separated her ass cheeks to expose her tight, ass hole. The puckered flesh was a pretty pink beige, and it contracted slightly when I first swiped at it with my tongue.

"Yeah," Nate sighed as he sat on the edge of the bed, his eyes intense. With one hand, he fisted his dick as he watched me start to eat Heather's beautiful little asshole.

I could feel the tension in her thighs quickly releasing as pleasure began to overtake her. Soon, I speared that tiny hole with just the tip of my tongue, and she began to bounce back against me, urging me deeper. Her moans rose to fill the room, and I placed a single finger against her throbbing, wet pussy. I wanted to eat her ass until she came, but I knew that I couldn't. It was so tight that it seemed to suck me in every time she pulsed back toward me. I wanted my dick in there, the need overwhelmed me, and I rose up, pausing just to slide the head of my dick against her wet, gleaming hole.

Wordlessly, Nate nodded his authorization, not that I would have let him go first, but it was nice that he acknowledged it. Heather twisted her head back to look at me over her shoulder. With her ass in the air, so open and ready for me, I feared I was going to come before I got inside her. Yet I knew the exquisite sensation that awaited me. I nudged against her opening, shifting my weight to bear forward slightly. It was the perfect height and angle, with just a ring of tight tissues separating me from the sweet spot that awaited me.

Surging forward, I continued to charge the entrance. I didn't want to go too fast, but I couldn't wait any longer. Finally, the tension allowed me to slide past it, then immediately constricted again and held me tight just behind the head of my dick. I bounced against this, thrusting gently but firmly until her ass began to suck me in deeper, quickly taking my full length.

Suddenly Nate shifted, lying flat on the bed and sliding beneath her. I felt the pressure of his dick against mine as he entered her pussy. Heather moaned desperately, submitting to the insane sensory excess of two brothers, plowing both of her holes at once.

My mind went blank with bliss as I filled her tight hole, synchronizing with Nate to fill her almost to splitting before we pulled back, then plunged inside again. Both of us, together, with just this beauty between us. We could go on forever, but the pleasure that built between us was too much.

Finally I couldn't wait anymore and unleashed my load deep into her body. Nate hilted himself inside her and roared as we came simultaneously.

When I withdrew, my cum leaked out a bit, mingling with Nate's on the white sheets. I grabbed a towel from the adjoining bath and dampened it, taking my time to clean her, soothing her leisurely stretched flesh.

"That was... amazing..." she sighed vaguely, her voice far away.

Nate stroked her hair, tucking it behind her ears. He glanced at me, smiling and at ease, and I found myself smiling back.

***

Heather's POV

I dumped nearly an entire box of Epsom salt into the bath before slipping off my robe and settling into the warm water. A sigh escaped my lips as I leaned back against the porcelain tub back. This was exactly what I needed because, after the way Tony and Nate invaded me, I was sore all over. We went at it for so long, and now both my pussy and asshole were begging for some much-needed rest and relaxation. Thus, the warm bath. Gingerly I shifted my weight, tender and feeling a bit lose in my joints. I could never have imagined what two men inside me at once would feel like. I would have said it was impossible. And yet, there we were. The moment Tony told me to roll over onto my belly, my heart was gripped with fear. And yet, something told me to try it.

But as his tongue did things to me I'd never even imagined, I felt my body come alive. I needed more, and more, and then Nate was ready. He was ready to give me the rest of what I needed.

Somehow, I made room. Somehow, my hips and pussy found a way to accommodate both of their thick, beautiful ebony dicks. It was beyond incredible, the kind of stimulation you could only get this way. But even sweeter was when Tony went to get a washcloth to clean me. With his smile, he lovingly parted my folds, wiping away every trace of fluid and leaving me feeling fresh and relaxed.

There I was on a private island, being fucked into oblivion by two amazing men, my husband, and his brother.

We'll call it a fairytale.

* * * * * *
***

16 Escorted Pleasures

I instantly regretted the idea as soon as we arrived. When we arrived at the resort, I lost all interest instantly. My eyes widened and would have popped out. Everyone was wearing little to nothing. Men had tight boxers that flaunted their bulging dicks while the women were wearing lingerie or bikinis that covered little to nothing. I gave my husband a questioning look, but he just grinned at me and pulled me along. The female escort noticed my discomfort and gave me an encouraging smile.

"In De Luna's resort, we often encourage nudity. Everyone here is free to express themselves and flaunt their assets," she winked at me.

At some point, we stopped walking, she reached her hand to her back and unzipped the gown she was putting on, and when it dropped, she revealed the lacy lingerie she wore underneath.

My husband turned to look at me, and he winked. I rolled my eyes in his direction. I tried not to check out the body of the escort. Her chocolate skin was tempting if you asked me, and her supple breast and wide hips were enticing with every step she took. She kept on walking till we reached the room assigned to my husband and I. She must have noticed that I was checking her out, but she didn't seem to care.

When we entered the room, I sank into a chair, glad to be away from where the nudity was in full display, but to my shock, the escort surged closer to me. In one smooth movement, she twisted to lift a leg and slide onto my lap, facing me, draping her arms over my shoulders. Automatically, my hands found her narrow waist and caged it between my fingers, holding her as she pulsed gently against me.

It was almost like I could read her thoughts. She was curious, courageous, and yet, I seemed to have underestimated her. Her lips hovered just millimeters away from mine, open to allow her sweet, gentle breath to float over my mouth. She tasted good, and we paused for a few tortured seconds, just barely apart, just tasting the space between us, letting longing fill us like a gate suddenly opened. She arched her back to kiss me, moaning gently as our lips began to quickly explore each other with mounting intensity. Her thighs clenched over my hips.

I found myself in an immediate, primal frenzy, touching every part of her. Her breasts contracted under my palms, nipples turning to hard pebbles. Her flanks are thick and yet yielding under my fingers. Her slit was blazing hot behind just a few wisps of fabric.

When I opened my eyes, hers were half-open too. Our gazes locked onto each other as though the connection had been there this whole time, like an ethernet connection, simply waiting to be plugged in. It felt so natural and correct. I couldn't believe what had just happened.

But then, a chime. It took me a moment to remember where it was. I held her hips and removed her from my lap. Her eyes search mine, frantic and suddenly self-conscious.

"What is it? Did I do something wrong?"

I shook my head at her and turned to look at my husband, Marcus. What I was expecting was a look of disgust, but it was not there. He had a smirk on his face, as if he was amused by what he had witnessed.

"What's your name?" I asked the escort. Gone was the confident and bold lady who could seduce anyone with just the way she walked. It had been replaced with a petite lady with tears pooled in her eyes, and it seemed like she was going to burst into tears anytime soon. If she did, I wouldn't know how to handle the situation, and Marcus was sprawled up on the bed like he wasn't there. It seemed like he was watching a show.

"Tasha. My name is Tasha." She replied hurriedly.

"Calm down, Tasha. You are an escort, right?"

She nodded in affirmation. There were two meanings to the word escort. An escort could also mean people whose service was to have sex with people, and they got paid in return. The good thing was that an escort could decline an offer if it wasn't best suited for them, and they were not forced to do whatever they didn't like. From the looks of things, Marcus must have hired her services. That's why he was hardly fazed about her presence.

"Why don't you go for now? You can return later in the evening," I tried to convince her.

She blinked and turned to Marcus. It was until he nodded that she took her leave.

"I guess you deserve an explanation about all of this," Marcus started, and I nodded at him. I wasn't upset that he had tried something like this. It wasn't the first time we were letting someone in on one of our sexual fantasies. I felt like I should have been informed in advance.

"I'm so sorry, babe. I planned all of this specially for you. That's why I didn't tell you about it."

***

Marcus' POV

I left the bed, which was warm and comfy, and approached Bella, she looked upset, and I felt hurt. Ever since she got pregnant, we had not had time for ourselves, so I planned a little vacation.

We spent the weekend at a resort and had even ordered the services of an escort to make the whole weekend spicier.

She cupped her belly where our child was, safe and sound. She was in her first trimester, and her hormones had shot up to the peak. "It's fine. You should have told me about it. The girl was shocked by my reaction. I felt really bad."

I hugged her small form and inhaled the scent of her shampoo from her hair. I was hungry for her, so hungry I practically wanted to drain her of this delicious taste. I wanted her body wrapped around me. I want her arms clutching my shoulders. I picked her up, hooked her legs around me, and carried her to the bed. I dropped her onto the bed and watched as she bounced. Her face was flustered, and she was panting a little bit. It was exactly what I wanted.

My utter excitement caused me to lean down, press a hand against her chin and press my lips against hers. She let out a moan before pressing her body against mine. I didn't waste time because I didn't have the patience. I hooked her legs around me, our lips never ceasing their connection. Bella's body pushed against me, desperate to find friction, and I didn't blame her. I wanted to be doing the exact same thing, honestly. I began to undo my belt and let my pants fall down my legs and pool at my ankles. Bella watched with intrigue, "I like it rough and fast, but for our child, I'll try to be gentle."

"That's okay."

Bella peeled the shirt off her body in no time. I undid her bra and marveled at her breasts. They were huge before, but now that her body was undergoing changes, they were becoming quite massive, with the nipples crying for attention. So, I gave in, wrapped my lips around them, and started sucking on a nipple while my finger was working the other. A gasp left Bella, and she arched her back, her eyes wild. I moved to the other nipple to give it the same treatment. She let out a moan as I sucked her breasts.

When I was satisfied, I helped her take off her jeans before I pulled down her panties. My finger ran along the length of her pussy, and she inhaled sharply. She was wet and ready for me, exactly what I wanted. Her lips turned upwards, but they were soon letting out the softest mewls while I ran my tongue along her slit. I began to feast on her, swirling my tongue and sucking on her clit. She was writhing like crazy in an attempt to get away from me while simultaneously thrusting her hips against my mouth and begging me for more. One of her hands found my hair, and she yanked it on hard, but I didn't care.

She could do whatever she wanted. She arched that back of hers and let out a loud moan, she tightened against my tongue, and I began to thrust my tongue in and out of her stronger, watching her lips part as she began to rub her thighs together. I separated them firmly and allowed myself a deeper angle inside of her. That was her last straw. She exploded around me and cried out as she did, doing a small chant of my name.

My hand came back up to fondle her breast while my lips

connected back with hers, and I pushed myself inside of her, all in one go. I increased my pace and thrust inside of her the way that I wanted to. She felt heavenly, tightly wrapped around my dick. I pushed into her over and over again, and she began to moan loudly against me. That was my cue to ravage her absolutely. I thrust continuously, and my lips were back around one breast while I tweaked the other one with my fingers.

It didn't take long for her to cum again, and a few pumps later, I followed after her. I carried her to the bathroom and we cleaned up together. Room service came, and it was a very pretty lady wearing a short skirt, crop tops, and boots. I could see Bella engaging her in a short conversation before she left.

"What were you guys talking about?"

"Nothing much"

Bella POV

Someone showed up and sat beside me. "A penny for your thoughts"

I laughed lightly and saw that it was Tasha, she had shown me two different sides of herself today, and this one was a completely different one. She looked calm and serene, tranquil like a lake.

"Then you have to give me the penny before you can have a chance to know my thoughts."

She looked around, probably for a penny, then gave me a mournful smile. "I don't have a penny here."

"Then maybe you can know my thoughts some other time?" I

raised one of my eyebrows at her expectantly.

"But- fine." She wanted to protest but couldn't get any word out.

"I'll let you in on my thoughts, but first, why don't we get to know each other since we'll be working together later," I winked at her.

She looked away. I could see her expression shy. She was really cute. "I'm Natasha, but everyone calls me Tasha. I'm twenty-two, I work as an escort, but I don't do it often. However, your husband convinced me he was doing it for you to make your weekend memorable."

I could see that she was being sincere with me. I couldn't help but to like her. She was a little bit taller than I was and chubby. Her brown skin gleamed and shone under the rays of the sun. She was the true definition of an ebony queen, and she had various personalties that were likely to entrance anyone that came in contact with her. She could easily get a great role if she chose to join the movie industry, and I would be happy to recommend her to a few agents and directors if she was interested.

"I'm expecting." I ran my hands over my flat belly. My pregnancy wasn't visible yet, so she just glanced at me as I rubbed my hands over my stomach.

She looked genuinely happy. "Congratulations! Can I hug you?" I shrugged and made a move to hug her first.

"I see that you've decided to shed some clothes. You look sexier this way." It was my turn to be shy. I was considering wearing a casual outfit, but I didn't want to look odd in a place with so many people who flashed their bodies with pride. In the end, I wore a swimsuit that fully displayed my body but hid my important bits.

I had received some cat whistles from some of the men who saw me, but I decided to be oblivious to them. I was happily married, and I wouldn't indulge myself with someone else unless my husband was well informed. Some of them had even tried to strike up conversations with me to gain my contact number or something they could use to trace me in the future, but I subtly avoided their questions and went to a less crowded area to think.

"Thank you so much." I smiled at her, the pregnancy had come as a huge surprise, but Marcus and I immediately chose to keep it. We didn't even consider our jobs. The most important thing was that I was carrying my child—our baby. "I guess that is why he wanted to make this weekend memorable. My name is Christabel, but most people know me as Bella. I'm an actress, and my husband is a movie producer."

"Are you all famous? I'm not a fan of movies, otherwise, I'm sure I would have known you."

"We have a little bit of fame here and there, but who cares."

She studied me for a moment. "I'm guessing from that, you guys must be so famous then. It's nice to meet you. Can you probably sign me an autograph?"

"You're joking," I laughed, but when I noticed that she wasn't, I stopped, which meant that she was being very serious. "Fine. I can do that much. It's not a big deal."

"So how come there are no paparazzi trailing you? Are they watching you in secret? Are we on a live reality show?" She looked around expectantly, and I was quite amused.

"No, no, and no. Marcus and I came here alone. No one knows

where we are currently, so there is no one watching us." We kept on talking, and soon it was sunset, hand in hand, we returned to my room.

***

Marcus' POV

As soon as the ladies returned, we all stripped. I found myself staring and comparing both their features. Tasha obviously noticed, for she took a great handful and framed her face with it, pouting in the most extraordinarily sexy fashion.

"So, you like my hair, do you, darling?" she breathed, probably noticing how I stared at her lightly shaven pussy. "You will have plenty of opportunity to sink into it, I can assure you."

But it was my dick which she was attending to now, grasping it in her dainty little hand, turning it this way and that, giving it the minutest inspection. She knelt down to get a closer look, and I could feel her hot breath on the still-moist head of my dick. To my surprise, she took just the tip of my dick into her mouth, and I could feel her tongue open the hole at the end of my dick. Her tongue then swirled over the head, making me gasp and almost choke on the breath that was still coursing down my throat.

"What a beautiful dick!" Tasha said. "I will certainly enjoy mounting this one if I may." With that, she rose to her feet and, kneeling on the bed, she straddled my waist. I looked directly into her eyes as she pushed open her outer lips and rubbed her clit to generate some moisture.

A tiny spurt of juice flowed from her, and then she was guiding my dick toward her hot wet pussy. I squirmed to try and get a closer look at what she was doing, for even after all the experiences I had been subjected to by my wife. I still found the idea of being mounted by this incredible beauty exciting.

Bella obviously recognized my excitement, as she withdrew her nipples from my mouth so that I had an uninterrupted view of what Tasha was doing. Her nipple hung over my chest, her areolas dark and wanting, but I was too fascinated with watching Tasha to notice.

The gorgeous escort was slowly lowering herself onto my dick, inching her way down bit by bit. Her hair cascaded down over her shoulder as she watched with interest the rampant dick drilled into her. Her lovely face was a picture of concentration; she was biting her lower lip with the strain of holding herself up, and I could clearly see the well-toned muscles in her legs and torso, which stood out like ropes as she controlled the passage down.

From my point of view, I was amazed at how incredibly tight she felt, just like Bella. Her outer lips strained to accommodate my dick, and as she sank down, so they seemed to be pulled into her by the pressure around her pussy. However, she was thoroughly enjoying the experience as she let out little gasps, which even I could tell were gasps of delight. Eventually, she was there. I saw the last millimeter of my dick disappear inside her, and then she was wriggling down on me, determined to insert me more thoroughly into her. She smiled down at me when she looked up from her work.

"That is quite sexy," Bella breathed. "Now you just lie there and feel Tasha's little pussy muscles start their work on you." All the time she was speaking, I could feel her pussy muscles working on the length of my shaft. But nothing could have prepared me for the sensations produced by the vice-like grip of her pussy. The rippling feeling as I was being roe was more than I could stand, and I cried as the nerve endings in my dick were stroked and caressed by her movements.

Bella, by now, had become agitated by the lack of attention being paid to her tits, and she used my discomfort to try and get me back to the breast. She turned my head towards her torso and fed the big hardened nipple to my mouth. Obediently I swallowed the puckered flesh and savored the sweetness. But still, I could not believe the sensation that was coursing through my body.

Tasha was having a marvelous time stroking up and down, ensuring that she was fully impaled on my dick, but also enjoying the fact that I could do nothing to escape her skillful hands. My dick was receiving the most unbelievable treatment. I knew I was rising toward a climax more quickly than normal.

My suckling on Bella's nipple was starting to become irregular and try as she might to get me to concentrate on her rather than Tasha, it was clear she was fighting a losing battle. She realized that I was getting close to the limit, and she was determined that Tasha should climax before me. She breathed in my ear and whispered.

"No cumming until I say so. Just because you are excited at the thought of shooting your seed into that gorgeous lady, we will not have you lose your self-control. You have got to allow her to climax first!"

I jolted back to reality with a start. I fought the desire to shoot into Tasha's wringing pussy and, with all as much self-control as I could muster, tried to concentrate on Bella's tit. I chewed lightly on the nipple and heard her sharp intake of breath.

"Ow! That hurts! Don't you dare bite me – just suck!" she commanded between moans. But her words were drowned by a great shout from lower down the bed, and I realized that Tasha was climaxing heavily. The sensations coming from her pussy were quite beyond anything I could describe, but I knew that I had lost my self-control.

I grunted as the thick cum roared out of my dick and found its way into Tasha's pussy. My eyes were tightly shut as I concentrated on shooting my cum into this lovely girl who was still keening and moaning on top of me. A tiny bit of me knew that I would incur the wrath of Bella for not cumming on her order, but at this time, I could care less. The only thing that mattered was to unload myself into Tasha, and this I aimed to achieve.

Someone had their hands on my balls and was massaging the last drops of cum from me as I collapsed into Bella's lap, spent from my exertions. Having watched the competition between Tasha and myself, Bella was still determined to reduce the pressure in her breasts and once again fed her nipple into my mouth, ordering me to suck. As I panted, I could feel great jolts of pleasure erupt from within her, fueling my hunger still as Tasha still remained impaled on my slackening dick.

***

Bella's POV

Marcus merely growled and pushed my knees apart. "Now I'm going in for the real deal." Then he buried his face in my drenched folds, and I let out a scream as shudders wracked my frame. He was thorough and utterly sensuous, licking wetly at my pussy before pushing in deep. Then he nibbled lightly on my clit before dropping down to leave his tongue over my ass hole.

"Wha--?" I gasped, jerking my head up to stare at him. "OMG, what are you doing? That's off-limits!"

But Tasha merely pushed me down gently, capturing my lips with her own. "Nothing's off limits when it comes to your body. All of this belongs to him, and it's going to be fine. Just let him do what he needs to."

By now, my frame was wracked with pleasure, and I plucked at my nipples as Tasha pushed her breasts into my face and her nipples at my mouth. I blinked a bit in confusion as my asshole and pussy were licked by my husband. I latched onto her nipples and started sucking them like I was thirsty, earning another deep suckle on my clit.

"Good girl," Marcus rasped from below. "You're doing great, baby. Suck that shit." Then with a chuckle, Tasha reached into the bedside drawer for a bottle of lube. Sure enough, an industrial-sized tube appeared, but she also pulled out a black dildo that made my eyes go wide. The toy was at least ten inches long, glistening, slick, and shiny in the light. I let out a muffled "mph!" in protest and arched my back, but my mouth was embedded in Tasha's breast, and I was literally pinned in place.

She grinned and smoothed her hand over the turgid rubber. "Don't worry. I'll give it to you slowly. It's not going to hurt one bit, I promise."

What the hell? Marcus looked me in the eye. "I need to give you a reason to keep your mouth closed before we put this in, baby. I know you can."

I shook my head furiously in protest, but Marcus was already kneeling on my other side, the tip of his dick probing at the corner of my mouth. I lifted my face from Tasha's breast, and he slipped his dick into my mouth immediately. Tasha leaned forward to ghost a hand over one nipple before reaching down to pinch my clit.

I squealed as pleasure rocketed through my sweetest spot. Marcus laughed and then met her eyes over my prone form.

"Keep going," he rasped harshly. "She's really wet and can take it."

He grinned and continued to slide his massive dick into my throat. The sides of my mouth ached, and I was sure my cheeks bulged like a chipmunk, but I also felt oddly proud that I'd accomplished this.

"Mmmm," I moaned headily as Tasha stroked my clit in praise. "Mmmm."

She caressed the huge dildo again and got it lubed up before circling the toy around my clit.

"Does that feel good," she smiled innocently. "You like that?"

I bucked my hips, flashing my pussy hole as a signal that I wanted it. Sure enough, she slid the black toy in a few inches, getting it soaked.

"Fuck," she hissed. "Your pussy takes dick really good."

But then she pulled the toy out and dragged the head down to tease my ass. What the hell? No, I'm not ready! In surprise, my back arched as my eyes bulged again.

"Mmmm!" I squealed. "Mmmm!"

But Marcus and Tasha were relentless. Tasha pulled the toy out and gently poured lube on it before grinning and pointing the tapered tip at my asshole.

"You can do it," she said in a soothing voice while beginning the pressure at my bottom.

"Legs apart, honey. Push out like you're going to the bathroom, and it'll go in easier."

OMG, I couldn't believe it was happening. I was currently sucking on a dick with my creamy curves on display and being teased by a girl. Not only that, but my bottom was exposed and in the process of being penetrated by a big black toy. With a low moan, I raised my knees so that the dildo could get in easier.

Tasha nodded with approval. "That's it," she said, her eyes fixed on where the toy entered my body. "You're doing great," she praised. "I love seeing that ass being ravaged. That does it."

The dirty words made me horny as hell at this point. Then, the huge dildo slid all the way in, impaling my round cheeks. The penetration was so thorough that I paused for a moment, unable to breathe.

OMG, OMG. Was this really happening? Was my ass crammed full of a massive rubber toy? But it was, and soon Tasha began to slide the rubber in and out of my ass as I sucked hungrily on Marcus's dick while he played with my nipples, obscene slapping sounds filling the air.

"Mmmm!" I groaned on a particularly forceful upswing. "Mph! Mph!"

"Yeah, baby, you're taking it good," Marcus rasped, his eyes glued to where the toy entered my ass. "That's it. Keep going."

"She looks amazing getting fucked in the ass," added Tasha, also watching the show. "Who knew she could stretch like this?"

I closed my eyes and lifted my knees even higher as my ass was violated, and when Tasha tweaked my clit, that did it. I soared over the cliff, screaming as the world dissolved around me in a shower of sparks.

"Mmmm!" I screamed as my ass was repeatedly violated. "Mmmm!

Marcus gave it up as well, and I felt his dick jerk as it began pulsing heavily in my body.

"Fuck!" he hissed, ejaculating down my throat while Tasha was still twisting my clit with her fingers. "Oh shit!"

She shoved the dildo deep one last time and then latched on my pussy, sucking and drinking up my liquid. We cried and moaned, our voices twining around each other. I'd never come so hard before, as she made me cry out with joy. But finally, the shudders and exclamations slowed, and Marcus pulled out from my throat, his massive lengths gleaming. I coughed a bit, and he quickly stepped out to pour me a glass of water.

"Here, sweetheart," he said in a low voice. "Are you okay?"

Meanwhile, Tasha returned with a warm, damp rag and gently removed the dildo from my ass before tenderly stroking my ravaged parts.

"You were incredible," she murmured before lowering his head to kiss me tenderly.

"Absolutely wonderful."

It was then that I let out a small giggle because this was a dream come true. I'd been naughty with a man and a woman, and in fact, the taste of Marcus' semen was still in my mouth. But I loved every moment of filth that I shared with them, and now, I just want more.

***

Marcus' POV

I took Tasha's hand and applied the lube to it. I didn't have to guide it this time as she knew what to do. She took her hand and slid it along Bella's clit, into her pussy. Bella moaned louder as the hand disappeared inside, finally stretching her a little bit. Tasha started to suck on her breast while she worked her fingers in unison, pumping in and out of the little woman's pussy.

It definitely wasn't stretching her enough to be painful, as Bella started to cry out in orgasm. I positioned myself behind Tasha and slipped inside her soaking wet pussy. I kept in rhythm with her pumping her fingers in and out of Bella and softly thrusting into her as I watched as she sucked Bella's nipple with relish. She began thrusting into Bella once again with her fingers. I removed my dick from her to let her concentrate on giving Bella another orgasm.

I moved over and started sucking on my wife's available breast while Tasha continued to work on the other one. I wasn't sucking for more than a few seconds before She grabbed the back of my head as her entire body went tight. I lightly bit down on her nipple, making her cum even harder. I watched her juices squirt out of her as the fingers went in and I heard the wet noises coming from her pussy as they pulled back. Bella froze once again, screaming from yet another orgasm.

The next morning, I opened my eyes to the already bright bedroom, and I looked down to see my wife with my quickly stiffening member in her mouth. I looked over to my left to see Tasha still asleep, and I started to run my hand over her curvy ass, slowly waking her up so she could also watch Bella sucking on me. She moved up, resting her pussy on my dick, it disappeared inside of her well-stretched pussy with a little effort, and the heat and wetness still felt very nice.

Then, she hung a breast over my mouth, and I invaded her nipple once again. Tasha moved downright next to me and started to suck on Bella's other nipple. She moaned loudly as she held onto the headboard, grinding on me while getting both of her breasts sucked at the same time. She twisted her hips to try to get my dick to fuck her in the best way. The tip of my dick was hitting the end of her pussy, which felt pretty good to me.

I took a long suckle from Bella's nipples before my head fell back in satisfaction, and soon her pussy walls tightened as she was cumming. Tasha, feeling left out, left Bella's breast, and she drew nearer to my head and made sure her pussy was a few inches away from my face so it gave me easy access to strum her clit and slip a finger inside. She was so tight. Her walls choked my finger to the point that I wondered if I would hit her sweet spot if I pushed a little further in.

Bingo!

She came all over my hand, then my mouth dropped back on her pussy and licked up every bit of her cream. She cried out, threw her head backward, and thrust her hips forward. She could not stop the orgasm that ripped through her, and her juices coated my face as she came. She muffled her cries with her hand to avoid screaming the room down.

I couldn't see her face because I was gulping every last drop of her sweetness. She came so hard that I had to pull my finger out but kept my mouth there until she was spent, taking everything I could from her.

***

Bella's POV

After Tasha left, we had time to ourselves, and Marcus and I debated taking a shower together. I closed my eyes as the spray hit my face. It felt so warm and relaxing. Even better was the feel of Marcus' hands sliding around my waist. I sighed and leaned back on his chest. "This is so nice."

"Yes, it is," He whispered, kissing my neck from behind.

"Let me help you." He rubbed my skin so delicately as he evenly distributed the lather over my body. This was so perfect and addicting. Every inch of my body was caressed, worshiped. He swats my ass, and I wiggled it a little.

"I think you need to learn that I'm in charge." The tip of his dick brushed past my ass, moving slowly down to my center.

He thrust in, claiming me from behind. He leaned over with his chest pressed against my back, sending him deeper inside my pussy. He gripped my chin harshly.

"You're so fucking sexy. I love the way your body fits mine. Kiss me, and I'll make you come."

I tilted my head a little more and kissed him. He pulled back with his hands skimming over my breasts, down my sides to my hips. One hand slipped under and pressed against my clit. I moaned and pushed backward, sending him fully inside me. There was a mix of pleasure and pain which I enjoyed, so I did it again.

17. Crossing The Lines

Three's A Crowd.

He's hot, that's what my body tells me.

That was Jeff, my best friend, and with him was Carter, another hot guy. I had a crush on them both, but Jeff's was much more serious. I wanted him badly, and I knew he wanted me too, but I'd probably never have him at this rate. We'd been flirting regularly for a while, and things, I was sure, had come to a head.

I made my decision late last night. I'd seduce him and fuck him. It really was that simple. I couldn't always wait for him to take the lead, or he never would. He feared ruining our friendship, but I wanted him too. You couldn't ruin something consensual.

My decision hadn't been hasty. It had taken months of consideration and years of crushing on him. Now we were away from the trappings of our small town, we were at college, and this was my chance, and I wasn't letting it pass me by. I got off my desk and made my way to him, skirting the other students who were sitting around.

"Look who made it over," Jeff said when he saw me. He'd obviously noticed me lurking around.

I bent over them and gave Carter a kiss on the cheek, all the while keeping my brown eyes on Jeff. He was staring at me just as intently.

"Carter, how have you been?" I said grandly, finally looking at him.

"Stop playing," he said, laughing.

"But why? I've missed you, my boy," I said, continuing in character.

"Jada, you should stop, settle down, we need to talk" Jeff sounded serious, his face as serious as I've ever seen it. I settled down immediately, almost worried myself.

"What's wrong?" I asked him.

"Not much. Carter and I will be going to my uncle Tim's cabin in the woods for the weekend. Would you like to come along?"

"That's sudden," I said, leaning against my seat.

"I know, but Uncle Tim's leaving for Colorado to visit grandma this weekend. He wants us there to keep an eye on the place," he replied, peering at me.

"I've got tests next week. When do we get back here?" I asked. I should've known my plans couldn't be straightforward. This trip hadn't been planned for.

"Late on Sunday or early Monday morning, depending on when we leave the cabin," he told me.

"How secluded is this place?" I asked. I didn't want to be cut off from the rest of the world completely. It just wasn't my scene.

"Just us. There's no other cabin within miles, just animals and trees. You'll love it. It's quiet out," he said.

On second thoughts, maybe it would be perfect, just the three of us, no other human to watch my humiliation if Jeff said no. Plus,

Carter would be there too, and I had a very vested interest in him too. I turned to him.

"You're coming, aren't you?" I asked him.

"My two favorite people in the world in one place? I wouldn't miss it for the world," he said, winking at me.

Carter was handsome, popular, and rich, the perfect boy. He was a light-skinned black boy, the tight curls of his brown hair always styled to perfection. He had a white father, but his mom was black. They always said they'd seen the future—the modern couple.

Jeff, on the other hand, was darker skinned, his chocolate eyes piercing. I shivered slightly, thinking of those eyes. His black hair was cut short. He was the smartest of the bunch, and valedictorian at our high school—perfect son of a doctor father and a psychologist mother. His uncle Tim owned a cabin in the woods outside town. He lived there alone, trapping during hunting season and generally keeping to himself. He was rich beyond reason. He just didn't like human company, not a lot.

"Hey Jeff, I need to get to my next class, but can you come by my place later?" I asked, sidling closer.

"Why?" He asked.

"There's something I think you'd love to see," I said to him, leaning closer and brushing up against him. Jeff could be incredibly blind when he wanted to be. But I was going to open his eyes. First him and then Carter and then the two of them—together if I could.

"When?"

"Whenever you're done with class, give me a call," I replied, getting off the desk.

"I'm not invited?" Carter asked, a comically hurt look on his face.

"You will be," I said as I leaned over to peck him on the lips before making my way to class. He didn't know what was coming to him. But he would soon too. Very soon.

I swaggered away from them towards my next class. I was 23, but you'd have never known. I'd been called the vixen, the siren, and whatever else you can think of along that line. And I'd been best friends with those two for years. Well, three years is still years. And now I wanted them, both, but Jeff first, he had been my best friend first, and I wanted the first pleasure to be with him.

***

The apartment was ready, and I would be too. I just needed to get a little more stuff set up, like the red lighting and the aromatic candles. This room had to look like a house of sin. It would, after all, be just that before Jeff left here.

I walked down to my closet and stood there, undecided. I swung my head back and forth, considering both outfit choices. I could either be a cute bunny or a sexy cat. It was ridiculous, I knew, but I wanted it to be immediately obvious what was going on. Jeff could only say no once.

I picked up the red outfit and slipped into it. It left little to the imagination, the trim skirt barely skirting my ass cheeks. I'd noticed his eyes on my butt, and I assumed he loved them. I'd be playing them off with this tonight. But I'd also played the part of the cute best friend quite perfectly in the last year, and the bunny outfit was fit for that.

I looked hot in red, I thought, the deep color in obvious contrast to my brown skin, making it pop in ways Jeff was sure to notice. I was nervous about tonight, but it wasn't like me to not go after something I wanted, and I wanted Jeff. I set up the candles and lit them. Jeff had sent me a text to let me know he'd be arriving any moment now. Everything had to be ready before he got here. I needed to be set, my mind prepped and ready. The fragrance from the candles pierced the room almost immediately, the musky scent complimenting my outfit perfectly.

I heard the doorbell ring then, and I slipped my legs into my sexy little kitten heels before leaving the room to get to the door. The heels had been a gift from my mother. She just hadn't intended for them to be so taken advantage of. I pulled the door open and beckoned him in. He'd been turned away and on his phone.

"What's this about?" Jeff said, his eyes still on his phone, and he walked into the room, "and what's that smell?" He added, sniffing like a hound dog.

"It's the smell of sex, My Lord," I said, my voice a sleepy echo.

Jeff looked up and then froze. He looked surprised—no, shocked. His lips in the shape of a perfect O.

"What do you think you're doing, Jada? Are you expecting someone?" He asked, unconsciously running his eyes down my body. I gave a small smile and posed, spreading my legs a little. He looked away fast, his hands going to his head.

"I'm seducing you. Is it working?" I asked, moving closer.

"Yes, no! I meant no. Why would you want to seduce me? I'm your best friend!" he said, taking a step back from me. That was useless. We both knew by now he would be spending the night.

"Well, I want you, and from the look of things, you want me too. It's really that simple," I answered.

"What about Carter?" He asked.

"Well, I'm not looking to date you, just to fuck, besides Carter might get his chance since you're so worried about him," I informed him, a sly grin on my face.

"Oh, this is crazy, Jada. I'm just gonna go," he said, turning away from me and moving to the door.

"You don't have to leave, what? Are you jealous of Carter already? Besides, you can't leave here with that hard on. You gon have blue balls," I said. "I could deal with that, just that."

Jeff stopped at the door and slowly turned to face me, his face dotted with sweat, the look of indecision on his face the replica of what I must've had on mine earlier.

"Fine, just the blow job," he said finally.

That's what he thought. He wouldn't leave here till morning. The blow job was just the beginning of a long night.

"Who said it would be a blow job?" I asked as I made my way to him. I put my hands on the lapel of his jacket and pushed them off his shoulders. They landed on the floor, polling around our feet.

"What are you doing now, Jada? You don't need to get me naked," he said.

"But what's the fun in that?" I asked, turning to the bed and pulling him with me. I patted the bed when I got to it and made him sit his ass there. Assuming a position of subservience, on my knees in front of him, I proceeded to slowly unbutton his shirt, all the while keeping my eyes on his. He probably still thought he could wrest control from me, and I wanted him to keep that illusion.

"Not the shirt," he said, placing his hands over mine. I raised both hands in surrender and moved over to his zipper.

"This better?" I asked.

"Just get it over with," he said, his voice lusty.

"Is that any way to talk to your helper?" I asked, even as I pulled down his zipper, my hands already moving to stroke his dick. Oh, he's huge. Not a disappointment down there. No wonder the girls loved him so. He'd also been prom king in high school.

"You're very well hung, not that that's a surprise," I told him.

"Well, you never did tell me you'd been thinking about me so often, Jada," he said sarcastically, even as his eyes widened with my stroke down his hardening length.

"Aren't you just lucky I've been thinking of all this? You seemed to like that," I said, looking up at him with an innocent smile. I yanked his belt open and tried pulling his pants off.

"Is that necessary?" He asked, looking at me suspiciously.

"Will you let me do my job or not, Jeff?" I told him, yanking off the pants. I waited for him to lift his toned ass off the bed before pulling it off him completely. Next, I attacked his boxer briefs, pulling them off just as fast. I wanted to get at him. Now he was still willing.

With both bits of clothing out of the way, I attacked his dick, my hands eagerly stroking the hard length of him. His massive black dick curved at the tip. I'd heard about it but never seen it. Lucky me, I'd heard they gave the best orgasms.

"Look who's so willing and eager," I said, speaking to his dick. I bent my head and put my mouth to his head first, sucking that over and over again. My tongue ran over his top while my hands stroked the rest of him. Slowly, ever so slowly, I pushed the rest of him into my mouth and kept pushing until I felt him hit the back of my throat.

Jeff moaned aloud, his voice the croaky break of a man in deep pleasure. I repeated the action, this time letting myself choke on him, waiting just until I felt him hitting the back of my throat before I ran my teeth softly down his sensitive pole. Jeff groaned, his hands moving into my hair and resting there.

"You like that, Jeff honey?" I playfully asked his dick, even as I dribbled spit on him and resumed sucking. I wanted him to blow his nut so I could get him into the bed. Jeff could be stubborn, but he was my friend, and I knew his weaknesses. And butts were number one on that list. I'd be naked by the time he came around.

I bent over him, pulling down the strap of my outfit to give him a go at my boobs. Being a solid c cup, my boobs stood perky, and my nipples a chocolate color. I loved them, and I'd be the first to admit they looked good. I'd gotten them from my mother though hers were d cups and perky till now. Jeff's eyes were closed now, the look of pleasure on his face, everything I had dreamed of when fantasizing about this night into existence.

I increased my pace now, my lips tightening around him as I tried to get his whole length into my mouth. I stroked what my mouth couldn't cover, my hands and mouth working together. Jeff's hands in my hair kept my face attached to his dick while he moved his hips, sometimes slamming his dick into my mouth like an avenging spirit, sometimes going slow. I felt his balls tighten. I wanted to take his cum in my mouth. A little taste of the thing never hurt anyone.

I moved faster, my hands squeezing his balls to hasten him on. I felt his hands tighten in my hair painfully before he yelled out.

"Fuck Jada, you might want to take your face away. I'm awfully close," he said.

"Do it in my mouth. I can take it," I said, opening my mouth wide as my hands stroked him even faster.

He pulled my mouth back to his dick and made me continue sucking while he ran towards his orgasm, his body quaking on the bed. I wanted patiently and, before too long, felt his cum sprout into my mouth. It was salty and snacky, like a salty meal. I swiped my tongue over him as he came, taking the cum on my tongue.

"Fuckkkkkk," He screamed again, his hands leaving my hair to hold my head over his dick like I could possibly want to be anywhere else but here.

He blew his load and then slowly came off his high, looking at me with new eyes.

"How long has this been in your head?" He asked as his breath finally steadied. I
was still on the floor in front of him, his cum swallowed.

"Months, I guess, been working up the courage for a while now," I told him as I got off the floor and joined him on the bed. "Are you mad?" I asked.

"Well, I'm certainly surprised, but mad? This is exactly something you'd do, seduce your best friend. besides, this orgasm has been one of my best," he said, giving me a smack on my ass. I wiggled closer as I giggled.

"You'll spend the night, won't you?" I asked.

"Are you sure about all this?" He asked, peering at me intently.

"This took a lot of work, I assure you. If I was going to change my mind, I would've been a long time ago," I informed him as I straddled his thighs.

"Then yes, I'll spend the night. Let's see what we can get up to," he replied with a smile on his face.

"About Carter? I do plan on fucking him," I told him.

"Why? I'm not good enough for you?" He asked mischievously, pulling my tits out of the lingerie cups and running his thumb over my nipples.

"No, because I've always wanted to, besides he's always had a crush on me, unlike a certain Mr. Someone on this bed," I said, already feeling the effect of his hands on me. This would be good.

"Some people wear their hearts on their sleeves, others don't," He said as he pulled up to latch his lips onto my tits, his eyes on mine.

I threw my head back and gave a soft moan, the feel of his hot mouth on my nipples like a hot pad on sensitive skin. He continued, sucking at me quite forcefully, his tongue joining the fun. I moaned silently, the sound lost in my throat.

Jeff stretched his hands behind me to find the clasp holding the outfit together. I gave a giggle and let him search a bit.

"Where's the damned clasp?" He asked, his voice tinged with frustration.

"It's right in front of you," I answered, pointing at the little string which I'd tied like a bow in front of the outfit. Jeff rolled his eyes and pulled slowly on the string, the off shoulder slipping down my shoulders. I pulled it down myself, baring my breasts to his hungry gaze.

"You look good, really good," he said, his face smashing into my boobs, rubbing across them. I wanted him, fast.

***

Jeff's POV

This wasn't Jada. This woman was nothing like her. This was a fully ripe woman, willing and ready.

Her boobs were dark, the areola a lighter shade of skin, her nipples were distended, the tips already tight.

I leaned in and kissed them softly, my tongue on them, flicking out to brush over them. Jada had straddled my thighs, her weight a delicious pressure on me.

I've always wanted this from the very start, but Jada never seemed interested until a few months ago. She'd started craving my attention or brushing up against me when we were together alone. But I'd still never seen this coming. Not in a million years. Not that I didn't want it, of course.

I bit her nipple, and her back arched towards me, her boobs covering my face. The smell of perfume filtered into my nose, the scent an arousal on its own.

"You want me now?" She asked softly.

"I've always wanted you," I replied, "just never thought I'd be doing anything about it."

"Well fuck me already," she moaned against my ears.

"Your wish is my command," I answered, already pulling the skirt off her. Jada was sexy, the hot girl vixen with flawless skin. And she was mine now.

I pulled the skirt off completely, she had nothing under it, and it was all I could do not to slam into her right then. Rather I sucked on my finger and penetrated her slowly. She was wet, and that was all the invitation I needed to slip into her. I raised my hips and pushed her down onto me.

She pushed me down on the bed and got on top. I raised my hands and watched her bouncing up and down on me, her ass slapping against my thighs as she landed on me. Her eyes were wide, her moans filling the room. I crept my hands towards her ass cheeks and squeezed them tightly. Her cries increased as I groaned at the pleasure coursing through my body.

My dick felt huge, the pleasure bursting through my body incomparable to anything else. Jada was fast, her body moving up and down on my shaft, her eyes closed as she bounced to a rhythm only she could follow. I clenched my jaws and began pushing in roughly, my jaws clenched.

"Fuck Jada, you're really tight," I told her as my dick went in and out of her. Her moans became louder as my pace increased. I sat up from the bed and bent her over, my dick slipping into her again without pause.

This way, I could control how deep or how fast I went, and I did just that, slamming into her so fast that my thighs hit her butt cheek with every pound in. Jada was screaming now, her voice a pitch I'd never heard before now.

I pushed her back into the bed, her back arching deeply to provide me with deeper depth as I rammed into her pussy with extreme force.

"Fuck Jeff, I'm damn close," Jada moaned as she shook on the bed. I increased the lengths of my thrust as my body ran toward orgasm along with hers. My balls were getting hotter, the heat moving up through my body, about to burst out like waves on the beach.

"Go ahead, I'm fucking close myself," I told her even as I continued my thrust. I couldn't have stopped them anyway. Jada shook once more, and she started shuddering, her movement jerky as she went through her orgasm. Her body went limp on the bed, her back shaking as she got off her high.

I could feel my own orgasm coming on, my balls tightening as I tried constraining my thrust. I didn't want to be too rough. No need to hurt her now, but my hips were thrusting of their own accord. My knees trembled as my orgasm hit me strongly. I bent over Jada and held her to me, blowing my load inside her, my dick slamming in and out all the while.

I shuddered once and fell on the bed, my body joining hers in a supine position on the bed. She got off and lay her head on my chest, her hands splaying over my nipples. She was still breathing hard, my breath pumping in and out in tandem with hers.

"You liked that?" She asked softly, almost as though she was insecure. This was more like the Jada she was around Carter and me, but no wonder she had received a reputation as vixen. That had been hot.

"I loved it, Jada," I replied, raising her head with my fingers and kissing her softly. Her lips were soft and pliable, and she responded like she'd been waiting all night to get here. Her lips opened slowly, accepting my tongue into her mouth as I pushed it in. She kissed me back, her tongue mingling with mine in our private dance of passion.

"You think we can do that again soon?" She asked, panting against my lips.

"Definitely," I said, smacking her ass with my hands. Her brown skin glistened temptingly in the light, an invitation to keep at it.

Jada pouted, her lips. I couldn't resist. I planted another kiss there, watching as her eyes closed when she kissed.

"Question, please, how long have you been planning this?" I asked when we broke apart.

"Don't ask," she said, giggling mischievously.

"I do want to know. This had to have taken a lot of thought, the candles, the outfit, everything," I said to her. And to think I'd never even gotten a whiff of the plan. It was surprising, really. I could sniff out things like these from a distance.

"Well, you were never going to do anything about it, so I decided to help you along," she said.

"Well, thank you, ma'am," I said, stretching out on the bed. "I appreciate your fervor to fuck me."

"You don't regret it?" She asked, her voice insecure again.

"Well, you did say something about Carter. Was that serious?" I asked her. Carter was our best friend. The last member of our trio, and I loved him like a brother, and that was exactly the problem, I wasn't interested in sharing my woman with my brother.

"Very much so," she said, wiggling against me, her breasts rubbing against my chest. That was probably deliberate, knowing Jada. She could very daintily tease a man to distraction.

"Why? Aren't I enough?" I asked her.

"Well, I've always wanted a taste of him. I like you, Jeff, you know I do, but I want him. I must have him," she said, looking at me with pleading eyes.

I looked at her intently, I couldn't understand her sudden obsession with Carter, but I also didn't have the energy to talk about it much. It was getting late, and my eyes felt heavy already. I needed to sleep.

I gave her a soft kiss on her forehead and pulled her head to my chest, splaying my hands on her waist.

"We'll talk about this later, okay?" I asked her.

"Alright, don't go thinking you'll change my mind, though," she said, her eyes blinking heavily.

"We'll talk about it later, Jada. Sleep," I told her, pulling my eyes closed. I threw my legs over hers and found my way to sleep.

18. The Cabin

The sun was shining brightly as I followed in Jeff's car down the winding road that led to his uncle Tim's cabin. Carter was dozing off in the backseat, but I was too excited to sleep. I had never been to a cabin in the woods before, and I couldn't wait to see what it was like. As we drove deeper into the forest, the trees grew taller, and the air grew cooler. The road became bumpier, and Jeff had to avoid hitting any potholes.

But finally, after what felt like hours, we arrived at the cabin. It was a quaint little wooden house with a sloping roof and a front porch lined with rocking chairs. The front door was painted bright red, and there was a wooden sign above it that read "Tim's Cabin." I couldn't help but smile at the sight of it. Jeff pulled into the driveway, and we all climbed out of the car. I stretched my legs, taking in the fresh forest air.

The cabin was surrounded by trees, and there was a small stream running nearby. It was so peaceful, so serene.

"Welcome to my uncle's cabin," Jeff said, grinning from ear to ear. "I told you it was beautiful."

"It's amazing," I said, nodding in agreement.

Carter finally woke up, rubbing his eyes. "This place is awesome," he said, taking in the surroundings.

We walked up to the front door, and Jeff unlocked it. The inside of the cabin was just as cozy as the outside. There was a fireplace in the living room, with a plush couch and a few chairs arranged around it. The walls were lined with shelves filled with books and trinkets. There was a kitchen on one side of the room and a staircase leading up to the bedrooms on the other.

"This place is perfect," Carter said, grinning. "I can't wait to spend the weekend here."

I agreed, feeling grateful for the opportunity to experience this little piece of paradise in the woods. We walked into the room and went exploring. Jeff led the way, pointing out the guest rooms and letting us know to avoid the master's bedroom. Carter went out the front door to the car.

"I'm just gonna pick up the bags," he said.

Jeff immediately pushed me against the wall and attached his lips to mine. We hadn't been together since the other night we had been together.

"Carter's right outside," I said against his lips.

"Do you think I care?" He asked, devouring my lips.

Jeff had been acting a bit jealous lately. He seemed to mind my intention to fuck Carter sometime later. I wanted Carter, and I'd have him, but Jeff was getting mad about it. Jeff clasped my hands and pulled me down the hallway. He pushed open a door and dragged me inside the room. It was a bathroom.

"What about Carter? He could walk in on us!" I asked him.

"I don't think he matters much. You'll be fucking him later anyways," he said jealously.

"You could always join us," I said suggestively.

"I'm jealous enough as it is, so no," he answered, pulling up my flirty little skirt and turning me towards the wall. I pressed my hands against it and waited for him to stick his dick inside me. Then I waited and waited.

"Jeff, stop teasing," I told him.

"It's how I feel about you and Carter," he told me before stepping in behind me and using his body to press me into the wall. He pushed his erect length against the crack of my butt, and I reacted by pushing my butt against him.

"Do it already," I moaned, the anticipation getting to me. Jeff fisted my skirt in his hands and made me arch my back before slipping inside me, his body hard and ready, stretching me as he pushed in fast.

"Do it faster," I moaned. Carter was somewhere around, and I didn't want to ruin his surprise by letting him catch us together in the bathroom.

Jeff obliged, his body stroking in and out at a wild pace, my boobs pressing into the wall with every stroke of his dick. I shuddered, my whole body riding a huge wave of pleasure. Jeff held me securely, his body an anchor. I heard the door opening, and Jeff must've too because he increased his pace, pulling in and out as fast as he could, the sound of his legs slapping against me loudly in the bathroom.

"Fuckkkkk," I moaned aloud, immediately biting my lip to stifle my moan of pleasure. I could feel my body shaking as I got closer to my orgasm, my moans steadily increasing. Jeff stretched his hands around me to rub roughly against my pussy, even as he spread my legs and went ramming in.

"I'm close, Jada," he groaned, his voice stifled against my hair.

"Good," I panted back, his hands on my clit now, hurrying me to orgasm. I felt my back arch involuntarily, and then my orgasm broke over me. I whisper-screamed, the effort to keep silent a turn-on in its own right. I felt Jeff shaking behind me as he came inside me, his breathing loud as he groaned his orgasm.

He turned me towards him and kissed me softly, running his hands over my boobs as his body slipped out of mine.

"I needed that," he said, looking down at me for a moment before he attacked my lips again.

We heard footsteps outside the hall and sprang apart. Damn, it must be Carter, and he would come across us with the look and aura of sex everywhere. Jeff quickly arranged his clothes and stepped out of the room into the hallway.

"Did you guys find it?" I heard Carter ask outside. He and Jeff moved on down the hallway. I released a sigh of relief and set about making myself presentable.

A moment later, I pulled the door open and stepped out, following the sound of their voice to the kitchen, where they had started laying out the snacks we had brought along for the weekend. They were screaming together as though trying to discover who had the loudest voice.

Oh, they were discussing football.

"As always," I said to them with an eye roll." You just couldn't wait a moment, huh?"

"Well, you sort of disappeared on us," Carter said, looking up at me. "I was getting worried."

I looked at Jeff, wondering what he'd told Carter. He smiled and gave me a little wink.

"I'm sorry about that. I had to use the bathroom for the moment," I said, settling beside him.

"What happened to the snacks?" I said, staring at them. That was the strange thing. They should've been ripping into the snacks by now.

"They're in the cupboard. Jeff's being a dick," Carter said with an eye roll.

I turned to Jeff, and he was staring at me as though just waiting for me to say a word. I stared at him as I leaned into Carter and gave him a little kiss.

"I could be your snack," I said to him softly, giggling when his eyes widened.

Jeff rolled his eyes and moved over to a cupboard. He pulled it open and took out some snacks from the cupboard. He threw them at Carter, who jumped up and caught them in mid-air.

"He can eat that," he said to Carter. He picked a pack for himself and opened it. He picked out the snacks and ate into them, crunching loudly.

I got a pack from Carter and started eating too.

"Who's cooking dinner?" Carter asked as he stretched out, his head on my lap. I smoothed back his dark hair and placed my hands across his chest.

It's called prepping. I didn't want him to be too surprised when I approached him later.

"How'd your classes go?" I asked him.

"Not great, Prof. Ross is kicking balls in philosophy," he said, wincing.

"Do you need some extra lessons?" I asked him. "My friend Asia is a Philosophy major, and she runs tutoring classes for students who need them at 100 dollars every month. I could ask her to help you out."

"I could use some boosting. Exams are coming up soon," he replied.

"I'll send you Asia's number, do not bother my friend," I told him as I raised a threatening finger.

"Yes, ma'am," he said, raising his hands in surrender.

"You've been awfully quiet, Jeff," I said, finally noticing his silence. He looked sullen, sitting there by the fireplace alone. It would be night soon, and I was looking forward to seeing Carter's reaction to my naked self.

"Well, you've barely said a word to me. Carter has all your attention today," he replied.

"Jealous much?" Carter said, laughing.

"Well, it's the truth," he said, laughing too. Jeff couldn't stay mad at Carter for long. They'd been friends before I'd joined the trio. I just had a crush on Jeff from afar for much longer.

I looked away from Jeff and continued my conversation with Carter. He was my baby now, and his sulking somehow made him even cuter. I just hoped he'd join us later. It would be a beautiful night. When the darkness had dropped, and the crickets outside the cabin became noticeable, I got off the couch and walked to the room I'd chosen for myself. I wanted to be ready before it was too late.

I'd packed the bunny outfit for tonight. It was cute, and that was exactly what Carter would fall for. The soft daddy's girl always turned his head. I slipped out of my skirt and pulled the bunny outfit over my body. I'd had it resized a while ago, so the skirt barely skirted my butt. I wanted his attention on my body, and going nowhere immediately, he stepped into the room.

I had forgotten to pack the candles, so that was shot. I moved over to the windows and pushed them open. I wanted the crisp breeze outside seeping into the room as well as the light of the moon outside. I pulled the dress around me and wrapped the long ties around my body. The ties were a bit long, so I folded them over twice and tied them across my navel. Sliding the headband over my hair, I walked to the door and called Carter.

"Hey Carter, gimme a hand here!" I called out to him. A moment later, I heard the clatter of feet coming down the hallway.

He knocked at the door before pushing it open and stepping in. I turned towards him, and he gave a dramatic gasp and turned away.

"Oh, I didn't know you were in such a state of disarray," he said to me mockingly.

"Oh, stop teasing. I need help getting out of this," I told him, walking towards him. He turned to me and asked what to do.

"What's this outfit anyways?" He asked as I showed him how to get the hooks. It wasn't a mistake that I had picked an outfit with a thousand little hooks, sweet little girls needed help from their men. Also, the hooks were the only thing holding the top together. He would be shocked when the top fell into his hands when the last look gave way. I couldn't wait.

I watched his face as he slowly worked at the hooks, his face a mask of concentration, he pulled the last hook, and I watched silently as his eyes latched onto my boobs for a long moment. He didn't say a word, just kept his eyes where I'd known they would be. He looked up at me and then looked away flustered.

"You certainly seem to be enjoying the view," I said pertly, my eyes following his to the movement in his shorts. There was a tent being built right in front of us.

"That's very normal. You're beautiful," he said as though reassuring himself more than me. "I'm sorry, though. I shouldn't objectify your body."

"Look who learned some ethics," I said. "And what if I want you to objectify me?"

"Do you?" He asked, his brows arched.

I trailed my fingers down his body and ran them to his dick, my fingers stroking his dick through the shorts. Silently, I held my hands out to him and walked him to the bed. Pulling his shorts off, I pushed him onto the bed, kneeling in front of him.

Almost reverently, I stroked his hardening dick as it began to expand in front of me. Carter gave a gasp, and his dick became even bigger. I wanted to kiss him so bad, his lips above me torture I couldn't deny. And why not? He wasn't resisting my attention. Getting off the ground, I grabbed the back of his head and put my lips to his, my tongue reaching in to tangle with his.

I kept at him, kissing him back when he pulled me closer to the bed to deepen our kiss. Breaking from him, I stroked his dick again, my hands pumping faster than before. I kissed a trail of kisses down his body and to his dick. I gave him a tentative lick before pulling him into my mouth, and my hands stroked at him as my lips went on down on his hard length. Carter groaned aloud, his hands fisted on the bed as he pushed himself down my throat.

He kept going until I gagged around his dick. He groaned again and pushed even deeper.

"Stop," I said, staring up at him. I liked to experiment, but gagging was too much for me.

"I'm sorry about that, forgive me?" He asked, a sorry look on his face.

I put my lips around his dick and continued sucking at him, my head bobbing as I swallowed his length. Suddenly he pulled out of my lips and tapped the bed beside me.

"Get on. I want to taste you," He said, a hot look in his eyes. I got off the ground as commanded and got on the bed. He put his hands on my legs and spread them apart.

He kissed up my thigh and took a moment to inhale at my pussy lips.

"Girl, you smell so damn good," he swore before slowly licking at my lips, his tongue making a rough scrape against my pussy lips. He groaned loudly and attacked me. His tongue nipped and lapped alternately, giving me waves and waves of pleasure. I felt my head lift off the bed, my hips pressing up into his mouth.

"Fuck, you're good," I moaned into the room. I felt my body quiver, and I realized I was close. I wanted him inside me when I came, and I would come apart very soon.

"Come on, fuck me already," I groaned aloud at him. It was all the invitation he needed to get off and stroke his dick into my wet pussy. His dick slipped into my wet hot pussy, raising all the hairs on my arms. I felt my body explode, my legs shaking out of sync as wave upon wave of pleasure came over me.

"Fuckkkkk, I'm cumming," I screamed into the void, my legs raising on their own to clasp around his hips. He pressed forward until his hips were pressed against my ass cheeks.

He increased his strokes, his thighs slapping against me fast, my body responding all over again. I'd be on the edge soon enough, and I could feel my body quivering against him.

"Damn, you're tight, so fucking tight," Carter said, his breathing harsh as he increased the pace of his strokes into my body. He held my hips tight and pounded into me faster, accentuating his hard thrusts with harsh groans.

Sooner than expected, I felt my body quickening, my hips pushing up harder against him as my body went stiff under him. He kept thrusting.

"I'm gonna cum, and I'm doing it inside you," he said as I bucked against him, my orgasm washing over me like waves at sea. I felt my walls pulsing around him as my body stiffened on the bed. A moment later, I heard his shout of pleasure as he came.

"Fuck, oh fuck," he groaned aloud into the room. No way Jeff couldn't hear his shouts of pleasure or my moans as I came. I felt bad about that, but not bad enough not to give off one more squeeze of Carter's dick before relaxing into the bed.

I closed my eyes as I waited for my breath to even out. Carter fell into bed beside me, his breath leaving his body in giant gasps. I ran my hands over his chest and stared at him. He was several degrees hot, no need denying it, and he could fuck really good. What wasn't to like?

I came out of my trance to hear footsteps walking down the hallway.

"Fuck, that was Jeff wasn't it?" Carter said, a worried frown on his face.

"We can always ask him to join the fun," I pouted at him in reply.

"He'll never agree to that," Carter said, his frown deepening.

"Would you mind?" I asked him softly.

"I believe I should, but maybe not. He's Jeff, after all," he said with a single shrug. He gave me a soft kiss and got off the bed, smacking my ass on his way to pick up his shorts. He slipped his legs into them and pulled them around his waist.

"I'll go speak to him," he said before opening the door and walking out of the room.

I didn't understand Jeff's jealousy. He'd always been cool with me and Carter spending time together. Besides, he never would've done anything about our attraction to each other if I hadn't taken matters into my hands.

I'll speak to him in the morning, I decided, before closing my eyes and slipping into a deep sleep.

***

Jeff's POV

I was usually not always jealous. In fact, I was never jealous, which was why this behavior seemed quite shocking to me. Besides, Carter was our friend, and she never hid her intention to have him too. I rubbed my hands across my face and got off the bed.

I walked out of the room and down the hallway to Jada's room. I needed to speak to her about Carter and our relationship. She could have him here just cause she wanted to, but once out of here, she had to be exclusively mine. No sneaking around with Carter.

Carter had tracked me down yesterday to tell me about her decision to fuck the two of us together, he wanted it, as did she. I was the reluctant party then, I just couldn't understand the craving, and I'd told him that exactly. Besides, Jada couldn't take the two of us at once, not to brag, but we were pretty well hung. She might be sore for days.

I rounded the corner and stopped short. There was no mistaking the sounds coming from her room. Jada was moaning quite loudly. Apparently, Carter had spent the night. I moved to the door faster and sneaked a peek into the room. I felt like a voyeur and a pervert, but I couldn't help myself.

Jada was riding Carter's dick, and her face turned away in reverse cowgirl position. I stared at her face, and there was a look of sheer pleasure stamped on there. I felt my dick expanding, my body heating up from watching Jada rise on fall on Carter's hard pole. I reached my hands into my sleeping shorts and stroked my dick, my fist on it pumping as I tried recreating the pleasure taking place on the bed.

What the fuck? I was aroused from watching a girl I liked being rammed by our best friend. Sick, but I couldn't help it. I wanted to be on that bed with them, my dick plunging in and out of her wet pussy as I drove myself to orgasm. Jada stiffened on the bed and turned her head towards the door, her eyes latched onto mine, almost as though she knew where to look.

I must've been moaning louder than I had thought. She lifted a little finger and beckoned me into the room. Carter was groaning on the bed. Obviously, he would soon be on the edge of an orgasm, and from the way he was moving his head back and forth, it would be mind-blowing.

Immediately I got to Jada, she replaced my fist with hers, wrapping her hands around my dick, pumping her fist up and down, her strokes in tandem with her up-and-down motion on Carter's dick. Carter's eyes opened, and he looked up at me for a moment as though surprised before he gave me a bold wink and went ramming into her again.

I couldn't help it. I felt my dick thickening even more in Jada's clasp.

"Oh, someone's naughty. You enjoy watching me fucking another man?" She asked, looking up at him with hooded eyelids.

"Isn't that what you wanted all along?" I asked her before wrapping my hands over hers and stroking my length faster.

Jada got off Carter and bent over on the bed, her shaved pussy wet and thrust towards Carter's dick. He pushed into her from behind, continuing where he had left off.

"Come on, stick it in my mouth," Jada said, snapping her hands toward me.

I got on the bed and moved in front of her. She opened her mouth and took me in. I shuddered slightly as I felt her warm mouth wrap around my sensitive tip. She pulled me out and sucked at the tip, her mouth making suckling sounds as she worked me with her tongue. Her lips found the crease where the tip joined the body, and she circled her lips there, sucking wildly.

I bucked my hips into her mouth, my body no longer obeying my commands. I pushed harder, and she struggled to accommodate me, her lips widening to take my sudden surge into her mouth. Carter slid into her one last time and came, his body shaking as he released his hot seed inside her. He slid out of her and lay back to watch her suck me out.

"Come on, fuck me already," Jada said, taking her mouth off me and offering me her pussy instead. It was wet and ready, the hole already glistening with ropes of Carter's cum. For some reason, my mind didn't want to comprehend, that image aroused me even further, sending me scrambling to her and then inside her. It was just as I had expected, warm, hot, wet, and just ready for me. I slipped in and then out, my body pushing back in just as fast as Carter's had.

"Fuck," Jada swore, her voice breaking on her last moan. Carter got off his ass and rubbed his hands over her clit and nipples at the same time. I kept up my pounding, my dick a large piston that just couldn't get enough.

The added stimulation pushed Jada over the edge, and she came all my dick, her voice echoing across the room as she screamed her orgasm. I smacked her ass loudly, my hips sliding in and out as I neared my orgasm. Soon enough, I felt my balls tighten as my seed burst out of me and into Jada. I groaned aloud and slammed into her one final time. Jada was breathing hard, her raspy breath very loud as she came off her high.

I was breathing beside her, my breathing just as hard as hers. Carter laughed out loud.

"And to think the day just started, this has officially been declared the house of sin," he said with a wicked look on his face.

And he was perfectly right, too. Spending the whole weekend here exploring the woods and Jada would be great, absolutely a great way to spend a weekend. It would be beautiful, just until reality intruded.

19. Desire

DEVON

"How do I look?" Jeanine asked as she turned around slowly.

I bit my lower lip as I stared at her. She was wearing a beautiful sunflower dress. It looked so good on her caramel skin. It made my heart thump hard against my chest as I watched her. How could she be this beautiful?

It was supposed to be impossible. She was grinning, and her perfect white teeth flashed at me. I couldn't help it. She had just put me in a trance, and I didn't want to get out of it. I accepted it because it was from her.

I didn't mind whatever she did to me. It was worth it. What was on my mind right now was crazy. I imagined the kinds of positions I was yearning to put her through. It was embarrassing for me, but I knew she would welcome it.

I loved the way she got nasty. It pleased me greatly. Jeanine was probably waiting for my answer, but I still couldn't say anything because I was still taking my eyes off her. If only she knew how edible she looked right now. I thanked the stars for the day I met her.

"You looked dazzling," I finally said.

"Oh, baby. Thank you," she said as her cheeks heated up.

I smirked at her. She turned around and faced the mirror

admiring herself. I couldn't help but admire her too. We were shopping at the mall, and she had decided to try some new clothes. I sat in front of her as she looked at herself in the mirror. Sometimes, I wondered if Jeanine knew how beautiful she was. Her caramel skin looked so delicious, and her brown eyes were even more impressive.

Whenever they stared at me, I would feel a cold sensation trickle down my spine. It was a good sensation, and I still couldn't get used to it. Jeanine turned back to me, and I focused my eyes on her. She came closer and sat on my lap. I chuckled as she did, and I took in a deep breath, inhaling her fragrance. She smelled so nice.

"You like the dress?" I asked.

She nodded her head slowly. I chuckled again. She was acting childish because it was something she wanted me to get for her. I loved it when she acted this way. It made me want to grab her and kiss her lips. Those lips were sexy and tasted as they looked.

"Do you want another?" I asked.

"You would get me another?" She asked.

I looked at her and saw her brown eyes looking down at me in surprise. I felt my body shudder in excitement. My dick began hardening. I was glad that she hadn't noticed it yet. She would have wanted us to have some fun right here. And I wouldn't mind, but it wasn't the right time.

"Babe? I would get anything you desire," I assured her.

I could see a smile spread across her lips. She was pleased with my words. Her hands came to my cheeks and held them. They were so warm. I closed my eyes and savored the sensation that spread across my veins. My dick was now fully bloated, and it was throbbing.

At this point, if she asked for anything, I would give her. And I meant anything. I opened my eyes, and I found her still staring down at me. I thought she was yearning to kiss me. I frowned at her, and she chuckled. I wasn't pleased with it all. My frown had said it all.

"Baabbee? I thought you wanted to kiss me?" I asked with a sad expression on my face.

"Don't worry. I'll give you more than that when we get home," she assured.

I still frowned at her.

"But I want one right now," I pressed.

Her eyes went down to my pants, and she saw the bulge. She looked at me and bit her lips. The surprised look came next. I knew what she was about to say. But then, no words came out of her mouth. Her hand crawled down from my cheek to the bulge in my pants.

She held it softly, then massaged it slowly. I felt electricity spread through my body, I knew the site of my bulge made her horny as well. I couldn't wait to go back and explore her body like the internet. She didn't stop massaging it. I closed my eyes and leaned back on my seat as she massaged me slowly.

I could almost feel myself on another planet. My soul seemed to have left the mall. I opened my eyes and looked at her. I realized that we were in public, and this time, I came to my senses.

"Babbbeee. We can't do that here," I reminded her.

She pouted her lips and looked at me.

"And why is that?" She asked.

"You know," I replied.

She sighed and let go of my bulge. Immediately, I wish she hadn't. I wanted her to grip it once more and never let go. I wanted to browse through her body. I wanted to touch every part of her that would make her scream my name. But all that couldn't happen here. It wasn't right.

"Devon. Come on," she said.

I was surprised that she used my name. It meant that she wasn't pleased with me.

"Don't worry. Let's get home first," I said.

She smiled at me and kissed me on the forehead. She stood up from me to probably get the dress off. As she left the changing room, I looked at myself and noticed a stain on my pants. She had made me wet already. Damn! I couldn't help it. Couldn't I?

She was so sexy and gorgeous. I couldn't resist the opportunity when I had one. I relaxed in my seat and waited for her to return. My mind was already thinking about what we would do when we got home. I was ready to explore her, I wanted to be inside her already. I couldn't be tamed.

I looked at my pants again and saw that my bulge had come back on again. I would have to hold it down till we got home. I glanced at my watch after a while and sighed. Why was she taking so long? Jeanine came out of the changing room with a smile on her face. She had the dress all wrapped up in a bag.

I stood up from my chair and headed to her. She reached into her Jean pocket and brought out my credit card. I stared at her, completely flustered. Had she used my credit card to pay for all that? When did she even take it from me? It must have been when she had been massaging my bulge. I got my card from her and placed it in my wallet.

"Are we done here?" I asked.

She nodded at me, and I held her hand.

***

JEANINE

We stepped into the house, and I closed the door behind us. As I turned around, Devon held me by the waist and pinned me to the door. I was surprised but also happy that this was what was going to happen. I had noticed how aroused he had been at the mall. I knew he wanted me badly, and now we had the time to ourselves.

He was smiling at me, and my body shivered beneath me. His smile was so beautiful, and it usually brought a warm sensation to my chest each time I saw that smile. It was a dangerous weapon—Devon's smile was my kryptonite. I could feel my body getting heated. His suspense was killing me. Was he going to kiss me or what?

"Babeeee," I said. "We haven't even gone in yet."

"We will soon," he said.

I knew what he meant by that, and I chuckled. He finally brought his lips to mine and kissed me softly. Immediately, I felt weak, and my body gave in. My grip loosened on the Valentino bag I was holding, and it fell to the floor. I wrapped my hands around his hard body and invited him to do more.

His lips were soft and inviting. I wanted more. He knew this, and I was confident that he would give me what I asked for. Devon's hands went down to my waist and gripped my ass cheeks. I moaned in his mouth. I loved whenever he did that.

He broke out from the kiss and looked at me. I bit my lower lips and stared into his brown eyes. He was my desire, and I had to have him. He reached for me once more and began kissing me on the neck. My hands rose to his back and held him tight as he sent fireballs of pleasure through my body. Why was he taking his time? The suspense was killing me, and I didn't know how long

I could hold myself back, I wanted him in me, I wanted to feel him expand my walls. Whenever he went slow, it tortured me and made me want him even more. Maybe that was what he wanted. On the contrary, I did love that feeling.

Devon stopped kissing me and moved away from my neck. He was now looking at me once more. His brown eyes pierced through my soul. I knew what that look meant. It was inviting. And who was I to resist? I picked up my Valentino bag as he stretched his hand to me. I smiled and held his hand. We walked to the room in silence.

When we got in, he closed the door behind us. I threw my bag on the floor, and his hands held me from behind. I felt his tongue on my ear next. I bit my lower lip as a shudder ran down my spine. I was getting wet already. This wasn't how it was supposed to start.

Devon stopped halfway and turned me around, and I moved willingly. He reached for my shirt and pulled it off. My breasts leaped free, and he smiled. Then, I reached for his shorts and took them off his body. His well-chiseled abdominal muscles stared back at me. I almost choked on my breath. He was extremely sexy. I couldn't hold it back.

I unbuckled my jeans and pulled them off my legs. I was only in my lace panties now. Devon smiled as he stared intently. I went on my knees, and helped him unbuckle his jeans, then he stepped out of them. I stood up and chuckled at him. He didn't seem pleased, and I loved the frown on his face.

He still wasn't smiling, and I couldn't stop laughing at him. I finally stopped and reached for him, I wrapped my hands around him and hugged him. We were only in our underwear, and I could feel his bulge against my thigh. He was so hard and ready, he was probably throbbing. I was eager to get that in my mouth as I looked up at him, and he was staring at me with a frown still on his face. Then, he reached for my lips and kissed me.

He wrapped his hands around me and pulled me closer, his body was warm and hard. He kissed me slowly, and I could feel my excitement rise. I wanted him badly. His tongue moved inside my mouth, searching for what only he could find. I let go of him to control my body and do with it as he wished. I was his now.

He let go of me, and I knew what to do next. He was certain I would do it, but I had to appease him because I was yearning for it. I went down on my knees slowly and reached into his underwear, and pulled out his dick. It was fully hard and ready. It was so warm, and I could feel it throbbing in my palm. The tip was wet from his precum, and he smiled at that. He was ready for this.

I brought out my tongue and tasted it. It was salty and sticky, my favorite combo. I ran my hand across his big dick gently. I could hear him moan slowly from above me. His moan triggered me. I loved when I made him sound like that. I was certain no other woman could do that to him. He was mine, and I knew how to take care of him. I looked up at Devon, and he had his eyes shut. It made me chuckle softly. He was enjoying this, which meant I wasn't going to stop.

I was going to please him even more. I carried my tongue to the tip of his dick and tasted it. He opened his eyes and looked at me. I was teasing him, and he didn't like it. It was payback for him kissing me on the neck. That had been torture. He knew that, yet he had exploited that weakness.

"Jeanine," he called.

I laughed and looked up at him as I stroked his dick gently. He closed his eyes and moaned out once more. I looked at him and spread my mouth and introduced his dick into it. He was large, and I could feel him fill my mouth already. He was heading down my throat, and I had to stop it. I paused and ran my tongue underneath his dick.

Devon opened his eyes and looked at me, his eyes widened. He was probably flattered. I took him out of my mouth with my eyes still looking up at him, like I was worshiping him and his big dick, and I knew he loved that so much. He placed his hand on my head and gave me those eyes I couldn't resist.

I placed him into my mouth once more and began sucking him gently. My mouth was like a vacuum, and I felt my responsibility was to wipe all the lust—like dirt—off his dick. I pushed his dick further into my throat and let my saliva wet him. Devon moaned out, indicating that he was pleased with my work. I moved my mouth around his dick and used my tongue as a base for him. I spread my tongue underneath and let my saliva wet there too.

"Oh, my God!" Devon exclaimed. "Baby."

I moved his dick in and out of my mouth as I sent tremors of pleasure running through his spine. He was trembling now, and I could feel it. I let go of his dick, and it got out of my mouth. He looked down at me and placed his hand beneath my chin. He raised it, and I spread my tongue out. He placed his dick into my mouth again and began thrusting it deep into my throat.

His dick expanded my throat, and I could not help but gag all over his dick. With each gag, he moaned out. He was enjoying this, and so was I. I loved the way his dick expanded my throat muscles. I wanted him to go even deeper. It was like he read my mind.

Devon adjusted himself and pushed his dick further down my throat till all of him was inside my mouth. I gagged once more as my lungs cried out for breath. I didn't heed their needs, I was fully focused on Devon. He stroked deeper into my throat, and I could feel my lungs. I gagged on his dick even more, and he held my chin as his thrust continued. I began seeing multicolored specs and felt I would pass out soon.

Devon finally let himself out of me, and I struggled for breath. As the air got into my lungs, I felt a stabbing pain with each breath I took. My saliva had run down my mouth and into my breasts. Devon smiled when he saw this. He seemed impressed. He was stroking his dick gently as I tried to recover my breath.

When I regained my breath, I began stroking his dick. It was slippery and warm. I wanted more. I placed his dick into my mouth and began sucking again. I stroked it as I sucked it. Devon pulled my head into his fist as I sucked his dick impeccably. He moaned as I moved him deeper once more. I let him go down my throat and gagged on it. He immediately got out, and I gasped for breath. Devon tapped on the cheek as I stroked his dick.

"Damn, Jeanine," he said.

I always made him speechless with my head. I stood up from the ground, and he carried me to bed. He let me lay on it. Then, he left me and headed to the closet. I knew what he was going for. He brought out one of my dildos and closed the drawers. I was already wet from sucking his dick. Seeing him bring out a sex toy made a new wave of excitement rise in my body.

He wasn't kidding when he promised to take it to me when we arrived home. Devon slid off my panties, which were already soaked. He spread my thighs apart, and I moaned out. I was waiting and dripping on the sheets. He brought out his tongue and poked my clit with it. I gasped in pleasure as he did. My body was shuddering already.

Why was he doing this? It was his turn now. I had to surrender my body to him. It was the rule I always made before we had sex. I laid back in the bed and let him take control. Devon picked up the dildo and placed it into my vagina. I could feel the toy widen my walls. He moved the object in and out of me, twisting it at intervals. This made me go crazy.

I gripped the sheets as Devon administered substantial doses of pleasure to my system. I felt like I was underwater. I was drowning in ecstasy, and there was no way I could escape. The funny thing was that I didn't want to escape because I was enjoying every second of what he was offering to me. I didn't want him to stop.

Then, Devon placed his wet tongue on my clit, and I felt a jolt of electricity run through my spine upwards. I screamed out in pleasure as he played with my clit and, at the same time, penetrated me with the toy. He was torturing me, and I didn't want it to end. I could feel my body shudder in excitement. Something was coming.

It was a sensation. A familiar one, but my brain couldn't fathom what it was because it was scrambled at the moment. My whole body grew rigid suddenly, and my walls contracted around the dildo. I orgasmed and spilled my juice on the sex toy.

"Devon!" I cried as I climaxed.

Devon brought out the sex toy from in between my thighs and showed me. It was covered with my cream and juice. He brought it to my mouth, and I sucked the dildo dry. Devon smiled as he watched. He mounted on top of me, and I knew what was coming. Devon began stroking his dick gently. I knew it was coming in. I wanted him inside me already.

"Come on, baby. Fuck me. Please!" I begged.

A smirk flashed across his lips, and he moved closer to me. Next, I felt my thighs go up in the air before I felt his warm turgid soft bone enlarge my walls as he penetrated me. I moaned and pushed my head back onto the pillow as he widened my walls and browsed deeper into my pussy. Then, Devon began his thrust slowly. He spread my legs, and I could feel my walls make more room for his dick. His dick swallowed up the space and moved in and out of me slowly. I gripped the sheets and looked at him as he moved in and out of me.

"Oh, baby! Fuck me!" I ordered.

Devon clenched his jaws and sped up the tempo of his thrusts. He was moving fast now, and there was no slowing him down. He bent my thighs further, making them reach my chest. My walls were completely opened, making my body vulnerable to his every thrust. Our connection became more slippery and divine, making neither of us want to stop. I looked at where we were joined and saw my cream coating his chocolate dick.

It felt so good watching it go in and out swiftly as he purged the lust out of me. I felt like I was in wonderland. I rolled my eyes as I received his every thrust, his groin slamming against my thighs at the end of every thrust. I was moaning his name, and I didn't realize when I had started screaming it. He wasn't slowing down, and I didn't wish him to. I wanted him to treat me like I was his.

Next, I felt his hand around my neck. He was choking me as I lifted my waist slightly to meet his every thrust. It was insane. Then, he slowed down till he fully stopped. I looked up at him, seeing the beads of sweat on the chocolate brown skin on his forehead. He still looked beautiful even though he was trying to catch his breath.

Devon pulled out of me slowly, and I felt my walls trying to stretch back to their normal shape. I looked at him and saw him still very hard with my cream painting his dick.

"Bend over," he ordered.

I nodded and rose from the bed. I turned around and bent over, arching my waist and puffing my ass cheeks upwards as my pussy awaited penetration once again. As soon as I felt his touch on my ass cheek, I shivered. Then, I felt him widen my walls once more as his dick stepped in. I moaned out, and then, he began his thrust quickly. He didn't slow down at all.

Devon pumped his dick in and out of me with every thrust greeting deeper into my waiting pussy. I balled my hands into fists and moaned out as I collected each stroke from him. Devon slapped my butt cheek, and I moaned out in pleasure. He held my waist and began exploring the deepest portions of my vagina. I couldn't help it. He slapped my butt cheek, and I bit my lower lip. He pushed my waist deeper into his hand, and I arched even more. I felt his dick spread through my walls and get into places he hadn't visited. He was at the very end of my walls.

Devon didn't slow down. He continued pounding my vagina, his waist slamming against it with each thrust he completed which added to the pleasure I was receiving. I could feel a torrent rise in me. I was heading toward another orgasm, and I couldn't hold back. It wrecked my body like a tornado.

"I'm cummminggg!" I screamed.

"Oh. Me too, baby," he said.

Climax hit us together, and I spilled my juice on his dick. Devon's warm juice poured inside me, filling my vagina. I loved that feeling every time. When he was done, he pulled out, and I slumped on the bed, completely wasted.

20 Comfort

.

DEVON

I came out of the bathroom with a towel wrapped around my waist. Jeanine wasn't in the room anymore. She had been in bed with me a couple of minutes ago. Anytime we were together, we could always feel the lust burn in us. It was a hunger that had always demanded to be fed by us. Not having that hunger this morning was strange, but I was okay with it.

When I woke up this morning, I found her on my chest. That was the best place she could ever be. It was hard and warm, and she always enjoyed it. My hands were wrapped around her while she slept. She was warm, and our bodies together made the connection more comfortable. This was interesting because I had been looking at her while she slept.

Her face looked so peaceful while she slept. I still thanked the stars for the day I had met her—It was actually one morning, though around 2 am into the morning. She had pulled up at the bar I had miraculously been inhabiting at that period. The first time I saw her, she wasn't this beautiful. Perhaps it was because she wore a pair of ash-colored joggers and a tank top. On her waist was a sweater which she had pulled off when she had stepped in. Her face had been so rough, and so was her hair which fell all over her face.

I had been minding my business and sipping my drink when she walked to the counter. I didn't notice her until she talked with the bartender. That was when I turned around and saw her face. She had been dead gorgeous when I first saw her. Though she looked like she had jumped out of a nightmare to get here, she looked so beautiful. Her curves stood out, and I drooled when I looked at her behind.

She was a sight to behold. Her caramel skin caught my attention easily. *How could she be this sexy when she wasn't trying?* That had been my question when I had first seen her. I had been wholly intrigued and had to do what every man would do when he was with a fine lady like her. I offered to buy her another drink. She initially rejected me, but eventually, she came around after raking her eyes through me.

I felt the reason she had rejected it the first time was that she hadn't looked at me. To me, she felt like a woman who wasn't really into men. She contradicted that point later on. We had talked for a while before I got her number. That was how we had met.

I was smiling at myself in the mirror and combing my hair as I thought of that. That was one of the best days of my life, meeting Jeanine. She turned out to be a real blessing. To me, she was heaven-sent, and she chuckled every time I told her that. I was still dressed in nothing but my towel wrapped around my waist, so when I was done with the combing, I reached into my closet and bought a pair of new underwear.

I slid them on and took off the towel. Then, I jumped into a pair of shorts and closed the closet afterward. There would be no need for a shirt. I purposefully didn't wear any. I stepped out of the room and hurried downstairs. The house seemed empty. *Where was Jeanine?* Surely she wouldn't be going anywhere today because it was a Sunday.

When I walked towards the kitchen, I heard a familiar sound. I walked in and found her standing behind the gas stove. Her black hair was packed up into a bun, and her ass cheeks were bulging out of her joggers. Damn. She was so sexy. She was wearing a singlet on top of all that.

I bit my lower lip and walked towards her. She didn't even realize that I was here yet. It was nice to creep on her. I chuckled silently as I walked towards her. When I arrived, I wrapped my hands around her and pulled her close. Her ass cheeks landed on my dick, and I sighed with satisfaction. It startled her. She turned around to see me and smiled. Then, a drop of oil from the frying pan landed on my upper arm. I let go of her as the stinging pain coursed through my body. I stepped away from her and the gas stove as I grimaced in pain.

"Babe?" She stressed as she realized I had been the one that crept on her.

I was rubbing where I had been stung by the oil. She rushed to me in concern.

"What was that?" She asked. "Here. Let me see," she requested.

I was still rubbing the injured spot. She took my hand off impatiently to look at the spot. There was nothing there. Not even a bruise, but it had stung like hell. Jeanine twisted her lips with dissatisfaction as she saw that there was nothing there. She thought I was probably lying.

"Stop that, Devon," she said.

"What? It hurts," I said.

She rolled her eyes at me.

"If you wanted my attention, you should have just said so," she said. "I'm a little busy right now."

I sighed and shook my head as she headed back to the gas stove. She didn't believe me. How could she feel I was lying? I sighed and sat up on the counter as I held the area I was supposedly injured. It didn't hurt anymore. But that was a sign that I should have put on a shirt.

I had been planning to seduce her, not knowing she would be busy with breakfast. Everything looked like it was ruined now. I held the edge of the counter as I swung my legs aimlessly. I was bored, and the aroma of what she was preparing made my stomach grumble. I wasn't hungry for the food she was preparing. I was hungry for her.

I wanted to feast on her before breakfast, but that seemed impossible now. I watched her as she fried the chicken next. I was beginning to get hungrier, and all I could see was food I couldn't touch. If only she knew how hungry I was. Maybe I could take a piece of her and then a piece of chicken afterward. I stepped down from the counter and acted like I had left the kitchen as silently as possible not to alert her.

Then, I walked silently behind her and headed toward the chicken she had fried. I reached for one and picked it up. Immediately, I felt a burning pain in my fingers, and I dropped it back, groaning. Jeanine turned around swiftly and caught me by the arm, taking back the piece of chicken. She looked at me sternly.

"Baby! What are you doing?" She asked as she came towards me.

"I was just trying to get your attention," I replied.

She reached for my finger, and the hot chicken burned. I should have known that they were still so hot. Jeanine looked at it and then looked up at me with a smile.

"If you wanted my attention, you should have just said so," she said.

"You told me that you were busy," I reminded.

"I'm never too busy for you, my love," she said.

I could see the emotions burning in her brown eyes. They were so sexy, and they made my dick swell up slowly. I was turned on just by her eyes. Jeanine was special. I didn't know what to do to myself if I ever lost her. Jeanine turned away and headed to the gas stove. She turned the chicken around and waited for a little longer. Then, she turned off the stove afterward.

She placed the rest of the raw chicken in the fridge when she was done and walked back to me, still holding my finger. Only by watching her move through the kitchen my dick got harder. I was ready to feed my hunger. I didn't know if Jeanine would want to have sex with me now too. She looked at my finger and placed it into her mouth. It was my index finger. She sucked it slowly, and I could feel my blood boil in excitement. I knew what she was doing, and I was falling victim to it. I couldn't stand that. My dick was throbbing now.

"Does that feel better now?" She asked as she took it out of her mouth.

I held her by the waist and pulled her closer to me. She gasped in surprise as she felt my dick against her thighs. She ran her hands on my chest, caressing me. I knew it would turn her on. I placed my lips on her and kissed her roughly. She held me and kissed me back. My hands left her waist and headed down to her ass cheeks. I held them tight and squeezed them softly. She moaned out in pleasure. I was getting there. Jeanine broke out from the kiss and looked at me.

"Do you want to have breakfast now or later?" She asked.

My mind wasn't interested in breakfast anymore. My body wanted her, and I had to heed its calling.

"Later," I replied.

She nodded, and I slammed my lips against hers. I squeezed her ass cheeks again, and she moaned in my mouth. I could feel her trembling beneath my touch. She was getting excited too. I could feel my blood boiling. My lust was raging, and I wanted to be satisfied. It was hungry and needed to be fed. I had to heed it.

I moved her to the counter and lifted her to sit on it. She reached for my dick and began caressing it as I kissed her, sending tremors of pleasure through my body. I was going insane, and it would be hard to return from such an enticing sensation. I held her shoulders and kissed her passionately. My tongue moved inside her as I explored her mouth.

Jeanine reached into my shorts and brought out my dick. It was throbbing in her grip. I could feel it. It was hard, and I could see my precum poking out of the tip. I broke out of this kiss and bit my lower lip as she massaged my dick softly. It was driving me insane. Her hand was warm and soft. I felt my soul leave my body as she stroked it gently. This was torture. I thought we had passed that already.

"Baby!" I called out softly.

She knew I was getting weaker by the second, prompting her to do it more. She began stroking it a little bit faster, and it was driving me crazy. I could feel my nerves fire up all around my body. I was sensitive to her every touch and every stroke. There was only one way this was going to end, and this was going to be in a powerful orgasm.

I could feel the orgasm lingering around and knew it would be only a matter of time before it came. I closed my eyes and leaned backward as Jeanine stroked my dick. Her warm hand wasn't helping matters. It was making orgasm creep in on me. Then, she stopped. I opened my eyes after some seconds to see what was going on. She let go of my dick and stepped down from the counter. I was confused. What was she doing? She went to the sink and washed her hands under the faucet. I watched with my dick still out.

"Babe?" I called, confused. "What's going on?"

Jeanine turned to me with a smile while wiping her hands with a hand towel. I stood there, surprised and unhappy at the same time. My dick became flaccid, and I stared at it helplessly, hoping that she'd come back and I wouldn't have to place it back into my shorts in disappointment.

"Let's have breakfast first," she said.

Now I was utterly confused. *After all that?*

"What?" I exclaimed wide-eyed.

***

I laid back on the couch with Jeanine in my arms as we watched Netflix. I was still mad at her for what had happened in the morning. Why had she left me that way? I felt like I had done something wrong, but it wasn't. She had said countless times that

I didn't do anything. And I knew Jeanine very well. Even though I made her mad, she wouldn't be able to stay that way for more than five minutes.

She was obsessed with me the same way I was obsessed with her. It was a mutual feeling, but I was still displeased with what she had done. She owed me an explanation, but sadly, none came. She didn't say anything about that throughout the day. I was starting to get pissed. I was silent as we watched another episode of a martin she genuinely loved so much. She lay in my arms as I struggled to keep up with the show. I was getting tired and wanted to get some rest. It would be a nice payback if I left her alone in the living room and headed to bed, but I wasn't going to do that. It wasn't worth it.

Jeanine turned to face me. I didn't lift my eyes from the television. Maybe ignoring her would make her pissed, too. I always gave her my attention. Not doing that now would make her feel something was up with me. That was exactly what I wanted. I wanted her to know that I was still unhappy with what had happened.

She sighed and turned to face the television. She wiggled herself in my arms, and I adjusted to make her feel more comfortable. Her comfort was my concern. I was cold tonight, but I was certain she enjoyed spending time in my warm embrace. She kept silent and continued with the next episode. I clenched my jaws. It hadn't worked.

I thought she wouldn't be pleased with me not paying attention to her. Maybe it was time I headed to bed. I couldn't last another episode of martin. Jeanine turned to me once more. I didn't look at her. She didn't look back at the television. She looked at me, hoping that she could get something out of me. I was certain that if she asked me anything, I would say or do it.

"Babe? What's up with you?" She asked.

I didn't reply to her. My eyes were still fixed on the television. Suddenly, the show became interesting. I could see her frown from the corner of my eyes. It was working.

"Devon?" She called again.

I gave her no response. Call me petty, but I was happy with it. I wasn't that eager to reply to her, which was weird. She placed her face on my chest, not wanting to watch the show anymore. I felt like I had overdone it. If she wasn't watching her favorite show, this was worse than I expected. I turned my attention to her and lifted her face from my chest. She didn't look at me. Her face was still bent down. She was probably feeling sad right now.

"Babe. I'm sorry," I apologized.

She still didn't look up at me. I placed my hand under her chin and lifted her face. Then, her brown eyes gazed at me in the dark room. The only source of light was the one coming from the television. She was sad.

"I'm sorry," I said again.

"Why would you do that?" She asked.

I sighed.

"I was just being petty," I replied.

Her face switched into a stern look. I had to confess now.

"I was still mad about what you did to me at breakfast," I said.

She nodded her head in understanding.

"Let me make it up to you," she said.

My cheeks heated up as I heard that. I knew what was going to happen next. She laid back on my chest and brought her face to mine. I wrapped my hands around her to generate some warmth between us. Jeanine placed her lips on mine and began kissing me gently.

I closed my eyes and felt her lips on mine. My body was heating up slowly. I could feel the blood rushing into my dick and making it hard. It didn't take long before I was fully erect. Jeanine kissed me even more, and I moved my tongue inside her.

One of her hands left my chest and went down to my shorts. She held my dick, and I moaned in her mouth. She broke out from the kiss and went down slowly. I watched her with delight. I could feel my dick throbbing already. It was getting ready to be devoured by my mistress. Jeanine pulled down my shorts, and I slipped my legs out of them. She threw it away, and I chuckled. Jeanine then reached into my underwear and brought out my dick. I was ready for an amazing round of head. Last night was insane. She had driven me crazy with her mouth work.

Jeanine kissed the tip of my dick, and I shuddered in excitement. It was about to go down. She placed my dick into her mouth next, and it was warm and wet, I gasped and laid back on the couch. I was ready, but she hadn't begun yet. Jeanine moved my dick in and out of her mouth as she stroked it gently.

Her tongue laid underneath my dick and gave me a sensation that I didn't feel often. I moaned out into the room in pleasure. My body was getting excited, and I could feel the pleasure she provided running like electricity throughout my body. I was on another planet entirely. Jeanine increased the tempo of her sucking, and I opened my eyes to look at her. She was working me out. I could barely see her, but she was working wonders below me.

I quickly packed her hair and held it up in a ponytail. She took my dick out of her mouth and chuckled. I didn't want her to stop. I placed my dick into her mouth and began working my way between her jaws. I closed my eyes as I stroked my dick in her throat.

I could feel her throat clamming around and letting go and doing it all over again as she gagged on my dick. It made me go insane. I finally let go of her and took my dick out of her mouth. She gasped for breath, and I relaxed, stroking my dick slowly. Then, I could feel her rise beneath me and sit on my dick.

She was still clothed as I saw her silhouette take off her shirt gently. Then she stood up from me and took off her panties. I reached for my waist and slid off my underwear immediately, flinging it away. I laid back on the couch and waited for her. Jeanine came back and sat on me again. I could feel my dick lying across the entrance of her walls. She was wet already.

It usually happened when she sucked my dick. Jeanine placed her hands on my chest and began caressing it. I moaned out softly and closed my eyes. Then, she raised her hips slightly and picked up my dick which was still bold and hard. She placed it inside her slowly, and I felt my dick spread her walls apart as I slipped into her pussy. Jeanine moaned slowly and sat back on me as my dick filled the space between her walls.

She bit her lower lip and began working her hips on me. She moved upwards and downwards slowly at a steady tempo. She was warm and wet, and I could feel my dick throbbing inside her. It was somewhat crazy and unexplainable. I heard her moan out, and my body shuddered in excitement.

I held her waist as she rocked me like she was riding a carousel. She placed her hands on my chest, increasing the tempo of her thrust. I could feel her ass cheeks slam against my groin with each thrust she produced. I smacked her ass cheeks with my palm, and she moaned out. Our slippery and warm connection delivered huge pleasure flowing through my veins.

I didn't want it to stop. I wanted to take control of myself. It was her chance, and I knew she wouldn't disappoint me. Jeanine slowed down and paused to catch her breath. I knew she was tired, and it was my turn now. I arranged myself properly and lifted her ass cheeks.

Then, I plunged my dick deep into her pussy. Jeanine screamed out in pleasure. I clenched my jaws and began penetrating her roughly. She couldn't resist the moans that sprang out of her mouth like melodies. She didn't know she was screaming my name and singing to me.

"Oh my goodness! That's it, babe! Pound me!" She begged.

I moved in more profoundly, and my thrusts began faster. I bent her over and made her head rest on my chest. That opened her even wider.

"Devon!" She screamed as my dick ate up the space her walls provided.

I moved my waist upwards and let my dick plunge in and out of her with extreme force. She had wanted to make it up to me. This was just perfect for that. She had given me the keys to her body, and now I was in total control. I was the dictator and did whatever I pleased with her because she was mine, and I was hers only.

I clenched my jaws and wrapped my hands around her. I could

feel her trembling. It meant that orgasm was creeping in on her. This was her final lap, so I had to make it worth it. I lifted my waist from the couch to make myself comfortable and began my thrust again. Jeanine gripped my shoulders and began screaming my name once more.

The neighbors were probably hearing her right now. My waist slammed against her ass cheeks roughly with each stroke I adorned her with. It made a clapping sound which complimented her screams like melodies in a duo. I could feel Jeanine's nails digging into my skin. She was causing me harm, but that didn't stop me from intruding on her walls. Her body was trembling now, and I could feel her body go rigid. She was about to orgasm.

"I'm cummming!" She screamed.

Her walls gripped me right as she climaxed on my dick. Her body became limp against me, but that didn't stop me from thrusting. I could feel a torrent rise in me. It made me shudder in excitement. Our connection became more slippery, and it made it even more divine.

I didn't want anything to put us apart. My torrent came like a volcano. I could feel it boiling up from beneath as it approached the top. With each thrust I gave her, I could feel it rise higher. And then, I couldn't hold it back. My whole body shuddered in excitement as my volcano exploded. I burst my seed inside her with full force as I climaxed. Jeanine moaned as my seed spilled inside her. When I was done, I let go of her and laid back on the couch, wasted. We both kept silent as we recovered our breath.

"That was amazing," she said, and I couldn't agree more.

21 A Throuple

DEVON

The doorbell rang, and Jeanine was already rushing downstairs to see who it was. We both had an idea of who it would be. There was only one person that would be able to pop up at the house without letting us know. Come to think of it, we rarely had visitors, it was just us against the world. We lived alone without problems from the outside world, and I loved that.

As Jeanine ran to the door, I opened my closet to look for something to wear. I was still wrapped in my towel and worried about what I would wear. Jeanine and I had been discussing having a few threesomes to spice up our love life. Tonight we would experience one of the first ones we had in mind. When Jeanine had first told me about the threesome, I thought she had been bluffing. It was when she assured me of choosing who I wanted to have sex with that I knew that she was serious. I had thought that choosing her best friend would send a clear message that I wasn't that interested in it, and she would break it off.

But she had accepted and had chosen Chris, my boss, as her partner. That was going to be the strangest threesome. As for Phoebe, we both knew that she had a crush on me. I didn't need to think about how she reacted when Jeanine called her and invited her over. She was counting her blessings. Her fantasies were about to manifest themselves. Who knew what she would do to me if we ever had sex? I gulped hard.

This was all my fault. I should have never told JeanineI agree. Now I was going to pay the price for that. She would share me with her best friend, and in turn, I would have to share her with my boss. When I told my boss about this yesterday, he grinned like a kid on chrstmas about to open gifts. I had seen him talking to Jeanie at a party we were all at a few months back, but I felt it was nothing serious.

Jeanine wouldn't give him attention. Her attention was my possession, and mine was hers. I knew I had offended her by leaving her alone at the night party to speak to some coworkers. This was probably payback. A little sacrifice was me having sex with her best friend and her for a considerable price which was having sex with my boss.

I decided on a black shirt and pair of jeans to go downstairs in. As I entered the hallway I could hear their voices coming from downstairs. They were mumbling and giggling about whatever they were talking about. The nervousness seemed to increase as I got closer to the kitchen where they were sitting. I avoided eye contact with them as I made my way over to the fridge to get something to drink.

" Um excuse me sir, you can't speak" Phoebe asked playfully.

"Of course I can, it looked like you ladies were in a serious conversation and I didn't want to interrupt" I said walking over to give her a hug to lighten the mood even more.

I had to face my fears. It was just a one-time thing. There was no need to get unccmfortable about it.I made my way to the living room to get comfortable while they finished their conversation. Little to my surprise they got up and followed behind me. Phoebe raised her eyes at me when she sat down. I could see the naughty smile on her face when she looked at me. She was probably thinking about the different positions she would put me in when we had the chance. I shuddered at that.

Phoebe was almost as gorgeous as Jeanine, but she wasn't my type. She had beautiful black hair which stopped at her shoulders, and her brown eyes were dazzling. I walked down to a different couch to give the girls space to talk to each other. I decided to focus on television. I picked up the remote and switched the channel.

The highlight of the football game last week was on, and I decided to watch that. I didn't have the opportunity to watch the game earlier because Jeanine didn't let me get out of bed. She hadn't had enough of me that evening. I watched Jeanine and Phoebe through the corner of my eyes and saw Phoebe staring at me lustfully again. I returned my focus to the television. Her look was tempting, and I could only imagine all the naughtiness she had in her thoughts.

"So, Phoebe, would you like me to get you anything?" Jeanine asked.

"Yeah. Some orange juice will do," she replied. "I know you always have that."

Jeanine chuckled as she stood up from the couch.

"You know me too well, girl," she said as she left the room.

The room became silent as she left. I knew that Phoebe was still staring at me. I decided to have a look. I turned to her, and she still had those lustful eyes on me. I gulped hard and tried to focus my attention on another thing. I didn't want to be looking at her throughout the short period that Jeanine would spend in the kitchen.

"So, Devon. How are you doing?" She asked.

"I…I'm fine," I stuttered in reply.

She smirked at me.

"I know why you chose me," she said.

I couldn't believe that she was bringing that up. Why would she think that I liked her that way? Well, I had chosen her. It was my fault. I didn't have any other person in mind to choose from. The last set of women I would choose would be my coworkers. It would send some suspicions to Jeanine, and I didn't know how I would feel having sex with people I work with. It could make the rounds in the office, and I didn't want that.

"We shouldn't be talking about that," I said.

"Oh, come on, Devon. I know you have a crush on me," she said. "It's fine. You ain't bad yourself."

I clenched my jaws and tried to pull myself together. I also hoped that Jeanine would come back soon and end this madness. My prayers were answered as Jeanine came back seconds later into the room with a glass of orange juice in her hand. She handed it over to Jeanine and sat back down on the couch. I returned my focus to the television, but the highlight was already over. I cursed under my breath.

"I hope you and Devon got along?" She asked.

I turned to her and gave her a questionable look. What was she trying to insinuate?

"He's cool," Phoebe replied.

Jeanine gave me an evil smile. I didn't particularly appreciate where this was going at all.

"Hey, Phoebe. Come with me. I want to show you something," Jeanine said.

"Okay," Phoebe said, rising from her seat with the glass still in her hand.

Jeanine stood up, too, and they both headed upstairs. When they did, I sighed in relief and relaxed on the couch. I was alone now, and that was enough for me. I was not too fond that Jeanine was using this to torture me. It was my fault in the first place. I shouldn't have doubted her, now she was making me pay for that.

What had even brought this silly idea into her mind? I wondered. Was it because of Chris? I didn't think so. Jeanine didn't even look at him twice. She wasn't even looking at him when I arrived. So what was it? An impulse idea? Most likely.

I sighed and smacked my forehead with my palm. Minutes passed, and I hadn't heard from either of them. What were they still doing upstairs? It was time we got into action so that I could get it out of my system. I wanted to move on from this fast. This would probably be in Phoebe's head for a lifetime. It was all my fault.

I sat back on the couch and waited for them, but they still hadn't returned. The whole house seemed quiet because I didn't hear their giggles and voices anymore. That was it. They were stalling this. I had to go in and check up on them. I stood up from the couch and headed up the stairs.

There were still no voices coming from up there. This made me worried. I arrived at the door and heard some muffled sounds from inside. Were they talking in low voices? I opened the door and stepped into the room. What I saw surprised me. Jeanine was on top of Phoebe, and they were both naked. They seemed to be touching themselves already. You could tell from the 69 positions there were in.

To my greatest surprise, I felt my dick spring up. It stood hard and erected. I looked at it, completely amazed. I was intrigued by the position they were in. It turned me on instantly, and I wanted to join them immediately. Jeanine looked up at me and smiled. Her smile made my dick throb. Phoebe got up from underneath Jeanine and looked at me. She scanned my entire body and then stopped at my pants. I saw a smile spread across her face.

"Someone looks hungry," she said.

I chuckled slowly. I couldn't believe that she could be this beautiful naked. Her breasts were perfectly round, and her hips were amazing. Her ass cheeks were almost similar in size to Jeanine's. I could feel my blood boiling. I had to get in now. There was no holding back anymore. I had been crazy to think that this would be awkward. Maybe it was going to be perfect after all.

"You guys started without me," I said.

"We couldn't keep waiting for you," Jeanine said. "So we had to warm up ourselves for you."

I bit my lower lip as I watched them stare at me completely naked. I reached for my shirt and pulled it off. Phoebe looked at my dick, biting her lip. I knew she was dying to have a taste of it. She turned to Jeanine with some pleading eyes, and Jeanine nodded at her. She smiled and turned to me, crawling out of bed.

She crawled slowly to me and arrived at my knees. My dick was throbbing beneath my underwear. I couldn't wait to get started on this. She came to kneel in front of me. Jeanine joined her on her knees as well. I can't describe the feeling at this moment. But

I can tell you that I was definitely a king on his throne. a
"I see why you two are best friends," I said.

They both giggled. Jeanine turned to Phoebe and kissed her. I
watched them patiently, my dick throbbing hard against my
underwear. I drooled as they kissed each other passionately. An
idea came into my mind. We should be doing this often. Phoebe
broke out of the kiss after a while. I thought that they had
forgotten about me for a split second there. Phoebe bit her lower
lip and touched my dick. I closed my eyes and gasped in
excitement. She caressed it slowly while it was still in my
underwear. Jeanine was loving the site but she didn't hesitate to
assist Phoebe in pulling it out to get a better view.

She reached for my pants and unbuckled them. I waited patiently.
Jeanine was the best dick sucker I knew. Phoebe would have to
do something better or extraordinary to impress me. She entered
my underwear after unzipping my pants and brought out my dick.
It was hard and bold. I could see her eyes widen in disbelief as
she pulled it out. It was better and bigger than she had expected,
I guess. I could only smile at her, thoroughly amused.

"Just the way you describe it Jeanine" Phoebe said

She must have been discussing with Phoebe how big my dick
was. Phoebe bit her lower lip and stroked my dick gently. Her
hand was so warm, and it was soft also.. She stroked me gently
and then spit on it. She made it slippery and continued stroking
it. I was floored. I could feel my blood boiling in excitement.

She hadn't even really begun yet, but I could feel the excitement
rushing through my veins. I gulped hard. She was going to
conquer me. I couldn't let that happen. Jeanine couldn't make me
submit from head, but the lips on Phoebe made me question if I
would be able to contain myself.

"I didn't believe Jeanine when she said you were this big," she admitted.

I knew that Jeannie had been talking about me. That just confirmed my suspicion. Maybe they had been planning this threesome before now. Perhaps that had been the reason she had brought the idea. Jeanine was smart. Very smart. I had to hand it to her.

"Then you know that it would be difficult to satisfy a man like me," I said.

Phoebe turned to look at Jeannine, and they laughed at me. It confused me. Jeanine looked up at me, barely able to hold her laugh.

"You would be surprised," she said.

I didn't know what she meant by that. Phoebe continued stroking my dick while Jeanine observed. Then, she licked the tip of my dick, cleaning the precum off it. As her tongue touched my dick, I felt a jolt of electricity flow up my spine. Damn! Her touch was so mind-blowing.

Phoebe chuckled before placing my dick on her wet warm tongue. I gasped and closed my eyes. She wrapped her mouth around my dick and began sucking it. I had to open my eyes and look at what she was doing. Jeanine was watching her sternly. She was doing something indescribable with my dick in her mouth. It felt like my knees would buckle at any moment. I couldn't give up just yet. Jeanine pulled back her hair and held it for her as she sucked me. *Friends helping each other*, I thought.

Jeanine took my dick from her and placed it into her mouth. I sighed in relief as my dick entered into familiar territory. I held Jeanine's head as she took my dick down her throat. She was deepthroating me already. This looked like a competition to me. Phoebe didn't want to be left out. She went underneath me and began sucking on my balls.

I closed my eyes and moaned out in pleasure. My body was shuddering with the amount of pleasure that it was being fed by these two. Who said that threesomes couldn't be awesome? I pushed my dick downwards into Jeanine's throat, and her throat muscles made way for my dick. I could feel her gag on my dick while Phoebe was sucking up my balls. Phoebe had taken me by surprise. I had to start looking at her differently from today onwards.

Phoebe scoffed at her as she stopped sucking my balls. It seemed like she hadn't been impressed by Jeanine. She held my dick and began stroking it roughly. Jeanine's saliva was still on my dick, making it slippery and warm. Phoebe placed it into her mouth and began sucking it again. I moaned out as my dick visited the insides of her mouth once more.

I held her hair and pushed my dick into and out of her mouth. She let go of my dick and let me do the thrusting. She opened her throat, and I pushed my dick in and out of her mouth. Jeanine got under and continued sucking my balls. I was in heaven already. I stopped thrusting and took my dick out of her mouth. I stepped back to look at both of them. Both of them had saliva drooling down their breasts. It was a lovely sight, and I couldn't help but smile. I began stroking my dick silently as I watched them.

"Damn. That was the shit," I confessed.

"I told you," Jeanine said, rising to her feet.

"So, are you impressed?" Phoebe asked, standing up too.

I smiled at her.

"Definitely," I replied.

"Then let's get to business," Jeanine said, getting closer to Phoebe.

She wrapped her hands around Phoebe and began kissing her. Phoebe smiled and kissed her back passionately. They grabbed each other's breasts and squeezed them pleasurably. I stroked my dick while watching them. Then, they broke out of the kiss and lay on the bed.

Phoebe lay down while Jeannine sat on her face. I knew Phoebe was going to give her the time of her life. I could see Phoebe's pussy calling me. I knew she was trying to tease and who was I to resist? I rushed to the bed and pounced on her. Jeanine reached for the drawers as Phoebe sucked on her pussy. She brought out her vibrator and closed the drawers back.

I smiled and licked Phoebe's clit. I felt her shiver. I placed my fingers into her walls which were so wet and warm and began thrusting them. I placed my tongue on her clit and played with it. Her body shuddered with excitement as she played with Jeanine's pussy. Jeanine was shuddering on top of her. Phoebe was doing a good job.

I took out my fingers and placed my tongue into Phoebe's pussy. I wiggled my tongue inside her, and she shuddered in excitement. I could feel her body trembling above me. I laughed in my mind. I was returning the favor from earlier. I could feel her walls contract around my tongue. Her body grew rigid, and she came on my tongue. Phoebe looked at me, panting.

"Give me your dick, Devon. I want that!" She begged.

I smirked and stroked my dick silently. Then, I placed my dick in her pussy and could feel her walls spread apart as they ushered me in. She was so tight. I raised her hips and moved inside her. Jeanine handed her the vibrator, and she began using it on her.

The buzzing sound erupted into the air in collaboration with Jeanine's moans. I clenched my jaws and made my thrusts deeper. I could feel her walls twitching on both sides of my dick. I reckoned another orgasm was around the corner. I lifted her legs higher and plunged in more profound. She screamed out as I reached the ends of her walls. I poked them with each thrust I gave her. Jeanine, on the other hand, was trembling.

"I'm cummminggg!" She screamed before squirting on Phoebe's face.

Jeanine sighed and lay back on the bed. Phoebe's legs were trembling. I could feel her getting wetter on either side of my dick. I increased the tempo of my thrusts.

"Yesssss! Don't stop, Devon! Don't you dare!" She screamed. "Fuck me!"

I raised my waist and plunged deeper. Her body trembled with excitement as I went deeper. I could feel her body go rigid below me. Her walls twitched again, and she orgasmed, spilling juice on me.

"Fuck!" She screamed as she climaxed.

I stepped out of her walls, and she laid aside. Jeanine came into view, and I smiled at her. She came and lay in front of me, spreading her thighs wide. I plunged my dick into her, and her walls welcomed me. I began my thrust immediately, not slowing down. She was already warm and wet from her last orgasm. Phoebe rose from the bed and sat on Jeanine's face. Jeanine placed her tongue inside her and began wiggling it.

Phoebe closed her eyes and rode her face. I, on the other hand, was busy pounding hard. My dick plunged in and out of her, and her cum began to coat me. I raised my hips and moved in more quickly. I could feel my body trembling in excitement. I couldn't orgasm, not this soon. I clenched my jaws and concentrated on my thrusts. My waist slammed against her thighs which each thrust I administered to her.

Jeanine began trembling below me. Phoebe had now leaned over and was rubbing the Vibrator on her clit, also watching my dick ramming in and out of her best friend.

"Baby Fuck!" Jeanine screamed.

I knew she wouldn't be able to take it anymore. And so I had to finish her off. I spread her legs wider, and her walls opened up even further. I moaned out as I reached the end of her walls. I slammed my dick in and out of her, and she was screaming. Her walls twitched, and I felt them grip me tightly.

"Baby! I'm..." she tried to say, and she orgasmed.

It wrecked her body to the point that she couldn't speak. I got out of her, and Phoebe took the vibrator off. I stroked my dick and waited for who was next. Phoebe smirked at me and stepped forward. She turned around and arched her waist for me. Her ass cheeks spread out, and it intrigued me. Jeanine got below her and placed her tongue on her clit. I rammed my dick into her walls and began my thrusts once more. I felt my hips slap against her ass cheeks with each thrust I administered. Her ass cheeks were soft, and I couldn't help but smack them.

"Fuck! Spank me harder!" She said,

I spanked her harder this time, and she moaned out. I plunged in deeper and continued thrusting in and out of her. I could feel her shivering below me. She was heading towards another orgasm. I couldn't hold back any longer too. Her ass cheeks were too soft. I felt a torrent rise quickly above me. It was a strong wave heading towards shore with great speed. My body trembled as orgasms crept into my veins. When the wave approached me, I got out of her quickly.

"I'm cumming. Quick!" I said.

They both got off the bed and went on the knees before me with their tongues out in unison. I closed my eyes and sprayed my seed on their faces as I climaxed. I shuddered in excitement as my seed splashed on their cheeks and foreheads. When I was done, I sighed and looked at them. They both had my cum on their face and smiled back at me. It was a beautiful sight.

22 Double Dose

JEANINE

I was getting excited already. Chris wasn't here yet, but I wanted to get to the best part already. Devon had had his turn, and it was now mine. He had devoured my best friend and me. She and I had a great show for him, and he had the time of his life last week. This week, it was going to Chris and us.

I was still wondering why I had chosen Chris, of all people. I didn't like him. The same man that I had been snubbing at the party that night, but now, I was about to have sex with him. It looked like he had won without trying. Devon had done so wrong to choose my best friend.

I had always known that Phoebe wanted to fuck him. She had begged me multiple times to let her have a one-night stand with him, and I had rejected that every time. You should have seen the excitement on her face when I told her I wanted to do a threesome with her and Devon. Her dreams had come through.

If I wanted a threesome with someone special, I would have gone with his brother. His elder brother, Dishon, was close to being as sexy as him. Sometimes, I wondered what they were fed in that family. Even his sisters were damn sexy.

I couldn't lie that I had enjoyed the threesome with Phoebe. We had done so many nasty things to each other that day, and surprisingly that had strengthened our bond. I was planning on another threesome with her. I didn't know if Devon would be excited. I knew he didn't like Phoebe, but I was confused when he chose her.

I was sure now that he had changed his mind about that. Phoebe had opened both of us to different areas of our bodies. How was Phoebe that good? Maybe I had underestimated her a little. Phoebe was the one who had given me my first blow job lessons. I knew she would make Devon's eyes bulge, and it did.

Phoebe also made me go crazy when she touched my walls. Remembering her wet tongue inside my walls made me shudder in excitement. I had to get back with her for another threesome. After the three of us had finished the sex, we had all laid on the bed and dozed off till evening. By the time we had woken up, Phoebe was gone. I had asked her why she had left, and she had told me that she didn't want to intrude in our privacy. That was so sweet of her.

I finished dressing up and turned around to look in the mirror again. I looked perfect. I was surely going to mesmerize Chris. I could see the way he had been staring at me when Devon had left to talk to his coworkers. He had been looking for the best opportunity to pounce on me, and he had found one later. Thinking about Devon, I wondered how he felt when he told Chris about the throuple.

He had told me that Chris had accepted so quickly that he had been amazed. That had been the same thing that happened with Phoebe and me. What did he expect? People were waiting for us outside if we ever broke up. The thought of seeing Phoebe with Devon made me shiver. I couldn't let that happen.

I blew my reflection in the mirror a kiss and stepped out of the room. I hurried downstairs and found Devon inspecting the food I had prepared earlier. At first sight, I thought that he was trying to have some before Chris arrived. And then I realized that he was being paranoid. He was anxious about this like I had been last week. He would get over it soon enough.

"Babe? What are you doing?" I asked.

"Just cross-checking," he replied, walking away from the kitchen.

I raised an eyebrow at him.

"Cross-checking what exactly?" I questioned.

As he opened his mouth to speak, the doorbell went. He closed it quickly while I looked at him sternly. The doorbell went off again, and I left him to answer it. That was probably Chris. I arrived at the door and swung it open. It revealed Chris in a white shirt and a pair of jeans, smiling at me. He looked so much younger in this. His black hair was brushed perfectly, and his brown eyes were shining. He looked cute, to be honest. He had that bright smile on his face, which I had found uncomfortable that night.

"Jeanine," he called sweetly. "So nice to see you again."

"Chris. What a pleasant surprise," I said sarcastically. "Come on in."

He nodded and stepped into the house. I closed the door behind him. He walked into the living room and took a seat on the couch. Devon walked into the room and smiled when he saw him. Chris stood up to meet him.

"Devon, my man," he said, shaking him.

"What a pleasant home you have here," he added.

Devon laughed as he shook his hand. I wondered why Devon

was always so formal with him. Maybe it was because Chris was his boss? Or perhaps he was trying to impress him too? I didn't know.

"Thank you, sir. That means a lot coming from you," he said.

Chris let go of his hand, and they sat down. I watched them from behind. Devon signaled me with his eyes to come and have a seat with us. I just wished I could tell him that I didn't want to bother them, but I had to go and sit with them. It would probably be boring because they would talk mostly about work, and I didn't know what to do. I sighed and finally took a seat on a different couch.

Devon looked at me with an evil smirk. He was doing the exact thing I did to him last week. I loved it when he always wanted to pay me back. He looked so cute every time he did that.

"So. How's it going?" Chris asked.

"Nothing much," Devon replied. "Work just gets more tedious with each week."

"You know, Devon. There's a vacancy for the manager of the productive unit. I would like for you to take that position," he said.

Devon's eyes almost popped out of their sockets. He was startled, and so was I. I turned to Chris, and he looked at me. He gave me a wink at the end, which made me frown. To me, I felt like he was about to use Devon.

"M…me, sir?" Devon asked, stuttering.

"Yes, Devon. You're hardworking, and you surely have a way with words. It would be good for the company's growth," Chris replied.

It looked like Devon was froze. He had been unresponsive for some seconds, and I was starting to get worried about him. He was probably trying to process what was happening, just like at the party that day. This was big for him, and I was so happy for him. However, I had my doubts that it was completely legit.

Chris was probably playing him and was after something at the end. And I was guessing that something was me. It was sad because no matter what he would do for Devon or me, I wouldn't dare date him. He was cute, I could give him that, but he wasn't my type. I was sure that he had his way of charming ladies at his company. Sadly, those charms wouldn't work on me. My eyes were fully fixed on Devon.

"Are you certain about this, sir?" Devon asked, finally waking up from his trance.

"Never been more certain, Chris replied.

"Jeeezzz! Thank you, sir," he said.

Chris chuckled slowly.

"Don't thank me yet. First, you have to apply for the position," he said. "I want to see your credentials."

"I will do just that," Devon said.

Chris smiled at him and then turned to me. I was giving him a suspicious look. Maybe it was legit, after all and his request from Devon made me almost believe him. Almost. Devon was smiling widely now. He was probably lost in thinking about how he would fit in his new office. I was happy for him. He deserved to be this happy. I just hoped that Chris wasn't playing with his feelings. I would be so mad if I found out.

"So, are we going to eat or not?" He asked.

"Sorry. My bad. Let's go over to the dining," Devon offered, rising to his feet.

Chris rose, too, with a smile on his face, and we all walked to the dining. Chris and Devon took a seat while I picked up the meal and began dishing it out. It was my famous chicken casserole, and I was sure Chris would like it. Chris was already drooling when I dished out the food. I didn't know if it was real or if he was doing so to make me feel good about myself.

I wanted him to taste it first. Chris picked up his fork and dug into the casserole. I took a seat beside Devon and began eating too. Devon was too excited to know what to do next. He was still holding his fork and smiling down at his food.

"Babe. Come on," I said. "Dig in."

He scratched his head as he snapped out of his reverie. He looked pretty embarrassed.

"Sorry about that," he said.

"It's fine," I assured him. "You deserve this."

He smiled at me and began eating. Chris, on the other hand, had gotten further in his meal. He seemed to be actually enjoying the meal. That made me smile. I knew that he would be impressed with the casserole. It was my grandma's recipe. I could never share it with anybody that wasn't in the family, not even Devon, at least not until we got married.

I began eating my dish, and I could feel my tongue dance in

excitement. I was blown away by my dish. It looked like I had made it perfectly this time.

"Damn, Jeanine. I have to hand it to you. This is delicious," Chris confessed.

Devon chuckled as he ate. I wondered what amused him.

"Seems like you underestimated her," he said.

Chris laughed.

"I sure did," he said.

I rolled my eyes and concentrated on the dish. Chris was almost done with his dish. Devon, on the other hand, was halfway through his. I ate gently, savoring the work of my hands. I felt so confident making something this good. Maybe I had upgraded the family's recipe. That would be a big deal for me.

Chris finished his meal and wiped his mouth with the napkin as he leaned back on the seat. Devon and I were almost done with ours. When we were all done, I picked up the dishes and went to the sink. Devon and Chris retired to the living room to talk more. When I was almost done with the dishes, I heard someone come in. It was Devon. He wrapped his hands around my waist and kissed me on the back of my neck, sending shivers down my spine.

"Babeeee," I said.

"Shhhh," he hushed.

"Your boss is in the living room," I said.

"I don't care. Let's ditch him and have some fun upstairs," he suggested.

"But what about the…."

I was stopped with another kiss on the neck. My body was trembling beneath his touch. I wanted more. So, I cleaned the last dish and placed it in the cupboard. Then, I motioned for him to come to me with a smile on my face. He kissed me on the lips, and it felt amazing.

"Fine. Let's go," I accepted.

He flashed a smile at me. He held out a hand for me, and I took it. He grabbed me and rushed me out of the kitchen. I could hear the television sounds coming from the living room. Chris was probably glued to the program he was watching. This gave Devon and me an advantage. It also gave me a realization. Devon would never share me with anybody. I liked that, but it also gave me another insight. He was probably more insecure than I was. Maybe he had been talking about himself that night. It was so amusing now that I had realized it on my own.

We rushed up the stairs and headed into the bedroom. I got in, and Devon closed the door behind me. I turned to him and saw him smiling devilously as he leaned against the door. I wanted to ask him to get over here but decided against it quickly. It would ruin everything. I would go to him personally. I walked to him and wrapped my hands around his waist. Then, I closed my eyes and kissed him.

He was so excited. I could feel his muscles flexed beneath me. He was enjoying this. Why wouldn't he? Devon wrapped his hands around me, breaking my grip, and kissed me back roughly. I loved that. He was as eager as I was. I wondered what was making him this excited. Then I remembered that Chris had offered him a better position at work. I loved that he would bring that excitement to the bed. I was going to enjoy this.

I pulled out of his kiss and reached for his shirt. I pulled it off roughly, and he helped me. Next, I went on my knees quickly and unbuckled his jeans. They fell to the floor, and he stepped out of them. He was rock hard already, and I was drooling as I stared at his dick. It was large. He was ready for this.

I reached into his underwear and brought out his dick. It was large and warm. It was also throbbing in my hand. I bit my lower lip as I stared at it. I looked up at him, and he smiled down at me. I was about to worship him once again. I placed a kiss on his dick, and he moaned out.

Suddenly, the door behind us swung open. It was the bathroom door. My heart almost leaped out of my mouth. I turned around and saw Chris standing by the door, completely naked. He was hard as well and surprisingly large. He wasn't as long as Devon, but he was as thick as that. I looked at Devon in surprise, who was laughing at me. They had deceived me. I had thought that Chris was watching television in the living room. I didn't know that while I had been in the kitchen, they had plotted this. Their plan worked because I was so surprised.

"You guys almost started without me," Chris said, coming forward.

"Baabbee!" I said to Devon.

He smirked at me in response.

"You're going to have quite a feast," he told me.

I giggled at that. I sure was going to. Chris came and stood beside Devon. I stared down at both of their dicks. They were both thick and large, but Devon's stood out because he was longer. I bit my lower lip and was confused about who to suck first.

Since Chris was our guest, I decided to give him a special treat and go for him first. I shifted slightly to his side and held his dick. It was large. I spit on it and began stroking it gently. Chris bent his head backward and moaned out. He was living the dream. He was going to have sex with me. That was what he had wished for since he first saw me at the party, and now he would get that.

I placed his dick in my mouth and began sucking it. Chris grunted in pleasure, and I loved my tongue over his large dick in my mouth. Devon, on the other hand, watched us as he stroked his dick gently. I was eying his next. His chocolate brown dick would always be more attractive and dangerous than any other I would ever encounter. I stroked Chris as I sucked him gently. He pulled up my hair into a ponytail in his hand and held it up for me. Then, he began pushing his dick deeper into my mouth. I could feel it go down my throat.

I relaxed my throat muscles and let him go deeper. Chris gasped as he felt his dick go deeper down my throat. I held my throat muscles back and let him go even more profoundly. I could feel him cuss under his breath. I began gagging on his dick as my lungs cried out for air. Devon, on the other hand, kept on watching with a smile on his face. I could see Chris' eyes roll backward in pleasure. He was going insane. Phoebe would be proud of me. Chris took his dick out of me, and I gasped for breath. His dick was soaked with my saliva.

I coughed a little, then headed to Devon. Devon smiled as he saw me come closer. He knew what was about to happen. I opened my mouth wide and brought out my tongue to welcome his long and turgid soft bone. Devon stroked it one more time before placing his dick on my tongue. He slid it on me slowly and sighed in satisfaction. I finally covered my mouth around his dick, and he moaned in pleasure. Devon moved his dick in and out of my mouth as he sought for satisfaction. His dick poked the end of my walls because I hadn't opened my throat for him to get in. My throat was probably going to feel sore after this, and I was probably going to need some meds. I was going crazy for both of them.

Devon got out of my mouth and let me breathe. I gasped for air and breathed it in slowly. My lungs pinched with each breath I took. I didn't know how long I could last with this pain. Chris watched us while stroking his dick. My saliva was still on it but was about to dry up. He came closer and gave me his dick. I held him and began stroking him gently. Chris moaned out in pleasure.

Devon placed his dick into my mouth and slid it down my throat. He was thrusting slowly, moving toward the ends of his throat. Damn. I had rarely seen him go that deep before. I couldn't hold it back anymore. I gagged roughly on his dick, and he moaned as he continued thrusting deeper. I was going crazy. I felt like I was going to black out any time soon. I was stroking Chris' dick and swallowing Devon at the same time. Talk about multitasking.

Finally, Devon stepped out of my mouth, and I gasped for breath, coughing roughly. I let go of Chris' dick and tried to catch my breath. Devon and Chris stepped back to give me some space. I stood up from the floor slowly, feeling quite dizzy. They both were looking at me with concerned faces. There was nothing to be worried about. I had done this more than a hundred times. I would be more than just fine. I smiled at them, and they stared at me as if they had just seen a ghost.

"What? Are we going to get this party started or what?" I asked.

They looked at each other, wholly flustered, and shrugged. I smiled when I saw that and laid back on the bed. Chris stepped forward first. He stroked his dick gently as I spread my legs.

Devon, on the other hand, climbed the bed above me and began stroking his dick too.

Chris placed his dick into my walls, and I moaned out. His huge dick spread my walls apart, stretching them to a certain point. I reached for Devon's dick above me and began stroking it. Devon bit his lip and closed his eyes as I stroked him to pleasure. Chris lifted my legs and barged in deeper. I screamed out in pleasure. Then, he began his thrusts quickly. He didn't even start slowly. He went straight to the point. I could feel his dick ramming in and out of me. It sent tremors of pleasure down my spine. I was trembling already. My pussy was already wet from sucking both of their dicks.

Devon surprised me today. I thought he had been insecure about everything, and I had been quick to judge him. He looked like he was enjoying sharing me with his boss. His boss was ramming my walls to kingdom come while I was sucking his balls and stroking him.

I felt his hands on my breasts. My body shivered. He squeezed them softly, and I moaned out. Both of them were administering a substantial amount of pleasure throughout my body. I didn't want that to end.

I felt like I was on a different planet. Chris lifted my thighs even higher and plunged deeper. They were using me in search of ecstasy, and I loved that. I felt like a slut to both of them, which was enticing. Being used as a tool for sexual pleasure was more enthralling than I had thought. My whole body grew rigid, and my walls constricted around Chris' dick. I orgasmed, and I cried out in pleasure.

Chris took his dick out of me and stroked it. I let go of Devon's dick, and rose from my lying position. Devon laid down and invited me. I smiled and lay on top of him. Devon placed his dick into my walls, and I felt him go further than Chris. I screamed out in pleasure. I could feel Chris behind me. I wondered what he was trying to do there. Then, I felt his dick barge into my ass.

I yelled out into the room. He was stretching my walls out already, and so was Devon. I felt weak already, and my body was trembling beneath them. Devon started his thrust first before Chris joined in. They didn't start slowly. Devon was also ramming in and out of my walls, and Chris was doing the same to my ass.

They were both pounding me, and I couldn't do anything but let them take control of me. I was lying there while they forced their way in and out of my holes. I could feel myself juicing out from both holes. They were digging the lust out of me deeper in search of pleasure for all of us.

Devon pushed deeper, and I screamed out. Chris got the signal and also forced himself deeper. He was at the end of my walls. I screamed out in pleasure as my body trembled continuously. I was heading toward orgasm, and it was going to be a powerful one. I could feel it coming in.

It took control over my body, and I burst out on Devon, squirting on his lower body. Devon got off me, and so did Chris. It looked like they were about to cum too. I got on my knees on the bed, and they spilled their cum simultaneously on my face and breasts. When they were done, they sighed in relief. I opened my eyes and saw them give each other a look that seemed like a high five..

23 Passion

DEVON

I opened my eyes and gazed around. It seemed like I had a slight headache. My head was thumping a bit, and I wondered why. What had happened last night? I couldn't recall. I rose from the bed and looked out the window on my left. The sun was rushing into the room, and it looked pretty bright.

I slid back down on the bed and lay to my right. Jeanine was sleeping beside me. She looked tired as well. I still couldn't fathom what happened last night. How did we end up this tired and wasted?

I looked into the sheets and saw we were still in my underwear. That meant that we hadn't had sex. Then what had happened? Frustrated that I couldn't remember, I lay back on the bed and sighed. I was raking through my thoughts to find out what had happened last night, but all the memories I was getting weren't affiliated with it.

They were previous memories. I relaxed and closed my eyes, and maybe everything would return to me in time. I turned to my right and saw Jeanine smiling peacefully. It was like she was smiling in her dreams. At least she was having the time of her life there.

That brought back memories of two days ago. That was when we had a threesome with my boss. It had been so crazy that it left me in awe. How could I have agreed to that? I was chuckling softly now too. I couldn't lie that it had been so good. It was better than I had expected.

It looked like Jeanine had taught me a lesson for doubting her. I would never do such a thing again. It had been all my fault at first. It had indirectly started with me, but I didn't believe I would be doing a threesome with my boss. I wondered how he was going to see me at work now.

I closed my eyes and tried to relax. Yesterday was a Saturday. Where would I go on a Saturday with Jeanine? Then it hit me. Everything came flooding back. As I remembered each scene, I became more embarrassed with myself. How could I let myself do such a thing? It had been Jeanine's idea. It had to be. I would dare do that.

I realized that I had gone to a bar last night with Jeanine. I got drunk, and we sang karaoke at the bar. It wasn't very comfortable because I had been the lead singer, and the whole bar had been screaming our names afterward. I opened my eyes and placed my hand on my forehead. What the hell was that? Why had I gotten so reckless? Who had driven us home then?

I shook my head as I realized how irresponsible I probably was. It shouldn't be happening to someone like me. Jeanine had wanted someone mature since she was older than I was. But I had met my immaturity taken over, and I had disgraced ourselves at the bar last night. I didn't think I would be going back to that bar any time soon. It was best for us.

The chants were even more absurd than I had expected. I heard Jeanine moan beside me. I turned to her, and she turned around sleepily and kept her hand on my chest. Then, she moved her face to my chest and sighed in relief. I couldn't help but smile when I watched her sleep on my chest. I placed a hand on her hair and caressed her slowly. A sigh came from her again, and she opened her eyes.

Jeanine looked up at me, and I was displeased that I had woken her up. She looked so beautiful while she was sleeping. She was smiling at me now and knew she somehow remembered what had happened yesterday. Maybe she had been the one that had driven the both of us home. I'm sure she had fun watching me sing completely drunk. That had been so absurd. To think of that moment made me displeased. She was still smiling at me, and I was confident that she laughed at me inside.

"Good morning, baby," she greeted.

I gave her a stern look, and she didn't hide the fact that she was holding back her laughter. After a few seconds of angry stares, she burst out laughing, and I shook my head in disappointment. I felt so embarrassed about that.

"Why did you do that to me, Jeanine?" I asked.

"Do what?" She asked, still laughing.

I frowned at her.

"You know exactly what I'm talking about," I replied.

She was still laughing, and I was getting impatient and embarrassed. I folded my hands and looked away, not wanting to look at her and laugh at me anymore. Jeanine finally stopped after a while and wiped the tears off her face. She had begun tearing up while laughing. It must have been one hard laugh. She looked up at me and burst out laughing once more.

"Okay, Jeanine, I'm done here," I said, attempting to stand up from the bed.

She held me back, and I paused. She was still laughing, and I clenched my jaws to let her laugh it all out. After a few seconds, she finally stopped. She looked up at me, and I raised an eyebrow at her.

"Are you done laughing?" I asked.

"Babe…I'm sorry about that," she apologized.

I didn't accept that so easily. She had had so much fun watching me embarrass myself rather than help me. It wasn't fair at all.

"Why didn't you stop me from doing that to myself?" I asked.

"I tried to, but you didn't let me," she replied. "You were too drunk and were shouting at the bartender to hook us up next on the karaoke. I was embarrassed at first."

I sighed and frowned at myself. It sounded like something I would do if I were drunk. I guess I had disgraced her first before I embarrassed myself. Why had I even had so much to drink? Was it for the fun of it? Or was I trying to brush my mind off something? My guts were telling me it was the latter, but I found that hard to believe.

Jeanine moved closer to me and sat on me. She was so warm, and when she placed her hands on me, I felt my blood boil up. The recent times we had had sex, it had been with other people. Now we had each other to ourselves once more. It was better this way. Maybe having threesomes was just to ensure each other's trust. Now that was settled, it was best we got back to riding solo.

"I'm sorry, baby," she apologized. "I guess I should have stopped you."

"Shhhh," I hushed her, placing my index finger on her lip. "You don't have to apologize for anything. It was my fault."

Jeanine chuckled, and I wondered what was on her mind. I was sure that she was thinking about karaoke again. I frowned at that.

"I can't lie. You have a great voice," she said.

"Oh, come on, Jeanine. Didn't get me started," I begged.

"It's just a compliment, babe," she pointed out.

"Well, I don't want that kind of compliment," I said, looking up at her.

She chuckled hard, and I frowned one more time. She stopped soon and placed her hands on my face. They were warm and soft. I closed my eyes and felt them in my face. They were sending sparks throughout my body. I was in the mood now. I was feeling my dick start to grow turgid. I was sure she could feel it, too, from underneath her lap.

I felt her lips join mine as she kissed me. I was so pleased by the kiss. I closed my eyes and savored every moment of it. It was mind-blowing. The fact that we were together alone once again brought back a certain desire. I could also feel the comfort come back too. After the throuples we had had, I was certain that we were satisfied with the double doses we had gotten from both Phoebe and Chris. There was no need to feel insecure anymore. We were satisfied with one another and trusted each other fully.

Jeanine broke out from the kiss, and I opened my eyes to look at her. She was staring at me as I opened them and was still caressing my cheeks. I saw her bite her lower lip, and I knew what was coming next. Her brown eyes shone courtesy of the sunlight that washed on us through the window beside us. I felt her eyes penetrate the deepest and darkest places of my heart and illuminate them. She was special to me.

Jeanine stood up from the bed, and I could see her panties shape her ass cheeks perfectly. She was looking back at me and standing in the sunlight, which made her caramel skin shine. Damn! She was sexy. Covering her breasts was nothing, and she looked like a model advertising underwear. How could she look this sexy effortlessly?

"You want to join me?" She asked, heaving towards the bathroom door.

I didn't need to be told that again. I rose from the bed, and my stiff and swollen dick almost stuck out of my underwear. When she saw that, she couldn't help but chuckle. She opened the door and walked into the bathroom. Not wanting to waste time, I got into the bathroom after her and closed the door behind us.

Once in the bathroom, she had already stepped out of her panties, and I saw them heading towards my face. It landed there perfectly, and I could smell her. She smelled so good, and it seemed soaked already. I took the panties out of my face and sniffed them repeatedly. I looked ahead and saw her turning on the shower in the bathtub. I threw her panties to the floor and quickly took off my underwear. My dick bounced and stood rock hard.

She gestured for me to come forward with her finger, and I didn't disobey. I got into the shower and hugged her from behind. I could hear her moan as my dick rested on her ass cheeks. The water was warm and perfect for the conditions. Jeanine bent over and held the wall, arching her waist.

I bit my lip as I stared at her round cheeks. I smacked them softly before introducing my dick into her. I felt it spread her walls apart, which were so warm and wet. Damn! She had been ready for me all along. I didn't know how long I would last inside her. I began thrusting immediately. I was starting slowly, then realized I had to up the tempo. She was too warm to go slow.

"Oh yes! Fuck me, Devon!" She begged.

I placed my hand on her waist and began penetrating her faster. Jeanine held the walls and cried out in pleasure. My hips slapped against her ass cheeks with each thrust I gave her. My body was trembling with pleasure, and so was hers. I could feel Jeanine trembling already. She was getting wetter, and I knew it would only be a matter of time before she orgasmed.

I dug in deeper, and her body began shuddering. As I slammed my dick in and out of her, I could feel a tightness to her pussy. It wasn't coming as slowly as I had expected. She was ready to let go and so was I. I was going to burst in a matter of seconds.

"I'm cummming, Devon!" She cried.

"Me too, baby!" I said.

Her body grew rigid, and she orgasmed, spilling juice on my dick. My body grew numb as the orgasm took total control. I climaxed and shot my cum inside her.

***

JEANINE

I stepped out of the bathroom last. I was still feeling weak, and my legs felt like they were about to give out in moments. That had been a powerful orgasm. The sex had been short, but the orgasm had been amazing. There was an element in there that we hadn't ever experienced. If we had experienced such, it would have been a long time. That element was nothing else but passion. The feeling had coated us while we dug up each other to satisfaction.

It had been intense, and I loved every second of it. It was nice to finally have the feeling of each other in our arms once more with no third party. I couldn't deny the fact that the third party's involvement had been tasty and terrific but having just each other to ourselves once more gave me a fiery feeling. I felt alive while Devon was inside me, and I was dying to have such a feeling.

Maybe he would give that to me later. I was hoping for that. I had to tease him a little bit, and he would oblige. He always did. He yearned for me as much as I yearned for him. That was the reason we were inseparable. He understood that he was mine and that I was his.

I walked into the room with a towel wrapped around my chest. Devon was on the bed when I stepped in. He was on his phone texting someone. I reached for the closet and swung it open. Devon had already dressed, and was back on the bed. After burning out so many calories in the bathroom and consuming so much alcohol last night, I was starving, and I guess he was feeling the same way too.

I had to get ready and go down to prepare breakfast. My stomach was empty. I reached for my favorite ash-colored tracksuit pants and them on. Then I wore my tank top and closed the closet. I turned around, and Devon was still on his phone. Whenever he was on that thing, it looked like his mind had been swallowed into it. I had to get his attention quickly. I reached for the towel and threw it at him. It landed on his face perfectly.

A few seconds later, Devon rose from the bed and took the towel off his face, giving me a perplexing look afterward. I smiled widely at him, and he threw the towel away. I frowned at him.

"Hey. That was my towel," I said.

"You have like a zillion of those in the closet," he pointed out, returning to his phone.

" Yea right. I need your help to make breakfast," I said.

"Why would you need my help for that?" He asked, not looking up from his phone.

"Devon," I called impatiently.

"Yes?" He responded, not looking up from his phone.

That was starting to get on my nerves. I folded my hand and looked at him.

"Devon!" I called again.

He looked up at me finally and saw that I wasn't pleased with his attitude. He sighed and turned off his phone, getting off the bed. I smiled when I saw that.

"Fine," he grumbled.

I turned around and walked out of the room. He came down behind me sluggishly. I needed his attention in the kitchen to keep me company while I made breakfast. He had to be there. I didn't know why I needed that in the first place. Maybe I was falling for him all over again. It wouldn't be wrong. I would love to experience that sensation again.

When I first found out that I had been in love with him, I felt so alive. My emotions had been raging, and my mood had been boiling. It felt so good as I stared at his brown eyes. I could also remember my heart thumping hard when he gave me a trademark smile. That had made me want to dissolve in front of him.

I wondered how he was feeling too. Was he going through the same thing I was right now? I doubted. If he were, he wouldn't be so focused on his phone. I walked into the kitchen and looked at it. It was as clean as I had left it last night. Last night had been a bit blurry, but I had managed to get the both of us home safely. I couldn't believe that Devon had gotten that drunk, and I also couldn't blame him for that. It happened to the best of us.

Devon came into the kitchen and sat on the counter. I turned to him and furrowed my eyebrows. He shrugged his shoulders only and reached for the fruit bowl picking out an apple. He bit it and watched me.

"So. What's for breakfast?" He asked.

Without replying, I reached for the fridge and opened it, bringing out the crate of eggs. I placed them on the counter and closed back the fridge. I found Devon watching me tentatively. I rolled my eyes at him and turned to one of the cupboards where most of the cooking utensils were kept. I opened it and reached for one of the frying pans. I tried to reach for it, but it was somehow stuck.

I pulled hard and finally pulled it out. Just as I was about to close the cupboard, I saw two pots falling out of the cupboard and heading for my forehead. Before I could react, a hand appeared and held the pots together. I turned around and saw Devon holding the pots. He looked down at me and smirked. He kept the other pots in the cabinet and closed it.

"You should be careful," he said.

I looked into his brown eyes and felt myself go numb. The only thing I could do was nod at him in response. He looked at me worryingly once more.

"Are you okay?" He asked.

I nodded at him. He reached for me and held me by the waist. Our eyes were staring at each other. It looked like the world around us had paused. It looked like a movie. I thought that this only happened in fiction. Then, I felt Devon lower his head toward mine. I knew what was about to happen.

I could feel my heart thumping again. I closed my eyes and waited for impact. I felt Devon's lips come in contact with mine. It was warm and inviting. I couldn't help but kiss him back. I could feel the fiery sensation coming back. It was burning through my body and making my blood boil. I was getting excited, and my body began shuddering.

The kiss got intense, and he lifted me off the floor. The way Devon often lifted me from the floor always made me feel so feeble. He carried me away from the cabinet and placed me on the top of the counter. He broke off from the kiss and looked at me. I could see the burning sensation in his eyes. He wanted this too. I grew excited as I realized this.

He kissed me again and placed his hand underneath my chin, raising my face. I gave him access to my body completely to do with it as he pleased. Devon broke out from the kiss again and looked at me. I smiled at him.

He reached for my tank top and pulled it off. I let it slip off my body. He kept it on the counter, and my breasts popped free. He gazed at them and kissed them. I closed my eyes and held the back of his neck as he sucked on them. I felt my body on fire as he squeezed and sucked my breasts.

He was already driving me insane. I didn't know how much longer I could take it. Devon didn't slow down. He pulled away and made me rest on the counter. I laid back and let him take control. He reached for my tracksuit and pulled it downwards. I let it go, and it fell to the floor. I was fully naked now because I had no panties on. Devon reached for my legs and spread them apart. I moaned as I felt my legs open up. Then, I felt his tongue on my clit. I held back my moans as he played with it.

He was sending tremors of pleasure through my body. I didn't want him to stop. The passion element kicked in, and I could feel myself get wetter and wetter by the second. Devon took his time on my clit before putting his fingers into my pussy.I couldn't take much more of this.

Devon stopped for a while, and I wondered why he did so. Then, I felt a swollen object open up my walls. It stretched them, and I screamed out in pleasure. It was his dick. It was so warm and puffy that my walls gripped him tight. I could hear him moan right before he began delivering his strokes. I sat up and widened my legs to give him more room. His dick barged in deeper and headed to the end of my walls. I could feel him there already. He was ramming in and out of my pussy the same way he had always done.

"Oh, baby! Harder," I said.

He held my hips and increased the tempo of his thrusts. I bit my lower lip and bent backward as Devon stretched me out. My whole body was trembling, and I was on the verge of climax. I could feel a fire burning the insides of me. I was satisfied. I wanted this and more. I wanted him forever.

The climax came quickly and wrecked my whole body. My muscles grew rigid, and my walls spammed as I climaxed. I could hear Devon moan in pleasure. I felt him grow larger inside me, and a few seconds later, I felt his warm cum dripping from my walls. We both sighed, and I kissed him on the forehead. He reached for me and hugged me tightly. I loved him so much that the last weeks reminded me that I would never love another man the way I love Devon, and I was certain that no other woman would please him the way I did. We were meant for each other, which meant that we were inseparable. And inseparable was what we were going to be.

24. Silent Studies

Walking into the library was the easy part. There was an unspoken signal between the two of them, or at least she hoped so. This evening might be the time he finally made a move, and she was craving for him to do so. Jay was one of the older librarians, and a complete silver fox. As part of her college career, Aniyah hadn't exactly been a saint, and she'd discovered that she really enjoyed older men.

Thanks to her upbringing, having a man who was confident and sexy because of his intelligence was a total turn on. As soon as she talked to him for the first time to ask a question about a periodical, she saw his eyes drift to her tight sweater and felt a tingle between her legs. It wasn't like she was totally demure but having the innocence of youth inside her made her ignore the fact maybe he was standing a bit closer to her than he needed to, his hands gently on her lower back or her shoulder while he helped her go through the files on the library system to find what she was looking for.

Impossible to resist, one time she'd intentionally worn a shirt that showed off an impressive amount of cleavage, and as he stood over her, she could almost feel the eyes burning into her breasts, especially because her bra cups were clearly visible. That outfit had caused a couple of guys to almost walk into poles on her way home. The outfit she was wearing tonight was even sluttier, and there was a reason for that.

She wanted him, and Aniyah wasn't going to be denied what she was craving. When Jay stood over her staring at her breasts and she caught his eye, she glanced down and saw a generous bulge under his pants. He quickly adjusted, but it was enough to show her what he was packing, and it was more than enough for her. If it wasn't for the people around her the first temptation was just to unzip him and pull out his nice hard dick to start sucking it.

Maybe that would be possible tonight. But more than likely, what she really wanted to do was find a secluded part of the stacks where nobody was around and see if she opened the door, how quickly he would walk through it. She'd had sex in public before, and what Jay didn't know was that it was the easiest way to make her pussy explode. The thrill of possibly being caught just fueled her libido to an out of control level.

"Hi Jay, I'm really glad you're working tonight." She said as soon as he came over. "I need some more help and I'm hoping you can assist me."

His smile was devastating. She knew he probably had a line of co-eds out the door wanting to fuck a sexy older man, but she didn't care. Tonight was her night.

"I'd be happy to, like always Aniyah. What do you need help with? More research?"

It was time.

"Actually...I think what I need is you to show me where a certain thing is. I'm pretty sure it's somewhere private and I want to make sure I get it." If that didn't tell him everything he needed to know, then he was an idiot. The outfit plus the words were definitely enough.

Thankfully he wasn't a stupid man, and picked up what I was putting down right away. His smile broadened and when he slid his eyes down my outfit.

"I think what you need is probably up a few floors." He said with a smile. It was melting her. "I can definitely show you where you need to look."

"Sounds good." Aniyah sighed. Thankfully he was taking the lead and seemed to know exactly what she had in mind. Jay walked towards the elevators. Because it was still relatively early, there were lots of students still coming in and out, but Aniyah had intentionally arrived late enough that people would be leaving as well.

He pressed the button for the top floor. Looking at her, he continued to flirt a bit.

"I've seen you quite a few times before. You must be a really good student to spend this much time in the library." His eyes lingered on her blouse, and Aniyah felt her nipples tighten.

She giggled. "I don't know about that. But I will try my best. Whatever my professor wants, they get." It was an obvious innuendo of course. Standing so close to him, she could almost feel the tension between them. The elevator doors opened and Jay led her out. Aniyah was slightly disappointed that there were a few people studying at one of the large tables and a couple of people wandering around the stacks. It meant maybe her plan couldn't be executed and she'd have to think of something else.

"I think what you're looking for is over here." Jay led her across the massive floor and to a more secluded area. Aniyah's suspicions were confirmed when she saw that the subject matter in the area was something incredibly obscure. There was no way anyone was likely to even be looking for books on 13th century furniture.

They walked down an aisle together and finally Jay stopped, both of them trying hard not to make it obvious that they were looking around. Aniyah stepped back against the stack and locked eyes with him. "I hope you can help me find what I'm looking for."

Knowing that it was time, she trailed her hand down the center of her blouse, showing him clearly that she wasn't wearing a bra. Jay gazed into her eyes with his sexy dark orbs and when he stepped closer to her, she could feel lust between them.

"You can touch me. It's okay." Her whole body was quivering with anticipation and when he smiled she knew that she had him hooked.

He stood there silent again, and then she felt him step closer and his hands started to explore her body. Sliding down the front of her nightgown he grazed them across her hard nipples and hefted her breasts in his hands. Moving to her thighs he slid the skirt up her legs.

Her legs were spread just wide enough to give him access with his hands. As his hands explored her inner thighs, massaging them they eased closer to her lace covered pussy, which she knew was dying to be touched. But she still felt the need to play out her fantasy.

"Please…touch me. Just be quiet…" As she gasped, his hands gripped her harder and he moved them up her thighs. Silently his fingers dragged against her swollen lips and Aniyah gasped. "Oh, please…yes…"

He pushed a finger against her lips, her damp panties easily pushed aside, and because of how wet she was it easily penetrated her, sending a shockwave of pleasure through her pussy. Just having him use it like a come-hither motion, barely touching her inner walls was enough to almost send her over the edge after all the anticipation she was feeling. And the fact she couldn't close her legs was incredible.

"Yes…yes…more…" she moaned as he began to play with her dripping wet pussy with tantalizingly slow movements. When he found her clit she couldn't help but release a loud gasp. He was good at listening. Finding her swollen nub with his fingers he began to circle it while he played with her swollen lips.

"I…oh…fuck…yes…please, make me cum…" she heard herself moan. But just as she was about to ride over the edge and crest into a glorious orgasm he stopped and pulled away.

It was as if he already knew her body perfectly, the cues telling him when she was about to cum. And then he denied her every time. Gently playing with her clit until she was ready to scream and then pulling away. As much as she thrashed, trying to get him to complete her wave he kept denying her. It was torture of the most wonderful kind.

Finally, he stood up and she watched him undo his pants. Aniyah realized he hadn't even really spoken yet when he finally said something. It was deep and powerful. "Get on your knees, little girl. Open your mouth."

Her entire body was on edge. The blouse she was still wearing brushed against her rock hard nipples and her pussy was already soaked. Idly she realized that her thighs were already damp. He was so close to her, she knew exactly what he had in mind.

Looking around, she knelt down and felt the harsh fabric of the carpet on her bare knees. It felt slutty as she took his dick into her hand. It was just as big as she suspected it might be, and looked delicious. Already rock hard with veins scattered across his skin.

The head of his dick slid against her lips and she eagerly opened them. It smelled musty and delicious. He grabbed her hair and quickly forced himself into her mouth, almost choking her right away. Tears sprung to her eyes but she didn't want to stop. There was a massive rush of adrenaline that caused her entire body to flex.

He was pretty big. Bigger than she was used to, and her cheeks had to stretch to accommodate him. But it was glorious how hard he was. She could taste his need and smell the musky scent of sweat all over him. His hands gripped her head while she began to suck him.

"Fuck...yeah, take that dick." He gasped. Aniyah wrapped her lips firmly around him and sucked hard, fighting against the breath and using her tongue to slide underneath his shaft. Without her hands available it was harder, but still incredibly exciting to have a man fucking her mouth. Especially in a place where anyone could walk around the corner and see her being a total slut.

Her hands crept up and cupped his balls while they clenched, but as his dick continued to invade her lips she sucked him harder than any man she could remember. His erection was thick and long, and she knew if he put it into her pussy it would stretch her perfectly.

Pulling on her hair again he began to fuck her mouth harder, the head of his dick slamming into the back of her throat with a glorious choking sound. Tears sprang to her eyes, but like a truly skilled lover, just as she was about to lose her breath, he let her go and breathe. After one breath he would slide himself past her lips again and fuck her mouth hard.

She moved a hand between her legs, eagerly touching her dripping wet bare pussy, but quickly he reached down and grabbed her shoulder. "No touching yourself, kitten. Not yet. Bad girl." A shudder passed through her. Pet names were another bullseye for making her pussy drip.

Without being able to touch herself it was like torture. All she could do was submit to whatever he wanted to do.

Finally, he pulled out of her and grabbed her arms, yanking her to her feet. As he did his mouth crushed down onto hers, his tongue easily sliding into her mouth. Sliding a hand inside her blouse, he teased her nipples and then pinched one hard, making her gasp into his mouth. Her gasp quickly became a moan as she pushed into him.

Standing up quickly, she moved as if to try to escape. But he was waiting for her movement and grabbed her around the waist. His powerful arms were no match for her small body, especially since she didn't actually want to get away from him.

"No, please…not here…" She cried, struggling against him. He grabbed her arms and pinned her against the stacks. She knew exactly where he was planning on taking her. It was so incredibly hot to feel like this powerful man was going to claim her for his own. Her body was like a rag doll to him, his strong hands controlling her easily. His physique belied a strength with ropy muscle under his clothing.

It was like she was a small child, and he was overpowering her. Which was exactly what she wanted. He was almost reading her mind and it was making her even crazier with lust for him. As he slid a hand under her skirt again, this time her panties were grabbed, and he yanked hard. They tore easily and with a gasp the tatters fell towards her feet.

His powerful hands spun her around, and before she knew it her hands were apart on the stacks and he had her pinned. She could feel his dick pressing against her skirt. Aniyah couldn't resist squirming and trying to get away like she had before, but her struggles were half-hearted.

She was facing through the books, hands above her head. Finally in one more violent act he grabbed her skirt and she felt him yank it up, exposing her bare ass. Her ass had already been exposed to the world, but now her entire lower body was naked and would be visible to anyone who walked into the aisle.

Looking through the openings between the books, she could see that there were people studying not even twenty feet away that had no idea a young co-ed was getting fucked by one of the librarians.

She felt him move closely behind her, his rigid dick trailing saliva down one of her ass cheeks. As she tried to bend over further to give him access he pushed her feet wide. Not he was in position, but for whatever reason wasn't shoving his dick into her. "What...what are you doing?" she begged.

A hand suddenly spanked her ass out of nowhere, making her cry out in surprise and sudden pain, but the warmth of it quickly spread through her body and her pussy flooded again. He spanked her other cheek, making them both bloom with warmth. The noise almost echoed within the confines of the stack and Aniyah knew he was taking a risk with his dominant moves, but it was just making her even crazier for him to finally fuck her.

She was totally helpless. His dick pushed between her ass cheeks, but his hands moved under her blouse to her naked back, raking down the exposed skin. He grabbed hold of her hair and firmly pulled her head back, making her gasp again. It was so incredible to have no way to prevent what she knew he was about to do.

It was all deliberate, the slowness. Almost like torture as his hands spread apart her ass cheeks and exposed her pussy that was now so ready to be fucked. He spanked her a few more times, each one eliciting a gasp and a wave of pleasure. There was nothing she could do, her arms above her head and her legs spread wide while her ass was propped up invitingly.

 Then finally he slid back and she felt his hands spread her again. The head of his dick brushed against her pussy lips again, and just the anticipation and eagerness she had to feel him inside her almost made her cum immediately. She realized he was about to fuck her without any protection as well. It added another forbidden element to the whole encounter. There would be no way to stop him from shooting his hot load inside her body.

Pretending to struggle, she pushed her hips back. "No…please…don't…" but all it did was force her pussy around the head and suddenly his dick had her spread wide. The thickness was exhilarating and the fact she was finally feeling herself get fucked made her crave more. Trying to push back, all she was desperate for was him to get totally inside her and make her cum.

The way he was tantalizing her, just the first inch or two of his dick resting in her pussy was too much to take. "Fuck me...yes, please fuck me..." she sighed, the hiss in her voice hopefully telling him that she was his to claim.

With one hard push, suddenly he forced himself into her, his massive thickness stretching her wide and filling her. No hesitation at all. And she felt her body respond. Immediately her pussy tightened around him, and she came hard, crying out in both exhilaration and pain at the same time. As if he had anticipated it, his mouth snaked around and covered hers just as she screamed, muffling the cry that surely would have been heard on the floors below.

Her legs almost buckled underneath her, but she was basically being held up, impaled on his impressive dick as he sat there, not moving. Her pussy was vibrating like she'd never felt before.

Like he had been all along, he sat deep inside her still. His dick pulsed in her pussy and she almost begged him to keep going. With only one hard stroke he'd given her a shattering orgasm, she could only imagine how much more he was capable of.

It was incredible how skilled he was. He began to simply move inside her one or two inches at a time but stayed deep. Then he would pull out and tease the outside of her pussy with his thick dick. His control was incredible. He was sighing gently but also kept a forceful hand on her head.

Not even being able to see him looking into her eyes while his dick claimed her was erotic enough, but when she saw that somebody was wandering through an aisle close to them, definitely within earshot, it sent her body to another level and she started to feel her orgasm build again. This time though, he was anticipating it.

He bent forward and whispered in her ear. "This fucking pussy is all mine. You are only allowed to cum when I tell you." With those words he pushed himself back inside and Aniyah clamped down on him, suddenly shooting towards the edge of another orgasm but somehow she managed to hold herself back. Squeezing her pussy hard, she clamped down on his dick and heard him gasp softly into her ear.

"OOOHHHH....fuck...please...please...I need to cum....fuck..." she begged. His control was relentless. "Please..." She started to use her muscles to fuck him gently. Both of them were trying to maintain some level of quiet as his dick in her pussy was driving them both to the edge like a roller coaster going over the first ridge.

He slid out until just the tip was inside her again. Pushing just the head inside her he almost teased her pussy again. It was incredible. "Fuck...please...please...I need to cum..." her entire body squirmed underneath him, but she was trapped. He had total control.

His hand went to the back of her neck and then finally he said the words she was dying to hear. "You can cum now, you little slut." But with those words one hand gripped her ass and another her neck and he began to fuck her hard and deep again, his dick searing into her like a hot iron rod. It took him three strokes to make her explode.

And this time it was literally explosive. Her pussy erupted like a fountain, squirting hot juices all over his dick while Aniyah wailed loudly, her entire body bucking up into him while he continued to fuck her pussy hard through her dripping wet orgasm.

"OH...oh...oh, fuck..." she gasped. His dick was unrelenting, plowing deep into her. His hand spanked her ass hard while he rode her fast and deep, her entire body jerking. As fast as she had climaxed and squirted all over him, she came again, this time her body gushing another dribble around him.

His grunts increased in volume and frequency, and she could feel him becoming more urgent inside her. All she could imagine was that he was about to cum inside her, almost a perfect stranger. And it was actually what she wanted. To feel his hot cum filling her pussy without being able to prevent it.

Obviously he decided he was going to cum all over her instead. "Fuck...yeah..." his voice hissed into her ear and Aniyah could feel his dick swelling inside her. The anticipation of his hot load filling her pussy was something she had been craving since they started.

She felt him pull out of her. Then splatters of cum landed hot and wet on her lower back and all over her ass cheeks. It felt like rope after rope of sticky cream covering her skin. A couple of drops dripped down her ass crack and she knew that there would be stains on the carpet from her squirting and his hot load.

Aniyah was almost disappointed that he hadn't erupted inside her and made her completely his, but she understood the need to cover her with his seed. It was like he was claiming her for his own. As his sighs stopped, she felt his fingers trace the coating on her back and rub it into her skin. "There you go. So fucking good. You look so good covered with my cum."

He took a few fingerfuls of his cum and began to rub it all over her pussy and ass. "Next time, I'm going to fuck you right…here." As he said it his finger slipped into her tight hole. Aniyah whimpered. She wanted him to claim her there immediately.

She could still feel her heart hammering in her chest. What was going to happen to her now that he was done? Would the fantasy dissolve? Did she even want to try to face him in any kind of reality after what they had just done together. There was no affection. It had just been him using her body, which was exactly what she wanted.

And she was craving it again right away. But they had to be careful. The anticipation of almost being caught was enough for now, and Aniyah knew that it wouldn't be the last time. After all, there were five floors to the library and each one got them closer to the crowded hub that people were constantly in. Every floor would be more and more risky for them to enjoy each other.

He smoothed down her skirt and adjusted her blouse, but deftly picked up her panties and slipped them into his pocket. "I'll save these for later. For now, you're going to enjoy walking home with your ass coated with my cum." She shivered with delight. A truly dominant man. Finally, It was everything she had been looking for.

They walked down the aisle together, but she slipped in behind him as they approached the elevators. There were a couple of other people studying at a table, but both of them had headphones in so likely there was no way that they had been heard. Even so, being heard and maybe caught was something she wouldn't have minded. And now that she had a taste for his dominating dick, He was definitely going to get a chance to do it again.

Just as they walked out of the elevator, she turned to him. "Thanks so much for helping me. Can I ask you again if I need more help?" It was mostly for the benefit of the other staff members behind the desk, but it was also a way for her to reinforce that he wanted to see her again.

Walking behind the desk, he pulled out a card and wrote something on it. "Here's my number. Just let me know when you're coming back next time and I'll make sure I'm available."

"Thanks again, so much!" she gushed, maybe a bit harder than she needed to. Turning around and walking away, she could feel her sticky thighs and her swollen pussy, and knew that it would only be a matter of a day or two before she texted him. There was so much more she wanted to explore with such a knowledgeable man.

25. The Bachelor Party

It was a decent gig that came Tracee's way, entertaining a party of people during a tour and getting paid almost *double* the amount she would normally get. She was excited before it even started and practiced a few points that would help make it special.

Whilst everything seemed fantastic at first, Tracee's nerves began to well when she arrived at the location they specified everyone would meet up at. The building seemed more like a club than anything, a large blacked-out window taking up most of the front of the building, so Tracee couldn't be sure. Hesitating with the thought they mixed up the address at first, her thoughts were stopped when a man came out of the front door, looking quite red-faced already and pointing her out.

"Hey, you're the guide, right?"

The man's voice was tinged with inebriation, he had clearly been drinking before this, and her own fears were soon met by the man as well.

"Wait, what's with the get-up?"

He points out the obvious, seeing the juxtaposition of an overly-dressed ghostly guide next to a half-drunk man in jeans and t-shirts. Nevertheless, Tracee takes a subtle breath before responding, trying to maintain the proper attitude.

"I'm Tracee, your tour guide! Shall we get started on our ghostly adventure~?"

There was a brief pause as the man stopped smirking to himself, processing what she had just said, a confused face staring back. Then his face turns to frustration, pacing back for a moment whilst talking to himself.

"What the fuck is this? A **ghost** tour?!"

He composes himself after a small meltdown, the man's face softening as he turns back around to speak with Tracee.

"Okay, my name's Don first of all. Second of all, this is supposed to be a *sexy* tour. You understand?"

Tracee caught her gasp before it came out, but was visibly shocked by his sudden outburst.

"Yeah, that's what I thought. This is a big mix-up, *or* a 'fuck you' from my future wife..."

Kicking his foot against the sidewalk, Don sighs to himself, motioning Tracee into the building.

"Look, just come inside, let's figure this out."

Eager to get this sorted out, Tracee joins him inside, feeling the cold air melt into the warm embrace of central heating, the faint sound of music muffled by the walls. The room gave way to another, sort of a private area that was blacked out by the front window, letting them speak privately.

"Okay, so look, I'm not saying you're not hot, because you *are*."

Tracee blushed at the sudden compliment, feeling embarrassed.

"We were just expecting... well..."

Don stumbles over his thoughts, trying to find the best way to say things.

"Shit, we were expecting a stripper to guide us around town and have a bit of fun, alright?"

Tracee's eyes widen, her beat-red face only deepening, confirming Don's thoughts of the mix-up.

"It's my bachelor party, so it's kind of the norm, you know? But fuck, what am I supposed to do now?!"

He clearly looks dejected, Tracee feeling for him somewhat under the circumstances, but unsure of what to do. They stand there for a few awkward moments, both pondering as to what to do next, Tracee still shying under his gaze under the sudden compliment, but also with the thought of 'entertaining' him. After it had gone on too long, she gave into her urges.

"You know, I'm already getting paid a lot for this… Why don't I just *fill in* for her~?"

Don's reaction was priceless, a shocked expression that quickly faded into a look that made his intent clear. He was peering across her body, imagining what was beneath, and from the smile, he seemed to like the idea as well. Don came closer to Tracee, smirking as she began breathing heavily, both of their thoughts coming to fruition as he clasps his hand around her waist, leaning in for a kiss…

All of a sudden, the door to their private room swings open, a rowdy group of half-drunk men calling for Don.

"Hey! Are we getting moving now?"

Tracee sees Don roll his eyes before turning around to speak with them, not letting go of her.

"Yeah, just give me a minute, we'll be outside in a few. And turn the light on! It's fucking dark in here."

The men nudge one another, pointing at Tracee, knowing full-well what's about to go on between them, plunging her further into the embarrassment over the whole situation. They do as he says, turning away and flicking the switch on before leaving them alone.

With them gone, Don turns back to her, leaning into her ear, whispering softly.

"Well Tracee… would you like to feel me inside of you?"

His words were dripping with confidence, and Tracee couldn't help but shiver from being spoken to so closely like this. There was little hesitation to her answer, already knowing the answer himself, she knew he just wanted to hear her say it.

"Yes… please fuck me~"

Tracee's almost surprised with how her words came out, but he clearly enjoyed them, adjusting himself to give her what she wanted. She heard the zipper of his pants come down, trying to catch her breath as she turned around and pressed up against the cold glass window.

"W-wait! We can't let anyone see!"

Don chuckles to himself before leaning back in, making her tremble with each word.

"Don't worry, they can't. It's only one-way~"

Her heart relaxed somewhat, looking outside and seeing the men file out into the street waiting for them, adding to the perverse nature of what's going on. Whilst she was distracted, Don adjusts the both of them one last time, hiking Tracee's dress up her body as he strokes his dick. Then she finally felt it, the sensation that she had been craving since she locked eyes with him, she felt his dick, glistening with precum, pressing against her pussy.

In a sudden moment of clarity, Tracee's eyes widen as she remembers where she is, focusing her eyes and looking forward, a cold rush overtakes her. She finds herself locking eyes with the group waiting for her, who she had spoken with only a moment ago, as they intently stare back. A horrific thought entered her mind as they stared at each other… that she didn't care… lost completely in the moment, the temptation was too great, and she felt herself slipping away from her pride.

That temptation soon took hold, Tracee's body betraying her previous morals, thrusting her hips down to feel his thick dick **impale** her body, stretching her tight pussy around him in a single thrust. She couldn't hold in her initial moan of pleasure, clenching her fingers onto her dress as he took her hint, beginning the first of many thrusts into her tight, eager hole.

As Don collects his thoughts that had been scattered by her desperation, Tracee's squeals fall in rhythm with his thrusts, both of them intending to walk out of this room a pair of wet messes. That whimper of pleasure was almost a signal for him to give into his carnal lust, the slow pace he had been holding himself at breaking away as he suddenly began pounding into her. Holding onto her for leverage, Don hears the sound of Tracee's skirt ripping in his hand, looking down before discarding the cloth to the ground. The gentle whimpers of pleasure melted away into lecherous moans of ecstasy, Tracee's mind completely overwhelmed with the sudden rush of pleasure building between her legs.

It felt as if he had flipped a switch in her head, something she had never felt before, every movement sending a crashing wave of pleasure across her body, leaving her trembling beneath him as he continually thrust into her.

His dick relentlessly stretched Tracee's quivering hole with each time he bottomed out, her legs had long-since become like jelly, even if she wanted to change positions or move at all, her mind was utterly unable to even think about taking herself away from this brain-melting scenario.

He himself was struggling with which part of her body to admire, feeling his tension reach its limit with each glance down at her smacking down against his hips. Throwing his restraints to the wind, he lurches forward, forcing himself to thrust **deeper** into her pussy, listening to her sweet squeals of ecstasy as she struggles with her guilty pleasures..

Though lost in the sea of arousal, she could still tell that he was nearing his limit, his breathing becoming erratic against her skin, and his thrusts much quicker. Tracee's pussy was practically **begging** for him to fill it up, and all of a sudden, she had her wish. The tip of his dick erupted as he came inside of her, the sensation of his cum surging into her pussy was too much, the warm kiss of his load forcing its way into her hole sent Tracee over the edge, and with what little strength she had, she clutched to the window, trying not to lose her footing.

All the while, she can't help but shake the cold gaze the men shot at her, guilty beyond belief as she voluntarily sinks into a blissful orgasm, smiling to herself as tears formed in her eyes, conflicted in her haze. They continue watching on, smirking as Tracee can feel her eyes roll up, tongue slightly hanging out from her mouth as her orgasm quakes across her body. In her fit of pleasure,

Tracee can't stop from trembling in Don's grasp, taking in a breath too deep for her corset to handle, hearing the buttons give way to her ample chest.

Her orgasm felt as if it had ruined her mind in a single moment, leaving her screaming out to the ceiling in pure bliss. Even though she was overwhelmed with pleasure, she couldn't stop the dread in her chest at what she was doing in front of everyone, their blank faces telling her all she needed to know. It was as if every pleasure in the world was forced onto her, despite her dread, and Tracee couldn't resist its pull, sinking further into it as he continued thrusting into her, drawing it out even more.

Don is busy enjoying the sight of Tracee's ass rippling with each smack of his hips against hers, his dick practically *kissed* by her pussy, begging for his load to erupt inside of her again. Before long, he couldn't hold back, tipped over the edge so soon again, the sights urged him onto his second orgasm. Digging his fingers into her cheeks, Don bottoms out inside of her, feeling his dick throb with pent-up desire, surging cum inside of her needy pussy once again.

Tracee feels her mind shatter in an instant, her pleasures washing over her without control. The feeling of his cum staining her pussy sends her over the edge again, her eyes rolling back further as her pussy spasms around his shaft, practically **milking** the poor guy for every drop of his thick load.

Completely exhausted, Don lets Tracee slowly slip down to the ground in a heap, still spasming slightly from their session together, and leans down to plant a chaste kiss on her cheek before slumping next to her, gasping.

The two of them sit down on the ground for a few seconds, both looking at her outfit, once so well-presented, and take in how badly they had ruined it. Tracee now looked as if she had just crawled out of a thorny bush, rips and tears all across her dress, barely holding her tits beneath the fabric and her skirt looking more like a stripper's outfit, which fit her new role.

"Come on, we can't leave them waiting or they'll come barging in again."

She knew he was right, but standing up was difficult enough, let alone whilst trying to keep her dress from exposing herself even more. Once she stood up, she realized it wasn't *that* bad. She had to pull her top-half up every once in a while, and her skirt was a lot more mini than when she left, but it was serviceable at least.

Don leads Tracee back outside, joining his friends as they cheer for him, each of them knowing what he had just done to her. After a few high-fives and pats on the back, the group turns to Tracee, awaiting her guidance on where they'd be going first.

"O-oh, right! If you'll all come with me, we'll start our little tour~"

26. Two Halves

Things were often rough around the place, and depending on what sort of job you had, there came special benefits. One of those people that enjoyed an important job was Tone, unfortunately not lucky enough to have been involved in a high-demand trade, though he had a knack for picking up just about anything put in front of him, to some degree of course. His anthropology skills rarely came into play, and being honest with himself, they never actually came into play at all, but he still manages to be of use.

One of those uses was Tone tinkering away as usual on a myriad of pipes, finding which one of them was not working was his role for the day. Whilst lost in it, he hears a familiar sound, mixing with the sound of his friend Toya, was the voice of the woman he had been fawning over for a while now.

She was somewhat well-known, mostly because she was currently drumming up plans for the camp to have a sophisticated water-purifying system, rather than the rudimentary systems they have in place already. Even *looking* at her was a treat, like meeting an old-world celebrity in person, she just had that kind of aura about her.

Suddenly, Tone feels his head ringing loudly, an echo striking in his brain as Toya bangs on the pipe above him.

"Hey! Stop banging on those pipes for a minute!"

Grumpily, Tone appears from beneath the twisting mess of pipework, eyes widening as he stows away his anger, catching a glimpse of Cecelia next to her. Toya waves her hand for a moment, snapping him out of his trance, she's always been somewhat aware of his feelings for Cecelia, but thankfully has kept it quiet for his sake.

"She says that since things are coming from overflow, the problem's further down the line."

Even moments like these seem like treasures to Tone, seeing her stand there and smile, like a picture in motion, she's a true beauty he holds dear...

Snapped out of it once again, Toya flicks Tone's forehead, eliciting a nudge from Cecelia, who disapproves of the workplace brutality taking place.

"It's about lunch, anyway, let's head back and you can take care of it later."

Already turning away, Toya motions for Tone to follow, who, still slightly drunk on love, starts packing his tools and heads further down the line of pipes.

"Hey, didn't you hear? All the good food will be gone if you don't hurry!"

Smirking at her joke, Tone declines the offer and heads off to find the problem, intent on impressing Cecelia in any way he can, or at least become a strong, reliable man in her eyes. Even though he has the skill to speak several languages, Tone would find himself unable to even find a *toilet* if left alone in the Russian sectors, the same going for Cecelia unfortunately. So, despite his aching heart, he has no choice but to bear with it, admiring her from afar whilst standing only feet from the woman.

Time passes and Tone eventually finds the issue, fixing it rather promptly, most of the hard work involved actually *finding* it, the rest being pretty simple. Despite that, before Tone is even able to pull his greasy face past the mess of pipes, Cecelia has managed to hurry her way over, a big smile on her face. Tone was beside himself, immediately greeted by her soft, angelic expression, it was almost like payment in smiles.

Though after the initial joy of it, the usual awkward air descends on them, Cecelia's smile disappears as the words she wished she could say in thanks weren't able to come to her lips. Tone still has to clumsily pull himself out of his office, carrying his toolbox over-shoulder whilst stumbling over a few pipes, almost causing a second leak whilst he's at it. Now things become even worse, both of them staring awkwardly, making vague gestures at one another.

Thankfully for both of their dignities, Toya notices their plight and quickly makes her way over, chuckling to herself before Cecelia verbally *jumps* on her, dumping the gratitude she had been holding onto her. Toya instinctively motions for her to slow down, taking in her words before relaying them back to Tone.

"Right! Cecelia wants to thank you *so* much for fixing the problem this quickly, she's really grateful and all that good stuff."

Tone gives Toya a slightly annoyed look, knowing she likely fudged the last bit, but still appreciative of her efforts on their behalf.

"Uhm, can you let her know that it's no trouble, and that if there's anything else she needs, that she just needs to ask!"

Toya smirks to herself, seeing the poor guy's sincerity, she turns to Cecelia and begins translating it back, Tone noticing how Cecelia takes everything to heart, her eyes widening and almost glistening as she speaks. After a brief pause, she nods, wiping one of her eyes and turning to Tone before lunging forward and wrapping her arms around him for a brief embrace. For that moment, Tone felt the toils of his day melt away, forgetting the slight aches in his body and instead being filled with a warm bliss in his heart.

Good things can't quite last forever, and her embrace soon ends, and Cecelia bids farewell to Toya, then waves once again to Tone, a faint smile constantly on her face as she walks with a slight skip in her step.

"Well, she certainly appreciates my work I guess…"

Toya shakes her head at Tone's remark, patting him on the back before extending her free hand, dangling the small lunch she brought over for him. The two of them exchange a grin and recline against the pipes, sitting down whilst Tone picks away at his paltry meal. Soon the conversation turns to recent events, Toya exclaiming something suddenly.

"Oh, Tone!"

She shoves him gently, causing him to cough on his food.

"I forgot to mention, the camps are going to be holding a little get-together, sort of like a big festival between us all!"

Tone looks up at her, wondering why it was news enough to try and choke him. After finishing his mouthful, he speaks up, wanting to know more.

"So, what's happening at it exactly, are we all going to hold hands and dance?"

Toya laughs at his attempt at humor, giving him another nudge, only lighter this time.

"Well, whatever it is, you'd better get practicing so you don't let Cecelia down."

Despite being a lighter nudge, she somehow found another way to cause Tone to choke on his food, patting his chest to help it go down before speaking again.

"What do you mean?! She's not going as well, is she?"

She just looks at him in a faux sense of bewilderment.

"Of course, she is! You asked her out to it after all."

There's a brief pause in the air, Tone staring up at Toya blankly, about to speak before she interrupts.

"Is that not what you told me to say to her just now?"

Once again, Tone loses whatever he was about to say, his brain no longer scrambling for his next sentence, instead just lingering in the moment, waiting for it to pass.

"Ah! Sorry, my English, is not so good, must have misunderstood!"

Her joke cracks Tone out of his silence, a laugh slipping past his lips, Toya being the woman he relies on most to translate for him. With her joke stripping down his mental block, he comes back to the realization that she had just set him up with Cecelia… and she said yes!

That was it, Tone's workload instantly became second on his mind. Finishing his meal, he shakily stands on his legs, Toya doing the same, though less jittery, and watches Tone turn to face her.

"You've **got** to help me learn something!"

Toya shrugs her shoulders, looking Tone dead in the eye.

"I could teach you how to fold paper planes if you'd like."

There's little space for Tone to collect his thoughts, and Toya knows that damned well.

"No, you idiot! I need you to help me learn Russian, at least a little bit so I can talk to her..."

Toya stands stalwart, looking coldly at Tone as she speaks.

"I *could*, but I'm not sure an *idiot* could help you."

With a heavy sigh, Tone realizes how much help Toya had already been, and apologizes.

"Look, I'm just worked up, sorry ab-!"

She doesn't let him finish, wrapping her arm around his shoulder and practically dragging him away.

"Well, that settles it! Let's get you educated, my friend!"

The next few days for Tone were spent buried in books, helped out occasionally by Toya whenever he met a roadblock, not wanting to pester her too much as she already laid the foundation of the language out for him. Most of his phrases were helped along with translator on his phone, whilst the literature helped with more formal lessons.

Before it felt like he even had a chance to learn to say 'Hello', the event was upon them. The entire day was spent brushing up as best he can, both with his physical appearance as well as his Russian lessons, Toya giving him a once-over before practically **shoving** him in the general direction of Cecelia.

The moment he laid eyes on her, Tone's chest felt tight. Cecelia was dressed in a form-fitting red dress, hugging her waist in a way he rarely saw at work, her body sending a shiver of arousal across his body, but he wasn't going to let that be his focus. With shaky confidence, Tone stepped forward, looking somewhat stiff before Cecelia melted his hesitations away with her smile.

"Good evening, Cecelia, you look... fantastic."

Her eyes widened, the sound of her language coming from his lips was almost too much for her, as if hearing him for the very first time, Tone could see her stifle a few tears. The night flowed magically from there, the two exchanging a few conversations, almost as if it was a gimmick between them.

Toya watched on out of the corner of her eye, enjoying her own side of the event whilst the new couple were lost in theirs.

"I've always wanted to hear you like this!"

Her words made sense in his mind, then processed into what she meant by them, and Tone felt the familiar rush causing his face to redden. It was almost too much, thrust so quickly into the arms of the woman he had admired for so long, he could hardly contain himself. Without entirely thinking, and with the event ending, Tone stares into Cecelia's glistening eyes and does his best not to fumble his phrasing.

"Cecelia... would you like to... go in private?"

It was crude but got the message across. Her smile turned from joyful to mischievous, a silent affirm as she led him back to her dormitory.

Every moment that they toured the place was like a prelude to their evening, both knowing in the back of their minds what was going to happen back at her room. The entire time was like them both pretending it wasn't going to happen, but secretly, they both were craving the moment they stepped foot inside of her room and could sink into their depravity.

Finally, the time came, Cecelia leading Tone up by the hand as they giggled to themselves. Once inside, Tone felt himself pushed onto the bed, smiling up at Cecelia as she smiled back, placing a finger on her lips as she disappeared into the bathroom. It was a few minutes before she came back out, but he felt his heart rush with excitement at the sight of her.

She was gorgeous, every bit as perfect as his imagination led him on with. Cecelia was feeling the intensity of what they were delving into, but it was a constant rush that urged her forwards, her desperation coming to a fevered pitch once she finally lays her eyes on him, as if her fantasy was standing before her. Without a single hesitation, she stepped closer to the bed, letting him gaze over her body as she stripped his clothes off.

As her hands traced across his body, Cecelia fell to Tone's gentle kisses, coaxing a few whimpers from her lips, guiding her to slow down as they simply held each other, savoring the feeling of finally being close enough to feel each other's heartbeat. It almost brought a tear to Cecelia's eye to be here, in her own little slice of heaven that was tucked away, she leaned into each of Tone's kisses. His hands explored her body greedily, causing her face to flush, still getting used to being able to feel this amazing sensation in private. Still, her desires grew more and more with each moment, and she couldn't hold back any longer.

"Let's see~"

Not sure what she meant at first, Tone's eyes widened at the realization of what she was talking about. Finally alone together, his heart is now racing at the scenario he had found himself in, there with Cecelia as he adjusts himself on the bed, finally able to look down at her as she sinks to her knees.

It's as if she's unwrapping a present on Christmas, almost ripping off his zipper as she tears away at his clothes, finally seeing his bulge, still throbbing beneath his boxers.

"Holy fuck…"

It seemed as though Cecelia was trying to stop herself from speaking, but let out her surprise anyway, moving forward and finally pulling down his underwear, letting his half-hard dick pop free from his pants.

"How did you hide **this…?**"

It was *beyond* impressive, something she had never seen before, at least not to this extent. Lost in the sight of such a dick throbbing in front of her face, she gazed over the head of his dick, imagining how intensely it would stretch her throat. Cecelia felt a subtle heat growing in her chest, and quickly threw her top over her head. In a swift motion, her tits were almost exposed for him, threatening to burst free from her bra at a moment's notice, he could barely take his eyes off of them, causing his precum to steadily drip from his tip.

Left there in awe, Tone is speechless at the scene playing out in front of him, and Cecelia has found herself lost in arousal at the *thought* of taking his dick inside of her, and leans forward, her tongue hanging out, ready for it. His feelings having built up over so long, it's nearly **orgasmic** when Cecelia finally lets her lips seal around his shaft, looking up at him as she smiles through her sucking, sinking his dick deeper down her throat.

Finally, Cecelia had taken every inch down her throat, her body trembling by this point, eager for release. Though what she *didn't* expect was Tone to get *even harder!* Seeing her like this had melted away any hesitations for him, and with Cecelia spearing herself on his dick, he felt the throbbing only intensify.

She, on the other hand, felt his dick press against the back of her throat, pushing past anything she had felt before, and began gagging on him. Not wanting to give into this absolute monster, Cecelia clenched her throat and began pounding her face into his crotch, savoring the sounds of Tone openly moaning at the sensation. Each time she throated him again, Cecelia felt herself retching from how much it had grown, thinking she wouldn't be able to finish him off, but was saved with the sudden feeling of his dick spasming in her mouth.

Knowing that he was about to cum, Cecelia pulls her head back until just Tone's tip is in her mouth, then sucks gently and moans around him, coaxing his load onto her tongue. The first shot was incredibly powerful, hitting the roof of her mouth before the ones that followed simply flowed across her tongue.

Cecelia let it fill her mouth at first, enjoying the feeling of how much he was letting out, but soon realized he wasn't stopping and quickly gulped down her first mouthful before anything spilled out. It was incredibly thick going down her throat, but she still had to focus on the next few shots as she pulled back, the tip of his dick **throbbing** in front of her as the next few surges of cum covered her face.

Tone was left still hard, Cecelia stealing another glance before standing up again, opening her mouth to show him she had swallowed, then flashing him a smile before running her finger across her cheeks, licking his cum off of her hand and swallowing loudly. Tone was struggling with his feelings in the afterglow of his pleasure, having just experienced his first time together with Cecelia.

With her little show finished, Cecelia finds herself *trembling* with arousal at what had just happened, looking at his dick as it continued to twitch, calling for her to crawl across him and start riding it without control... Whilst lost in her thoughts, he snapped her out of them as he began crawling up from the bed, making his way up to her body before locking eyes with Cecelia.

Silently, the two of them were in a sultry dance, Tone stripping her down until her body was laid bare for him. With her luscious figure to admire, he couldn't help but let his thoughts run wild. She was something that he had been craving to see for so long, he felt his dick throb painfully having finally been able to see her like this. With his arousal reaching its pique, he finally lets Cecelia hear what she's been waiting for.

"Cecelia... would you like to feel me inside of you?"

His words were dripping with confidence, and she couldn't help but shiver from being spoken to so closely like this. There was little hesitation to her answer, already knowing the answer himself, she knew he just wanted to hear her say it.

"Yes... please fuck me~"

Cecelia's almost surprised with how her words came out, but he clearly enjoyed them, adjusting himself to give her what she wanted. In a single motion, Tone falls backwards whilst clutching to her, pulling the both of them back onto the bed, then rolls over to have her beneath him. It was then that she finally felt it, the sensation that she had been craving since they walked in and locked eyes, she felt his dick, glistening with precum, pressing against her pussy.

He had clearly been pent-up throughout the evening, his breath already becoming ragged as he tightly gripped her body, his fingers sinking into her thighs, ready to take her. His first motion was gentle, sliding his dick between Cecelia's legs and letting her take the first few inches slowly, but as she adjusted, he quickened his pace, now rhythmically gliding inside of her.

Her whimpers only urged his arousal to build, and by the hungry look in his eyes, she may have sent him into a frenzy. Cecelia could only let out a surprised whimper before being pulled onto all-fours, her ass positioned into the air as he began **pounding** into her quivering hole, dripping her juices down her thighs with each thrust.

Her surprised and loud moans quickly filled the room, each cry of pleasure in rhythm to his frantic poundings. Cecelia's eyes were soon rolled up into her head, tongue lolling from her lips as she helplessly came on his dick, stretching her pussy out so roughly that she couldn't resist the pleasure, even if she wanted to.

She couldn't help but moan gently, her body trembling with pure bliss as he continued fucking her from behind. That whimper of pleasure was almost a signal for him to give into his carnal lust, the slow pace he had been holding himself at breaking away as he suddenly began pounding into her.

The gentle whimpers of pleasure melted away into lecherous moans of ecstasy, Cecelia's mind completely overwhelmed with the sudden rush of pleasure building between her legs.

It felt as if he had flipped a switch in her head, something she had never felt before, every movement sending a crashing wave of pleasure across her body, leaving her trembling beneath him as he continually thrust into her.

His dick relentlessly stretched her quivering hole with each time he bottomed out, her legs had long-since become like jelly, even if she wanted to change positions or move at all, her mind was utterly unable to even think about taking herself away from this brain-melting scenario.

He himself was struggling with which part of her body to admire, feeling his tension reach its limit with each glance down at her body. Throwing his restraints to the wind, he lurches forward, burying his dick between her cheeks, listening to her scream in bliss at being filled so suddenly.

Though lost in the sea of arousal, she could still tell that he was nearing his limit, his breathing becoming erratic, his thrusts becoming more frantic, and his grip tightening. Cecelia's pussy was practically begging for him to fill it up, and all of a sudden, she had her wish. The tip of his dick erupted as he came inside of her, the sensation of his cum surging into her pussy was too much, the warm kiss of his load forcing its way into her hole sent Cecelia over the edge, and with what little strength she had, she clutches tightly against the sheets, moaning loudly as he continued pumping her full of his load.

Her orgasm felt as if it had ruined her mind in a single moment, leaving her screaming out to the ceiling in pure bliss. It was as if every pleasure in the world was forced onto her, and she couldn't resist its pull, sinking further into it as he continued thrusting into her, drawing it out even more.

He couldn't help to stop, fantasies flooding his mind of how he wanted to fuck her, to use every inch of her luscious body until he could barely move. Each thought only urges another throb from his dick, desperate to fill his partner and claim her for himself.

Pure ecstasy washed over her body, leaving her a shuddering

mess as he continued pumping her full of his load, a few shallow thrusts all he had left in him before the two of them were simply exhausted, he finally pulling back and gasping loudly, dropping to rest his head against her, leaving them panting beside each other. Their pent-up arousal taken out on one another, they were left there to bask in the afterglow of their intense session, barely able to string together a sentence as she breathed softly onto his neck.

Looking up and seeing him also struggling to recover was somewhat comforting to her, knowing that they had just shared an evening together that both of them can look back on fondly. Even as she has his cum leaking from between her legs, his dick still half-hard against her thigh, Cecelia couldn't help but wrap her arms tightly around his back, holding him closely as her heart quickens.

Though her idle cuddling didn't last, Tone gained his second wind as he adjusts himself to claim something that had filled his mind for so long, Cecelia's tight pussy was still waiting for him. It was a thing he had been pushing for in his fantasies, but it was always a faint thought, but now in the moment, lost in pleasure, he couldn't stop himself from exhausting himself claiming it.

As she felt his wet tip press against her tight hole, she didn't offer up any resistance, if anything, he felt the wiggle of her hips, coaxing him to take what he wanted once again. With no reason to hold back, he does just that, sinking his shaft between her cheeks, listening to the gentle squealing from her lips as he pushes further inside, feeling her struggle to accept his shaft.

After several shallow thrusts, he finally found purchase in his movements, bottoming out completely as Cecelia catches her breath in her throat, unable to even moan with the sudden intrusion. Only she didn't need to say anything, Tone understands how badly she wanted this from him as well, he began his manic thrusts into her pussy, watching as her cheeks slapped against his hips with each thrust, squeezing her tightly in his hands as his orgasm began creeping up on him quicker than he thought.

The tight squeezing of her hole around his dick was too much, double with the whimpers and squeals from her lips, he was painfully coaxed to his orgasm, quickly bottoming out as he gripped onto her tightly. Her hole was suddenly flooded with his thick load again, mixing with his last, causing Cecelia to squirm involuntarily at the sudden rush of cum inside of her, a shiver of perverse arousal coursing through her body.

After a few moments, he was finished, letting her sink into the bed like a used toy, she couldn't stop her spasms whilst trying to recover. Though they wanted to stay like this forever, they knew they couldn't stay, even as Cecelia was still twitching from the overstimulation.

Both of them understanding, Cecelia was urged back to reality by Tone's idle groping of her naked body, a smile on her face as she's reminded of the passionate afternoon they had just spent together. Whilst they both wanted to stay, likely going for another session, Cecelia knew she couldn't stay too long, and treasured the final few minutes they could spend together, gently making out as they giggled beneath the sheets.

The time soon came, Cecelia giving him one final chaste kiss before staggering to her feet. Tone gathered his clothes as Cecelia took her time in the shower, the steam leaking into her room an almost tempting offer to join her. Finally, she made her way out whilst drying her hair, embraced affectionately by Tone the second she was free, both of them savoring a final moment together in the secluded pleasure they stole for themselves.

"You can stay tonight…"

Cecelia whispered it into his ear, still clutching to him tightly, her grip was almost desperate, as if wanting to hold onto this moment for as long as possible. With her shaky hands gripping to his body, Tone couldn't say no, silently reciprocating her embrace, holding her tightly as he fell backwards onto the bed, Cecelia still in his arms. She lets out a surprised yelp, only making Tone smile when he begins play-wrestling with her on top of the sheets, rubbing her towel across her head so she can't see.

"Such a jokester!"

The limited words he can understand still brings Tone joy, a constant smile on his face from finally being able to communicate with the woman who held a firm place in his heart. Finally letting her see past her towel again, Tone leans forward for another kiss, holding her tightly whilst the two of them descend back under the covers, their warm bodies writhing together as exhaustion soon overtakes them.

Come morning, Tone is the first to awaken, barely able to sleep in the first place with the object of his affection lying quietly next to him. He was unable to stop himself from gently stroking her hair, trying to ensure her restful sleep, even at the cost of his own. It was like he was lost in a dream, given what he had desperately clung to over a simple prank that he now *has* to think of a way to thank Toya for.

Hmmm...

Even as she began rousing, Tone didn't stop stroking her hair, nestling closely behind her as Cecelia's eyes fluttered open. The look on her face when she awakens from one dream to another is enough for him, seeing her precious smile after seeing him still there told Tone all he needed to know, and they both leaned in for a kiss, wishing it would never end.

Though like all things, they both know it has to, and reluctantly rise from the bed, looking over before falling back into the sheets. Both of them giggle together, wrestling lightly as an excuse to explore one another's bodies, savoring the heat between them, the subtle sensation of being close to one another. Cecelia herself was still in disbelief that she was here right now, holding the same feelings that Tone had kept close for so long, but just as unable to display them.

None of that mattered now though, with both of them locked in a gentle embrace, even the morning's duties couldn't separate them. They knew how each lunch could be spent together, the lessons to bridge the language gap even further, and the nights they would be able to spend together were all before them. They both wiped away a tear at the prospect, exchanging a final kiss before parting for their days, aching for the moment they would be together again.

27. Office Passion

Tokyo felt her mind wandering again, the sound of the typing surrounding her. She zoned out, her body relaxing as the sound sped up. Being in an office 8 hours a day was driving her crazy. After her commute, she barely had time for herself. She tried online dating, using the apps but that ate into her precious time even more and usually resulted in lackluster dates. Guys who still lived at home, guys who had baggage, guys who wanted to go straight into her panties.

She just wanted someone who understood her, who understood the stress that came with being a professional, who understood her time was limited. She pushed her long brown hair into a loose bun and massaged her head.

She felt like it had been ages since she had had sex, much less been touched or kissed. She was usually too tired to even touch herself at night, her mind too distracted by the stress of work and everything going on in her life. Can you imagine, wanting sex so badly and needing it? Craving it. But so tired that your brain and body would mutiny against your pussy, making you pass out cold most nights without even an effort to get off.

She spent her days in the office and her nights, going over the plans for the next day at the office. She was caught on a hamster wheel, going in circles, day in and day out. It was driving her crazy.

"Hey, Tokyo, you got a minute," a deep voice came from the doorway of her office. She jerked, looking at the man. Her body responded quickly, as it always did when AJ was around her. He had light brown hair that had volume that most women paid for. His dark brown eyes were hidden behind wireframe glasses that he nervously pushed up as he looked at her.

"Sure, AJ, come on in," she smiled, noticing the shirt tight across his chest.

"How can I help," she asked, steepling her hands together. He was younger than her by at least a decade but that made no difference to her. They always did say that women hit their stride in their early 40s. That's why cougars existed, after all. She wanted him so badly; she could feel her pussy clench every time he was close. She chuckled softly to herself, looking at the shy nerdy guy waiting for her in front of her desk.

"There's this problem with one of my programs and I'm not sure how to fix it. I was hoping you'd be able to help me. I know it's getting late already but I can buy us some food. We can get this figured out together," he said, smiling tightly, the hope of assistance in his eyes.

"Oh, I can definitely help you," she said, hoping the innuendo wasn't lost on him. She watched as he nervously swallowed, his cheeks turning an adorable shade of red.

"I'll come back in a few minutes, okay? Gonna go grab my laptop," he said, standing and walking out of her office. She sucked her teeth softly, watching his ass as he left. It had been too damn long. She was going to take this opportunity if she could.

"Hey, AJ, you just had a birthday, right? Big 3-0? I got you something for your birthday," she said, crossing her legs slowly, her short skirt riding up. Aj's eyes traveled down her body and up again.

"Uh, yeah. 30," he said, trying to loosen his tie from his throat. He turned quickly, bumping into the door facing. Tokyo held in her laugh, watching as he left, returning ten minutes later with a satchel holding his laptop over his shoulder.

"Welcome back. Let's see what we can do," she said, motioning to the desk. They had their heads down for the next hour, as people left the office for the day. A low rumble from Tokyo's stomach made them stop, realizing how much time had passed.

"What do you want for supper," AJ asked, pulling out his food. Tokyo bit her tongue, sighing softly. What she wanted wasn't something you could order on an app. She paused, thinking back to her online dating scenarios. "Okay, maybe you could order it," she corrected herself with a smile.

"Yeah, I planned to," AJ quipped, making Tokyo realize she had been talking out loud. She felt her cheeks flush.

"Get whatever you want. I'll eat anything," she said, her eyes trailing over his body. Aj stared at her, his eyes falling to her breasts.

"Anything," he asked, a small smirk on his face. She raised an eyebrow, wondering where that shy nerd had gone. Maybe after work hours, he transformed into someone sexy and in control.

"Anything," she said, licking her lips slowly, leaning forward, moving her hips around in the hard chair. She arched her back slightly, trying to look as if she was innocently stretching when in reality, she was pressing her breasts forward for him to stare at more.

"Would you like your birthday present now, AJ," she whispered, licking her lips slowly. He set his phone down, his eyes glued to her mouth.

"I hope it's something I've wanted for a while," he said, standing up from the chair. Tokyo looked up at him, her hands reaching for his belt, their eyes never losing contact. She could feel her body waking up, realizing what was finally going to happen. Her pussy was already soaked; she could smell her arousal and hoped AJ could too.

She pulled her lower lip in with her teeth as he raised a hand, cupping the back of her head. He reached up, pulling the glasses from his face, transforming how he looked with such a small action. Tokyo gasped softly, able to see the fire and passion in his eyes. His jaw was set in a hard line as he watched her.

She quickly pulled his slacks down, taking the black silky boxers with them. His fingers tangled into her hair, squeezing and pulling it slightly as she neared his hard dick. It was thick and angry looking, the head a deep red.

She opened her mouth, putting her tongue out like a welcome mat for him. He slammed deep into her throat, making her gag softly. Who was this guy and where had he come from? Her fluttered closed as he began fucking her mouth, bobbing her head against his groin roughly. Tokyo grabbed his hips, holding him close to her as she sucked her mouth tight against him.

"Oh, God," AJ sighed, his stomach clenching.

"You are such a good little dick sucker, Tokyo. You want this so bad, don't you," he said, slowing his thrusts. Tokyo moaned softly, the words running up her spine, unexpectedly affecting her.

"Oh, you like that, do you? You like when my words aren't as nice as I look," he said, sneering down at her. The coldness in her voice made her try even harder to please him, making her move her head even faster.

"Good girl. Such a slut, just like I knew you'd be," he said, both of his hands gripping her head. She could feel his ass clenching as his body tensed. She knew he was getting closer, and she chased that feeling.

"No, stop, this isn't how I want it to end," he said, pushing her back away from his body quickly. Tokyo leaned back, surprised. She had tasted the salty pre cum in her mouth and knew he had been getting close. For a guy to bring things to a halt, so he could focus on her. She felt her heart jump a little, a breath stuck in her throat.

He pulled her up, his hand pulling her head back to offer her throat to him. His mouth worked against it, nipping and biting as his fingers moved to unbutton her blouse. She could feel her pulse in her ears as her long hair tickled the top of her ass.

"AJ, tell me what you want," she whispered, looking over his shoulder at the open door to her office. The thrill of knowing someone could easily walk by and discover them sent a thrill through her body, an electric current going straight to her clit.

AJ moved back, pulling his slacks up over his ass, and put his dick back into his briefs. Tokyo groaned, loving that untucked look, where the material hung open, giving him a casually sexy look.

"I want you to bend over. I want you to beg me," he said, guiding her to the side of the desk. She pressed her back against his chest, the feeling of his hard dick pressing into the small of her back. She moaned, wiggling her ass slightly, teasing him.

"I said, bend over. Now," he ordered, his voice firm. She looked at him, at her insubordinate employee. Hearing the steel in his voice was driving her crazy, knowing how he was around everyone else. She felt like she was getting to see a secret side of him, that he kept hidden behind a wall of quiet nerdiness.

She obeyed, bending and pressing her upper body to the desk. She could feel her breasts flattening in the cups of her bra, trapped by the lace and wire. She could sense him behind her, slowly sliding his hands over her ass.

"Do you want this," he asked quietly, his hands cupping her body, squeezing them gently.

"God, yes," she moaned, pushing back slightly against his hands. His fingers trailed down to the bottom of her skirt, tugging it up over her hips. Tokyo moaned, the cool air hitting her skin. The black thong was between her cheeks, separating them nicely into two tight globes. AJ's hands moved over them, his hands warm and form. His fingers clenched, digging into her skin. Tokyo moaned, whimpering slightly.

"Please," she begged softly, unsure of what exactly she was asking for.

"Do you want this," AJ repeated firmly. Tokyo nodded, gulping.

"I want this," she said, her voice wavering slightly.

AJ brought a hand down onto her exposed ass, the sting making her jump forward. Her body connected with the desk, unable to escape.

He brought his hand down again, rubbing the spot softly after the blow. Tokyo sighed, her body on high alert now. She had never really been one to be spanked. She had never been one to do much actually, aside from the plain vanilla stuff. This was different and she kind of liked it, she decided.

"Please," she said, her pussy clenching as she waited for his hand. He did not disappoint, landing the blow dangerously close to her pussy. She felt her eyes welling up as she raised to her toes.

"Have you had enough, Tokyo? Or do you want more from me," AJ said, his hands gripping her hips. She could feel his fingers digging into her skin.

"I want more. Please, AJ, I want more," she begged, reaching behind her, searching for him.

She felt his fingers pulling at the material of her underwear, felt them sliding down her legs. She quickly stepped out, kicking them away. The sound of his zipper being slid down was loud, as she braced herself on the desk. Her pussy clenched, knowing what was about to happen. She almost moaned in excitement.

AJ slammed into her, pressing his dick into her pussy. She groaned, feeling it struggle to stretch for his size.

"Oh my God," she moaned, closing her eyes tightly.

"You've wanted this for a while. Don't deny it. I see how you look at me, like the slut that you are," he said, running a hand down her back. Tokyo nodded, struggling to pull her blouse from her body.

AJ traced the straps of her bra, his fingers leaving behind fire everywhere he touched. She was so keyed up, she was surprised she hadn't come twice already. Her pussy was soaked, making her as slippery as she had ever been.

"You're right. I have wanted you," she said, as he slowly started to thrust into her. He buried himself in her with a grunt.

"Say it again," he said, between clenched teeth.

"I want you. I want you," she moaned, her body rocking against the desk as he fucked her. She could hear the wet sounds of her greedy pussy, taking him all in hungrily. She could feel her ass spreading as his body hit hers, the slaps of their bodies colliding the only sound she could hear.

She had needed this, need this connection to anyone. She could feel the stress dripping off her body like the juices dripping from her pussy.

"AJ," she moaned, feeling his hand go around her throat, pulling her body back to his. He had unbuttoned his shirt and she could feel his skin on hers. The nerves in her body responded, coming alive joyfully. She felt him kick between her feet, making her legs spread wider. Her feet slipped, her heels twisting slightly as she moved to obey.

"You want this," he said, his hand running down her back, unsnapping the bra. Tokyo felt it slide from her shoulders and saw it land on the desk. The cool air made her nipples tighten.

"I want this, AJ. I want you," she said, looking over her shoulder at him. He licked his lips slowly, before pressing his mouth to hers. She felt his hand twisting her neck, trying to gain better access to her mouth. She moaned, pulling back with a gasp.

Her lips felt bruised. He pulled her back his chest, his arms moving around so he could cup her breasts.

She reached behind her, holding his head to her neck as his teeth grazed her skin. His fingers kneaded the softness of her breasts, pressing them tightly against her body.

"Do you like the pain, Tokyo? Does it make your pussy nice and wet for me," he whispered, his lips moving against her skin. Tokyo moaned, her knees getting weak. He held her, stronger than he appeared to be. She would never judge a book by its cover again, thinking of all the guys she had skipped over in the dating apps that might have surprised her, much like AJ was doing.

"The pain," she replied, her eyes closing softly on her cheeks. She did enjoy it, toeing that line between pain and pleasure. The endorphins would race through her body, making her wonder if what she was feeling was turning her on or hurting her. Maybe both.

He rubbed her nipple with his thumb, making her jerk back towards him. Her clit twitched, her thighs tingling. That was different, she thought to herself.

He did it again, rolling the hard nub between two fingers, tugging slightly. He reached his other hand around, sliding it slowly down her stomach. She could feel her muscles fluttering under his touch, his large hand moving slowly. He came to her pussy, pressing through the wet patch of hair and found her throbbing clit. She moaned, her body trying to escape.

"Oh, Tokyo, just enjoy this. I know I am," he whispered, moving his fingers in slow circles. She moaned, her hips jerking forward to urge him to move faster.

"AJ, please," she begged, whimpering softly. She was standing, pressed against the edge of her desk, with her skirt bunched around her waist. He stood behind her, his button-up shirt open with his slack unbuttoned on his hips. She could see his dick peeking out the top, the head shiny with precum.

"Since you said please," he chuckled, his breath warm on her ear. His fingers began to move quickly, his other hand pinching the nipple in the same rhythm. She could feel her pussy clenching, her body twitching as the orgasm built in her body. He swiped his fingers down, gathering the juices from her pussy and returned to her clit, the lubrication making it that much more sensitive.

Tokyo groaned, arching her body back and he touched her. He moved his fingers down again, sliding them into her pussy, thrusting them up into her, holding her body to his. Tokyo could feel her thighs trembling, her ass clenching as her body began to take control away from her. She took a deep breath, letting go of the reigns that she usually held on to so tightly. She tried to control everything in life and looked where that had gotten her; sex starved being fucked in her office by a man ten years younger than her.

She felt the walls of her pussy clenching, pulsing as she grunted in reply to the actions. She could feel the small gush as her pussy squirted, the liquid sliding down her thighs.

"I want more," AJ said, his fingers moving back to her clit. Her body was sensitive, her pussy already on high alert. He twisted and tugged at her nipple, running his tongue up the side of her neck.

"I have thought about you so many nights. I have thought about what your pussy would smell like, how you would taste. I have thought of your breasts in my hands. I have thought about my dick sliding into your pussy. Every fucking night since I started working here," he whispered, circling her clit rapidly. The

orgasm came out of nowhere, her body already primed from before. The words pushed her over, her breath catching in her throat at the thought of being wanted so much by someone.

"Did you...touch...yourself," she panted, her body weak against his. Her knee shook and she felt as if she would fall at any second.

"You bet your ass I did," he said, running his hand slowly across her body. She could feel the wetness from her pussy and watched as he raised his fingers to his mouth, sliding them in between his lips. Her eyes opened wide, watching as he moaned softly at the taste of her.

"Now, I'm going to come in you like the slut you are," he whispered, turning her to face him. She spun, feeling her hair move behind her, the scent of her shampoo heavy in the air.

He grabbed her waist, lifting her to the edge of the desk. She could feel her pussy, slippery against the cool surface. She spread her legs, watching as he pulled his hard dick out again. He looked even harder than he had before.

He tangled a hand into her hair, pressing his forehead against hers.

"Are you enjoying this," he whispered softly, his lips moving against hers as he spoke. Tokyo moaned, her mouth reaching toward his. She pressed a hand to the back of his head, feeling the softness of his hair. She pulled his face closer to hers, her lips attacking him with desperation. She wanted to show just how much she was enjoying what he was doing for her, to her.

She moved to the edge of the desk, her hands moving down to his hips. She pulled at him, feeling him move closer to her. She reached down, touching his hard dick, a sigh coming from both of them. It was hard, pulsing slightly in her hand.

He groaned, his hips pressing in toward her.

She spread her pussy lips, watching as his dick disappeared into her slowly. She locked eyes with him as he slowly thrust into her, wrapping her legs around his waist. She felt that they had both done what they needed. They had both conquered that mountain and fulfilled that need. They were coming down from that high now, moving slowly and enjoying each other's bodies without the furious need to come.

AJ slid into her, thrusting slowly, holding her to his body. Her breasts were pressed against him, her pale skin a contrast to his sun tanned body.

She sighed, inhaling his scent deeply, cologne mixed with sex and sweat. And her. She could smell herself on his body, as if she had claimed him as her own. She licked her lips, a lazy smile on her face as he pressed deeper into her, readjusting her hips as his thrusts became harder.

"Mmmm, yes," she cooed, tangling her fingers in his hair, pulling his face closer to hers. He opened his eyes, staring at her as he fucked her, his hands grasping onto her ass.

"God, you are such a fucking surprise to me," she said, arching her back to him. He smirked, thrusting deeper, accented with guttural groans.

"You have no idea, Tokyo," he said, closing his eyes as he started to jerk faster and harder. Tokyo squeezed her legs around him tighter, enjoying the feeling of his dick sliding in and out of her body, her juices letting him go much further than she'd expected. She watched his face, watching as his thrusts got.

more swallow. She could feel his stomach tighten up as she ran a hand slowly down his chest toward the place they connected.

"I want it all," she whispered, watching her words push him over the edge. He grunted, his body pressing into her. She could feel the warmth filling her pussy, his hands holding her close. She sighed, tipping her head back, feeling his body twitching as he finished.

He stood there, regaining his breath, his face buried in her hair. She wondered if she smelled like him, if he thought about her claiming him.

He pulled away slowly, tucking his semi hard dick back into his briefs and buttoned the slacks. She pulled her blouse back on, her fingers shaking slightly as she buttoned it up.

It was like watching a magic show, watching AJ return to the nerd she had thought he was before. He pulled his jacket back over his shoulders and pulled his glasses from the pocket. Her mouth dropped a little, watching the man she had just fucked disappear completely, hidden behind the façade of a quiet sweet guy.

She pulled her skirt down over her ass and looked around, trying to find her underwear. She had kicked them but they seemed to have disappeared.

AJ looked at his phone, realizing how late it was.

"We can finish this project tomorrow. You must be starving," he said, his eyes glancing down the front of her blouse where her nipples pressed against the material. She grabbed her bra from the desk and crammed it into her purse, smiling at him, narrowing her eyes at him slightly.

"I could eat," she said, her eyes moving down his body. She knew they had just had sex but the chemistry between them had electrified the room. Her stomach, however, disagreed, letting out a loud rumbling sound. It sounded like a small lion trapped in her body, warning whoever was listening of its discontent.

"Let's go eat," he said, gathering his laptop into the satchel, and walking towards the door. She was amazed at his transformation, the wide shoulders that she had just held curving in slightly to put out a tired front. She felt a shiver run through her body at the thought of his dick, the same dick that had emptied into her. She could still feel it, thick within the walls of her pussy.

As they walked, she started to wonder if it had been a dream. The guy next to her didn't seem like the same person who had fucked her and called her a slut. As they neared their cars, he looked at her and smiled, bringing an item to his nose. He inhaled deeply before handing it over to her.

"I knew you'd be delicious," he said, a small smirk on his face. Tokyo laughed, catching her thong and tucked it into her pocket.

"Where do you want to go eat," she said, biting her lip innocently.

"I don't care. I'm starving," he said, smiling at her and she opened her car door. She looked at him and motioned for him to get into her car. He quickly followed.

28. Work Troubles

After starting work here so soon ago, Craig was still rather new around the building and had taken up an offer from Olivia to basically ensure he didn't get lost in the endless halls. The offer was nice enough, though he could quite easily tell the ulterior motive. The overly touchy nature and subtle clinginess was enough, she was *absolutely* vying for his attention, and he sort of enjoyed it.

"It's nice talking to someone from my hometown like this…"

As Olivia was practically clinging to his arm, doing little to hide her apparent affection, Samantha made a quick turn around the corner, bumping into the two of them.

"Sorry!"

Looking up, she locked eyes with Craig, and instantly he knew there was going to be a bit of a conflict between the two of them. Ever since showing up, these two had been showing obvious interest in him, but worse yet, have been showing a distaste for being around him at the same time, some apparent conflict between them.

"What're you doing with this *dry* thing, Craig?"

Olivia has a look of annoyance across her face, having anticipated a little competition for his attention, but not from *her*.

"At least I actually have some warmth to me, ice *bitch*!"

There's a moment that it seems as though they may jump on one another at any moment, and Craig's mind races to come to a conclusion that'd settle this without a fight. Almost as if a lightbulb shines above his head, he comes up with an idea, a strange one, but perhaps the girls would agree to it.

"Ladies, there's no reason to fight over who's warmer! It'd be much easier to *prove* who holds the most inner desire…"

Olivia's eyes widen slightly, hearing his lecherous suggestion unfold.

"Why don't we go back to my room and have a little competition. I'm sure a *fine woman* like yourself would have no issue competing, right?"

Samantha takes the comment to heart, curious as to what's in store, and adamant to show up Olivia and take something from her, but also something she wants herself. She clings to his other arm, and Craig ends up escorting the two girls back to his room, letting them in before sitting on the bed and explaining the contest.

"Now, the two of you are clearly interested in me, there's no denying it. So… let's see who would be able to take *my* desires better! Both of you strip and let's see how long you can last."

The mere notion of it is enough to make Samantha blush, recoiling back slightly before looking at Olivia, who had already unclasped one of the straps to her top.

"What? It's not exactly *common* but it's a normal enough contest between lovers. You're not already thinking you'd lose, are you?"

The slight awkwardness Samantha was holding onto soon dissolved into bitterness at the notion of her being any lesser than someone like her. With much more elegance than Olivia, she slowly took the time to slip her clothes down her body, the paleness of her skin emphasized by Olivia's tanned body next to hers. In a few moments, both had completely stripped down, their naked bodies on display for the man before them.

"Good. Now, let's time an hour, and see who's still left sane by the end of it."

He reaches across to his table and turns a sand timer, the grains falling through the elaborate glass spiral as Craig reclines back on the bed, anticipating the show before him.

Without much hesitation, Olivia had already begun sliding her hand up Samantha's thigh, to which she slapped it away on instinct.

"Do **not** touch me, you filth!"

As she opens her mouth to speak again, Olivia can't help but smirk at the absurdity of what she's saying.

I'm the filth after she stripped with me?!

In response, she silences whatever Samantha was about to continue saying with a harsh slap on her round Ass, loud enough to make her tremble on her feet from the sudden shock. Samantha tried to bite her lip to silence her squeal, but it did little to stifle the sudden sound escaping her lips, which was much to the delight of both Olivia and Craig.

Seeing them smile at her outburst was turning her cheeks bright red, clearly flustered, Samantha wasn't thinking clearly enough to react to Olivia, still recoiling from everything happening so suddenly. This gave Olivia plenty of time to lurch forward, knocking Samantha off balance as she took her place on top of her.

"Not much of an *elegant woman* when you're so *beneath* people, hm?"

The insult clearly struck a nerve, Samantha throwing one of her hands toward her face, but was caught with ease, instead both of her arms were pinned above her head as Olivia lowered her head to Samantha's face, bringing their lips together in a forced kiss.

It only lasted a second, Olivia breaking it to whisper in the squirming girl's ear.

"I'm going to make you scream"

With those words swimming in her head, any response is cut off as Olivia dives back to encompass her lips with her own, letting

Samantha whimper into her own mouth as their tongues battled for power. All the while, Olivia repositions herself on top of Samantha, until her leg is between both of hers, then grinding her knee against Samantha's pussy, feeling her writhe beneath her once she understands her plan.

Samantha desperately squirms as she loses the battle for dominance in her mouth, forced into submission in more ways than one, the pressure building between her legs soon becomes too much, and moans begin escaping her lips. It's easily noticed by Olivia, who decides to break the kiss, leaving her moans unfiltered by her own mouth, and flashes a smirk toward Craig.

While they were busy battling with each other, he had stripped down his clothes, leaving him entirely naked while he sat on the bed, staring at the two girls wrestling together. His dick was throbbing between his legs, though he gave her nothing back as she looked on, silently telling her to continue.

"As you wish~"

Olivia takes the hint, looking back to her little captive, and deciding it's time to put on a show. She pulls her knee from Samantha's crotch, and instead straddles her thigh, holding her in place as one of her hands moves down between her legs. She thrashes beneath Olivia as her hand traces her pale skin, wanting to avoid succumbing to her teasing so easily, but currently helpless in this position, pinned by her opponent.

Samantha's eyes open, feeling the sudden intrusion of Olivia's slender fingers between her legs, teasing her aching pussy. She had already been grinding her knee against it, by now it was sensitive and ready for the attention, despite Samantha's reluctance. She couldn't hold in the built-up tension any longer, her pussy subtly grinding against Olivia's hand in a desperate attempt to gain pleasure.

"Oh~? Looks like the **whore** is a little over-eager, hm?"

Samantha's face shows disgust at her words, yet her body *begs* for more, which Olivia happily obliges. In a swift movement, she slides in a second finger and begins moving faster, pushing her pussy *back* into the ground as she picks up the pace even more, until she's ruthlessly finger-fucking her little slut on the floor. Samantha can't help but squeal on the floor, held in place by someone she deems lower than herself.

"This is what you want, isn't it? To be captive and forced to cum like a **slut!?**"

She practically spat the words down at her, almost as worked up as she was during the heated passion between them. The image forced into her mind, as a captive, held down as they have their way with her... it was too much in her state, Samantha threw back her head in pleasure as she spasmed on the floor beneath Olivia, her body caving into the frustration and cumming in her hand.

Olivia leans back, watching as Samantha cums on her own, on the floor through her orgasm, squealing to herself until it finally subsides, and she seems to have relaxed to the idea of the contest a tad more. The look in her eyes were of one lost in pleasure, and Olivia took advantage of this by positioning herself to start their little game, crawling across Samantha's body until her pussy hovered above her face, and quickly smothered Samantha, still moaning to herself, with her pussy. Olivia clenched her thighs around her face as she continued moaning between her legs, grabbing onto Samantha's pale thighs, burying her lips into her pussy, taking her first taste of her pussy.

Craig leaned forward, the sight of the two women finally battling it out in a sexual game for his amusement, as well as his favor, was causing him to begin leaking onto the floor, but he stared on dutifully, awaiting a clear winner once the sand had fallen.

The two women continued battling for dominance, Samantha's attempts slightly dampened by her hazed mind, still recovering from the rough and sudden treatment from Olivia, her pussy not given a chance to rest after her fingers had forced an orgasm out of her. Though she was determined to elicit the same from her opponent, squeezing her hands around Olivia's plump ass, she forced her pussy onto her tongue, shoving it **deep** inside Olivia's pussy. The deep, penetrative technique of Samantha seemed to be working, as before long, Olivia's thighs were trembling as they squeezed Samantha's face, and her juices were dripping down her cheeks.

"It's a lovely sight, girls, but your time is almost halfway up."

The sultry tone of Craig's voice was a reminder of the stakes at play, and not just the satisfaction of beating the other. Renewed with intent, the two of them seemed to pick up the pace quite a bit, Samantha's oversensitive pussy quickly becoming overwhelmed with Olivia's tongue, brought to a mind-melting orgasm once again, causing her to sink deeper in her submission toward her.

Thankfully for her, a moment of disgrace came to Olivia, as her own orgasm finally washes across her body, urged on by Samantha's unfiltered moans into her pussy, her tongue acting like a vibrator as she continued fucking her with it.

The two girls cried out together, wailing into one another's pussies as the other trembled in bliss, which began an unending cycle of orgasm after orgasm. They were both locked in a rhythm of teasing the other with their own orgasm, their moans sending them over the edge, which in turn did the same to them. Craig watched on as they were quickly reduced to whimpering, moaning messes before him.

With the game ending, he decided to give everything a bit of a fair chance, rather than have them become dribbling messes without him even playing with them. Craig stands from the bed, grabbing Olivia by the hair and removing her from on top of Samantha, letting the two recover on the floor by themselves for a moment. A wave of panting and gasping followed, both of them completely out of breath, but slowly coming to their senses now that the constant stimulation had ceased.

"Grab each other's hands and trib together. We'll see who comes out on top..."

His words are commanding and absolute, the girls hurriedly crawl to one another, exchanging sadistic looks as they lock fingers, pressing their pussies against one another before they begin grinding idly.

Their bodies were glistening with sweat after the intense session they had just experienced, but they were both still full of intent to win. Without any hesitation, they began gyrating their hips against each other, battling to force more stimulation on the other, while also trying to keep their own at bay. After a while of biting their lips, pretending as if they weren't slowly slipping down the slope of ecstasy, Samantha was the first to cave, giving way *just* for a moment, but long enough for Olivia to take the advantage, forcing a moan out of her.

That was enough to turn the tables in her favor, quickly forcing Samantha to the edge of her orgasm, which Olivia felt no mercy over shoving her into that pit of pleasure.

"Go ahead and cum. We both know it's all you're good for!"

Her taunting words didn't help her situation, apparently having the desired effect, Samantha quickly tipped over the edge and fell into pleasure once again, her eyes rolling into her head as she thrashed against Olivia's pussy, her orgasm overwhelming her body.

As Olivia enjoyed the sight of Samantha's chances slipping away, it seemed appropriate to take a moment for herself, grinding away into her spasming pussy as she enjoyed the sight of her victory. Perhaps enjoying it *too* much, Olivia soon felt her own orgasm edge its way closer, and after looking at her opponent, felt no guilt in voluntarily letting herself go over the edge. She was even encouraged by Samantha's thrashings, grinding harshly between her legs, eliciting a shrill whimper as Olivia caved to her pleasure, crying out to the ceiling as her pent-up orgasm finally quaked across her body.

It was earth-shattering, every inch of her body was shaking in pure bliss as she watched Samantha's suffering. But in that moment, she saw a glint of defiance, and as she felt Samantha's hands grip tighter to her own, she understood why.

"That's a good girl, submit to your Queen, you little **bitch!**"

It was like something primal had awakened within Samantha, her grinding became powerful and directed solely toward forcing moans from Olivia's lips, which they succeeded in doing. The once powerful and in control Olivia was quickly turned into a whimper mess, her orgasm giving way to many more, lost in a sea of unending pleasure as Samantha refused to give her a moment's rest.

Before long, Olivia was reduced to a quivering, babbling mess opposite her. The confidence and taunting words had long-since melted away, replaced with whimpers and squeals as she came minute by minute. Her thighs were **soaked** in her own juices that had mixed with Samantha's, trembling madly, but still held in place by Samantha's firm grip.

It was maddening to have this amount of pleasure forced on you, Olivia's mind quickly melting away as little was left but the burning urge to fall deeper into this pit of pleasure, which was happily given to her by the sadistic woman.

"That's it! Cum for me you slut! Cum for me!"

She was clearly drunk on both pleasure *and* power, watching on as Olivia desperately tried to wriggle away from her grip, but was held firmly in place, forced to look up at Samantha's sadistic gaze down at her. The minutes bled away as her orgasms quickly overwhelmed her. Olivia was soon a wet mess, tongue hanging out of her mouth, eyes completely hazed over in pleasure, and a lead lost to the Queen currently dominating her into the floor.

Much like Olivia had done to her before, there was little mercy in her eyes, instead nothing but pent-up hatred being let out all at once. Samantha was soon laughing down at her with each orgasm, seeing as Olivia was becoming much more vocal with them, having given up the guise of being the one in control.

Samantha wasn't sure how long she was held under Olivia's control, or even how many times she came, so she doesn't allow for a moment of rest, not for either of them. The floor was practically soaked with their mixed juices, and their bodies were covered in a glistening sweat between them, emphasized by the gentle lighting of the room. Without realizing the last grain had fallen to the bottom of the glass, Samantha continues grinding against Olivia's limp body, and even Craig allows for another few moments so he can enjoy the sights.

Deciding it was finally enough, Craig clapped his hands loudly, snapping the girls out of their trance and signaling the end of the game. Much to Olivia's obvious delight, hard to notice through her twitches and spasms. They're both helped to their knees by him, before he sits back at the end of the bed, ready to explain the end of the game to them.

"Well Olivia, I'm sure you know how far ahead you were at first…"

She bites her lip and struggles to hold back her squirming in an effort to remain composed.

"But Samantha took it away once you lost yourself, the numbers may embarrass you, so simply put, you lost rather handedly."

It didn't come as much of a surprise, but Olivia still couldn't help but slump dejectedly, trying to ignore the smug look on Samantha's face, a look that she made *very* clear to her by crawling in front of her, throwing taunts and jeers her way.

With the game concluded, the victor clear to everyone, Samantha can't hold in her smug face, even between the occasional twitches of her own pent-up pleasure from her triumphant come-back.

"Looks like he'll have no use for your pussy after all~"

Samantha crawls closer to Olivia, having already started to recline on the floor in both shame of losing and relief at the chance to rest after being tortured by her for so long. Though as Samantha gets closer and she's forced to look up at her wicked, lust-filled grin, she's suddenly pulled out of view. Olivia props herself up on the floor, watching as Craig had stepped off of the bed and had grabbed Samantha by the hair, pulling her ass into his lap as he knelt on the floor.

"I've been watching long enough… time to take what's **mine!**"

Samantha had his hands grip around her waist, forcing her down into his lap, grinding his thick dick against her quivering pussy. The desperate, pathetic wailing of pleasure from her lips made Olivia smile, she may not have won, but it's still a beautiful sight to see her go from so smug to so broken this quickly.

The game was over, but Olivia could still enjoy the view of Samantha bouncing on Craig's lap, her almost limp body spasming as he forcefully slammed into her. Before long, Craig had shoved Samantha to her hands and knees, and was pounding into her from behind, the sound of his hips slapping against her ass was filling the room, as well as her wet pussy being stretched by his dick relentlessly. Her arms soon gave out, and her body fell to the ground, ass still in the air as Craig didn't relent in his fucking, using her like a toy as she helplessly came on the ground, eyes long since having rolled up into her head.

Her moans didn't stop, as if every moment she had spent cumming was resurged back to the surface, forced to show itself for Craig's pleasure. Underneath Samantha's Sea of pleasure she was feeling, was a slight hint of humiliation at being fucked so brazenly before the woman she had only just finished teaching to submit to her. She's not able to focus her eyes long enough to look up at her, but it's easy to imagine the look on her face right now, which makes her next orgasm dig that humiliation even deeper, but no less intense.

Olivia watched on as she frantically fingered herself to the sight of Samantha being treated like a common whore, someone who was degrading her not moments ago, was now looking more like a whore than she could have imagined. Maybe losing isn't so bad after all? Olivia and Craig share a sly smile with one another, before they both sink back into their pleasure, the night only just having started.

29. Uncompromising Situations

Diana could still feel the tension in her body as she opened the office door and walked into the parking lot. Mark's car was right across the lot from her and she hoped she'll be able to get there without anyone noticing. They didn't want to spark rumors, that's for sure. So far it seemed that their colleagues didn't notice their connection or the way they spent so much time together – they worked in the same department, so it wasn't that obvious. And, if Diana was honest, she wasn't worried about them noticing when both she and Mark had much more important people in their lives who could see that something was off.

Finally, Diana was at the car's door. She quickly opened it and dived inside, looking at Mark. His smile was wide, but he was grabbing the steering wheel so hard his knuckles were white. He also was nervous, of course, he was. It would've been strange if something like this was a usual occasion for him. This thing between them was bright, new, and sparkling, making them both feel like shy teenagers – both of them just wanted to dive into it, not thinking about anything else. That was impossible, of course. Mostly because both of them were already taken.

"Are you ready?" Mark asked, taking Diana's hand and looking her in the eyes. His finger ran over her fingers, avoiding a ring with a big diamond on one of them. Diana remembered that she was engaged, and Mark did too, there was no point to remind about it one more time. And it's not like Mark didn't have a wedding ring of his own.

For a moment Diana went quiet, not thinking about what was

going to happen, but about the consequences. Was this worth it? She felt this temptation before, but she was able to successfully fight it. Not this time, though. Now that she thought about her fiancé's disappointed face, she still felt heartbroken, but not enough to refuse herself. She wanted to know how this passion would feel once unchained and she was willing to risk everything for it.

"Yes," she nodded, smiling back. "I'm ready."

Mark started the car and they drove out of the parking lot. It felt final as if there was no turning back after, and Diana felt at peace with that. She wanted to be there, in that car, next to Mark, feeling his presence and knowing that she was about to get much more of it.

"Where are we going?" she asked, finally realizing that she didn't know that huge detail.

"To my house," Mark simply answered. "Anna is... I mean, I'll be alone there for a couple of days, so there is nothing to worry about."

They couldn't talk about their partners, of course. At least not now, when the air was so thick between them, so full of promises and longing. It felt unreal that they finally were there, at this point, when all of this was about to become possible. Diana just hoped that she'll get everything that she dreamed about and more.

This short reminder about Mark's wife made her think about her fiancé. Diana used the same excuse she heard all cheaters use – she was late at work, finishing an urgent report for her boss. Peter didn't seem to mind, he just sent her a message, saying that he hoped he'll be back home soon. Reading those words made Diana feel guilty again, but she still wasn't going to stop. She wanted it, she needed it, her whole body singing about that desire she felt. Diana just needed Mark to satisfy it and things would get back to normal. She knew it, she felt it in her bones.

They drove down narrow streets on the way to Mark's house in complete silence. Neither one of them wanted to break that fragile agreement between them, making the other one gets scared and jump the boat. Diana instantly figured out that they were getting closer – Mark started looking around, making sure his neighbors wouldn't see him in a car with another woman. Only once he drove the car into the garage and closed the door did he seem to relax.

"Let me welcome you into my house," he smiled, opening the door for Diana. Now that they were far away from the world, in a place where no one could see them, she didn't feel more relaxed. On the contrary, her body was as tight as a spring. It was coming, they both knew it, but no one felt brave enough to make the first step.

Mark looked a little lost as they entered the living room, as if unsure if it would be too forward to invite Diana into the bedroom. She looked at the couch, noticing the decorative pillows and thinking that it must be Anna who bought and placed them there.

"Do you want to have a drink?" Mark asked as they moved even closer to each other. They weren't touching, not yet just sharing space, sharing air between them.

Diana felt like her skin was burning, her whole body aching to get what she desperately wanted for so long. Mark was right in front of her, her breasts would've touched his chest if she took too deep of a breath.

"We can stop if you..." Mark started the sentence but couldn't end it – Diana's hands were already on his shoulders, her lips on his, her mouth moving, opening, as she kissed him. There was passion in these first touches, but still, some shyness, as if Diana wasn't sure what result she'll get by doing this. She found that out soon enough.

"Fuck, Diana," Mark said, for a moment pulling away, looking at her with his eyes shining. "I'm not sure I'll be able to stop."

She smiled, taking his hand and firmly placing it on her ass.

"It's a good thing that you don't have to," she smiled wickedly, pleasant heaviness already more than evident in her lower stomach. "Just forget about everything else and take me."

That was all the encouragement he needed. Mark kissed her again, this time putting all of the longings he felt for months into it. He opened her mouth, teasing Diana's tongue, his hands moving up her ass, to her jacket, pulling the useless thing off her shoulders. She heard it drop somewhere behind her but didn't care. The less fabric was between them the better she would've felt. Her fingers grabbed Mark's jacket while his lips and hands were driving her mad. Wherever he touched her, Diana felt her body just turning hotter, filling with more need for him. With their bodies being so tightly pressed together she could feel his dick, his hardness evident even through the fabric of his pants.

With his lips still on hers, Mark turned Diana around, making her step back until she felt the edge of the couch pressing into the back of her legs She sat down, trying to pull Mark with her, but Diana was unsuccessful. He was still standing above her, looking down and smiling, as he looked at her puffed lips.

"You're so fucking beautiful, Diana," he said, leaning to kiss her again, more gently this time. "You have no idea how much of a torture it was to look at you in the office, knowing that you can never be mine."

"But I am yours now," she said, barely breathing, as she felt his lips on her neck, his tongue teasing the tender skin. They both knew that they needed to be careful not to leave any traces, but Diana couldn't help but wish to feel his teeth there, pressing into her skin.

She pulled his jacket off his shoulders, her hands shaking as she opened the buttons of his shirt until Diana could put her palms against his chest, seeing so much skin – all of it for her to touch.

"No, you're not mine yet," he said, opening the top buttons of her shirt until it was open enough for Mark to reach the tops of her breasts. He kissed her soft flesh, while Diana moaned softly, just aching for more. She was so wet and aching between her legs that every moment when Mark wasn't touching her there felt like torture. "But you will be. The moment you feel so good you'd want to scream my name."

This sounded like a promise and Mark had so much desire to fulfill it – he didn't hesitate for a moment. Still not taking any other item of clothes off of her, he got on his knees in front of Diana, his hands laying on her thighs, as he looked up.

"I want you to be as loud as you can for me. I want to hear how good you're feeling with my mouth on you. Do you understand?"

Diana could only nod – her mouth went dry, her head spinning, as she thought about the things this man was about to do with her. She looked at him silently, as Mark took her shoes off, going for her stockings next, pulling his hands under her skirt. She lifted her thighs, helping him take it off. Just as slowly, Mark pulled her skirt up, to her thighs, until he could see her black panties right in front of him. Diana wore one of the sexy things, all see-through, with barely any fabric covering her ass.

"Spread them wider for me," Mark said, caressing his thigh. Diana never did anything faster in her life. She instantly choked on her breath, feeling Mark's fingers against her slit, teasing her right through the fabric. "Feels unfair, doesn't it? That I already know how much you want me and you're still in the dark."

Diana laughed. She wasn't about to be in this position, wasn't going to be the one who wanted it the most. She pulled her foot to the front of Mark's pants, pressing it over his hard dick.

"Oh, I'm not. I know exactly how much you want me. I'm just giving you the chance to show me how good you can satisfy me before I return the favor."

His eyes darkened at her words. It felt so strange, so new and sharp to be in this position, saying those words, when Diana thought about this moment for so long. But it was finally happening, her wait coming to an end, and she was planning to make the most out of it.

"Trust me, by the end of this you'd want to do anything for me."

Diana was about to protest, but it was already too late – Mark dipped his head between her legs, pulling her closer by the hips. He didn't take her panties off, just moving the soaked fabric to the side. He pressed his tongue fully to her pussy, licking her in a long stripe, making Diana shake lightly. It felt so good, she felt it in her toes.

"You're so needy," Mark said, his head still between her thighs. "So wet. I'm going to have a fun time playing with you."

And he really meant it. Mark started with the light teasing, using just the tip of his tongue to make Diana moan and whimper, grabbing onto his hand. The touches of his tongue were echoing through her whole body, making her feel weak. All her thoughts were focused on that intensifying sensation between her legs and Diana couldn't do anything about it.

Mark's tongue started moving faster, his tongue going over her whole pussy, from the hole to the clit, intensifying her pleasure. Diana felt her orgasm getting closer, her body getting tenser, ready to experience it.

"Mark," she moaned out, feeling his mouth covering her pussy, his tongue still teasing her clit. "Fuck, Mark!"

She knew that he loved it, loved hearing his name between her moans and it made him only go stronger. Her clit was in his mouth now, and he sucked on it, making Diana scream and arch her back. How much she needed it, and how long she waited for this release. As she felt her orgasm hitting her, Diana grabbed Mark by the hair, starting to move her hips, using her face, his tongue, to get everything out of this that she could. She was still moaning, still being loud, grateful that Mark allowed her to do it. When she was done, Diana just relaxed, leaning on the couch, and looking at Mark's face as he looked down. His mouth and chin were covered in her juices, and she couldn't wait to kiss them off.

"Come here!" she demanded, pulling him closer. Diana kissed him, sucking off her juices from his lips, enjoying her taste on Mark's tongue as her pussy was still throbbing after the things he did to her. "Get up! I want to show you how grateful I am."

Mark didn't protest even for a moment, instantly standing straight, putting his hands on Diana's cheek, slowly caressing it, as he watched her unzip his pants, pulling them and his boxers just low enough to let his dick out. Diana smiled, looking at his length, thinking that this was everything that she wished for during those long months of flirting – to have his hard dick in front of her as she was about to suck it. Her mouth started watering, as she put her hand around him, and started stroking him from the base to the tip. She used her left hand for it, her engagement ring shining as she moved it. She knew that it was wrong but seeing this only turned Diana more. She wanted to sleep with Mark long enough to break any rules and this was just one of them.

"Watch me," she whispered, leaning closer, opening her mouth for him.

And Mark did watch her. He looked Diana right in the eyes as she took the tip of his dick into her hot mouth, sucking on it until she heard him groan.

"Fuck, Diana," he said, visibly struggling with keeping control. "You're so unbelievably sexy."

She loved to hear it and she loved what her mouth was doing with him. She took him in deeper while stroking the rest of his dick using her hand, pressing tighter around the shaft to make him feel good.

She teased him with her tongue, enjoying his taste, the feeling of his hot dick inside her mouth. This was everything that she wanted for so long and now Diana was finally getting it. She knew that he loved it, she could feel it in his every breath, every groan that he was letting out while holding onto her head, as if trying to ground himself. She wondered if Mark would allow himself to finish into her mouth and, if not, she knew how to make it happen.

She moved away, letting his dick out of her mouth, while Mark looked a little lost. She just smiled back.

"Just trying to make it feel better," Diana said, starting to unbutton her shirt to take it off. She wore a matching black bra with see-through cups, but she needed it to be gone now. She took it off slowly – unhooking it, then sliding it down her arms, letting Mark enjoy every moment. Once he looked at her bare breasts there was a new look in his eyes, as if he saw something so beautiful that he couldn't take his eyes away.

"Come here now," Diana said, pulling him even closer and sitting him on the couch. "Enjoy this while you can."

She was the one on her knees in front of him now, leaning toward his dick. Diana put her full, perky breasts around his shaft, seeing the excitement in Mark's eyes as she did it. Slowly, she started moving them up and down, letting his tip show at the top. She didn't take it in her mouth, not yet. She wanted to see Mark desperate, aching for her before she would do that.

"Diana," his voice was low, full of desire. "Please, open your pretty mouth for me."

She laughed, licking his tip teasingly, but only once.

"Diana," he looked at her again.

"I'll do it if you'll promise to cum in my mouth," she smiled, moving her breasts faster around his dick.

"That I can give you easily," Mark smiled.

Diana opened her mouth, taking his tip inside, sucking on him, as her breasts were still stimulating his shaft. Mark was groaning, grabbing onto her hair in the search of relief. His hips were moving, trying to push his dick deeper into her mouth and when Diana knew that he had enough of her teasing, she let it happen. Mark fucked her mouth with abundance as if it was the only thing he ever wanted and now he was planning to enjoy it fully. Diana let him, because she wanted to feel it too, wanted him to thrust inside her, as she just let him do so.

Just a few moments later she felt it – his seed, filling her mouth. She still heard Mark groan as she was swallowing it, licking every single drop that was left off his shaft. She wanted all of it and she wanted more. Once she finished and their eyes met there was only one thought on her mind and Diana said it out loud.

"Just fuck me already!"

It seemed to be a signal Mark was waiting for all along – he got up and pulled Diana to her feet too, both of them taking care of each other's clothes. He was unzipping her skirt and pulling it down, while Diana was tugging his pants down. Once they both were undressed and nothing but the skin was between them, Mark pulled Diana to lay on the couch, spreading her legs and getting on top of her.

"I've been waiting so long for this moment," he said, kissing her neck, her breasts, her stomach. Diana moaned lightly, looking at him and trying to remember every little detail of this experience. His soft lips, his strong hands, the way he looked at her. Somehow Diana knew that this night, as she'll be lying next to her future husband, she'd only be able to think about Mark and his hands on her.

He moved up, his dick laying against her slit, making Diana want him inside like never before. She needed it with every cell of her body, her desire so strong that it was clouding her better judgment.

"Tell me how much you want it," Mark said, his hand on her breast, his thumb rubbing her nipple. "I want to hear it."

"Fine," Diana let out, putting her hands around his shoulders. "I want your dick inside me like I never wanted anything else in my life. I wake up and fall asleep with thoughts about the ways you can take me, fuck me, and make me moan. When you flirt with me at work I get so wet I have to go to the bathroom and take care of it."

Mark smiled, clearly satisfied with her words. Slowly, he pushed his hips forward, letting Diana feel the way his tip was getting inside her pussy, stretching her.

"Did you ever do it with him while thinking of me?" he asked, as more of his dick entered her hot slick pussy, making Diana whimper and close her eyes in pleasure. "Did you?"

"Yes!" she let out, overwhelmed by sensation. "I did… oh fuck. It feels better than any fantasy, I swear."

"Good," Mark smiled, kissing the corner of her mouth. "Because it's only the beginning."

He pulled her knees higher, pushing his dick fully inside Diana's pussy, letting her feel every inch of his hard length inside her. She took him easily with how wet she was, enjoying the way he stretched her. She moaned, grabbing his shoulders, hoping that this moment would never stop. She wanted this for so long and, finally, she was about to get her to wish.

Once Mark started pounding her everything disappeared. She felt his weight on top of her, his breath on her neck, his dick deep inside her, making her feel as good as no man was ever able to. All Diana needed was more of it, so she pulled Mark closer, putting her legs around his waist.

She moaned, pressing herself against him, asking to be fucked as hard as he could manage, but Mark wasn't giving her enough. It felt like he was afraid of hurting her, of testing her limits, but

Diana couldn't stand it. She wanted to be fucked deep and rough, so she could get up the next morning and still remember the way he felt inside her.

"Let me get on top," she said. Mark didn't stop, but he moved away, looking at her.

"Are you sure?"

"More than sure!"

He pulled his dick out, leaving Diana's pussy feeling unpleasantly empty. Mark then sat down, waiting for her. Diana smiled, finally about to get the control she needed. She went to straddle his hips, taking his dick in her hand and pressing it to her entrance. She left his length wet enough for her to take him all at once, but she wanted to wait, to tease, to make it even more exciting for both of them.

"Just do it," Mark whispered, grabbing her hips.

"So impatient," Diana said, kissing him. "I love it."

She moaned as she drove her hips down, taking his dick back where he belonged – inside her. She grabbed Mark's shoulders, starting to ride him faster and faster with every moment. Their bodies were meeting with wet sounds that filled the air around them, along with their moans, making it feel like nothing else really mattered. They both wanted only one thing – to satisfy their need that was growing long enough to devour them.

"Diana," Mark groaned, moving his hips to meet her, his chest covered in sweat. Diana could only look at him, at the way he was watching her as if she was giving him something he could never get before. "Slow down just a little or I'll cum inside you."

That thought didn't scare her at all — it only made Diana move faster, pushing her hips down, taking his dick deeper as she went.

"Do it," she said, a challenge in her voice. "I want it all inside me. Till the last drop."

It seemed to sound like a challenge to Mark, because a moment later his thrusts became stronger, his dick pushing as deep as he could while Diana still was riding him, trying to keep up with the rhythm.

"Take it," he said, driving her down again. "Take it all."

His words made Diana moan, her pleasure finding her as soon as she felt Mark spill inside her, making her pussy even slicker, full of his seed. She kept riding his dick, giving her body time to enjoy this moment, until her legs were too tired until she couldn't keep up anymore, just staying in his lap, hugging Mark.

"It felt amazing," Diana said, still breathing hard. "I always dreamed that it would feel this way and now I know it's even better."

"I'm glad that you feel this way," Mark smiled, kissing the side of her head.

It felt peaceful, and calm, both of them were happy at this moment. Until Diana heard her phone ringing. She looked at Mark with regret, getting up to take it. His cum was still inside her, leaking down her inner thigh, as she answered the call of her fiancé.

"Everything is okay, yes," she said, trying to sound calm. "I'll be home soon."

It was the first moment when it hit Diana — she just cheated on

Peter, and she broke his trust. But what was even worse is that it felt amazing. And she wanted to do it again.